This is Cat Devlan.

She has red hair—inherited from her buccaneer father
whose infamous death by hanging
she has sworn to avenge.

She has red hair—thick, long and lustrous, but
well-hidden beneath her turban
when she walks the decks as a man—
the captain of a pirate ship.

She has red hair—and violet eyes that can change
with her mood from steely grey
in anger to glowing amethyst
in moments of love.

She has red hair—and a temper to match when she
rages against the man who dared
to take her body against her will—
and dares to demand her heart as well.

This is Cat Devlan.

No man can win her except one
who knows how to . . .

CARESS AND CONQUER

Books by
Donna Comeaux Zide

CARESS AND CONQUER
SAVAGE IN SILK

Published by
WARNER BOOKS

By Donna Comeaux Zide

A Warner Communications Company

Dedicated with affection to
Fredda Isaacson and Jay Davis
with special thanks to
Ann Hoffmeister

WARNER BOOKS EDITION

ISBN 0-446-82949-8

Cover Art by Elaine Duillo

Warner Books, Inc., 75 Rockefeller Plaza, New York, N.Y. 10019

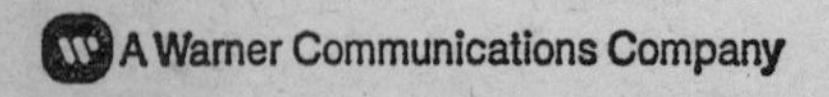

Printed in Canada.

Not associated with Warner Press, Inc. of Anderson, Indiana

First Printing: January, 1979

10 9 8 7 6 5 4 3 2 1

Prologue
New York, 1710

The eastern sky formed a bleak panorama; dark, rain-swollen clouds swirled in a tempest across its breadth as though nature itself were protesting the night's events.

A small figure huddled forlornly in the doorway of a shuttered tavern. A man approached, his quiet, furtive step unnoticed in the dark night. Suddenly the moon swept from behind a veil of black cloud, disclosing in its cold, white light the taut, stunned features of a young girl. She grasped her knees, rocking back and forth, oblivious to the newcomer's presence. With great, gray-violet eyes she stared emptily across the black water lapping at the dockside.

Catherine Devlan's delicate, heart-shaped face and sweetly turned, rosebud mouth held the promise of a beauty that would someday be described by some as breathtaking and by others as wild and untamed. Wind howled with a wild, wounded sound in the darkness as it ruffled the heavy, copper curls framing Cat's face and tugged at the boy's shirt and leggings that covered the thin twelve-year old body.

Fifty feet away, at the end of the dock, the moon cast its unrelenting rays upon a man whose features and gleaming hair were uncannily like Cat's. There could be no denial of the relationship between the girl and the man whose body hung, grotesquely swaying in the night winds. The handsome lines of his face were frozen in a death grimace, the rakish mustached mouth set bitterly against his fate. Brian Devlan, the famed "Red Devil," would never again sail the seas he loved so dearly. Never again would fat, richly laden merchant ships come under attack from his swift and deadly sloop, the *Devil's Revenge*.

Cat continued to rock. Her father's last, challenging laugh still echoed within her; it seemed to ricochet jarringly inside her skull. She would always remember him that way—the breeze ruffling the lion's mane of red-gold hair, back straight and proud as they laid the noose about his neck. Those who had raised the hue and cry against him, indeed, the same moralists who had previously backed him in ventures, stood milling about with self-righteous smirks twisting their faces. There had been a cry for him to repent; repent before he met his maker. Brian Devlan had slowly surveyed the crowd, his lips cynically mocking their power over him.

"I'll not repent, my fine friends," he'd cried in a clear, ringing voice. "I've done the bidding of many among you. If I go to the Devil, on my honor, I'll not be lonely there. I look forward to greeting you all at the gates of Hades!" With that, he had laughed, and the savage, reckless sound had sent shivers down the spines of those present.

Out of the whispering mob came a voice, a cold, unfeeling command. "Hurry the bastard to his due, then, if that's his desire!" The tall, thin, dark-haired man who had spoken so callously stifled a yawn with one perfectly manicured hand and added, "I, for one, am bored!" His words seemed to break the uneasiness that had held the crowd in thrall, and others were emboldened enough to jeer and add their taunts to his.

In a moment it was over. Devlan's life had been unmercifully choked from him. Cat had bitten down hard on her lip, stifling the outraged pain within. Never again would he lift her in his arms to point out the perfect symmetry of a gull's flight or teach her the names of the stars as they sailed through a night warmed by the trade winds. He was gone from her forever. Her lips tightened to control their trembling. She would pay them *all* back; especially the thin, dark man who had so cruelly derided her father in his dying moments.

Suddenly a voice penetrated her shell, a hand touched her. Without glancing up, she knew the large, strong fingers gripping her shoulder belonged to none other than Will Foster, her father's first mate and closest friend.

"How long have you been here, child?" he asked. "Brian sent me after you but you'd disappeared." When Cat ignored his inquiry, he asked again, in a sharper tone. "How long, child?"

Catherine glanced up, her eyes dry and glazed with pain. "Long enough," she said in a dry, raspy whisper, sounding years older than the youngster who had disappeared from his sight that morning. "Did you watch, Will?" she asked. When he admitted he had arrived at the last moment, she questioned him, desperate to learn the identity of the dark man.

"Who was he, Will? I've got a right to know."

"It'll do you no good to dwell on it, Catherine, child. Your father wouldn't want it so." The strong, deeply lined features of his craggy face were twisted with distaste. To the end of his days he would bitterly regret his inability to save his friend. Even now, the same men who had trapped Devlan were after him. He could almost feel them snapping at his heels, like a pack of hungry, vicious hounds.

"Devlan left orders for me to pack you off to France. Your grandmother'll be there to look after you. No one there'll connect the name with the Red Devil. He wanted you to get schoolin', so's you'd grow up a lady, like your mum."

"A lady!" Cat turned all the fury of her youthful scorn on Will. Her eyes blazed lightning as she rejected the idea. "Who'll avenge him, if I'm gone? I'll not let his death go unpunished, even if you would!" Great tears welled up in the wide violet eyes and cascaded down her cheeks, and she shook with sobs.

Will pulled Cat close into the shelter of his arms until the storm of weeping had passed. When she quieted, he set her away from him, lifting her chin with calloused fingers until the amethyst eyes gazed into his own warm brown ones.

"You have my vow, little one. Devlan'll be avenged." His voice was deep with rumbling anger. "The time'll come when those who sought his death will rue the day they plotted!" He shook his head at her spirit and fondly tousled her curls. "You can do nought at your tender age, and I've a vow to be keepin' to your father to see you safe away. I've ne'er broken my word afore and I'll not be startin' with a promise to him departed."

Cat clung to Will, allowing him to pull her to her feet. Dear, familiar Will—he had always been a second father to her. Indeed, he had been there as long as she could remember. Despite the sobering effects of watching her father hang and her vow of vengeance on those responsible, in Will's arms she was once again a vulnerable young girl. Catherine's mother had died four years before and her only close relative, her younger sister, Briar, was safe at home in the care of a governess. Briar was a lovely child, three years younger than Cat and the very image of their dead mother. Now she and Briar would share a new manner of life in far-off France, with a grandmother they did not know.

"Are we going home to Canterbury Hill now?" Cat inquired softly, more than willing to let Will take charge.

"Yes, girl. On the morrow, we'll start home. For now, I've got to get you out 'a this weather." He gently placed a hand on her forehead, felt the warmth of a coming fever and quickly drew off his coat to place around her shoulders. "Jack Gordon'll take us in for the night." He placed a protective arm around her shoulders, urging her down the cobbled street.

Cat stopped, turning her head to stare back at her father. Wind had set the body swinging and the rain had suddenly begun to fall, huge splashing drops that soon soaked the both of them. "I'll not leave him there, Will. We must take him down and see to the burial!" A single tear trickled down her cheek, blending with the raindrops.

The wind blew harder, and the slender girl shivered beneath Will's arm. "I'll take you to Gordon's and return with a few 'a the boys. Don't worry, love, we'll do it proper."

Cat raised her face and the moonlight caught the silver glint of determination in her gaze. "No," she contested solemnly, refusing to budge from the spot. " 'Twill be done with loving hands." She placed one small hand within his own. "You and I, Will. We must get him down *now!*" There was a stubborn set to her chin and Will knew her well enough not to argue. Many times he'd seen precisely the same expression on Devlan's face. He glanced about, making sure they were still unobserved.

"We must be quick then. If I'm caught like Devlan, there'll be no one to get you safe away."

It took them almost half an hour to bring Will's mount, loosen the rope, and settle Devlan's heavy body across the stallion's broad back. Another twenty minutes found them at the back door of Jack Gordon's small cottage on the outskirts of town. Jack could be trusted, for he'd served with Devlan's crew for six years before marrying and retiring to land.

Cat was exhausted by the time they reached the cottage and, despite the protection of Will's coat, soaked through to the bone. When Jack's plump, rosy-cheeked wife, Meg—whom everyone called Mother—cautiously opened the door to her warm, well-lit kitchen, the girl almost fell into her arms. Mother clucked in maternal sympathy and gathered the girl to her ample bosom while over their heads, Jack and Will exchanged worried glances. There would be problems for Jack if Devlan's body were found here. Will motioned silently to Jack and, as his wife showed Cat to a seat by the blazing fire, they left the room together.

At quarter to six in the morning, as the sun rose in a still troubled sky, Devlan was laid to rest beneath the soil of the earth he had trod with such lusty exuberance. The small group ringing the graveside was silent in its mourning. Will, who had known Devlan for over twenty years, spoke a few simple words of eulogy. When the grave had been covered, Cat requested a few moments alone. She knelt and placed a single, blood-red rose atop the mound of moist earth.

"I swear I won't forget," she wept. "I swear on Mama's memory, I'll return and avenge you!" She touched the dirt covering his body and, rising, ran for the cottage and the comforting arms of Mother Gordon.

Canterbury Hill sat on a high bluff, overlooking the Hudson River. Its lines were classically English; it had, in fact, been built by Devlan as an exact copy of his ancestral home in Devonshire, though on a somewhat smaller scale. It was still a large house for the area, and the granite that gave it such a warm, pink glow had been quarried and transported at great expense all the way from the Connecticut Valley. It sat majestically, crowning two thousand acres of lush, green, heavily forested land that Devlan had purchased from the Horton family. The house had two wings, one with a large ballroom, the other containing the kitchen and work areas.

Unknown to any, save Cat and Will, Devlan had had steps cut into the side of the cliff at the rear of the house. Camouflaged by bushes, the steps could not be seen from the river. They led up the cliffside from a small cove at its base. Countless times Devlan had anchored the *Devil's Revenge* in the cove and used the steps to enter the house without detection. They ended in a natural cave at the top of the cliff where Devlan stored his more valuable spoils. A narrow passage, excavated and shored by strong timbers, led beneath the house to a hidden cellar.

Through this passage Will and Cat now moved. Will led the way with a lantern held aloft with one hand as Cat followed tightly clutching his other.

It had taken them weeks to reach the house, a trip which normally might have been made in four days. Traveling stealthily by night, skirting the larger towns along the way, they'd still had several close calls with the militia.

One morning at a small country inn owned by a friend of Jack Gordon's, Will had narrowly escaped being caught. Cat, not yet recovered from the shock of her father's death, had been sleeping fitfully. She had awakened at the tread of heavy boots below, and crept carefully down the stairs to find the aleroom full of red-coated soldiers. She had quietly returned to their room to shake Will out of a deep slumber at the foot of her bed, and they had managed to slip from the inn into the deep woods behind it. They'd hurried on that day, never stopping to rest until they were miles away. In a small clearing where they had finally stopped, Cat hesitantly inquired what their fate would have been had they been captured.

"No sense thinkin' about it—nothin' happened, girl. We'll be home to Canterbury in a twinkle and then off to France." Cat frowned again at the mention of France. "You'll like it there once you gets used to it," Will reassured her. "High time you had some female companionship! Always worried about Dev, you'd never be able to make a proper place for yourself."

Now, Cat trustingly tightened her grip on his hand, allowing him to lead her forward in the damp, gloomy tunnel. She hadn't seen her sister in a year and wondered if they would have anything at all in common. Briar had always been such a dreamy china doll, content to play quietly with her toys. Mama had loved them both dearly, but Catherine's wild ways and nature had always worried her. Cat was well aware she'd never lived up to her mother's gentle standards. Though she'd loved her, Devlan had been the parent she adored and tried to emulate. Once when she vied for his approval with a demonstration of her skill at fencing, he laughed and picked her up to whirl her around in the air. "Little Cat!" he shouted in hearty affection. "I do believe you were meant to be a boy!" She thrilled at the admiration in his voice, noting the touch of longing it held because of the son he would never have. At the tender age of eight she solemnly vowed to make it up to him. She became superbly accomplished with the rapier, learned to throw a knife with deadly accuracy, and conquered the art of navigating by the stars—all for the approval of the man she worshiped, the man who would never smile at her again!

Suddenly the end of the passageway loomed before Cat and Will. At the top of three steps lay a trapdoor leading into the cellar. Will turned to her and held the lantern so that her features were revealed in its soft halo of flickering yellow light.

"I want no arguments on this, lass," he warned her soberly. "I'll leave the lantern with you and I won't be gone long, but I must see if it's safe ahead. You'll be all right till I return." Again, Cat's expression was doubtful, but she recognized the wisdom of his statement and acceded to his wishes.

"Do be careful, then," she said with a show of bravado that hid the slight trembling of her lower lip. The tunnel was dark and close, and she had no desire to spend more time than necessary in it. As he winked reassuringly and turned to mount the steps, Cat touched his arm with her fingertips. "Please hurry, Will!"

"Back before you miss me, lovey."

As she watched, he lifted the trapdoor and hoisted himself through it. He still carried the lantern, and for a brief moment she was in darkness. Icy fear clutched at her and she almost abandoned her promise to stay behind. Then he lowered the lantern again, and as she took it from his hand, he disappeared silently into the darkness beyond the opening.

It seemed to Cat that she spent an eternity sitting cross-legged on the uneven dirt floor, although Will was gone only twenty minutes. She purposely kept her mind a blank, unwilling to dwell on the happiness of the past or the uncertainty of the future. Once she experienced an eerie feeling of being watched and discovered a small brown mouse eyeing her just at the edge of the lantern light. They stared at each other, neither blinking, until Cat shivered and adjusted her cloak. The mouse scampered off into the darkness, and she was alone once more.

Finally Will returned. She heard his footsteps before she saw him and an involuntary sigh of relief escaped her. She hadn't realized how much she'd come to rely on the comfort of his closeness. Eagerly she stood up to light his way down the steps. "Is it safe, then?" she asked, anxious to enter the warmth of the house.

"No!" There were lines of tension radiating from his eyes and his long, thin mouth was stretched further into a grimace of distaste. He sat heavily on the ground, telling her to sit next to him.

"Catherine, I don't know how to tell you. Girl, they've taken the house, the land, everything that was Devlan's!" Will paused, seeing that the girl was puzzled and unable to comprehend. "The soldiers, lass. They're up there now, all over the house. I just missed bein' caught again. Some bleedin' official had everything that belonged to Dev confiscated."

Apprehension and disbelief stretched Cat's eyes wide, darkening them to midnight velvet. "And Briar?" she said in a dull monotone.

"Cook said she was sent off with a relative of your Ma's. A cousin by marriage who lives in North Carolina. A rich dandy by the description of 'im. It's not her I'm worried about, child. We'll have to leave *now.*" His tone emphasized the need to escape before they were caught in the area.

In a world that had suddenly shattered, Cat had placed all her hopes on the comfort and safety that Canterbury Hill represented. Now that also was gone. She was too tired to think. "Where will we go without money?" she asked in the same monotone.

"We needn't worry over that at least. Dev hid a

chest of gold and silver in the cave. We'll take what we can. No one'll ever find this place—the rest'll be safe till we return for it." He stood abruptly, filled with purpose. "Come, girl, I've a promise to fulfill." He helped her to stand and gently guided her back towards the cave. His voice came again out of the semidarkness behind her. "I'm makin' another promise, child—this time to you. We'll come back, you and I. Them bastards'll be sorry for this, they'll regret their bloody profits!"

Part One
North Carolina, 1718

Chapter One

A strong, sharp wind blew from the south, catching and filling the topsails of the brig, the *Black Falcon*. She was an old ship, an eighty-tonner built in 1695, but a proven scrapper who'd proudly held her own against two-hundred-ton frigates. There was nothing showy about her. The lean lines of her time-worn hull and rigging had been designed for one purpose only—that of speed. With the present winds, she was slicing through the crest of the waves at a brisk eight knots. Soon she would reach her destination—Ocracoke Island, lying off the mainland of North Carolina. The crew of sixty bustled about under the direction of the first mate, a husky man of presence and command, whose voice rasped orders with authority.

Suddenly the lookout shouted. "Ocracoke to the port bow!" All hands stopped briefly to glance at the narrow spit of land that had just been sighted.

Captain St. Marin stood on the bridge, shielding eyes against the glare of the sun in the west. Orders were issued to launch the pinnace, the small boat that would proceed them and sound the torturous channel that lay ahead. Once through the channel, they would be safe in a deep-water harbor that had few equals along the Atlantic coastline of America.

Slowly they made their way through the narrow, twisting channel, tacking against the wind as men in the pinnace ahead shouted the soundings. The tide was with them; indeed, it was the only way to approach the island from the southern side, and all hands were relieved as the soundings gradually deepened. The *Falcon* was soon anchored in the safety of the harbor and preparations were made to go ashore.

A knock sounded at the door of the captain's cabin. Seated at the huge, oaken desk, reviewing the privateering commission that lay upon it, St. Marin absentmindedly called out a command to enter.

"All lines secured, Cap'n," the first mate said in English. He had never learned to speak French and stubbornly clung to his South England accent. The rest of the crew were Frenchmen and understood his roughly bawled orders, more from the timbre of his voice than from the few garbled words of French he spoke. When the captain urged him to be seated, the huge man threw himself into a chair with more grace than a man his size would usually have possessed. He was a great lion of a man, six foot five, with enormous, muscular shoulders. With his brawny build, the mate had no problems keeping the rough, brawling crew members in line. Of less than average height and extremely slender, the captain possessed the skills needed to navigate the ship and the daring imagination to make her successful as a French privateer against the English. Together, the two combined the qualities needed for achieving success in their aims.

"You know the plan, then," said the captain. "We're off at midnight with the tide. We should reach the Nicholls plantation by dawn." Marin's eyes were narrowed and cold, speaking of their objective. "The men are aware of the penalty if the girl is harmed?"

"I stressed the point, Cap'n," the mate replied, grinning as he fingered the edge of a very long, wicked-looking knife.

"Good. I want no chance for anything to go wrong." There was a preoccupied air about the captain, and the man sharing the cabin was well aware of the reason. As he rose to leave he paused a moment to study the aristocratic features he knew so well.

"I'll let y' know when the landin' party returns. Shouldn't take 'em long to fill the water casks."

The captain barely heard him. Sitting tensed in an armchair of such mighty proportions that it seemed overwhelming, the solitary figure brooded in silence. The mate moved to the door, leaving the captain alone to reflect on the events that would soon come to pass.

In the light just before dawn, everything took on a gray appearance: the sky, the ocean, the mists upon the water. If someone had chanced to stand ashore at the Nicholls plantation, twenty miles southeast of Bath Town, North Carolina, he would have been awed at the sight of a ship emerging out of the billows of fog, a ship that was as gray and ghostly as the mists from which she had materialized. But no one stood ashore, at this hour; there was no witness as scores of men swung down the side of the ship to the waiting boats, and rowed silently to shore, and gathered on the beach to await the command to advance. At last it came, when Captain St. Marin stood on the sand, feet planted firmly astride.

"Onward, men, and remember my warning—death to the man who harms the girl!" The mate's order came in a low, growled whisper, and the crew moved stealthily up the beach toward the main house of the plantation known as Seahaven. Their plan was to strike swiftly like a snake, and retreat before the stunned inhabitants could awaken and form a defense. Behind them in the east, the sun began its ascent, lighting the sky with a pale violet pink that promised another steamy, humid autumn day.

As silently as possible, the men moved forward to surround the house. In the still, dim light of predawn they met no one and encountered no resistance until they reached the house. At the entrance to the kitchens, the captain and mate came upon a slave, a dark, imposing woman with a wide girth. She had apparently already been hard at work preparing breakfast for the household, for her round ebony face was frosted with a sheen of sweat. Her eyes widened, the whites showing clearly as she backed into the kitchen at the sight of the armed intruders. St. Marin and the mate entered, followed by ten of the crew.

"Secure the first floor," the captain ordered in a hushed tone. Drawing a sword from his hip scabbard, the mate flourished it in the air, and the cook's eyes widened even more.

"We mean you no harm, woman," he said in a low growl. "Tell us what we want and you'll live to see another morn. If not . . ." He waved the sword again, slicing the air for emphasis and leaving no doubt what the consequences would be. "Which room is the girl's?"

Clearly the woman was frightened to death, and yet her features showed the signs of an inner struggle. Whether it was loyalty to the family who owned her or the possibility of retaliation by her master, the two confronting her would never know. Settling her ample mass on a long bench before the fire, she sighed, and answered their question.

"Upstairs, suh," she drawled. Tears had appeared in her dark eyes and rolled unnoticed down the fat cheeks. "To the lef', third do' down 'de hall." She saw the two exchange triumphant glances, and as they rushed from the room, leaving her in the care of an exceedingly wicked-looking fellow with a brace of pistols stuck beneath his sash, she dissolved into a fit of weeping. Hugging herself, she rocked back and forth, mumbling, "Lordy, what is we goin' to do . . . what'll Masta' Charles say?"

Upstairs, exactly as the woman had indicated, they found the girl's room. Entering quietly, they located her bed by the half-light of early dawn and crept forward.

Quickly the captain moved to her side, placing a hand over the girl's mouth. Startled from a deep sleep, her eyes flew open, widening in horrified disbelief at the sight of the two strangers.

"Don't scream," ordered St. Marin. "We won't harm you." She began to struggle and the captain quickly ordered the mate to subdue her. A heavy cloak was thrown over her and she was lifted into the mate's muscular arms as easily as a feather. As the mate left the room with his light, still struggling burden, the captain raised a long, thin knife to skewer a note to the feather pillow, then paused to read it once more, a smile playing at the corners of the finely etched mouth.

Charles Nicholls, it read. *If you value the girl's life bring ten thousand pounds and meet me at Ocracoke Island tomorrow at dawn. Come alone.* The note was signed, *The Falcon.*

A long, loud scream from below broke the silence of the house. Racing down the stairs, the captain found one of the crewmen holding his sword at the throat of the old cook. "That's enough, Mauret," St. Marin snapped angrily. "By now you've alerted the whole house. We're off!"

The woman collapsed into a corner, shaking with fright at her close call. Word was passed to the men stationed about the house and grounds to retreat. When the men had all made for the safety of the beach, St. Marin began to follow.

Rounding the corner of the outbuildings came a squat, heavy-set man who appeared to be the overseer. He was about to shout orders to a group of slaves following him when he caught sight of the captain. His mouth dropped open in astonishment but he recovered quickly enough to draw the pistol stuck within his belt. Taking careful aim at his target, who had no chance of reaching any cover, the man shouted to one of the Negroes to alert the master.

Captain St. Marin reached for a pistol but the man raised his weapon higher and steadied on his captive's heart. "Don't try it, mister," he drawled. His narrow, piggy eyes stared at the captain. "You wanta' tell me what'cha doin here?"

Jules Lareau crept up stealthily behind the man holding the gun. The slaves saw him but none made a sound, perhaps hoping that their cruel taskmaster might be killed. The captain's face remained passive, watching the crewman stalk closer until he stood directly behind the overseer. Placing a sword at the fellow's neck, Jules laughed aloud, then ordered the man to drop his weapon. The overseer's face lost its triumphant leer and quickly turned a pasty white. The captain laughed and ran forward, clapping Lareau on the back.

"Well done, Lareau. I owe you one for this! Now let's be off—he sent a slave to alert the household." The pistol was retrieved from the ground and used to bludgeon the overseer unconscious, then the two hurried toward the beach and the waiting boats. Every moment was precious, for although they had plenty of men, their ammunition was limited.

The mate's frown lifted as he saw them coming. He grinned lopsidedly and admitted, "I kind 'a thought you might 'a needed help!" The girl had ceased to struggle and lay quietly in his arms.

The full light of dawn was now upon them. The boats quickly made the return trip to the waiting ship. By the time all were safely aboard, the beach was alive with pursuers. Looking back, the captain laughed and gave the order to set sail. The mate was instructed to take the captive to the cabin. Exuberation filled the captain. Except for the brief incident with the overseer, all had gone according to plan and soon, very soon, St. Marin would feel the thrill of victory.

The girl sat huddled in the captain's huge chair, wondering what would become of her. She knew nothing other than that she had been captured by ruffians for some unknown purpose. She had been sitting here for half an hour now awaiting—what? The captain's pleasure?

She'd heard stories of women captured by pirates and she shuddered to think what her fate might be and yet . . . the captain's voice had been gentle when warning her to stay quiet.

She ran a hand distractedly through her tousled, white-blond curls and tried to bolster her courage. Perhaps if she pleaded prettily enough the captain might return her. As if to interrupt her thoughts, St. Marin entered the room. A large wide-brimmed hat covered his head, almost hiding his features. His small size surprised her, for she would have expected to see a more muscular type as the leader of such a motley crew.

"Ah, Mademoiselle, I trust you have not been harmed or frightened too severely?" The captain's walk was strangely graceful, his voice almost melodious. He moved to the cabinet against the far wall, pulling forth a bottle of brandy and two glasses. He spoke with a French accent but his grasp of English seemed extremely fluent. "You will pardon the furnishings, please. It is rare that we have a lady of quality as our guest." He encouraged her to sip at the brandy to, as he phrased it, "calm your nerves."

"Mademoiselle . . . Devlan . . . is it not? I wish to reassure you we mean you no harm. I have left a ransom note for Monsieur Charles Nicholls asking that he meet me with a sum of money for your safe return. In the event that he is too penurious or cowardly to appear, rest assured you will be released unharmed!" He paused and threw the brandy down his throat. "Tell me, are you an only child?"

Briar Devlan was startled by the sudden inquiry concerning her relatives. After sipping the brandy she had almost been lulled into a feeling of security. "Yes, I . . ." She had begun to state that she was alone in the world except for her guardian, Charles Nicholls, but she felt a strange compulsion to tell this man, this gentle pirate, the truth. "I had a sister . . . . She . . . she disappeared at the time of my father's death."

"And no attempt was made to find this sister?"

"But of course! Uncle Charles searched everywhere, spent great sums trying to trace her, but to no avail. I haven't thought of her for years. Strange that I should mention it now—to a complete stranger." The girl stared down into her brandy glass, lost in thoughts of the past. "I was only nine at the time."

Captain St. Marin had begun to pace the room. "And what if I informed you that your dear 'Uncle Charles' was responsible for your father's death and your sister's disappearance—what then, Mademoiselle?"

The girl jumped to her feet, her hand lashing out to spill the brandy on the desk. "You lie! You don't know Charles—he would never have——"

The air seemed charged with lightning. The captain turned and stalked to the desk, placing both hands upon it and staring into Briar's eyes. *"I* lie, Mademoiselle? Not I! *I was there!"* One hand reached up to sweep the wide-brimmed hat away and reveal the heavy mass of red-gold curls that had been hidden securely beneath. "I was there, Briar Devlan. *I watched our father hang by the neck until the life was choked from him!* Charles Nicholls *was* responsible, and tomorrow at dawn, he'll pay for what he did!"

Briar was stunned but suddenly it all fell into place—the captain's grace and slender physique, the gentleness of voice. Only eight when she'd last seen her sister, Briar immediately recognized the blaze of golden hair. Without a doubt, it was Catherine who stood before her, attired in men's clothing. Her face drained white as she considered the violent charge her sister had thrown at her. It couldn't be. Charles couldn't be responsible for their father's death! Tears sprung into her wide blue eyes as she defended her guardian.

"You're wrong! Someone's misled you, Catherine. Charles is a strong man, but never would he deceive me so . . . not me!"

Cat unpinned her hair, allowing the heavy waves to fall to her shoulders. It felt so wonderful to relax and be herself. She sighed heavily and poured another glass of brandy. She had planned this for so long that now, facing her sister with the truth was almost an anticlimax.

"No, Briar. Whatever face Charles Nicholls presents to you, he *is* a ruthless liar and a scoundrel." She wearily sat in a chair opposite Briar and began to describe the events of that horrid day, eight years before, events that still remained as crystal clear as though they had occurred yesterday. She had hoped to spare her younger sister the anguish of hearing the tale, but apparently she had no choice.

As she finished, Cat added, "I found out much later that the man who had mocked our father's dying and the man who had taken you into his home to rear were one and the same. Unfortunately, Grandmère St. Marin held tightly to the reins and refused to allow me to leave France before my eighteenth birthday." Cat smiled, flashing even, white teeth in a heart-shaped face. "She found me a little trying as far as her matchmaking efforts were concerned. When I refused the Comte de Savan, she finally threw up her hands in disgust and allowed me my own way."

"Will Foster was with you this morning, was he not?" The sound of his voice had triggered a vague memory in Briar.

"Yes, I'd be helpless without him. He stayed in France with me all those years, working at Grandmère's estate. In fact, it was he who discovered solid evidence of Nicholls's deception. Here, if you doubt my word"—Cat stepped around the desk, pulling open the bottom drawer and laying several documents before her sister. She pointed to the first, a letter of commission signed by Sir Charles Nicholls and dated August 1708. "As you can see, Father was backed in a venture by Nicholls and two associates, Jonathan Winston and Pieter de Rysfield. Both died rather mysteriously within a year of father's hanging." She shuffled the papers and drew one to the top. "*This* was signed by de Rysfield as lieutenant governor of New York. As you can see, it's a warrant for Brian Devlan's arrest on a charge of piracy. De Rysfield owed his appointment to the machinations of Nicholls." She paused for effect and then continued, "They found him at the bottom of a cliff three months later."

Briar stared, shocked by the weight of evidence. "How do you know these aren't forgeries?" she demanded in desperate defense. "Charles had no reason to do such a thing!"

Cat had begun to pace the cabin once more. "No reason that *you* knew of." She whirled to face her sister, eyes ablaze with indignation. "It was greed, Briar, greed and revenge. He wanted Canterbury Hill! Didn't you know it was confiscated after father's death? Again, de Rysfield was responsible. The lands and house were deeded to Nicholls."

"You mentioned revenge," Briar mumbled.

"Yes. I would never have known if Grandmère hadn't brought up the subject. Charles was a suitor for Mama's hand. She spurned him and ran off with our father instead. Grandmère said the man worshiped Mama, but she would have nothing to do with him. He was furious when they eloped, and within three months had married Mama's cousin Thérèse."

"And I looked just like Mama . . ." Briar's voice trailed off to a whisper as she turned an ashen color. She tried to stand but fell back to the chair in a half-faint.

Cat was at her side immediately, calling her name and lightly patting her face. In a moment Briar came around, moaning softly. Her eyes flew open to gaze pleadingly at Cat's concerned features. "You can't hurt him, Catherine. For my sake, let him live, *please!* I can't explain but you *must* listen."

Cat was livid with fury. "After everything I've told you, you still defend him! Didn't you care anything for Father?"

Briar began to cry hysterically. "I'm going to have a baby . . . Charles's baby. You'd ruin everything for me —you can't do this!"

It was as though a white-hot flash of lightning had exploded before Cat's eyes. Her hand shot forward to connect with her sister's face in a resounding smack. The girl stared at her for what seemed an eternity before she threw herself forward on the desk and began to sob. Cat backed away, nausea beginning to churn deep within her. How *could* Briar have slept with the man who had killed their father! Cat stalked to the mullioned window of the cabin, staring out across the sea she loved as much as Devlan had. Her breath came raggedly as she tried to clear her mind and think sensibly.

Briar hadn't known about Charles, she reasoned silently. She hadn't known what a conniving murderer he was. The thought that Briar would bear a child of his made Cat shudder. Suddenly she remembered what she had learned in Bath Town, a month before. "Briar . . . darling, I'm sorry I hit you, I didn't mean to hurt you." Briar glanced up, her eyes swollen and red. Like a child, she wiped at the tears with the back of her hand. "Briar, tell me—does he know you're pregnant? The answer is very important."

Briar sniffled once and nodded her head. "I told him six weeks ago. We're going to be married soon."

Cat's mouth formed a thin, hard line, her eyes narrowing in disgust. "He *never* meant to marry you, love. Briar, how did you ever become involved?"

The girl glanced down at the desk, her hands nervously entwined. "He seduced me when I was fifteen. Thérèse had died a year before and . . . he was lonely. He told me how beautiful I was . . . ." Her mouth wavered as she finished, "it was Mama he saw in me, I know that now." She glanced up, a plea in her eyes. "Please Cat, he said he'd take care of everything, that I wasn't to worry."

"I was in Bath Town last month, seeking information for my raid this morning. Do you know a woman by the name of Cora Fitzhugh—an older woman, a widow?"

Briar seemed puzzled by the question. "Yes, of course. She owns the next plantation. Her husband died last year and left her quite well off. Why do you ask?"

"Because Charles Nicholls announced his engagement to the widow Fitzhugh five weeks ago—*after* you had informed him of your state!"

Briar's mouth rounded into an O of shock. Again the tears began, a cascade of them as she wondered aloud what would become of her.

"Is there no one you're interested in? Someone to love you and give the baby a name?" Cat inquired gently. She had come closer again and stared down at her sister with a mixture of pity and sorrow.

"Ryan would never marry me now," the girl sobbed. Through her tears, with gentle prodding from Cat, she explained that Ryan Nicholls was the heir to the Nicholls fortune, a nephew of Charles by his only brother. Ryan's parents had died when he was but a babe and Charles had raised him. It had always been understood that the two would marry. "Whatever will I do?" Briar sobbed, her hands covering her face.

Cat patted her shoulder, trying to comfort her. "I'll handle this, Briar. I think it would be best if I sent you to France. Grandmère will take care of you. No one need know about the babe. It'll give you time to think and consider what to do. After you have the baby, she can claim you're a widow and perhaps arrange one of her famous matches for you."

She helped Briar to stand and the two girls hugged each other, embracing for the first time. Cat suddenly felt the burden of being the older of the two and protectively placed an arm around Briar's shoulder, urging her lie down on the bunk and rest. "Don't worry about anything. I'll take care of it all," she assured her. Briar seemed happy to turn her worries over to a more competent person and smiled trustingly at her older sister.

Long after darkness had fallen, the cabin was quiet and still. Briar slept and Catherine sat in her chair, brooding over the changes in her plans. The moonlight shining through the windows lit her face in profile, highlighting the finely drawn features. The Comte de Savan had exclaimed over her, describing her to all who would listen as Venus incarnate. Slender, and taller than average, Cat's face and figure had set the court dandies to writing poems in her honor. Savan himself had written a poem which came to the attention of the king. Louis had sent for her, anxious to meet the young woman his courtier had described as fire and ice.

Louis had given her a private audience and then spent the night dancing with her at a court ball. Tongues had wagged, and the lovely ladies of the court had turned green with envy. Yet, despite her seductive figure and flaming hair, there was a distance, an elusive air of hauteur that surrounded her like a shielding cloak. Even as she smiled into a suitor's eyes, flirting and teasing, he sensed a reserve about her that could not be penetrated.

It was this combination of qualities . . . a body that promised the depths of desire and violet eyes that looked on the world with the innocent, withdrawn air of a convent postulant, that drove men wild and kept their interest long after it might have waned. Her flawless fair skin was a perfect setting for her eyes of violet ice fringed by thick, dark-gold lashes. The shading of her irises varied according to her mood. Happy and bright, her eyes reflected the cool twilight of a summer's eve. Angry, they flashed a darker hue, as though a storm had settled in. Reflective and rarely seen was the light ice blue of remembered pain, the pain of loss that had never left her those eight long years.

The shape of Cat's mouth almost seemed to do battle with the coolness of her eyes. It was warm and inviting, with a slight pout to the lower lip that teased in the most delightful manner. A delicate, sculptured nose and dimpled chin completed the aristocratic profile. There were few women who hadn't sighed with relief when they found she would no longer be in attendance at the court of the French king.

As a parting gift between friends, for they had never been more than that, Louis had given her a large emerald surrounded by tiny diamonds. She wore it now, around her neck on a slender gold chain. Often when she was upset, she would touch the jewel, and somehow it had become a very comforting habit.

Now, she sat fingering the gem absently as she tried to decide what course of action to take. With her newfound knowledge that Briar had become a liability to Charles, instead of a desirable asset, she knew he would never come to the rendezvous. In fact, she had played into his hands perfectly. She had rid him of his problem. In the morning they would have to set sail for Tortuga. The island had been her home for almost two years now and she had built a modest, comfortable house there. In the safety of familiar surroundings, she would be able to think and plan more clearly. Charles Nicholls had been afforded only a brief respite from his fate. The time would come soon enough when they would face each other over crossed rapiers. *Soon,* she thought, and the idea brought a wicked smile to her mouth. She had waited patiently for eight long years. She could wait a while longer. Only now, she would be avenging not only Brian Devlan, but Briar as well.

Chapter Two

Cat lay back, relaxing in her bath. The warm, scented water was finally beginning to ease the dreadful pounding of her head. She had awakened this morning with another headache and nothing seemed to ease the throbbing of her temples. She was well aware of the cause; only satisfying her long-nurtured lust for revenge would make the almost daily headaches cease.

At least she had seen Briar safely off to France, in Will's trusted care. Cat smiled to herself as she remembered the argument he'd given her.

"I can't go off for two months and leave you alone," he had protested stubbornly. "Suppose, just suppose, missy, that Nicholls sends a ship after you. You'd have no protection, what with the *Falcon* gone and me with 'er!" After much wheedling and many assurances, she had finally convinced him that she was in no danger, that she would use the time to rest and plan. After all, there was no way for Nicholls to locate her.

Lifting one slender leg from the water, she arched

her ankle and rested it on the tub's edge, soaping its length with her sponge. Slowly the silken, scented water was lifting her mood. If only she could devise a plan! Part of her problem was due to restlessness. For the past two years she had been physically active, and the thought of remaining here for six weeks until Will returned with the *Falcon* was enough to have caused her headache. Perhaps she should have gone with them. It would have been good to see Grandmère again. Still, by the time Will returned she should have a solid plan worked out in detail. This time nothing would be left to chance; this time Charles Nicholls would suffer the fate he so richly deserved. Perhaps she would have him strung from the yardarm. *That* would be justice indeed—to see him dealt the same fate he had allotted for her father!

Suddenly, without a warning sound, the door to her bedroom burst open. It rocked on its hinges, slamming back against the wall with resounding force. Startled from her daydreams of revenge, Cat whirled to see who dared to enter her room in such a manner. Her expression turned from anger to stunned shock as a tall man in black strode confidently forward, cutlass in hand, aggressively alert and obviously searching for an adversary. Cat had the briefest of moments to study the man as his eyes searched the room. He was well over six feet tall and broad-shouldered, with a narrow, tapering waist and spare belly. A black silk shirt was tucked within the waist of skin-tight breeches that covered lean, muscular legs. From the look of him, he'd make a fine pirate, Cat thought. His hair was thick and wavy with a rich, blue-black cast, tied back and framing a fiercely proud, hawklike face. His skin was darkly tanned, stretched taut over bold features that seemed fine, almost aristocratic. He was, by far, one of the most interesting specimens of manhood she had ever seen.

When he satisfied himself that the room harbored no opponent, he turned toward her. Cat sank lower in the water, suddenly aware of her nudity before this virile intruder. She positioned the large sponge strategically between her breasts, hoping it covered them partially from his view. He was even more handsome when he faced her. He smiled, obviously delighted with what he had found, and despite the defenseless position in which she found herself, she couldn't help noticing the deep cleft in his chin. She must be mad! Had anyone else entered her room so abruptly she'd have screamed with fury and yet here she sat, calmly contemplating the intruder's features!

The man sheathed his cutlass, smiled once again and made a sweeping, almost courtly bow to her. "Your pardon, madame. I had no idea I would be intruding upon your privacy!" His voice matched his looks. It was a deep, husky rumble and she involuntarily shivered.

Cat forced her racing pulses to calm, and a semblance of haughty disdain into her voice. "I assume I am safe from your blade, monsieur—or do you war on defenseless women?" His eyes, startling black coals, swept over her appraisingly before he answered.

"You seem fairly calm for one who fears the edge of my blade, madame—or is it mademoiselle?" His mouth twitched with wry amusement as he took a step forward. He seemed to be enjoying her helplessness.

Anger pulsed through Cat and she tossed a spirited retort. "I never said I feared you; you assume too much, monsieur. If you were to leave immediately, it would not be too soon!"

"I think not, mademoiselle. I have not satisfied my purpose in coming. Perhaps you would be good enough to tell me what you know of the captain of the *Black Falcon*. This is reported to be his house. Tell me his whereabouts and I shall leave you to your privacy, much though you might regret the loss of my presence."

The nerve of him! The arrogant fool taunted her with his virility. What excuse could she think of to rid herself of him? Quickly her agile mind searched for a plausible story. "The captain is gone. The *Falcon* has sailed to France, and you have missed your chance at her master!" There—that would set him back on his heels!

A black frown settled across the strong features. His

brows drew together as he glared down at her. Cat almost shivered under the gaze of those dark, angry eyes. Clearly he was not used to being thwarted. "And when will the good captain return?" he asked, his voiced deepened further by anger.

"I know not, monsieur. I do not even know why you trouble me with your pursuit of him. What has he done to you that you seek him?"

"He has kidnapped my fiancée, and left behind a ransom note, m'lady. The scoundrel is a craven coward and when I find him, I shall have the pleasure of running him through. What is your relationship to this dog?" He stared down at her, commanding an answer.

Cat had to think fast. She was becoming deeper embroiled in lies by the minute. There would be no harm in admitting she was the captain's mistress, cast off when he came to prefer Briar. That would surely be a knife thrust to this man's heart, for she deduced he was none other than Charles Nicholls's nephew, Ryan. She forced a sullen pout to her face, refusing to meet his gaze. "I . . . I am the captain's mistress, if you must know. At least, I was until . . . *she* came here, the one with blue eyes and white-blonde curls." She almost laughed aloud at the low growl of anger that he made. If she didn't control herself, she would spoil her handiwork!

"I suggest you step from the tub, madam. We have much to discuss."

Cat's head shot up. She was appalled that he would dare to suggest . . . "With you here! Indeed not!" she snapped. He had apparently gained control of his anger, for he now regarded her with a cool, studied gaze. As she watched, he crossed his arms at his chest and his mouth twitched with a cynical smile.

"Pretend I am your absent amour, *chérie*. You seem to be a very self-possessed young woman. It should not be too difficult for you to master your . . . modesty." He placed sarcastic emphasis on the last word and Cat's fingers burned to slap the sneer from his face.

"I will not," she repeated stubbornly.

"You will, or that pretty skin will shrivel like a prune, my dear." He drew up a chair and placed it before the bath. "I have plenty of time to wait. Shall we see who gives in first?" He sat, relaxed and easy, his eyes never leaving her face. Cat couldn't suppress her fury, and the frustration on her lovely features made Ryan smile.

Cat bit her lip, trying to think of a plan to foil him. She decided to give a little, to let him think he had the upper hand. "Well, then, monsieur, you win." She glanced up into his eyes, her long, thick lashes fluttering several times in a display of enchanting, helpless confusion. "Please, if you would at least turn your back a moment. Allow me the decency of wrapping a sheet about myself!" She smiled tremulously and was rewarded by the slight softening of his features. He stood, turning his back, and she quickly rose and stepped from the water. The sheet was around her in a second's time and she had just tucked the end into the valley formed by her breasts as he turned again to face her.

When he had turned away to allow her to step from the bath, Ryan had neatly positioned himself before a mirror on the opposite wall. The girl had covered herself quickly, but not quickly enough, for Ryan had caught a fleeting and highly tempting glimpse of white thigh and gently rounded breast. He had much to discuss with the wench. He had not accepted her story of being the captain's cast-off mistress. Briar was a lovely girl and might be a temptation to any man, but this girl was not a woman to be cast off by any but a deranged fool. He had more respect for the man who had arranged the raid on Seahaven and Briar's kidnaping than to believe such a fabrication.

Ryan opened the door of the room, shouting to Foxworth. The young man was his second in command and could be trusted to settle in the men and see to their well-being. He heard the sound of heavy boots treading the stairs and then Jeremy appeared somewhat breathlessly before him.

"Yes, sir. You called, sir?"

"See to sleeping accommodations for the men, Jeremy. Get them fed and post several guards. I'm not sure how long we'll be here. That's a good lad!" Foxworth touched his hat respectfully and hurried away.

Something, perhaps the deep quiet of the room, warned him. As he turned to face the girl he saw a flash of metal and managed to duck, just as a long and almost deadly accurate knife blade whizzed past him to stick and quiver in the door, exactly where he had just stood. In three long strides he was across the room. The girl stood near the bed, had stood there calmly waiting to watch her blade reach its victim. As he came toward her she made a wild dash, attempting to scramble across the bed and away from the fury reflected on his face.

Ryan threw himself forward, tackling the girl and pinning her to the bed. She struggled, screaming a torrent of abuse in French, kicking, biting, scratching in a show of wildcat fury. His anger matched hers and he easily caught her hands, twisting them high above her head. In the struggle between them, the sheet loosened, came free, revealing the soft white bounty that it had covered.

Cat ceased to struggle, mortified by her position. Not only had her attempt to wound him failed, but she was now his prisoner, helplessly pinned beneath him with nothing to protect her from that dark, sensual gaze. Their eyes met. She saw the flare of lust within his and knew there would be no escape. Her eyes closed as she caught her bottom lip between her teeth. Something, her pride perhaps, would not allow her to beg or plead with him, and she refused to allow one tear to escape her tightly shut eyes. But neither would she struggle, for that would surely add to his pleasure!

The girl's actions puzzled Ryan. One moment she had been a spitting tigress, the next a mild lamb awaiting sacrifice. Her lovely face was tense, pale, delicate as though in the one glance that had passed between them, she had accepted her fate. Only the rise and fall of her breasts with every breath betrayed an inner agitation. The sight of those soft, ivory mounds, gently asway with every deep breath, would alone have driven him to passion. He rolled from her, still gripping her hands above her head, and stripped the sheet away, revealing the glory of what he had only glimpsed before. Slender and fine-boned, she lay quietly, exposed to his gaze.

If he had thought briefly of releasing her, that thought now fled. His body would not allow him to let her go without tasting the sweetness that was surely hidden within her. Ryan lowered his mouth to engulf one rosy nipple. The captive girl flinched at the contact, her body trembled and then was still once more. He released her wrists slowly, waiting for a reaction. Her arms stayed above her head but her hands formed tightly clenched fists. Her eyes remained shuttered. Somehow he sensed she was expecting a violent attack and had resigned herself to it in a sacrificial manner. He had never resorted to force before, preferring his women warm and willing. Perhaps if he took his time, this one, this still and lovely creature, would warm to him.

Cat felt his weight ease from the bed—could it be that she would escape violation? She refused to open her eyes, though she would have loved to know the direction of his thoughts. In a moment she knew. He settled next to her, his body as bare as her own. The thick mat of crisp, curly hair on his chest brushed her nipples, teasing them against her will.

She commanded, literally ordered her body to show no reaction, and yet, dear God, his hands, his fingers swept so lightly across her skin, tempting her senses against her own volition. His lips found the tender spot below one shell-like ear and pressed a soft kiss. She shivered; her eyes flew open to find his face so near hers that their breath intermingled. Violet eyes met black. The vision of his handsome face dissolved from view as his mouth sought her trembling lips.

She who had always been aloof and untouchable, who had commanded the most jaded of Louis's courtiers with a mere flutter of her lashes, who had never known more than Savan's gentle, respectful kiss was soon to know the full measure of physical love between man and woman. It seemed he meant to leave her no illusions, for though he was taking possession of her body, his plan of mastery was gentle, teasing her into response against her will. She felt like sobbing, but again the devilish pride within her would not allow any show of weakness.

His hands now caressed her breasts, his mouth trailing light kisses across her belly. Cat shivered, unable to suppress the tingling feeling that was spreading across her entire body. Damn him! The quick violation of her body would have been enough to endure but this slow, sweet, wicked torture was killing her! Suddenly his mouth found her and her back arched with shock. She struggled to break away but his hands held her, pinning her to the bed like a captured butterfly. Cat's breath came in ragged sobs, her head twisting wildly from side to side. Her loins felt afire with a mounting tension that she had never before experienced.

Her body shuddered as wave after wave of pure, erotic feeling swept over her, a tide of feeling so strong it threatened to drown her in its wake. Quickly, all too quickly, the sensations ebbed, to be replaced by a knifing pain between her thighs. She screamed once, her eyes flying open in pained surprise before his mouth covered hers to cut off her protests, before his strength stifled her futile efforts to escape the searing pain. It too ebbed, until the same tingling flames of desire burst into a fire that seemed bent on consuming her. Finally Ryan collapsed and rolled from her, the passion aroused by the sight of her naked body now spent.

Cat lay sprawled on the bed, exhausted physically and emotionally. Never had she imagined the intense heights of lovemaking, and never had she experienced such throbbing pain. Ryan lay at her side, his hand draped across her below her breasts. His voice came, so low and husky she almost missed his question.

"Now that we know each other so intimately, Mademoiselle, perhaps you will tell me your name."

She whirled to face him, eyes wounded and glazed by

unshed tears, resentment emanating from her in unseen waves. Her hair was a wild, tangled mass, surrounding and framing her face in a bright halo of red-gold tendrils. She retorted spitefully, "Call me whore or harlot then, for *that* is what you've branded me!"

Ryan leaned over her, his face close to hers, and firmly took her chin in hand, forcing her to turn and face him. "It's Eve that I should call you, my nameless vixen, for it's not a whore I've made you but a complete woman. I had no idea you were a virgin."

"Would it have made a difference?" she questioned bitterly.

"Aye, possibly." His dark eyes glowed warmly. Evidently the bedplay had put him in an excellent mood. "But then again, it might not have. By your own admission, you were the mistress of our absent friend, the captain." One dark, winged brow arched in amusement. "By my own experience, mistresses are seldom virginal!"

"And I suppose you have a vast range of experience," she commented tartly. "How many other defenseless innocents have you despoiled, gallant sir?"

"Jealous, my love? You needn't be—you're by far the loveliest of the lot." He seemed to be enjoying her resentful attitude, and showed not the least touch of remorse. Remembering who he was, who his uncle was, added to the fire of her wounded emotions. That a Nicholls, of all men on earth, should claim her virginity was the bitterest brew to swallow. A tiny, mirthless smile played at her lips as she added his name to her plan of revenge.

Ryan lightly caressed the soft, rounded curve of her derrière and commented casually, "I see you've seen the lighter side of this. Good, I've never taken to wenches who weep and gnash their teeth after the damage's been done. Better to look to the future, sweet, it does get better, you know."

"I can manage quite well without your philosophy of life, Mr. Nicholls." Cat suddenly realized her mistake and silently cursed her loose tongue. She waited, breath held, to see if he had caught the mention of his name, a name he had not yet revealed to her.

"You were saying—what silence, my injured innocent? Come now, it's time those sweet lips spoke the truth." He sat up, pulling her onto his lap. "Now," he said, toying with the silky curls at the nape of her neck. "Unless you prefer an immediate encore of our love play, I suggest you answer my questions. Truthfully." His hand rested on her knee, his fingers tracing a light teasing pattern along her inner thigh. "How did you know my name, and what is your real connection with this rascal, St. Marin?"

Refusing to look at him, yet well aware of his close physical proximity, Cat gazed sullenly at a spot high on the wall. A part of her warned her to cooperate, for the man who held her so gently had an arrogant ruthlessness hidden beneath his genial manner. She was in his complete control for the time being, unable to seek help from any quarter, and she must play along to benefit her own designs.

"I am not St. Marin's mistress, but his sister," she lied glibly, praying inwardly that he would believe her. "As for knowing your name, my brother and your intended have been on intimate terms for over a year. Briar suggested making Charles pay the ransom." She cast a quick sideways glance at him to see his reaction, hoping the first statement would prick his vanity. To her keen disappointment, there was no alteration in his expression, and he merely continued his fondling of her thigh. "Doesn't your fiancée's infidelity cause you any distress?"

"Not at all, dear. We had no formal commitment to each other, only an old understanding of sorts. Your brother—if I am to believe *that* claim—was not the first to seek Briar's favors. I believe my uncle had that honor."

It was Cat who reacted with shock. "Then why did you come after her? Are you merely a lackey, doing your uncle's bidding?"

"Had I known she left of her own will, I'd not have

bothered myself. But then, I'd not have had the pleasure we just shared." He smiled smugly and bent to kiss her shoulder.

"*That* is a matter of opinion. I found no pleasure in your attentions!" His lips touched at her throat and then roamed lower, seeking the soft rise of her breasts. She squirmed uncomfortably, trying to escape his growing ardor. "Now that you know the truth, I suppose you'll be off, with nary a thought of what you've done to me. If my brother were here," she threatened, "he would slit your throat for what you've done!"

"Would he, now? Well, perhaps I should stay to meet him. Yes, I think I *will* stay and await his return." His arm tightened about her shoulders, drawing her close against his chest and his warm breath whispered against her ear. "If I'm to pay the piper, I might as well get my money's worth!"

Incensed by his arrogance, Cat struggled to avoid him, but as before, she had no choice in the matter. Her hands pushed ineffectually at his chest, her nails digging deep into his skin in an attempt to wound him. A deep rumble of laughter issued from his throat as he lifted her and deposited her back on the bed.

Ryan lay next to her, running his hands freely across her body, enjoying her efforts to struggle from his hold. "I'm going to enjoy my wait for this brother of yours, my sweet demoiselle. And soon," he promised, before his mouth descended on hers, "soon you'll come to enjoy it too!"

Chapter Three

Cat stood on the balcony of her room, looking out over the patio below. The house had been built in the Spanish style, with a central courtyard and garden. The heavy scent of tropical blossoms wafted to her and a small fountain gurgled pleasantly in the afternoon sun. There was nothing tranquil about her mood. She had paced for over an hour now, like a caged animal. Indeed, that was what Ryan Nicholls had made of her.

The past three weeks had been unreal. She spent her days cooped up in her room, a guard posted outside the door, her evenings seated across the table from Ryan as they dined and her nights sharing the fourposter bed. She knew not which was the worst, entertaining him at the table or submitting to him at night. He had not tired of her to any extent, though she had sullenly refused to tell him anything of her past life or to show any response to his lovemaking. Aside from the posted guard and the old colored man who served them dinner, she saw no one except him. As much as it galled her to admit it to herself, she did feel aroused by his lean, virile body. He was handsome and lithe, a man any woman would have desired, but the indignity of being a captive to his whims was galling. Her fingers curled into talons at her side as she imagined the target of his handsome, lean features before her.

"You wouldn't make a good card player, my dear. Your movements give you away." Cat whirled, startled by Ryan's sudden appearance behind her. "Imagining what you would do to me if you still possessed that deadly weapon? Would I still need caution in presenting my back to you?" His hand reached out to gently stroke her cheek as his dark eyes gazed speculatively into hers, seeking an answer.

Cat retreated from his touch, tossing her head back in a spirited manner. "Now, more than ever," she asserted. "But then I hold no hope that my knife will be returned *or* that you'll will present your back to me!" She wore a pale yellow dress of organdy, its bodice trimmed with a satin ribbon of a deeper hue. A matching ribbon caught the flame curls back from her face. She swept past him into the room and whirled to face him again. He lounged against the door frame, relaxed and easy, his long legs casually crossed at the ankle.

"How long do you propose to keep me a prisoner in my own home? You have no right—my brother might not return for months!" Her hands rested at her narrow waist, as she raged at him. When he didn't reply, she stamped a slender, slippered foot. "Answer me, you scoundrel," she demanded.

Ryan smiled. In three weeks time he had seen enough of the girl before him to admire her untamed spirit. When she had lost her virginity to him, there had been no display of tears, much to his relief. Though he had been rather cavalier in his treatment of her, she had refused to give in to weeping, but instead had alternated between stubborn silences and blazing, fiery tantrums. His lack of reaction now was adding fuel to her fury. He decided not to tease her longer. "As a matter of fact, I came to tell you I was leaving. I've neglected my work at the plantation too long, as it is. Would you not miss my devoted attentions overmuch if I were to leave you behind?"

"No," Cat answered emphatically. "In fact I would offer my services in packing your belongings to see you gone the sooner!" Her mood lightened considerably. She was to be free of him at last! No longer would she have to submit to either his vaunting arrogance or his physical demands. Soon, within three or four weeks, Will would return and the *Falcon* would be hers to command again. Then—oh, yes, then Master Ryan Nicholls and his horrid uncle would *both* feel the brunt of her vengeance!

"I do appreciate the offer, but you'll be busy with your own packing. I've changed my mind, love. I find the thought of parting with your sweet nature and willing body too dear a cost to pay." He stepped from the window to stand before her and his voice hardened into an indisputable tone of command. "We leave on the morning tide. I trust that will be enough time for you."

Cat's hands clenched into fists at her side. If only she had her cutlass or rapier handy she would carve out his heart if the bastard had one! Blinded with fury at his arrogant, high-handed manner, she swung her hand without thinking. He guessed her action and easily caught her wrist, twisting it cruelly behind her back and pulling her hard against him.

"Understand this, my dear, understand it well. Until now I have put up with your tantrums and tempers; they have even amused me, but now they grow tedious. From this point on, they will cease. Is that clear?" Cat refused to answer, refused to look at him, and bit her lip to draw attention from her aching wrist. His fingers tightened about her hand. "Look at me," he commanded. Slowly her head raised until her eyes sullenly met his. "We will leave a note for this brother of yours, telling him of your whereabouts. Though I admire his daring, I dislike his arrogance in absconding with what was technically mine. Perhaps his brotherly affection for you is more than his love for the fickle Briar. Only the next few weeks will tell. If he wishes to rescue you, he shall have to do so in person. This time, we'll not be surprised by a dawn raid!"

Despite the terrible pain in her wrist, Cat flashed a haughty, defiant smile. Without knowing it, he had played into her hands. While he was expecting a raid from the sea, she would be well situated in his own home. She would have her chance to strike at her enemies with total surprise. Interrupting her reverie, Ryan's mouth came down on hers, hard and demanding. He released her wrist, sweeping her into his arms and throwing her down on the bed.

Ryan's mood had swiftly changed to violence, as though her mystifying smile had set savage emotions in play. The dark, angry smudges of her eyes never left his face as he quickly stripped his clothing away. Finally he stood naked before her, lean and magnificently muscled, his features cold and relentless. With slow deliberation, he reached down to place his hands at the edge of her bodice. The material easily gave way with one violent tug until she lay naked amidst its shreds.

Ryan rolled atop Cat, seeking his pleasure on her immobile form. Suddenly she came alive and her violence matched his. She fought him with every natural weapon at her disposal, striking him with her fists, nails, any defense she could muster. He laughed without feeling, mocking her efforts to fight. This time he had no intention of leading her gently into passion. This was an assault on her spirit as well as her struggling body. He felt a fierce desire to vanquish the spark of fire and defiance within her, to master her and show no mercy in doing so. He positioned himself and plunged into her unprepared body. She screamed at him, every vile, hateful name she could imagine, until his mouth silenced her. Suddenly she bit down hard on his lower lip, drawing the sharp, salty taste of blood. Ryan drew back and his hand slammed brutally across her face.

"Bitch!" he snarled. He withdrew from her, grabbing her shoulders to flip her onto her stomach. Again he entered her, slamming from behind, again and again, as his fingers sought and roughly fondled her breasts. Ragged sobs tore from her until at last he finished. She huddled away from him, curled into a fetal position, her knees tucked up and her arms covering her face and the furious tears she shed.

Ryan lay on his side, his head resting on his arm, and stared down at Cat. The yellow dress lay in tatters around her. The beautiful mane of bright curls lay like a veil across her shaking shoulders. Staring at the reddened imprints his fingers had left on the tender ivory skin of her shoulders, he was struck by remorse. Something about her, the mystery surrounding her, the continued defiance before his greater strength, something had driven him to the violent assault. He reached out to touch her gently.

Cat recoiled from the touch of Ryan's hand. She inched further away and one hand swept the hair from her eyes. She glared reproachfully, like a wounded animal that still faced its tormentor. "I hate you," she cried. "I won't forget what you just did—I won't ever forget!"

A heavy sigh escaped Ryan. Better to let her be. He would keep her vague threat in mind, though, for once she *had* almost killed him. He rose from the bed and donned his clothing, quietly leaving the room to the girl, who still sobbed into her pillow.

Cat heard the door close and sat up immediately, glaring at it as though it were Ryan's back and her eyes were daggers. He was a monster, a brute who had used and discarded her like a worn rag doll. Every muscle in her body seemed to be afire with aching torment. She would pay him back. The entire Nicholls family was composed of selfish, ruthless brutes and the time to strike back for all their misdeeds was drawing nigh. They would both have time to regret their treatment of the Devlans. *She* would see to that!

Chapter Four

Cat had been assigned a room adjacent to Ryan's. It served only to still the gossip that might have spread among the servants and passed further to the servants of the other families in the area. The budding society of Bath Town, North Carolina, was still a close-knit and very proper group. For all practical purposes, Cat slept with Ryan. She would have been delighted to bar her door, but knew that the solid, heavy mahogany would have only temporarily kept her safe from him.

One of the hardest ordeals of her life had been meeting Charles Nicholls on their return to Seahaven. She was forced to smile, while her heart cried out hatred and her nails itched to scrape his face raw. In the years that had passed since that long-ago day when she first glimpsed him, he had changed little. He was even thinner now and his dark, wavy hair had begun to gray. His eyes were as black as Ryan's, but where the nephew was confidently sure of himself, the older man was coldly pretentious and overbearing. He seemed to view the world with a sneer, as though he alone were fit to inhabit it and others lived in it merely for his amusement or service. He had politely greeted her, bowing over her hand and touching it lightly with his cold, thin lips. Sheer willpower kept her from shuddering. She felt as though a viper had stung her. His eyes, sunken, lined versions of Ryan's own, surveyed her from head to toe and returned to rest on her face. Remembering his seduction of the fifteen-year-old Briar, she noted the brief flare of lust that sparked within the dark irises and thanked God that she was old enough to repulse a similar attempt.

Now she walked on the terrace behind the house, for when Ryan was absent, she had nothing to occupy her time. She was not even allowed the luxury of riding the horses in the extensive stables, so daily she walked the circuit of neatly trimmed hedges that had been laid out in precise, even patterns. Everything in the house and gardens reflected Charles Nicholls's cold, exacting standards. His rigid, hypercritical tastes were revealed in everything from the daily menu to the neat, white, starched uniforms worn by the colored servants.

"Ah, I thought I might find you here, my dear!" Cat whirled at the sound of Charles's voice by her shoulder. An icy chill settled over her as it always did when he hovered near. She drew her light shawl closer about her and commanded a smile to her lips.

"Sir Charles, how pleasant to see you! I had no idea you enjoyed the gardens." Despite an inner quaking, her voice came through calm and assured.

"I normally don't," he replied in a dry, crackling tone. "However, your loveliness so enhances the beauty of the gardens, I found myself unable to resist. You don't mind if we walk together?"

There was no polite way for Cat to refuse. The smooth, oily compliment had not been his first in the three weeks since her arrival. On every occasion that threw them together, he managed to touch on some favorable aspect of her face or figure. Glancing at his profile as they walked, she tried to imagine him wooing her sister.

He did have a tensile strength, a raw power that seemed to flow from him. She supposed it came from his position as a wealthy landowner. His title was a baronetcy, a fact that failed to impress her. She had known too many aristocrats of ancient and honored lineage in France to be awed by a mere baronet. She tried to look at him objectively, to see him through Briar's fifteen-year-old eyes. It was possible he might impress a naïve, inexperienced girl with his flowery compliments and promises. Cat shivered again as the thought of Briar's baby came to her.

"Your thoughts are deep and secretive, young lady. Would you not care to share them with an old man, lonely for company?" They had come to a wrought-iron settee and Charles motioned for her to be seated.

"My thoughts are nothing to interest a man of the world such as yourself, Sir Charles. The weather has turned cold and wintry and I fear it depresses me. Yet I did not wish to bore you with such a trivial subject."

The man leaned closer, his gaze sweeping over her every feature before he replied. He took one of her hands in his and brought it to his lips, lightly touching her fingers in a kiss. "No thought of yours would bore me, Eve, for I have been fascinated by you since your arrival! I must remember to compliment my nephew on his choice of women. Everything about you is a mystery, and I admit that you excite me the more for it."

"Me—exciting! Why, sir, I'm nothing more than a simple girl, an orphan alone in the world but for my brother. There is nothing about *me* that would interest someone like yourself!" The lies came easily to her lips, for she kept foremost in her mind exactly who she was dealing with. He would be less prepared when she finally revealed herself. If only Will had contacted her—surely he should have returned by now! She needed his assistance in her plan.

His eyes still burned with admiration and a deep flickering of desire. Cat withdrew her hand from his, unable to bear his touch, and clasped her hands together in her lap. "Tell me something, Mistress St. Marin. Have you relatives in France? It seems too much of a coincidence that your family name should be so similar to that of Briar's mother. This story of Briar's love for your brother doesn't set well with my mind. I knew the girl too well to have missed such a romance. After all, she was seldom away from the plantation." His gaze had lost its lovelight, to be replaced by shrewd deliberation.

Cat thought quickly in an effort to satisfy his doubts. "The girl may not have been absent from the plantation, Sir Charles, but surely there were times when business called you away. Would it not have been possible for Briar to rendezvous at such times, freely and unobserved by your guarding eyes?" She held her breath, waiting to see if the lie satisfied him. His mouth twitched as he digested her comment and he nodded.

"Yes, that could have happened. It's a shame the girl came from such a bad heritage." He reached out a hand, his long fingers touching hers. "Believe me, my dear, her lack of morals was not due to *my* failing. I tried my best with her, no one could have done more. But tell me, you failed to answer my question of your own background. Surely you could be no relation to Briar."

"I know of no relatives at all. As I said, my brother and I were left to fend for ourselves at an early age. The memories are quite distressing. . . ." Cat raised a hand to her forehead, as though trying to soothe away an ache. "Please," she said with a tremulous smile, "I know of nothing that can help you. I didn't know my brother was involved in any ransom scheme. He . . . always seemed to have the money to support us, but he sheltered me from its source. Until your nephew so high-handedly abducted me, I knew little of the outside world." She touched his arm, her lips trembling as her eyes glazed over with tears. "You do believe me, Sir Charles?"

It never failed. All a woman had to do was appeal to a man, any man, with helpless confusion and he fell over himself to reassure her. Charles Nicholls, for all of his worldliness and jaded appetites, was no exception. He rushed to assure her that he did, indeed, believe her.

"Of course, my dear, don't trouble your thoughts further. 'Fraid I went too far in satisfying my curiosity—a habit of mine I should control. As for my nephew, I'll have a talk with Ryan. Despite the problems we've had with your brother, I've no desire to see it adversely affect you. Consider yourself my guest. If that young pup bothers you, come directly to me."

Cat glanced down at her hands, controlling a desire to laugh in his face. Not only had he been pompous enough to judge Briar immoral but the randy old devil had placed himself as her protector, a role so vastly unsuited to him as to be ridiculous! She smiled instead, her long lashes fluttering a properly grateful reply.

"How ever will I thank you, Sir Charles? It means so much to me to have your protection!" His eyes glowed once again, briefly revealing the lust he suppressed.

"Your lovely presence is enough thanks, young lady. I shall remind myself to have a talk with Ryan."

"About what, uncle?" Ryan had come upon them quietly, without the notice of either. Cat turned to face him, wondering how much he had overheard. She felt a glow of triumph from having set uncle against nephew. It was time for her to exit.

"I think I should be going, Sir Charles. I feel a sudden chill wind." She glanced significantly at Ryan and finished, "and a need to seek shelter." She smiled at Charles, flashed a triumphant, fleeting grin at Ryan, and rose to sweep past him. Ryan's arm shot out, his hand grabbing her forearm. She gazed back at Charles, seeking to test his offer of help.

"Release the lady at once, Ryan!" Charles thundered dramatically, more for Cat's benefit than anything else. Ryan hesitated, surprised by his uncle's order. "I said immediately, you young pup!" Her arm was set free and as she pulled her shawl over her bright hair facing away from Charles, she flashed another, even more wickedly triumphant smile at Ryan and hurried toward the house. Minutes later she stood by the window in her room, gleefully watching the argument taking place in the garden. It was her first real taste of success and she exalted in it, dancing lightly about before she threw herself on her bed and hugged her pillow. This was only the beginning. If she could just manage to keep Charles from superseding Ryan in her bed until Will came. . . . It would be a fine juggling act, a delicate balance of one against the other; but she felt up to the challenge. A half hour later she heard the door slam in the room next to hers, Ryan's room, and smiled to herself. Now let him dare accost her!

The following week was the proof of her effect on Charles. Now she was given the privilege of riding, though she was still forced to have a servant tagging along. A colored maid, well versed in hairdressing and other niceties, was assigned for her use and a dressmaker arrived from Bath Town to create a ballgown for the upcoming prenuptial party for Charles and his fiancée. Though he was the epitome of politeness, Cat knew Charles had already entertained the idea of installing her as his mistress following his marriage. He wanted the best of everything, the added wealth that marriage to Cora would bring and a young and lovely girl to share his bed.

Ryan had bothered her only once. Soon after she had heard the door to his room slam, the connecting door to her room was thrown open. He stalked into the room and over to the bed. Cat lay there, unafraid and openly gloating.

"I must admit I underestimated you, my dear," he had said with cold sarcasm. His eyes swept across her features and then down her body, slowly rising to meet her eyes. His jaw was clenched and a muscle ticked beside his mouth, evidencing his inner fury. "You seem to have found a champion in my uncle." His eyes remained cold and black, though he smiled, baring a row of even white teeth. "I only hope you realize what you've done. My uncle has strong appetites where women are concerned. Should you find you need help from your . . . protector, you need only open that door." Stubborn silence greeted his offer. "Well, you've time to reconsider. I'll be willing to accept an apology at any time—day or *night,* should you feel the . . . urge. I am at your service, *m'lady!*" He made a mock bow and turned before she could sputter an angry retort. As the door closed behind him, Cat had picked up a brush lying at hand and thrown it with all her might. The loud crash it made as it hit the door was followed by low masculine laughter from the next room.

After that scene, whenever Cat and Ryan met, in the hall or at dinner, they were coldly polite. Tonight there were to be guests at dinner. Cora Fitzhugh and her niece, Marian, were invited. Cat had never met either and did not warm to the idea. She sat before her mirror, watching as Allie, her maid, artfully arranged her hair in a cascade of copper-gold curls that fell from her crown to her delicate nape. She had refused to powder her hair in the current fashion. She found the custom ugly and much preferred the high sheen and glow of her natural color.

"There, ma'am," Allie drawled, her accent slow and ponderous to Cat, who had grown up accustomed to the fast pace of the French language. The girl pulled the dressing cape from Cat's shoulders and stood back to admire her mistress. "Lordy, Miss Eve, you sho' is pretty. No wonder Masta' Ryan brung you home with 'im!"

Cat turned her head, admiring the girl's handiwork. Her hair looked elegant, setting off the low bodice of the green silk evening gown. A fichu of lace was tucked decorously between her swelling breasts. Staring at it, she suddenly changed her mind and withdrew it, exposing the dark, shadowed valley between the soft ivory cleavage. She cared not a whit about what the women would think. She had devilishly decided to remind Charles, even in front of his fiancée, what was within his reach and to remind Ryan of what was now beyond his. She stood, turning full circle before a larger mirror. Though normally she considered a corset uncomfortable and, in her case, unnecessary, tonight she had worn one. It had narrowed her small waist to tiny proportions and added to the daring décolletage. Allie handed her a white lace shawl which she casually draped across her shoulders.

She was about to leave the room to join the others below when she remembered her emerald. It would suit her dress perfectly. She dismissed Allie, waiting until the girl left the room before she opened the top drawer of the large wardrobe. Beneath her intimate apparel she had hidden the packet that held her most valuable possessions. Carefully she checked to see that it still contained the copies of the documents she had shown Briar. All were safely in order, including her privateering commission. She stared down, wondering briefly if she should burn it. If it fell into the wrong hands, she could be hanged. Suddenly there was a knock at the door. She quickly grabbed the necklace and replaced the papers in the packet. She could decide later what to do. With the packet hidden once more, she called, "Enter."

The door swung open, and Charles was there. He smiled as he caught sight of her, his gaze sweeping over her in admiration. "I grew worried that perhaps you had taken ill, my dear. Your beauty is more enchanting tonight than I have ever seen it. Please, allow me to escort you."

"Thank you, Sir Charles," she said with a brief smile and curtsey. "I wonder . . . would you help me fasten my necklace? Unfortunately, I've already dismissed Allie."

Charles came forward and just as he reached her, Cat lifted the shawl from her shoulders, revealing her high, proud breasts swelling above the silken bodice. She could hear him draw a deep breath, and she paused just a moment before handing him the necklace and turning to allow him to fasten it around the slender graceful column of her neck. The large jewel fell directly between the soft, ivory breasts. It lay there, winking a brilliant green, drawing attention to the surrounding beauty. Charles paused, his hands on her shoulders, and she felt his hot breath close behind her ear. He was breathing harder with every passing second and before he could put his thoughts into action she whirled away, turning to face him with a flashing smile. "We had best not keep your fiancée and her niece waiting, sir. I would not care to create a disagreeable first impression." She adjusted the shawl to cover herself once more and allowed him to offer his hand.

Cat swept down the long, steep staircase as though she were once again at the French court. As they approached the drawing room, she caught the low rumble of Ryan's laughter, followed by a high-pitched, feminine giggle. Charles said something to her, a witty epigram he had to repeat before she comprehended it. She forced herself to laugh, a clear bell-like sound that she hoped carried to Ryan. They paused at the entrance to the room and for the sake of propriety before his intended, Charles withdrew his hand from hers.

Cora Fitzhugh sat ensconced in a wing chair, appearing to Cat's eyes, like a great fat toad. There was nothing appealing in her face or bloated figure; and had Cat not hated Charles so, she might have pitied him his forthcoming marriage. As it was, she smiled brilliantly and strolled forward with Charles at her side. Ryan, when she happened to glance at him quickly through lowered eyes, seemed not to have noticed her arrival. Neither had the lovely girl at his side. This would be the niece, Marian, but Cat would have never guessed at a family tie between the petite brunette and her squat, ugly aunt. Ryan seemed absorbed by Marian and bent low to whisper into her ear. She threw back her head and again, the same high-pitched laughter tinkled forth.

Charles cleared his throat and all eyes came to rest on him. He took Cat's hand, introducing her to Cora first. The woman peered at her from eyes that had all but disappeared within folds of fat and issued a noncommital grunt. Next Charles drew Cat to Ryan's side and introduced her to Marian. The girl, whom Cat judged to be approximately sixteen, merely nodded haughtily, a somewhat knowing smile lighting her lips. "Ryan's been telling me about you," she said. "This should prove to be an interesting evening. I've never met a woman of your background before."

Cat would have loved to strike the back-water vixen. Apparently the emotion showed on her face, for Ryan coughed discreetly. She glanced at him to find one brow quirked in an amused manner and a slight smile playing at the corners of his mouth. He was obviously looking forward to a rivalry between the two of them. Well, she wouldn't disappoint him, but *she* was determined to be the victor.

"That doesn't surprise me at all, Marian. The nursery affords one such a small chance to mix with society. Possibly when you mature, you'll be allowed more exposure." Cat smiled slyly. Charles was growing more uncomfortable by the minute. He wasn't quite sure what he would do if the two young women came to blows. Of the two, he'd have wagered money on the redhead to come out ahead.

Marian seemed shocked that Cat would dare return her jibe. She opened her mouth, then decided against continuing for the moment and turned to Ryan. "Darling, shouldn't we go in to dinner now?" She batted her lashes, ignoring Cat and Charles. Cat noticed the same drawl, the peculiar type of speech that seemed common to all of these people. It was Charles's place to escort his fiancée to dinner. Marian obviously meant to snare Ryan and either leave Cat to fend for herself or take Charles's other arm.

It was Cat's turn to raise a brow. With a worldliness that the young girl before her would never possess, she was not to be outdone by fluttering lashes. Artlessly she shrugged a shoulder and the lace shawl fell to rest on her arms, exposing a dazzling display of soft, swelling cleavage. The emerald winked in the candlelight, an added attraction to draw the attention of the two men but one which paled in comparison with Cat's natural charms. Ryan did not offer his arm. He still suffered from her recent treatment and wasn't about to rescue her. Charles stepped in to avoid what could have become an embarrassing situation.

Offering his arm to Marian, he suggested she allow him to escort her and Cora both. "Soon we'll be related, my dear. I'd like to become better acquainted." Marian had no way of refusing without seeming rude to her host. Frustration flared in her dark-fringed blue eyes as Cat smiled serenely.

"Ryan." Charles raised a brow at his nephew, reminding him of his manners, then tucked Marian's hand within the crook of his arm and moved off across the room in Cora's direction. Marian glanced back once, in silent appeal to Ryan, and venomously met Cat's eyes.

Ryan made a short, curt bow, offering his arm to Cat. "May I have the honor, m'lady?" His expression had switched from mild amusement to chill reserve once more. Cat's eyes glittered, for she was enjoying her slight edge of power over him. They slowly made their way down the hall to the formal dining room with Charles in the lead.

"Are you regretting your arrogance in bringing me here, Ryan?" Cat whispered in an effort to annoy him and shake his aloof, detached manner. "Though I'm quite enjoying myself at the moment, you'll remember it *was* against my will."

"I am neither overjoyed nor regretful," he answered, stealing another glance sideways at her delightfully exposed charms. He had to admit she looked exquisite tonight, assured and poised, every inch a desirable woman. His forced abstinence had made him testy, but she seemed to glory in her ability to entice him and yet be safely removed from his touch. It irked him that she had managed to bewitch his uncle into protecting her. Ahead of them, Marian gave a quick glance back, pursing her lips in an angry pout at the sound of their voices. She was an interesting possibility, one that he had failed to pursue in the past but which now might be worth exploring.

At the dinner table, Cat was seated to the right of Charles, who had taken care to arrange their positions to his advantage. Cora sat at the opposite end of the table, with Ryan unhappily seated at her right, across from Marian. The only problem Charles had not foreseen had been placing Cat and Marian next to each other. He only hoped that he could draw Cat's attention throughout the meal and minimize the sparks that seemed to fly between the two young women.

Marian kept her attention on Ryan, concentrating on his handsome features and ignoring the brazen hussy at her side. To her mind, the older girl clearly had no background. The overbold manner of her dress alone indicated that. She still had not learned all the facts concerning the girl's strange appearance but was determined to prove her worthlessness to Ryan before the night's end. She smiled into Ryan's dark eyes, well aware that Aunt Cora's coming marriage would afford her many opportunities like tonight. After all, she was the sole heiress to Cora's considerable wealth and he held the same position in relation to his uncle. What could be more natural than an alliance between the two? She shivered, admiring his profile as he politely engaged Aunt Cora in an almost one-sided conversation. The wanton thought of what the marriage bed with Ryan would hold made her giddy.

Cat listened to Charles's boring dinner talk with only minimal interest. She was trying to imagine Ryan through Marian's eyes, wondering how she herself would have felt if they had met under more gentle circumstances. Beyond the fact that he was one of the most handsome men she had ever seen, he exuded bold confidence and an air of breeding that just barely hid a raw animal strength. An impish desire to taunt him with the inaccessability of her body seized her. She turned her full attention to Charles, smiling into his eyes and flattering him.

The older man warmed under the glow of her eyes, silently wondering when he could make his move. The girl was obviously taken with his authority and mature strength, something she had been unable to find in his nephew, despite Ryan's good looks and youth. She was hotblooded, this slender girl with flaming hair. Glancing at her high, creamy breasts, he imagined her naked in his bed, begging for his attentions. He would have to proceed slowly, though, for she was spirited and wild, resentful of force such as Ryan had used. The thought of subduing her when the younger man had not been able to brought a smile to his thin lips.

Suddenly he realized that Cora had spoken to him, and he turned to stare at her fat, wrinkled face, almost shuddering as he mentally compared it with the girl at his side. The idea of bedding the bloated old creature was repulsive. After the marriage contracts were signed, however, he would banish her to a room of her own and never go near her again. She questioned him now about some trivial idea for the coming party. It required all of his effort to smile in her direction and give some plausible answer. He had to be careful, for though the woman was a gross toad and a bore besides, she was in no way stupid. She'd been the guiding light behind her late husband's success and should he be too obvious in his attentions to the girl, the marriage would fall through.

Ryan had been discussing the island of Tortuga with Marian when she suddenly turned to Cat and stated loudly, "I understand the island is inhabited by ruffians and thieves, cutthroat murderers who call themselves the Brethren of the Coast. I suppose *you* felt at home in that atmosphere!" The silence at the table was deafening. Even Ryan couldn't believe his ears.

Cat turned slowly to face the girl, her eyes narrowed and feline. The air crackled as everyone awaited her reply to the challenging slur. Two spots of color stained her cheeks in anger. Finally, in a controlled voice, she defended herself. "Your view of the world and its inhabitants is somewhat limited by your experiences, Marian. Yes, I found myself at ease in the company of the men you mentioned. Ruffians though they be, they're proud men and free who came by their lives of crime, for the most part, escaping from the injustices of *your* world. We are not all born to the manor and must do what needs to be done to survive." She paused and sighed wearily, as though she were trying to reach a stubborn child. All eyes were riveted on her.

"I've dined in the presence of royalty and though I'm sure you wouldn't understand, I much prefer to break bread with those simple men you disdain!" She turned away from Marian, dismissing the girl as insignificant. "Sir Charles, with your leave, I would prefer to seek the quiet of my room. I fear I've developed a headache." Charles threw Marian such a withering glance that Cat almost felt sorry for her. Without resorting to the same bitchy techniques, Cat had made her point dramatically. As she passed his chair, Ryan rose and took her arm, his expression unfathomable.

"Allow me to escort you to your room, mademoiselle. I wouldn't care to have you faint before you reached it." He made his excuses to those at the table, conspicuously ignoring Marian. When they reached the hall and were out of range of the dining room, Ryan stopped her, his fingers gently raising her chin until her clear violet eyes gazed into his eyes. Cat felt drawn to him, like the strong, relentless pull of a magnet, and remained motionless until his lips touched hers.

The tender, persuasive kiss was unnerving, for everything about Ryan's lovemaking had been masterful and demanding. A dreamy, unreal feeling settled over her as she was slowly, gently drawn into his arms. His hands pressed the small of her back, molding her body to his as he whispered against her ear in a low, yearning groan. "You've driven me half-mad the past week! To see you and not . . ." The passionate claim trailed off unfinished as he kissed the soft, tender spot below her ear.

Cat shivered, her stomach lurching with a twist of answering passion, his nearness affecting her so that she was suddenly frightened, nay, terrified. She had no idea how much she'd missed the close physical contact with his lean, demanding body. When had the forced lovemaking turned to a necessity? Suddenly she was frantic to escape him, to run from the desire he aroused within her, an emotion that threatened to enslave her. Her own wild response, allowed free rein, would be her undoing, far more than his domineering actions of the recent past. She had to get away! Cat pushed at his chest, pleading with him, "Please, Ryan . . . let go of me!"

Ryan raised his head from the soft, sweet-scented skin of Cat's throat. He was puzzled by her outcry, for when he had kissed her, admiring the spirit she had shown in her own defense, she had seemed to melt against him. Now his hands dropped away, freeing her. Her expression revealed, not pleasure at his touch but a kind of wild terror as though the sight of him was loathsome. The rejection pricked his pride, replacing the sweet drift toward desire. The girl was impossibly mercurial, rapidly changing from warmth to ice, from passionate response to cold withdrawal. His pursuit of her was over. She stared at him a minute, then bolted, picking up her skirts to run toward the staircase, away from him or whatever she saw in him that terrified her.

Within the privacy of her room, Cat gave in to tears of frustration. She threw herself on the bed, weeping in confusion, ashamed of her response to a man she should hate, yet whom she found so undeniably attractive. Finally her tears subsided. He had meant to manipulate her and lower her defenses with tenderness only to have his own way, she decided, to gain his own selfish ends. A gentle knock sounded at her door and she quickly wiped away the traces of tears and composed herself.

The door was opened cautiously and Allie timidly poked her head around it to inquire if Cat needed her assistance. "Yes, please. I would like to retire now," she answered, grateful that the caller was only her maid. The girl helped her to disrobe and then sat her before the mirror to unpin her coiffure and brush the lovely curls into a gleaming mass that lay spread across Cat's white shoulders.

"Thank you, Allie," she said in dismissal. She had come to like the young girl, for she was always around to help and her manner never failed to be sweet. "I won't need you until the morning." The girl curtseyed but hesitated as though she wished to speak. "Is there something else, dear?"

Allie reached into the top of her starched white uniform, pulling forth a folded slip of paper. "Yes'm, I . . . I's tol' to deliver this t'ya, t'nobody else, ma'am." She held forth the paper hesitantly and Cat took it from her. Before she opened the note, she asked Allie to describe the person who had sent the message. "He was tall, ma'am, frightful tall an' old, wif' a funny way a' talkin."

Cat smiled at the description. To Allie's young eyes Will must seem old, and his clipped accent would sound odd. She thanked her, adding, "I hope I can help you out sometime, dear. *Please,* don't say anything about this to anyone." She smiled and the girl returned her smile, and hurried away.

Seated on the bed, she opened the note, recognizing Will's familiar scrawl. Thank God he had arrived safely! The note opened in a scolding tone and she smiled, imagining how he would berate her in person, like an old washwoman. He was staying in town, at the inn, and asked her to meet him at a clearing just west of the Seahaven boundary at ten the next morning. The *Falcon* was safely anchored in a cove south of Bath Town and would be ready for a quick leave-taking. He ended with a warning to take care. Cat hugged the note to her, longing to see Will's dear face once again. In an exercise of caution, she held the note over a candle, watching it catch and burn until nothing but ashes were left.

Over the past weeks, she had learned much about Charles. His world centered about himself and the pleasures his wealth afforded him. Cat had decided to expose him, rather than offer the quick, almost merciful death her rapier would bring. He would suffer far more by being publicly exposed as a scoundrel and murderer, and in addition would lose the wealth that marriage to Cora Fitzhugh would bring him. She intended to chip away the very foundations of his world, a world he arrogantly considered safe and settled. She would tell Will to lie low in town until the night of the party, a week hence. Before Charles Nicholls's friends and associates she would brand him the bastard he was.

Cat was dreaming. No, it was more than that, she was having a nightmare. First she saw her father, a noose about his neck as he stood before her. He held out a hand in supplication, begging her to seek vengeance on his enemies. A mist rose about him, obscuring the plea in his eyes, and suddenly Ryan stood where her father had. He spoke, telling her that she would never escape from him, that he would never let her be free. Then he took her hand, pulling her forward into an embrace, but when she drew close, it was Charles's face instead of Ryan's. It was Charles who tore her gown and pawed at her exposed body. She struggled helplessly but there was no escape and in the background she heard laughter, a high-pitched giggling laughter she recognized as Marian's. Charles was assaulting her and she struggled and screamed in a futile effort to break his hold. The nightmare dissolved into reality and the sound of Ryan's voice penetrated her terror. He bent over her, his hands gripping her shoulders, trying to awaken her.

Her wide, frightened eyes centered on Ryan's face, as the terror receded into the night. She was left shaken and trembling and it seemed the most natural act in the world for Ryan's arms to encircle her. She felt safe from the specters of her dream and continued to cuddle against him long after she had calmed.

"It was only a dream, girl. There's nothing here to harm you, unless it's me you fear." Ryan spoke in a low soothing tone, close to her ear.

He was reminding her of their confrontation! How could she explain the fear that had caused her to bolt from him? In a halting voice, she spoke, searching for the words to make him understand. "Ryan, I . . . about last night, I . . ." He had glanced down at her expectantly but as she gathered her thoughts into a clear pattern, she caught a flash of movement by the door connecting their rooms. Marian stood there, her dark hair tousled about her shoulders, a sheer, rumpled nightgown her only cover. She needed to say nothing, for her appearance said it for her. Cat bit back the confession she had been about to make and stiffened in Ryan's arms.

When she failed to continue but merely stared past him as though transfixed, he turned. The sight of Marian brought a dark, heavy scowl to his face. He ignored her, turning back to Eve, to find her white-faced and sullen, refusing to look at him. He released her angrily and stood. Cat looked up, just once. "I apologize for disturbing your . . . leisure, Master Nicholls! Please, don't delay returning to your bed partner," she insisted coldly.

Ryan swore silently. Again her manner had been soft, communicating a willingness to him. Each time she seemed about to trust him, something stopped her. Damn the Fitzhugh bitch! The girl had teased and flirted all evening. He'd consumed just enough brandy after dinner so that her pretty face and willing body had appealed to him as a fair substitute for this girl, an idea he would have rejected had he been more sober. When the distressed sounds of Eve's nightmare penetrated his heavy slumber, he'd rushed in, completely forgetting about Marian. How he wished now that he'd sent her packing after their tumble! He cursed again and stalked irritably back to his room. Marian awaited him in bed, her gown artfully arranged to show her charms and leaving little to the imagination. The girl irritated him with her clinging ways and empty head. Though she seemed to pale in comparison with the girl he had just left, Ryan spitefully decided to possess her once more, for he had already paid dearly for the night's love play.

Cat refused to glance up until she heard the door close. God, what a mistake she'd almost made! She would have admitted to a growing desire for Ryan and faced the consequences had that simpering bitch not appeared. What *was* she to him? Merely an outlet for his urges, just one of a multitude of conquests. Most likely her earlier rejection of him had piqued his interest or he would have already ceased to pursue her. If he could so easily seek another, so quickly find a willing playmate, he must value her as nothing more than a trifle to while away his time. Cat lay back, snuggling safely beneath the covers, and tried to cleanse her mind of the thought of Ryan and what lay beyond the connecting door. Before she drifted off to sleep, she vowed to herself to guard her feelings more closely in the future. There would be no repeat of the mistake she had almost made.

The next morning, following a restless, fitful sleep, Cat rose early and bathed before breakfast. She donned her riding habit and after a quick cup of tea, was at the stables by eight-thirty. The rest of the household slept late and she met no one but Michael, the stableboy. He had ridden with her before, assigned by Charles for her protection. The morning air was cold and damp and, as she strained an ear, she could just hear the sound of the waves breaking on the shore. The sound was a comfort and a reminder that she would soon be aboard her ship and far away from this dreaded place.

When they had ridden for almost thirty minutes, Cat slowed her mount and wheeled the spirited mare to address the boy. "Michael, I fear I've been foolish to come out this chilly morn without my cloak. Please ride back and tell Allie to give you my white woolen cape." The boy hesitated, knowing he had the strictest orders to stay with the young lady on all of her rides. "Nothing will happen, Michael," she assured him, dismounting and tethering the reins to a low hanging branch of a pine. "Hurry and be off, boy," she added sharply. "Sir Charles would be greatly angered should I catch cold due to your laggardness!"

The sharpness of her tone combined with the fear of angering Charles seemed enough to convince him. He wheeled his bay for home, but paused and glanced once more at her. "I'll be at this very spot until you return, only hurry!" For added emphasis, she shivered and hugged her shoulders. The boy took off at a gallop, racing down the road toward the house.

When he was safely out of sight, Cat remounted and set off galloping toward the rendezvous point. It only took her ten minutes, allowing her a short visit with Will and a ten-minute return. He stood in the clearing when she arrived and she brought the animal to an abrupt halt before him, jumping from the saddle into Will's strong arms. She hugged his neck for a full minute before she allowed him to put her down. Tears sprang to her eyes as she stood back and gazed at every worn, beloved feature.

"Here now, we'll have none a' that," Will chided, his arm curling about her shoulders. "The note you left me was sketchy, I want to know the *whole* of what's taken place." He led her to a huge fallen tree trunk and as they were seated, added, "I warned you, missy. You shouldna' sent me away. Briar's safe now in your Grandmum's care and it's you who's in trouble!"

When Cat had explained everything, Will growled in a bearlike fury. Had she not restrained him, he would have ridden straight up to the plantation house to call Ryan out. Though she refused to admit it, she had no desire to see that handsome, selfish devil bleed from Will's avenging cutlass. Her virginity was gone, a dim memory already and better consigned to the past. Remembering the shortness of the time, she quickly explained her plan for Charles.

"No, Cat. I don't like it one bit," Will grumbled stubbornly. "You, in the middle a' that viper's nest! Dispatch the devil and 'ave done with it! You don't know 'im as well as you think, girl. Sometimes I think you outsmart yourself. You'll find your pretty head in a tangled web and that black spider bearin' down on ya!"

Cat jumped up. "It's settled, Will. My decision stands! Now, I must get back or risk being found out. The night of the sixteenth, I'll meet you at the inn and we'll make for the *Falcon*." She hugged him tightly once more and affectionately kissed his rough cheek. Will watched Cat ride off. There was much of Devlan's fire and determination in the lass, perhaps too much for a woman. Despite her assurances to the contrary, he would worry until he saw her safely aboard the ship again.

When Cat arrived back at the stand of pines, the boy had still not returned. She waited another five minutes and began her ride back to the plantation. It was puzzling that he had not returned and when she arrived at the stables and found him still missing, she felt a quiver of presentiment. Because of his absence she was forced to rub down the sweating mare and curry the animal herself. Finally she finished, leaving the horse in its stall, contentedly grazing on a breakfast of oats. She walked slowly toward the door of the stable, preoccupied with the missing stableboy, when suddenly she found her way blocked.

The Nichollses' overseer, the same squat, sloppy fellow who had leveled a gun at her on the raid, lounged against the door, his arm stretched across its width. She frowned, more irritated than frightened, for as long as she was a guest at the house, the man dared not accost her. Her nose twitched. The man radiated a combined odor of unwashed sweat and stale tobacco. He grinned, still barring her way, and bared misshapen, tobacco-stained teeth.

Cat drew herself up, imperiously demanding that he move. "Your employer will hear of this, if you don't," she threatened. The man's grin turned to a leer as a beefy hand shot out to grasp her arm in a cruel grip. He dragged her into the shadows of the stable, shoving her back hard against one of the stalls. As she opened her mouth to scream, one of his filthy, sweaty hands closed over it, cutting off the attempt.

"I been watchin' you, woman." The fetid breath came harder as the gaze of his small, bloodshot eyes crawled across her body. "Y'think yer too good fer the likes a' me, don't cha? Well, you ain't, Miss High n' Mighty—I seen 'ya meet up with that fella' this mornin'! No need to tell Nicholls, though. You and me, I figger we kin share yer secret."

Above his hand, Cat's eyes widened in dismay and dawning terror. This horrid, sweating animal meant to blackmail her, to secure her silence while he . . . while he . . . she could not finish the thought. She closed her eyes as his free hand pawed roughly at her riding coat, tearing the buttons away as he impatiently sought her breasts. Her only chance was to scream, to lull him into thinking he'd won and then scream and try to run. It would be her word against his, should he carry through with his threat.

As his fingers cruelly pinched at her nipples through the thin material of her blouse, she sunk her teeth sharply into his other hand. She was rewarded by an angry, surprised grunt of pain and her mouth was set free. Cat took advantage of the moment to scream. Surely someone at the house would hear her! The vision of his swarthy, reddened face floated before her and, as his hand flew back to slap her, she closed her eyes, steeling herself against the coming pain. A startled grunt broke the silence and her eyes flew open to find Ryan behind the overseer, tightly gripping the man's beefy arm. Ryan thrust him backward and his fist connected with the broad jaw in a loud, bone-crushing blow that propelled the heavy man to the ground in a tangled heap of arms and legs. Ryan towered above him, legs astraddle, daring the man to rise and fight.

The resistance drained visibly from the overseer. He glared past Ryan to Cat and she shivered at the hatred and raw emotion of that glance, drawing her ripped coat close about her. "Get your things together, Jones," Ryan ordered coldly. "I want your sweaty carcass off this property within the hour. See my uncle's secretary for your wages but don't *ever* set foot on Nicholls land again." Jones slowly struggled to his feet.

"I's only after some a' what she offered 'er lover this mornin'," he sneered, and spit on the ground. "Ask 'er 'bout the man she met." He brushed at the straw clinging to his dirty clothing and glared once more at Cat before he stomped away to his quarters.

"The man's mad," Cat exclaimed as Ryan turned to face her, none of the cold fury in his expression subsiding. "He lied to cover his crude attack!"

"Did he?" Ryan questioned accusingly. "The lady doth protest too much!" He stepped forward, searching her face. "You had ample time to meet someone. Fortunately

Michael came to me instead of Allie, otherwise you would now be lying beneath Jones's sweating limbs." He scowled, grabbing her arm to drag her toward the door. "At any rate, you've cost me a good overseer. I strongly suggest you confine yourself to the house from this point." He imperiously pulled her after him, forcing her to run to match his long strides or suffer the humiliation of being dragged across the ground. When they reached the house, he released her, ordering her to her room.

Cat's fury was now an equal match for Ryan's. He had no thought for her feelings or any harm she had suffered, but instead worried over the difficulty of securing a new overseer! The arrogance of the man twisted her insides and her fingers itched to slap the arrogance from his face. The emotion showed clearly, for he stepped closer and glared a warning.

"I wouldn't try it. You're in enough trouble."

Cat had to grit her teeth to keep from spitting her fury into his face. She whirled away, angrily seeking shelter in her room. She spent the day there, though, not because of Ryan's threat. The seamstress, Madame Courais, had come for the final fitting of her ballgown. The woman was French and had taken extra care with Cat's gown for, as she put it, "a fellow countrywoman." The entire afternoon, as she fitted and adjusted the material, she kept up an animated conversation in French, regaling Cat with all the local gossip.

"You would not believe how gauche these transplanted English are, my dear! They expect miracles of me—I must prod and push their ungainly figures into the latest styles. Ah, but you, mademoiselle, *la belle magnifique!* It is such a pleasure to use my talents to enhance the beauty of your figure." She stopped chattering a moment, to stand back and admire her handiwork. The lines of the dress were simple and clinging. The dark, forest green brocade was fitted to Cat's narrow waist and sweeping folds of material belled forth in the wide skirt. White satin was inset and laced across the bodice with dark green ties. White piping edged the sleeves and the low, revealing décolletage. "Not a man at the ball will be able to keep his eyes from you," she predicted and added with a twitch of disdain, "I created a gown for Mademoiselle Marian also, but she will not hold a candle to you! That one has set her sights on Monsieur Ryan, but I doubt that she has a chance with you here!" The woman leaned forward and whispered confidentially. "I overheard Madame Cora in an angry exchange with her niece. Apparently she caught Marian leaving Monsieur Ryan's room early one morn!" She giggled, amused by the retelling of the juicy tidbit.

That night Cat dined in her room, exhausted by the long afternoon fitting and unwilling to face Ryan's sneers or questions. She sent Allie below with an excuse to Charles, pleading a headache. Retiring early, she fell into a deep, but troubled sleep. Near dawn she was awakened by a sound in the hall. Dazed and still half asleep, she was sure she had imagined the sound until it was repeated. Quickly, she slipped into her dressing gown. Still tying the belt at her waist, she drew open the door a crack and peered into the hallway. Allie leaned against the wall, a few feet from Charles's bedroom door, her eyes closed as she moaned in distress. A heavy sheen of sweat glistened on her dark forehead. Cat threw her door open, softly calling the girl's name. Allie startled at the sound, her dark eyes showing terror until she recognized Cat's concerned face near her.

"Miss . . . I's sorry. Didn't mean t' wake you!" Allie was tight-lipped with pain and faltered as she attempted to walk away. Cat was at her side immediately.

"Allie, Allie, what on God's earth——" She stopped, freezing at the sight of blood staining the back of the girl's rumpled white uniform. She gently took Allie's hand in her own and urged her toward the bedroom, quietly shutting the door, and seating her at the vanity. Lips pursed in anger, Cat searched for a towel and dampened it with water from the basin. Carefully unfastening the white dress, she exposed Allie's raw, bleeding back to the light. Cat had seen men fight aboard ship, had seen blood flow as men lay mortally wounded, but nothing touched her so much as the sight of this young, trembling girl with cruel whip lashes lacerating the tender skin of her back. She cleaned each welt of the already clotting blood, wincing each time the girl did. Clear of blood, her back showed signs of earlier cuts that had healed and scarred. Finally she bound Allie's back with strips of torn toweling and helped her to dress.

"Allie, I insist you tell me who did this!" The girl refused to meet her eyes and stared down at her hands, grasped tightly together in her lap. "Allie, was it Sir Charles?"

The girl looked up at the mention of Charles, her large, dark eyes full of unshed tears and a flare of suppressed rage. "Masta' Charles . . . he like young girls . . . he let me work in de house 'stead o' de fields an say I be grateful. Please, don' say nothin' ma'am, please! I be sent to de fields ta work."

Tight-lipped with fury, Cat assured the girl she would remain silent. She asked if she could assist Allie to her quarters, but the girl shook her head, clearly shocked by the thought of Cat coming near the slave quarters. She hurried to the door, pausing a moment to throw Cat a grateful look, then slipped out the door and away.

So, along with his other dissolute habits, Charles Nicholls forced his perverted attentions on young defenseless girls! Allie couldn't be much older than fifteen. The vision of Charles standing over her, whip in hand, made Cat nauseated. She almost changed her mind—he *deserved* to die a painful death. But no, she would stay with her plan. The public humiliation before his circle of friends and associates would cause the pretentious devil more suffering. And if anyone deserved to suffer, it was this despicable man who derived so much pleasure from the pain and sorrow of others. Tomorrow night would see his downfall at last.

Chapter Five

Charles had spared no expense to create a lavish party that would long be remembered. The guest list included over a hundred and fifty people, members of local society and others, old friends from as far away as New York and Connecticut. There was not a spare room in the house, for many would spend the weekend before beginning their long journey home.

The entire house was ablaze with the light cast by thousands of tapers. The ballroom sparkled, its parquet flooring shining beneath the glow of three huge crystal chandeliers. A raised dais had been constructed for the musicians at one end of the long, rectangular room and at the opposite end a sumptuous buffet had been arranged on three long tables. An elderly gray-haired slave stood behind the main table, commanding a staff of fifteen. Each was dressed in immaculate white and was assigned a separate area of service. Outside, liveried servants saw to the needs of each new arrival; and at the door to the ballroom, Cora's English butler presided, imperiously announcing each guest with a sharp tap of his elegantly carved staff.

Cat had joined Cora and Charles before any of the guests had arrived. The old woman resembled a raven, sharp-beaked and dressed entirely in black. She was apparently still in mourning for her late husband, and the somber color only served to emphasize the pasty white complexion and heavy jowls. She seemed in a warm mood tonight for she greeted Cat with a smile and a wish that she enjoy herself. The pleasantries took Cat by surprise. She had hardly heard the woman speak a complete sentence in the few times that she'd seen her. Marian acknowledged Cat's existence, nodding, tight-lipped and haughty. Apparently Aunt Cora had prevailed upon her to behave herself, for she made no attempt to issue any more acid comments on Cat's background or lack of one. Marian *did* look lovely, and, on the surface, virtuous, in white lace. Cat allowed herself a tiny, amused smile at the illusory effect. Ryan was aloof and withdrawn, the expression on his patrician features clearly bespeaking a desire to be elsewhere. He and Cat ignored each other, and he met Marian's overbubbly attempt at flirtation with short, clipped replies.

At the moment, Ryan could barely conceal his irritation. Marian had draped herself upon his arm and clung as though she were drowning and he was her last hope of salvation. The lovely, elusive redhead, whom he still knew only by the name of Eve, seemed to be enjoying the girl's behavior. Her tall slenderness was enhanced by the simple, elegant ballgown, and her soft white shoulders gleamed in the candlelight. Despite her distant attitude, Ryan felt a twitch of desire in his loins each time he glanced at her. Her bright, coppery curls were draped along the graceful column of her neck and waves swept back from her face, revealing the delicacy of her sculptured profile. She reminded him of a perfectly carved cameo he had once seen.

Despite his attempts to make the ball a success, Charles appeared lost in gloomy contemplation of his coming nuptials. Cat had seen him glance at Cora several times with barely concealed disgust. It appeared that none of the household shared Cora's high spirits but Cat herself. She revelled in this night, the excitement and anticipation coloring her cheeks with a touch of fire and setting the perfect, porcelain complexion aglow. Tonight was *her* night; it belonged to her by right and she would share it with all those who had suffered from Charles Nicholls's greed and selfishness. She sparkled in the brocade evening gown, a jewel in an exquisite setting.

The lilting strains of a minuet began the night's entertainment. The dancing had commenced though late guests still arrived. The tinkle of a spinet filled the air, accompanied by several violins and a harp. Ryan bowed formally before Cat, ignoring Marian's quick, offended intake of breath, and politely inquired, "May I have the pleasure, mademoiselle?" Cat toyed with the idea of refusing but decided it would be worth dancing just to irritate Marian. Slowly they began to move to the formal, graceful cadence of the dance. When they stepped close for a moment, Ryan whispered, "You seem to sparkle with an undercurrent of excitement tonight, my dear. Dare I hope that I am the cause of such a mood?"

Cat raised her chin, arched a feathery brow and smiled coyly. "Your vanity far exceeds your arrogance if you would believe so. I am merely pleased at the chance to join the company of gentlemen *at last.*"

Ryan frowned and ceased to converse, turning his attention to the other couples on the dance floor. It was apparent that his partner was the object of intense scrutiny by some of the young hot-bloods who were dancing. She moved gracefully, perfectly at ease and poised, so much so that he again wondered about her true upbringing. She had mentioned that she'd dined with royalty. Everything about the girl was a mystery, an intriguing potpourri of half-truths and lies. The dance ended. As Ryan escorted her back to her seat, he was approached by a man of roughly the same age, who slapped him heartily on the back.

"Ryan, you lucky devil! I insist upon an introduction to this fascinating creature you've discovered." Justin de Rysfield smiled, his thin, aristocratic features lighting with anticipated pleasure. Ryan paused, unwilling to make the introduction but unable to ignore the request. He'd known Justin most of his life and had gone through school with him in the north. Justin's father, Pieter, had been associated with his uncle in several business deals and their contact had thrown the two together. Justin was a cocky, arrogant fellow who had always attempted to compete with Ryan in every conceivable category.

Some of Ryan's displeasure communicated itself to Cat. She took advantage of the situation to extend her hand and smile radiantly at the stranger. "Ryan seems to have forgotten my name, monsieur. It is Catherine, Catherine St. Marin." There, that would serve him! She had confided her true name, something that Ryan had never been able to make her admit, to a total stranger. His frown deepened as Justin introduced himself. Cat controlled her shock at the name of de Rysfield and, as the music began again, accepted Justin's offer to join him in a dance. Her mouth twitched with amusement at the black scowl covering Ryan's face, a scowl that included her *and* her new partner.

Ryan watched the two dance, his heavy, black brows furrowed in irritation. The bitch had sensed his dislike of Justin and played upon it! Now, as he watched them, she threw back her head and her lilting laughter carried across the room to him. Ryan cursed, stalking off to the refreshment table for a drink. He'd be damned if he'd give her the satisfaction of showing any further irritation. If she must play games, he refused to be the source of her enjoyment.

Justin monopolized Cat's time the next hour. No others had a chance to dance with her. The buffet was announced and he left her just long enough to fill two plates with the tempting array of foods. Ryan appeared at her side the instant Justin left, reaching down to capture her hand and draw her to her feet. "I'd like to strike a truce, *Catherine,*" he said, emphasizing her name. He grinned, his dark eyes crinkling with high humor. "Come and dine with me."

Cat tried to withdraw her hand but found herself drawn along, almost against her will. "I cannot, Ryan. Justin has gone——"

"Justin will have to find another dining partner," Ryan interrupted impatiently, leading her along the hall toward the smallest of the three drawing rooms. Once inside he closed the double doors behind him and gestured to her to be seated. Two plates were arranged on a small table, two glasses of wine and a small candelabra. Cat couldn't resist an amused smile, for Ryan had been very efficient in a short period of time. The rapt attention she had received from Justin had to be responsible for this display of solicitude.

"I must be insane to be here with you," Cat contended, disconcerted by her own willingness to be swept along in his plans. "You've been rude and overbearing, arrogant and demanding, and yet I join you with so little protest." She knew the reason herself. When he chose to, Ryan Nicholls exuded a charm that few could resist. She had been intrigued by his approach and had gone with him, knowing that after tonight she would never see him again.

Ryan raised his glass in a toast. "To sweet insanity then, if that's the name of the emotion between us." His coal black eyes seemed to bore into her, causing a shiver to run up her spine. "There *is* something between us, Catherine, you know that as well as I." He glanced down at the table, his long, elegant fingers toying with the silver, then again his eyes sought hers. "You're merely struggling to resist our relationship."

Cat was indeed struggling, but it was an inner struggle. She was trying to break the hypnotic thrall of his gaze. His hands reached out to hers, covering her cold, slender fingers with their warm strength. She felt dazed and trapped, suddenly pulling her hand away as though his touch burned. "And what *is* our relationship, Ryan?"

She smiled, soft lips twisting with cynicism. "Are you offering me marriage, or just the sharing of your bed?" Silence greeted her question, as she had known it would. Thank God she was leaving soon, she thought, or Ryan would have had his way.

"I am not ready to offer marriage to anyone, Catherine. I can't make any promises or vows that I would not honor. I've felt your response, I know it's there. You have a deep well of passion, though you might try to deny its existence. I am offering an arrangement that might fulfill our mutual needs."

"I wouldn't find that fulfilling in the least! I was perfectly happy before you entered my life and I can manage as well again." Ryan's expression displayed quick displeasure and frustration, like a young boy denied a plaything. "If you'll excuse me, I'd like to return to the party. My appetite has deserted me." She started to rise but Ryan's hand shot out to grab her wrist.

"I usually get what I want, and I want you, Catherine. I took you once without fear of reprisal and I'll do it again. Do not be foolish enough to think my uncle could keep me from what I truly desire." He released her and smiled, cold, ruthless determination glinting silver within the midnight of his eyes.

Cat again thanked God that she would be leaving. The sure knowledge gave her the courage to answer with a calm, confident smile. "I invite you to try, Ryan, though I doubt your success." She whirled away from him before he could reply and swept from the room with a flare of green brocade skirts.

In the ballroom, Charles stood near his seated fiancée, idly listening to the repartee between Marian and a houseguest the Holborn family had brought to the party. When Ryan disappeared, the girl had attached herself to the man she astutely determined to be the most eligible bachelor present. Justin approached Charles, bowing politely to Cora and drawing his host into a conversation.

"Your party is delightful, Sir Charles," he flattered.

"I've rarely seen guests enjoy themselves so. You've outdone yourself. Haven't seen that lovely guest of yours, by chance?" Charles preened at the compliment though he had just been thinking the same thought. Most of the guests had finished eating and champagne flowed freely, setting a mellow mood. He had lost track of Eve and looked for her now. The musicians had just begun another tune when there was low exclamation from Marian's partner.

Paul DuMarial, the Comte de Savan, turned to Charles and drew his attention to a couple dancing across the crowded floor. "Sir Charles, forgive me for intruding but I'm sure I have seen an acquaintence. The young woman in green . . . what is her name, please?" Beneath his powdered wig, his straight blond eyebrows were raised in eager anticipation. The strong masculine features of the man were arrested with attention as he stared across the room at Cat.

"You have excellent taste, Monsieur le Comte," complimented Charles. "However, I doubt you know the young lady. She's a guest of my house, a Mistress St. Marin, but she has never told me she had traveled abroad."

"But, monsieur, I could never forget that face, though it's been two years since I last saw her. I sued for her hand, along with half the bluebloods in Paris. She would have none of us. Even His Majesty, King Louis, found her fair. She was a great favorite of his. That emerald about her neck is a gift from him. I had wondered where my Catherine had gone. Excuse me, please, I must renew our friendship."

Charles was in a quandry, completely puzzled by the facts Savan had revealed. "Wait, monsieur, a moment before you join the lady. By what name do you know her? It's very important."

"Why, Catherine Devlan, of course. The name you mentioned—St. Marin—it is that of her grandmother, Marguerite, an old and honored name in France. Now you must excuse me." He made his way across the room, leaving the small group behind. Marian gaped after him, her mouth beginning to purse with frustration. She had cultivated his company the entire night and now saw her chances of snaring a French count vastly diminished by none other than the same red-haired whore she had sneered at and slurred.

Charles's pale complexion had gone a deathly white at the mention of Cat's true surname. With a vast effort at control, he turned to Cora and excused himself, ignoring Justin, to hurry out into the hall. Justin himself was stunned at the name of Devlan, for he well remembered his father's role in the plot against Brian. He was amused at Charles's reaction and promptly followed the older man in an attempt to see what would come to pass. As he walked into the hall, he caught sight of the Frenchman greeting Catherine.

Cat had just finished dancing with a young, local dandy when she heard her name called in a low, familiar voice. She whirled, her violet eyes widening in stunned surprise at the sight of Paul duMarial. It couldn't be he, not here, across the wide expanse of the Atlantic, in a distant colony of England! Yet it was, his face aglow with the same admiration it had held when she had last seen him. "Paul, Paul—how good to see you!" she cried, allowing him to catch her hands and bring them to his lips in a soft kiss. Suddenly she remembered where she was, in whose house she stood, and the thought of her identity being revealed before her plan could work struck a chord of anxiety within her. She affectionately hooked her arm in his and urged him down the hall, seeking a quiet spot to question him and find out whether he had accidently given her away. In the long, velvet-papered hallway, there was no one in sight and she sat on a bench below the wide staircase, drawing him to her side. "Paul, how ever did you turn up in the colonies?" She spoke in French, conversing in a low tone so that no one might overhear.

His eyes searched her face, lovingly tracing every

soft, delicate feature, features that had remained in his memory these past two years.

"I was stranded here at the outbreak of war, my sweet. I've been with friends in New York for the past six months. Had I known you were here, I'd have rushed to your side. I had forgotten you were born in America. Is Sir Charles a relative?" He smiled, unable to take his eyes from her. "We must have a long talk, I want to know everything you've done since we last met." He brought her hands to his lips once more in a tender caress. "Tell me you haven't married, my love, that there's no one who's captured your heart. I would be consumed by jealousy!"

"The lady is unattached." Ryan had appeared at their side, almost without a sound. He was once more cool and aloof, and had startled Cat by his easy command of French. It was another fact that she hadn't known about him. Suddenly she remembered the furious abuse she had shouted at him that day in Tortuga. He had known exactly what she called him. She blushed at the memory, growing angry at his interruption.

"Monsieur Nicholls is quite correct, Paul. There is no one I've found who . . . compares with you." She smiled at her old suitor, well aware that her flattery of him would gall Ryan. She introduced the two and watched as they nodded, each measuring the other distrustfully. Good, it would serve Ryan right to be taken down a peg or two. He thought of her as a helpless child, unschooled in the ways of the world. Let him see that she was his social equal, if not superior! Paul had taken the seat next to her again and she placed her hand on his arm in intimate affection. "Paul and I are old friends, Ryan. We would like to be alone, if you don't mind." She paused to flash a glance at Ryan and measure his irritation. She was pleased to see his brow furrow with anger as he stared at her hand and stiffened. "We have so many fond memories to recall."

Ryan bowed stiffly, furious at the dismissal and the open affection she showed with the Frenchman. "Far be it from me to interfere with close friends. By your leave, Monsieur le Comte." He wheeled and stalked off toward the ballroom.

Paul had watched the repartee with an amused expression. Quite obviously there was an undercurrent of emotion between Catherine and the younger Nicholls. She had never reacted to him so warmly in the past. For a brief moment his heart lifted in hope that she might have missed him enough to entertain the thought of marriage. As he studied her and saw the naked feeling exposed in her eyes as she watched the man leave, he knew he hoped in vain. Whatever the emotion, hate or love, she seemed bonded in some lasting way to this Ryan Nicholls. He felt a small flicker of jealousy gnaw at his insides but dismissed it. If he couldn't have the love of this gorgeous creature, he'd do nothing to harm her regard for his close friendship. "Catherine," he said softly, gently lifting her chin until she gazed into his eyes. "I am an old friend." He gestured after Ryan. "Tell me about your feelings for this man."

Back at the refreshment table, Ryan seethed with fury. Catherine, the soft, sensuous bitch, had taunted him openly with her warm regard for the count. She, who had just flaunted her independence before him, now sat in close, intimate conversation with that French jackanapes. He knew that the man had never been her lover. *He'd* been the first to have that honor, but the soft light in those lovely amethyst eyes as she looked at Savan had twisted in his heart like a knife thrust. He'd been too soft in his manner with her. He tossed back a brandy and refilled his glass. No woman could treat him like a schoolboy, dismissing him with a regal nod of her head. Tonight, he decided, as the liquor sank to his belly, warming his blood. Tonight when the household had retired he'd take her to his bed once more. She was a wild vixen who required a strong hand and he had attempted to woo her gently. The coming night he would possess her, whether she resisted him or not.

Cat refused to tell Paul anything of Ryan. "I'd much

rather speak of you," she said, turning the conversation away from a subject that still confused her. They spoke of mutual friends and he entertained her with amusing anecdotes of the court life she had missed. The clock in the vestibule struck the hour, chiming ten times, and she suddenly remembered her purpose this night. Pleading a slight headache, she rose and excused herself. "I must lie down a while, Paul. The excitement of the night has given me an aching head. I promise, we'll speak again after I rest." He rose and leaned forward, pressing a light kiss at her temple.

"You're more lovely than I remember, Catherine, dear. I *will* see you again. Perhaps tomorrow we might ride together," Paul suggested in parting.

"Yes, that would be lovely," Cat replied, vaguely anxious to seek her room and the hidden documents. She withdrew, knowing he watched as she mounted the stairs. Her head *was* beginning to pound, though the cause of it was intense excitement keyed to a fever pitch. The moment she had long awaited was soon to come.

Halfway up the stairs, Cat paused as Allie called softly to her from the hall. The girl hurried toward her, her manner agitated and frightened. "Miss . . . I's sposed to give you dis," she stuttered quickly, thrusting a note into Cat's hand and turning to hastily retrace her steps.

"Wait, Allie—who is it from?" Cat called, but the girl had already disappeared into the kitchens. She opened it, her eyes darting to the signature. Charles had scrawled his name at the bottom. Even his writing was indicative of his nature, sharp, spare, and lacking in warmth or grace. She quickly read the note, her heart pounding in a race with her pulses. He declared that he held certain documents belonging to her. If she wished to retrieve them, she must meet him in the library at once. She paled, knowing that somehow, Paul must have revealed her secret. Charles was one step ahead of her and unless she hurried, he would destroy the papers that sealed his ruin. She fled down the stairs in a panic, slowing her pace as several guests strolled through the hall. She couldn't arouse suspicion by her behavior. Until she had the papers safely in her hands, she must control her emotions.

Cat knew the location of the library, though she had never had occasion to enter the room. Now she paused, taking a deep breath as she stood before the heavily carved mahogany doors. She needed all her courage to face the monster within. As she reached for the handle, the door swung open. Charles faced her, his expression a combination of exaltation and power. He reached out, grabbing her wrist, and pulled her in to the room. She whirled on him, allowing her own expression to show the hatred she'd been forced to hide. Her eyes blazed with fury as she demanded the return of her property.

Charles's thin, dry laughter curled from his throat like a venomous snake. He sneered, ordering her to be seated. In the fireplace, a blaze crackled and popped, for a second the only sound other than the breathing of the two people in the room. "I should have known you, should have connected the name and that blaze of hair. You're very like your father in temperament." He moved to the fireplace, turning to face her where she still stood. His hands were clasped behind his back, the shadows cast by the firelight darkening the hollows of his thin cheeks until he appeared to be the image of the devil, backed by shooting sparks of flame. "You're a fool, a silly chit who hadn't the sense to let well enough alone! You even think like Brian, Catherine. He was all emotion, never stopping to deliberate, never a cool, premeditated thought in his head."

"I insist you return my property immediately. Others have seen those papers. You won't escape your just reward *this* time." She faced him unafraid, head held high and color blazing in her cheeks.

Charles gazed down the length of his long, thin nose, and smiled, an evil gesture of conceit and power. "You're more than a fool, girl, you're mad if you think I'd return those documents!" He reached up to the mantel, grasping the papers he had laid there in one clawlike hand. "No, my dear, these papers will never be seen by another soul.

I've taken the liberty of separating your commission and placing it in a safe location. Despite your annoying attempt, I'm willing to keep it hidden should you agree to become my mistress."

"Never!" Cat spit the word out on the crest of a wave of nausea. The very thought was an abomination. "I'd rather be dead and rotting in my grave!"

Charles bristled at the rejection, his eyes hard and icy as they swept over her figure. "I think you might change your mind; I'll enjoy taming your shrewish temper. As for these"—he gestured with the papers, watching her start as he held them toward the fire. Slowly, taunting her, his hand moved closer to the flames.

"No!" Cat screamed and ran toward him, her arm outstretched to save the papers. His hand flicked and the fire flared as the documents landed and caught, blazing brightly as the flames licked at the brown, curling corners. Desperately she attempted to pull them away but Charles caught her wrist, forcing it cruelly behind her back.

His hand slammed against her face, stilling the hysteria within. She was forced against his reed-thin body and again nausea swept her and her skin crawled with the touch of his hands. His lips found her throat, and as his desire began to rise, he pushed her back, so that she landed sharply against the desk, bent half backwards with his body covering hers. His strength was amazing for such a sparrow of a man, the strength of evil, and though she struggled with all her might, she couldn't escape him. His thin, bony fingers were everywhere, at the nape of her neck, thrusting within the low bodice of her gown. Cat whimpered, an animal cry of pain and helplessness as his narrow lips closed over her mouth, his tongue invading its inner softness. Her mind went blank and she acted instinctively, for her own survival, all thoughts of revenge lost. Her right hand wriggled from beneath her, desperately searching the desk top for a weapon, anything to strike the mad, rutting beast atop her and stop his vile attack. Suddenly her hand closed on a sharp object. Without thinking, she closed her fingers and brought it forward. It plunged into his back and suddenly she was free, as he lifted his face in stunned disbelief and fell away to the floor. She lay there panting, quelling the panic that had almost drowned her in its swirling eddy. Cat was in shock, unaware that her hand still tightly gripped the letter opener she'd found. Blood smeared the sharp point and as her eyes focused, she dropped it, shuddering and distractedly running a hand through her tangled curls.

She rose slowly, still wary of the form crumpled on the floor. Charles's eyes were closed but he moaned, low and uneven, and she jumped at the sound, inching back from the body as though it were the incarnation of pure evil. She wasn't thinking clearly, she only knew she couldn't bear to be in the same room any longer. She ran for the door and made her way to her room. Her one thought was escape, to get away from this house and the threat that Charles held over her. She quickly changed to her riding habit. Tears poured from her eyes as she discovered her emerald missing. Charles must have pulled it loose in the struggle! It still lay with him in the library. She couldn't force herself to return, for by now he may have alerted the household. She had only grazed his shoulder—she must hurry and meet Will at the inn!

As soon as Cat bolted from the library, the terrace door had opened. Justin de Rysfield entered, slipping quietly into the room to see the outcome of the struggle he had overheard. His quick glance surveyed the scene, the disarray on the desk and Charles Nicholls lying crumpled at its foot. He smiled, for half of his objective this night had been accomplished for him; Charles was dazed and groggy, moaning from a slight shoulder wound. The girl hadn't hurt him badly, but as usual with men who enjoy the power of inflicting cruelty on others, the bastard was overcome by his own pain. Justin quickly searched the top drawer of the desk, found the commission that Charles had mentioned, and slipped it into his waistcoat. Then he knelt by the body, picking up the letter opener and staring at it. It seemed to fit the palm of his hand neatly. He noticed the emerald that the girl had worn, still clutched within the fallen man's hands. Prying open the fingers, he pocketed the jewel. Charles was coming around, moving more actively as his strength returned.

Charles opened his eyes to see Justin at his side. "You . . . you must help me, m'boy," he stuttered weakly. "That woman, the one I sheltered—she stabbed me, attacked me for no reason!"

Amusement lit within Justin's blue eyes. Even in pain, Charles remembered how to lie. "Oh, she had a reason, Charles. At least as much as I—we both lack fathers because of you." He bared his teeth in a grin as his hand rose and the sharp weapon glinted in the firelight, then plunged deep into the heart of the man who had killed his father. The hand rose and thrust again and buried the sharp instrument deep within Charles. The body twitched in its death throes, then jerked one final time and was still. Justin rose and backed away, making his exit by the same door. Twenty minutes later he stood in the hall, his features composed as he signaled for a servant. "I've not been able to find Sir Charles, boy, and I must talk to him. Perhaps you'll find him in the library. Tell him I'll be in the ballroom with Mistress Fitzhugh." The slave nodded, rushing off to find his master. Justin gave his reflection in the hall mirror one last perusal, calmly flicked the lace at the edge of his sleeves, and sauntered into the party.

Outside a chill wind blew, forcing Cat to draw her cape closer. She had managed to sneak down the back entrance without being observed, thankful the night was dark, lit only by a quarter-moon. She ran to the stables, quietly entered and searched the darkness for the stall that held her customary mount. Softly she rubbed the mare's velvety nose, soothing and quieting her. She didn't pause to saddle the animal but merely dropped a bit within the horse's mouth and drew the reins back, jumping easily astride bare-back. Once Cat had walked the mare beyond the stable, she patted her, flexing her knee to urge her forward to a gallop. Exhilaration filled her. She would soon be at Will's side and together they would sail the *Falcon* to Tortuga. She raced down the road toward Bath Town, refusing to look behind her. Briefly she wondered what lies Charles would concoct to cover his attack and wounding. Would Ryan believe him? Paul, at least, would be there to defend her.

Chapter Six

The old servant ran shouting from the library, his speech garbled and run together in terror at his discovery. People crowded into the hall, curious about the uproar, turning to each other to whisper behind their hands. Soon the news spread, reaching Ryan and Cora in the ballroom. The hushed crowd of guests parted to allow Ryan to pass. When he reached the library doors, he found old Jethro, the servant who had discovered the body, in near hysteria. He soothed the man, telling him to calm himself and relate what he'd found.

"It's Masta' Charles, suh," the old man said in a trembling voice. "I's sent to give 'im a message an' . . . an' I foun' 'im lyin' there by de desk. He's dade, Masta' Ryan, somebody done killed 'im!"

Ryan again reassured the old slave, telling him he was relieved for the evening and could go to his quarters. The frail old black tottered off, shaking his head and mumbling under his breath. Ryan frowned, entering the library to find Justin kneeling by his uncle's fallen body.

Ryan stood over the body, staring down at the mortal remains of Charles Nicholls. He felt no pain of loss, no sadness or hurt. His uncle had been a solitary, unloving soul whose cold, haughty nature had apparently brought about his death. Finding the killer would be difficult. Charles had made a great many enemies in his long, ruthless life. "How long's he been dead?" Ryan asked.

"I'd say roughly about twenty minutes or so. Sorry, Ryan, I know he was your only relative. Have the authorities been sent for?" Justin rose, gingerly holding the murder weapon in his fingers and dropping it on the desk. His lace cuffs were spotted with blood and he rubbed at the dark crimson stain, attempting to dull it. In the ballroom, while he had waited for the servant to discover the body, he'd been shocked to find blood on his sleeves, and had managed to hide the telltale sign until now. Having purposely handled the letter opener, he had provided an answer to anyone who might notice the blood stains. Before Ryan entered he had pulled the emerald necklace from his pocket and laid it on the floor near Charles's hand. It lay there now, sparkling in the firelight. He reached down, picked it up, and stared at it with mock surprise. Ryan had seated himself behind the desk and stared blankly into the fire.

"The murderer might still be here, among our guests," he commented drily, wearily rubbing a hand through his dark curls. "How in the hell do I go about asking these people if by any chance they happened to strike my uncle with a dagger?" He barked a short, mirthless laugh, glancing at the silent Justin. "What's that you have?" Justin shifted uncomfortably before he answered.

"Look, Ryan, there's probably a good explanation for this. It's Catherine's necklace—the emerald she was wearing. I overheard Savan say it was a gift from the French king. I'm sure if you ask her, there's a reasonable——"

"There'd better be," Ryan said angrily, rising to stalk to the door and call a servant. He instructed the man to find Cat and bring her to the library. Before he left, the slave told him that Cora had fainted and had been carried to the green drawing room. The guests still milled about in confusion and Marian had been asking for him. "I'll be out in a while to talk with them," he said. "Meanwhile make sure the champagne still flows. That'll keep them busy for a while."

Justin sat on the edge of the desk, watching Ryan pace before the fire in agitation. "You know the girl is Brian's sister, don't you?" he interjected slyly, knowing full well that Ryan had been absent when the news was revealed.

Ryan whirled to face Justin, shock spreading over his features. "What the hell are you babbling about, man! You must've been to the refreshment table once too often."

"I won't take offense at that, considering the recent shock you've had, but I'm *not* babbling. Ask Savan, if you don't believe me. She's Catherine Devlan, not St. Marin. I don't know the reason for her charade but there's no doubt the man knows her well."

Ryan's thoughts were racing, turning back in time to the day he'd seen Brian Devlan hanged. His uncle had taken him along to watch. Though he hadn't admitted it he had admired the rascal's bravado in the face of death. The older girl—now he remembered, her name *was* Catherine- -had disappeared following the hanging and no one had seen her since . . . until now. He knew it was true, the pieces all fit together. Perhaps she'd seen her father hanged and in some way held a grudge against Charles for his crude comments. He realized suddenly there was no brother who had raided the plantation; it had been Catherine herself who commanded the *Falcon*. He scowled, for the idea of having been duped by a young girl pricked at his vanity. She'd have a hell of a lot to explain.

There was a quick knock at the door. "The lady ain't nowhere t' be found, suh," the servant reported, adding that Michael had just come to the kitchen to say that a horse was missing from the stables.

"Damn," Ryan cursed, dismissing the man and turning to Justin. "I'm going after her; she can't have gotten far. Do me a favor, try and keep everything under control until I get back. I shouldn't be long. She must have headed for town."

"Of course, old boy," Justin replied smoothly. "I wouldn't be too hard on her though—you don't know yet what *really* happened."

Minutes later Ryan was astride his white stallion, Centaur, headed north along the sea road to Bath Town. He worked the animal hard, urging him to a gallop. Catherine had a half-hour's advantage; but her mare was no match for the huge, disciplined stallion and he had no doubt he would catch her somewhere along the road before she made the town. He remembered the "lover" she was supposed to have met and wondered if it had been one of her crew. How long had she planned all this? He couldn't believe she had the nerve to stab a man to death. Then he remembered his own close call in Tortuga. She had the necessary skill, there was no doubt of that!

Just past the boundaries of his land he caught sight of her on the road ahead. She heard the sound of hooves pounding in pursuit and glanced back once before spurring her mount to a breakneck speed. He had the edge, for the night was dark and he knew the road well. Cutting across a stand of pines, he decreased her lead by half, then steadily gained until he was close enough behind her to hear the hard breathing of the labored mare. A minute later he was beside her, easily catching the reins to pull sharply upon them and halt the mare. She whinnied, dancing about until his voice calmed her.

"Let go!" Cat cried out. "Whatever lies your uncle told you, you have no right——"

Ryan jumped down from the stallion, still holding tightly to the mare's reins. He grabbed Cat's wrist, dragging her roughly down. She tumbled almost falling until his arms caught her. "I've no right have I," he sneered, mindful that his uncle lay dead and she suspiciously had taken flight. "I suppose next you'll tell me you had a sudden fancy for an evening ride. You're going nowhere but back to the house. If I can sort through your lies, Catherine Devlan, we might yet find the truth of what took place tonight in the library."

"So, you know who I am," Cat snapped with a spirited toss of her head. His fingers still tightly clutched her arm, biting painfully through the riding habit into the tender skin. "Let go of me," she repeated, trying to struggle away. "You and your uncle have done enough harm to the Devlans to last a lifetime! There's no crime in concealing a name."

Ryan shook her, an irrational desire to hurt her pounding at his senses. "Don't pretend innocence, you're long past that. As for my uncle, he won't be able to answer any charges you make, you saw to that!"

"I don't know what you're talking about. Charles assaulted me," she argued, adding sarcastically, "It seems to be a family trait. I merely defended myself and fled from your wretched home."

"Stabbing a man twice in the heart seems more premeditated than defensive."

Cat smiled coldly, her hair a wild tangle of moonlit curls. "If he's dead, then some one else was present who bore him ill. The number who do must be legion. I doubt any will mourn his passing. Had I the presence of mind, I'd have stayed to applaud the devil's end!" She panted with savage emotion, her breath steaming out into the cold night air.

Ryan regarded her with a mystified gaze. "What did he ever do to warrant such hatred," he puzzled. "I know he took advantage of Briar, but she needn't have continued with him, Catherine. It was by her own choice."

"Choice, ha!" Cat spat. "What choice did a fifteen-year-old have with that satyr? After he'd ruined her, what chance did she have for marriage? Even now, with him gone, his vile deeds live on. Briar is with my grandmother in France, awaiting the birth of his bastard!" She boiled with hatred and bitterness, gasping for breath before rushing on. "Your uncle, the prominent, the respected Sir

Charles—were you aware that he took advantage of other young girls, that his tastes ran to cruel whippings to gain his pleasure?"

Ryan peered through the darkness, releasing her arms, knowing she hadn't finished. She stepped back from him, the blazing hatred in her eyes animately reaching out to envelope him. A heavy, stout boundary marker stood by the side of the road and she leaned against it, her shoulders thrust back as she continued the list of grievances.

"He killed my father! His influential friends arranged it all, everything down to the last detail, including stealing my inheritance. And you question why I hated him, why I'm happy to see him dead! He can no longer hurt another soul—*that alone* is reason enough to rejoice." She looked up at him through eyes that shone with a glaze of unshed tears.

"You're wrong. He was a ruthless businessman, a selfish man whose world revolved about himself, but he wouldn't have plotted a murder such as you describe. What proof have you?" The horses danced restlessly, aware of the violent tension in the air, and Ryan reached a hand out, soothing them.

Cat's laughter was harshly bitter. "You'll find proof in the ashes in the library fire. He found the evidence by rifling my belongings." She slumped wearily, every muscle aching from her battle with Charles. "I don't care if you believe me," her voice came in a frustrated moan, "I only want to leave this godforsaken place at last! If you want the mare, I'll walk to town."

Ryan stepped forward until he stood directly before her, staring down into her eyes, searching them in the moonlight. She had lied to him in the past, could he believe her now?

"You'll come back with me. If you're telling the truth, you've nothing to fear. The authorities will want to question you." His tone was relentless, unyielding, and as he took her arm, more gently now, surprisingly she made no resistance. All the fire and emotion had been spent. He lifted her to the back of the stallion, jumping up behind her, the reins of the mare in one hand, his other locked tightly around Cat's narrow waist. Only the slightest pressure of his knees guided the well-trained animal toward home. The journey was silent but for the soft clip-clop of the horse's hooves.

As they came in sight of the stable, the girl stiffened against Ryan's chest and he guessed at her aversion to repeating the tale to strangers. Her bright, silken curls scented sweetly with an exotic flower he could not name, teased his cheek. The nearness of her slender body recalled their most intimate moments and he suddenly found himself regretting his stubborn insistence that she return. Suppose she told the truth and wasn't believed? With no proof of innocence, she could be charged with murder and sentenced to the gallows. The thought of her vibrant beauty snuffed out so young by the hangman's noose and the lovely, supple body consigned to the earth made him sick. Could his selfish insistence result in the loss of something he had already come to treasure? She remained silent, though as he dismounted and lifted his arms to catch her, her trembling muscles betrayed her anxiety.

"Look, Catherine, I'm not sure whether to believe you. I believe you hated him enough to kill him. Regardless of that, I won't allow anyone to badger you with questions." He glanced back at the house, still blazing with light, gave the surrounding property a cursory glance, then his eyes sought hers reassuringly. "This belongs to me now—I'm the master of it all. No one would dare to disobey my commands. Remember that when we're inside." Ryan's hand reached out and Cat flinched, but he merely ran his fingers lightly along the lines of her cheek.

Cat could barely believe the tenderness of his touch. Was this the same Ryan Nicholls who had forced her against her will, who had never displayed an iota of concern for her feelings? His manner was confident and protective, shocking her from the apathy that had settled over her weary mind. She questioned his sudden change of character with spirited sarcasm. "What game are you playing now, Ryan—lord of the manor, protector of innocents? Somehow, I find it difficult to distinguish being abused by the local authorities or by you!" A sudden thought struck her and she threw back her head as bitter laughter bubbled from deep within her. "Or are you so vain that *you* must be my only source of torment?" Cat shook her head in sad wonder. "Ryan, I'm beginning to believe you'll follow in your uncle's footsteps. You might even improve on the finer points of his cruelty and hone them to a sharper cutting edge." She straightened her back, turning away from him to walk slowly toward the house. When he hesitated, she turned and smiled with mocking amusement. "Well, come then, my brave protector, you don't want to miss out on all the fun!"

It was a full half-hour before the constable and his men arrived. Cat had entered the house with Ryan at her side, forced to run the gauntlet of the remaining house guests. Her head was held high, back proud and stiff as she ignored the sly, whispered asides from the openly staring assembly. Pausing only a moment before the library door, she steeled her courage and entered. The body had been removed to an upstairs bedroom and only the pool of dark, wine-red blood soaking the richly patterned carpet remained as evidence of what had happened. Justin and Savan awaited them, and both rose at her entrance. Each began to talk, trying to override the other's voice and profess Cat's innocence to Ryan.

"Be seated, Catherine," Ryan ordered, frowning at the two men who had appointed themselves her defenders. It sorely tried his vanity that he had been cast in the role of judge and executioner. He walked to the desk, throwing himself wearily into the large leather chair.

The smile Cat offered the two was brilliant and a touch strained, as she accepted a seat by the warmth of the fire. She felt suddenly chilled, revisiting the scene of her argument with Charles. Leaning her head back against the high-backed leather wing chair, she closed her eyes and shut the sight away, withdrawing into herself to ponder her fate. The brief, exhilarating feel of freedom was behind her now, her flight cut off by Ryan's twisted ideas of justice and gallantry. His offer of protection was almost ludicrous in the light of what she would now face. At the moment she truly believed he cared to see her humbled, groveling for her life. Unaware that the three men in the room all studied her, she allowed her despair to flicker briefly over her features. She looked frail and waifike, dwarfed by the large wings of the chair, her hair a mass of wild, wind-blown tangles, the delicate copper-gold tendrils framing her pale, distraught face.

"This is an outrage, monsieur," Paul bellowed, moving to Cat's side and draping an arm across the top of the chair. "Catherine was gently raised. To subject her to an inquiry is . . . is abominable." He sputtered furiously. "I question your judgment and your supposed upbringing as a gentleman!" His deep blue eyes swept disdainfully over Ryan as he tossed his challenge.

"The count is right, Ryan, old boy. You've condemned the poor girl without evidence. Even if the constable decided there were no grounds for a charge, you've set her down squarely in the center of a scandal she'll never live down." Justin shook his head, feigning despair for his friend's lack of judgment. "I'd advise you to drop this before it's too late."

Ryan had been irritated by Savan's tirade, but Justin's added words of wisdom were the finishing touch that set the fuse of his temper ablaze. "When I need your advice, I shall ask it, Justin," he stated coldly. Cat had come out of her lethargic state and Ryan was suddenly aware of her gaze, the violet eyes appraising him through lowered lids. He was further infuriated by the twitch of amusement touching the corners of that delightfully pouting mouth. "You're enjoying this, Mistress Devlan," he sneered. "I vow you won't be so amused when the constable arrives!"

He rose, pacing the room in agitation. "Damn it, Justin, why am I suddenly the villain? You, yourself found the necklace. Unless I'm addled by the night's events, that suggests the lady was present. Why not ask *her* for an explanation?" He stalked across the room to stand in front of Cat's chair. "Well," he said with a deep scowl, "has m'lady suddenly lost her voice? Your defenders are breathless with anticipation!"

At her side, Savan stiffened in fury, his eyes narrowed at Ryan's sarcastic comments. He moved toward Ryan but Cat's hand closed on his wrist, resting there to restrain him.

"No, Paul," she insisted urgently. "I'll not have any further displays of temper on my account!" She left her hand on his arm, smiling sweetly to ease his indignant anger. "I *did* lose my necklace, and missed it only when I changed clothes. It was torn from my throat when——" Her voice faltered at the memory and a shudder visibly passed over her before she could continue. "When Charles assaulted me." Cat withdrew her hand from Paul's arm, clasping both hands tightly in her lap, eyes downcast, as the words tumbled from her in a dull, halting monotone. She described the scene, reliving each horrid detail once more.

"I meant to expose him tonight—*that* was my revenge. To expose him to scandal and public scorn for his evil deeds." Her head rose slowly until she glared reproachfully into Ryan's eyes. Her own glittered with righteous anger. "I had many opportunities to kill him, had that been my desire."

"You see, Ryan," Justin's voice came from across the room. "The poor girl just defended herself. I can hardly see a woman as delicate as Catherine repeatedly stabbing your uncle. There *was* a smear of blood on his right shoulder. Someone else, someone who also hated Charles must have found him dazed and taken advantage of the moment." Justin restrained his amusement as he carefully retold the truth.

"When the authorities arrive," he continued, "you must add your voice to ours in Catherine's defense." He threw her a reassuring smile.

"I told you once that when I need your advice I'd request it," Ryan snapped furiously, his gaze still fixed on Cat's defiant features. "The lady follows in her father's illustrious footsteps. She has a violent, unbridled temper and a high degree of proficiency with weapons."

Cat's eyes narrowed in disgust, her fingers whitening at the knuckles as she clenched them tightly together. "If you'll recall the circumstances, *Master Nicholls,*" she retorted sarcastically, "I would think even *you* could agree that my action was warranted!" She paused, adding a statement that was meant to wound him. "I would do so again. I only regret my blade missed its appointed target!"

Ryan bristled, wheeling to return to the desk. He slammed into the chair, cursing as he pounded the desk for emphasis. "Where the hell is that constable! My only desire is to have done with this ridiculous bickering. I strongly suggest we maintain silence until his arrival." The sweeping glare of his black eyes included all three in the command.

As if to answer his irritated query, there was a knock at the door, followed by the entrance of an officious looking man dressed in somber black. He cleared his throat, sweeping his hat off in a deep bow to Ryan.

"Master Nicholls, you have my sympathies. A dreadful shock, dreadful indeed," he puffed in an overly solicitious manner. "My men are stationed outside. I understand you suspect a young lady . . ." His rough, gravelly voice trailed off as he became aware of Cat's presence.

To all outward appearances, Cat was poised and calmly in control of her emotions. Inwardly she shook with sudden, unnerving fear. What if Ryan insisted on her arrest? She had deliberately antagonized him, and this official bumpkin seemed to fawn before him in awe. A sick dread churned in her stomach, rising like bitter gall in her throat. In her mind's eye she envisioned herself hanging, as her father had, until her breath was choked away. It was so unfair, a hopeless situation. Incredibly it seemed that history was about to repeat itself. Another Devlan would soon feel the bite of a rough hempen rope because of another Nicholls.

"Well, young woman, what have you to say for yourself?" The constable asked as she shook the desperation from her. He peered down over his paunch, judiciously studying her features, his hands clasped behind him. Cat felt a sudden hysterical impulse to laugh at the pompous little man who would decide her guilt or innocence. With difficulty she managed to stifle the feeling.

"I've already repeated my story twice," she said with quiet dignity. "I have no intention of repeating it a third time. Master Nicholls can furnish any details you wish to know. The hour is late, Constable . . ."

"Higgins, ma'am, Joshua Higgins," he told her, awed by her unshaken poise in the face of his questioning.

"Yes, Constable Higgins. As I said, the hour is late and I feel exhausted. I understand I'm not free to leave but I would like to retire. If Master Nicholls is worried that I might escape his clutches, you may post a guard at my door. If not, you may take me into custody now." She stretched her wrists before her, crossed together. A look of amusement highlighted the amethyst eyes as she arched a mocking brow at Ryan. "I suggest you tie my wrists, though. Ryan considers me highly dangerous!"

The barb found its mark and Ryan abruptly stood, his eyes flashing dangerously as he glowered at Cat. "I think we can postpone our discussion until the morning, Higgins. We'll all be more clearheaded after a night's rest." He walked around the edge of the desk and paused next to the constable.

"I . . . well, I . . . this is highly irregular, still, seeing it's you, Master Nicholls, I guess there's no harm in waiting till morning. We'll meet again, say at eight-thirty?"

Ryan had a look of resignation on his handsome, angular features. "Outside the door you'll find an old colored servant by the name of Marcus," he said. "He's been in charge of the house ever since I can remember. Tell him I said to arrange for quarters for your men and yourself. I'm afraid I have other duties to attend to before I can retire. As you suggested, we'll meet after breakfast." He dismissed the civil servant with a curt nod and watched as the man shuffled his bulk towards the door. "Oh, by the way, Higgins. We'll accept Mistress Devlan's idea of posting a guard for the night. That way we can be assured we will *all* meet in the morning."

Cat experienced a fleeting urge to scratch the snide arrogance from Ryan's face but she was too tired, too frightened and almost apathetic. What did it matter now, she thought dismally. Justin stared down at his hands, as though suddenly fascinated by his well-manicured nails. Only Paul reacted, attacking Ryan's attitude.

"*If* you were a gentleman," he jeered, reverting to his native French, "I would call you on the field of honor for your cavalier treatment of this young girl." He straightened his back, turning slightly away from Ryan in dismissal. "Seeing that you are not," he added coldly, "I will not sully my hands with your blood!"

The silence in the room was deafening. Even Justin, who had no command of the language, was aware of the challenge.

"Oh, I can find time to accommodate you, Savan. Say at . . . six tomorrow morning?" Ryan's manner was cool and matter-of-fact, as though he discussed the next day's menu instead of a duel to the death. "I must be done with it by six-thirty though. I hate to be late for breakfast—ruins my entire day. Is it settled then?"

A dull red flush suffused Paul's face as he realized his predicament. He had thought to embarass this crude American, make him appear the fool to Catherine, yet the man's icy black eyes had shown no fear and he had even mocked the seriousness of a death match. He had an unwilling respect for this man and though he had won his share of duels, he had a very strong desire to live to see his homeland once again. There was a long silence as he attempted to find an honorable retreat from almost certain death.

Without sensing Paul's inner turmoil, Cat came to his rescue. "No, I won't have it! Paul, if you still care for me, retract your statements!" She also slipped into the use of French, from a sense of habit. "Please, Paul," she pleaded sweetly. "For me!" Her eyes were liquid jewels as she gazed beseechingly at him and even if he had intended to go ahead with the match, he would have been forced to accede to her soft pleas. For appearances, he paused to consider her request. Desperately, she turned to Ryan, including him in her appeal. "Ryan, surely you don't value me highly enough to cause a man's death. Stop this now, before it goes too far!"

Ryan's expression was callous, his lithe, catlike body at ease. "It's out of my hands, *chérie*. Your friend made the challenge. If he wishes to withdraw it," he added magnanimously, "I will accept." His eyes glowed briefly with a touch of remembered passion. "And you're quite mistaken concerning the value I place upon you, my dear, quite mistaken."

A warm blush crept over Cat's face. The devil was mocking her again, reminding her of the intimate moments they had shared. For a brief moment she almost wished the two *would* duel. A headache was beginning to pound at her temples. Ryan was despicable, a ruthless rogue born to torment her. "Paul, please," she said, issuing a last plea for sanity. "Please, you're only adding to my distress!"

The nobleman shuffled his feet uncomfortably, refusing to look at his antagonist. Grudgingly he withdrew his challenge. "The hour is late, monsieur, and we are all under tension. For Catherine's sake, I retract my challenge."

Ryan laughed, easing the tension in the room. "I agree, Savan. We should all seek our beds at once. If you'll share Justin's room, we'll be able to put you up for the night." The new master of Seahaven ushered his guests from the room, closing the door after them. He still had many details to consider. The plantation, the funeral, all the responsibilities now rested squarely on his broad, muscular shoulders.

Cat closed the door to her room, wearily leaning back against its solid oak frame. God, she had thought she'd seen the last of it when she galloped away from the stable hours before. Paul had escorted her to her room, bringing her hand to his lips in a fervent kiss as he whispered of his loyalty and assured her that all would turn out well. Just as he had gently touched her cheek in a farewell kiss, a man had appeared at her door, a rough, burly sort, well armed and ready to stand watch over her for the night. Paul had bristled with righteous indignation at the man who took a seat next to the door and settled himself comfortably for the night. Again Cat touched Paul's arm, silently communicating a need to remain calm.

Now, she paced the room, dressed in a sheer, lace-trimmed night gown. She felt like a caged tigress and the tension of the night kept her from seeking the oblivion of sleep. By now, Will must know that her plans had gone awry. Would he try to find her tonight or at daybreak boldly ride up to the house in search of her? She prayed he would wait, for she had no desire to see him harmed because of her folly.

Somewhere in the hall a clock chimed the hour. Four o'clock . . . and she had to be up and about by six-thirty! She sank into the chair in front of the mirror, staring at her reflection. The fright she'd hidden so well in the library was now evident in her tight, tired face. Her complexion was pale and drawn, her eyes deep violet and wide with strain and tears formed at their corners. She bowed her head and covered her face, unable to face her reflection a moment longer. Will had been right! She had misjudged her own competence and all the well-laid, overproud plans had only led to her own downfall. She trembled violently, overcome with fury at her naïvete.

"You needn't worry, love. The good constable will almost certainly decide in your favor." Ryan spoke softly from the door joining their rooms. Cat's head shot up and she wiped hastily at her eyes, unwilling to let him witness any weakness. "The name Nicholls seems to awe him immensely."

"So, you've decided to believe me after all," Cat replied acidly. "And pray tell, what caused this change of heart?"

He sauntered leisurely into the room, slowly approaching her. "Did I say I believed you? No, Catherine," he added, reaching out a hand to lightly touch her curls. "I merely assured you that your pretty throat would not feel the roughness of a rope." He took her hand, prying open the clenched fingers to drop the emerald into her palm. "I believe this belongs to you."

Cat stared at the brilliant gem, opened her palm, and dropped it on the table. Suddenly the keepsake no longer offered the same, warm comfort it had before. She glanced up to find him observing her with a dark, discerning gaze. Her mouth twitched with the beginnings of a cynical smile. She had learned much these past months.

"Don't keep me in suspense, Ryan. What is it you seek in return for your . . . patronage? I've come to know that your every move is carefully planned to your advantage." She rose, adding defiantly, "Am I to be at your beck and call, ready to service you at any hour?" She began to pace furiously, her hands resting at her hips. Finally she stopped to confront him, her fury rising to a fever pitch as he studied her calmly. "Call Higgins now," she insisted. "Have him arrest me, for I will not play the whore for your pleasure. You took what was mine by force and have the power to do so again, but I'll not mewl and whimper to assuage your masculine vanity!"

Cat's eyes were a dark midnight velvet, her high cheekbones tinted with angry color. The candlelight gleamed, adding a halo of light to frame the long, curly mane of unruly red-gold waves. The agitated rise and fall of her breasts was enhanced by the cloudy, apple-green negligee. He had never seen her more defiant or more bewitching and desirable. His loins ached to possess her again, though he was growing more irritated by the moment. He had her at his mercy—one word from him and she could be carted away, a common felon accused of murder, yet she dared defy his offer of assistance. A blind, encompassing rage flooded over him, his pride pierced as though she had cast a knife blade at him. Who was she to deny his help? The impoverished daughter of a notorious scoundrel, a girl who should be trembling with appreciation!

"Your claim of innocence comes too late. You've already played the part. You cannot deny your response when I touch you. You're an accomplished liar, my pet, but your body speaks the truth your lips will not." His long, sculptured mouth was set with a mocking twist, his dark, brooding gaze boring into her eyes, daring her to deny he spoke the truth.

Why must he always taunt her! Her hand rose to slap the mockery from the handsome features. She found her wrist caught in a lightning grip. He held her effortlessly as she struggled, attempting to strike out at him with her free hand. That, too, was caught and bound with her other.

Slowly Ryan inched Cat backward until she was pressed against the wall. The heavily carved wood paneling bit into the tender skin of her back, as Ryan's body pressed close. He stretched her wrists high above her head, holding them easily against the wall with one hand. Her breasts rose and fell and rose again in a tantalizing display of temper.

Cat felt her defenses slipping away. As always, when he was near, his strength and virility seemed to act as a drug, draining her resistance until she became a puppet, a sensual creature who wantonly responded to his every command. Her gown was ripped away, to hang in shreds about her exposed body. Ryan's head moved relentlessly closer until she saw only his bold, rakish features. His mouth slammed against hers, his tongue a battering ram, easily breaking through the soft defenses of her lips, to enter and ravage repeatedly. Cat moaned, trying to twist her head away. Suddenly her lips were freed.

Ryan stepped back, leisurely surveying the ivory-sculptured body before him. The silken tatters of the gown hung about her, more alluring than sheer nudity. He took his time, impressing her helplessness upon her. The black silk robe he wore accentuated rather than concealed his aroused sex. As he untied the belt at his tapering waist, his penis rose like a magnificent animal, vibrant and engorged, possessing a life of its own as it parted the material. Her eyes widened at the sight, then closed tightly as she tensed.

Ryan stepped forward, closing the slight distance between their naked bodies. His fury had abated, replaced by a ravening hunger to taste again her sweet, scented, velvet skin. He proceeded slowly, as much to draw out his own pleasure as to create an answer of passion within her that would put the lie to her denial of feeling. His lips touched her throat, his tongue tracing a fiery path down the deep valley that divided her quivering breasts.

Against her will, for she had tensed to repulse any feeling within herself, Cat felt her nipples spring to life, the tender rose tips forming miniature peaks on the soft white globes. "Stop it, Ryan . . . for God's sake, stop!" she moaned.

"No, my love, for *your* sake! I intend to prove to you, once and for all, that you're a woman, warm and alive and meant to be loved. Now, hush," he commanded softly, his lips warm and seeking against her skin. He continued to tease her, his lips engulfing first one nipple, then the other, as his fingers gently probed the heated sanctuary hidden at the soft juncture of her thighs. Against her own will, she moaned.

"Ryan, please . . . I can't . . ." she panted, each succeeding breath harder to catch as Ryan's tongue and fingers worked their sensual magic on her body. She twisted in a last effort to escape, ceased her movements as the budding embers of desire burst into flame within her, tongues of flame that licked at her heart and soul, scorching her insides with its intensity. Ryan sensed her yielding and smiled against the creamy, satiny skin, his own passion growing unmanageable. The tension of resistance was gone from her body and he released her arms, bringing them to rest around his neck. Her expression was barely visible by the light of the low, sputtering candles, her eyes closed in resigned languor, lips parted and dry. She sighed deeply as the delicate rose-pink tip of her tongue darted out to wet them.

"Tell me what you want," he crooned, relishing the moment. "For once I want the truth from those sweet, lying lips!"

Cat's eyes flew open in shock and humiliation. She caught her lower lip between pearl white teeth as he pressed boldly against her. "I . . ." She was ashamed to finish, unable to voice the bold admission he insisted on hearing. His fingers caressed her, keeping the fires stoked and burning within. "Oh, God, Ryan," she sobbed, "Please . . . don't make me say it!"

"Yes!"

She closed her eyes, submitting to his will. "All right," she cried desperately. "I want *you,* devil that you are! That night I ran from you . . . I ran from what *I* felt! God help me, it's true!" She was thoroughly humbled by the concession. Her eyes flew open, her heart twisting painfully at the sight of his brief, triumphant grin.

In victory, Ryan meant to be generous. His mouth descended to gently capture her lips. The vocal expression of her desire for him allowed her to respond freely and she melted against him like a liquid jewel. Long slender fingers tangled in the ebony-black curls at the nape of his neck, graceful arms wound about his neck to pull him closer. Ryan's strong, dark fingers closed on her firm, rounded derrière, kneading the satiny flesh and cupping her buttocks to mold her body to his. In a moment he had lifted her, easily holding her slight weight and fitting himself to her until she had settled on his hard, throbbing shaft. Cat moaned against his lips, her own tongue battling in a love match with his as he began to move within her. Her long sinuous legs were twined about his hips, as her tight, moist muscles ensheathed him.

They moved to the beat of a sensual rhythm, drunk with passion, intoxicated with desire, panting, perspiring, melting within one another. A primitive, ageless drumbeat of love pounded as they strove together, again and again and again until they were swept by such a powerful burst of emotions, a deluge of primal, sensate response that they were both transported beyond the physical senses, spiraling effortlessly through a transitory world of pure feeling.

Ryan found his ragged breath, catching Cat as she

collapsed against him, spent and exhausted. Lifting her into his arms, he carried her to the bed, placing her gently at its center. He threw himself down at her side, pulling her close to rest against his chest.

Cat stared at Ryan through a heavy fringe of gold lashes. His even breathing soon revealed that he slept, his arm cast possessively across her. She was frightened, now that the tide of engulfing passion had ebbed. This overpoweringly handsome, lithe man at her side affected her as no other ever had. When she was near him, the sight of him, the masculine aromas of tobacco and brandy and the perfect animal grace in his lean body excited her beyond her control. Her lack of willpower would be her undoing, for she wanted more from him than the lust they had just satisfied. Despite his arrogance, his selfish demands and his vanity, she sensed a strength of will within him that satisfied her need for security. Ryan might command her, yet he could offer the protection and strong reliance she desperately needed. Could these feelings be love?

Dear God, no, she thought in terror. It was bad enough to discover that she could find fulfillment within his demanding lovemaking, but to love him, and risk rejection—could she bear that kind of aching pain? Silently she cursed the fate that years before had sent her forward on a long journey of revenge. Why couldn't life have been simple? Why couldn't she have met a good man who loved her and would marry her? Beside her, Ryan slept peacefully, stirring once to caress her in his sleep. He smiled contentedly, his even features relaxed and boyishly handsome.

Tenderly, Cat reached out to touch the tousled black curls. They lay in darkness now, for the candle had flickered out. Beyond the draped window, the first light of a new day was beginning to brighten the sky. She closed her eyes, allowing sleep to overtake her, dreaming, impossibly, of herself and Ryan, wedded and blissfully happy.

Chapter Seven

When Cat next opened her eyes, the bright rays of the morning sun beamed through the drapes. She stretched luxuriously, amazed that she felt so rested and content. In the light of day, her problems seemed much less awesome and overwhelming. She turned to smile a greeting to Ryan, only to find the spot where he had lain now cold and forsaken. Panic seized her. Had Ryan merely used her again, satisfying his flare of desire? He had seemed so warm and tender. She couldn't have been mistaken! Quickly she rose and pulled on her dressing gown, hurrying to the connecting door. A silent prayer echoed within her that he would be in his room, that he would see her and smile with warm tenderness.

Cat hesitantly drew open the door and found the room empty. In a display of quick temper, she slammed the door shut. He would have stayed to waken her if he'd felt anything beyond the lust that had made him seek her last night! Anger and hurt pride whirled within her; she felt dirty and used. She rang for Allie and ordered a hot, steamy bath. A good scrubbing was what she needed to remove all traces of Ryan's touch from her skin.

"Miss . . . I . . . I's sorry 'bout las' night," Allie stuttered hesitantly, her thin, dark face a mask of worried concern. "He . . . he made me do it!"

Cat quickly reassured her she bore no grudge. Charles must have threatened to send the frail girl to the fields and the hard, grueling labor of tending crops from dawn to dusk. "It's over, Allie—he can never hurt you again. I'm sure Master Ryan will prove less harsh." Cat had seen Ryan's easy manner with the servants. Even though at the moment she felt something akin to hatred for him, she was objective enough about his role as the new master of Seahaven. He would be just. There would be no more senseless beatings to cow the slaves. Ryan was intelligent enough to realize he could draw more work through fairness than intimidation. "Set your mind at rest," Cat said soothingly. "Now hurry, girl, I must be bathed and dressed by eight!"

In the hip bath, Cat scrubbed industriously at her skin until it shone pink and glowed healthily. In a physical sense, she was washing away the indulgence of the previous night, the shameful memory of her admission of Ryan's power to arouse her. In the future she would will her mind to control her traitorous senses; they had almost been her downfall. She would have allowed him to dominate her, to toy with her affections at his leisure until he tired of her and sought a new distraction. She recalled how quickly he'd taken Marian to his bed and it hardened her determination.

Allie helped her from the scented bathwater, toweling her dry and hurrying to fetch her most demure gown from the wardrobe. The impression she made today was extremely important, for she had vague doubts about Ryan's help. She must call on her own resources and present a mien of modesty and delicacy to the constable. There was no doubt in her mind that the man was malleable and could be handled if it was done with any subtlety.

The dress was a cream muslin, sprigged with tiny embroidered violets that drew attention to her eyes. Its high, straight-edged bodice concealed all but a slight, teasing impression of the soft swell of her breasts. Long, fitted sleeves ended in a froth of lavender lace at her slender wrists and the wide skirt, belled by satin petticoats, created an entrancingly feminine rustle as she moved.

Allie dressed her and then swept the long gold waves into a knot of curls at her crown. At each temple, tendrils of silken copper escaped the coiffure to soften the sedate effect of the style. Finally, her preparations completed, she examined herself carefully in the mirror, satisfied with the appearance of the innocent, modest young woman who returned her gaze. She praised Allie for her skill and dismissed her.

A few touches of her favorite perfume made a finishing effect. The scent was a fragrant blend of rare narcissus and iris blossoms. She had originally brought a dozen bottles with her from Paris. Now she held the cut crystal to the light and sadly noted she was nearing the end of her next to last bottle. The sweet, lingering scent warmed at her pulses, forming the perfect complement to her attire.

Cat started for the hall door, pausing as she reached for its handle. The guard must still be seated there! The thought of being escorted below like a common criminal was galling. Instead, she turned on her heels and swept into Ryan's room, intending to exit quietly through his door and escape the guard's attention.

The room was dark and somber, in a color scheme of deep royal blue. The dark mahogany furniture was heavy and well made, but sober and almost austere in its style. Clearly Ryan considered the ornate, fragile styles favored by the gentry too feminine for his tastes. Everything was neatly in place and revealed little about Ryan except that he was meticulous about his person. She had learned a little about his upbringing from Justin, but she was intensely curious to know more. The two had been together at the College of William and Mary in Virginia. There appeared to be a low-key rivalry between them and she'd played on it a bit when she'd flirted with Justin.

She wandered to the dresser. It was bare except for a few personal belongings arranged in neat order. Nothing to learn there! Opening the heavy wardrobe, she found it filled with a vast array of fashionable attire. He was clearly proud of his lithe body and vain enough to clothe it in the latest fashions.

Suddenly there was a knock at the door. Cat whirled almost guiltily. A moment later it swung open and Justin walked in, his attitude one of stealth as he quietly shut it. He turned to face her, a sly, scheming smile slowly spreading across his face.

"Ah, I'm so glad I caught you, dear. I've something very important to discuss before the inquiry convenes." He glanced over to the door of her room and gestured towards it. "Perhaps it would be more discreet to talk in your room." She tilted her head, wary and unsure of his motives. "You're perfectly safe. Ryan is busy downstairs and what I have to say won't take long."

What could Justin possibly want with her? Cat walked into her room, curiosity building with each passing second. With an overassured manner, Justin offered her a seat and waited until she was settled in a chair before he spoke.

"I know how distressing this episode must be, Catherine! You have my heartfelt sympathy." Justin's long, thin mouth pursed with the right touch of compassion. His pale blue eyes flickered over her figure and returned to her face. "I mean to offer you a way out of it, if you'll trust me."

Cat greeted his offer with uneasy skepticism. "Why should you involve yourself, Justin?"

"I have my reasons, dear. I *know* you're innocent, whereas poor Ryan would merely like to believe you are. But that is beside the point. If you'll follow my lead, I'll establish a believable alibi. All you'll have to do is appear distressed, shed a few tears from those lovely eyes, and agree with what I assert. Simple and effortless, no?"

Cat was even more skeptical. She barely knew Justin, had spent only an hour in his company, and yet he offered to lie to save her. Why? The thought echoed again and again until she voiced it. "Justin, why would you make up a story? Why are you so sure I didn't kill Charles?"

He sighed patiently. "You only wounded him slightly in your attempt to escape his clutches. At the most, it would have caused the old lecher a restless night or two." Justin's lip curled with a sneer. "I had the honor of ending his useless life. You do agree it was useless?" The sneer widened to a cold, ruthless grin as he admitted, "I'm afraid I eavesdropped on your confrontation from the terrace. Aside from the appeal of your obvious charms, the corrupt bastard had animal instincts, assaulting you the way he did. Disgusting!" He appeared to shudder at the memory.

How could he sit there and calmly admit his guilt? Cat stared incredulously, transfixed by his nonchalance. With her newfound cynicism, her decision to *think,* instead of *feel,* she inquired distrustfully, "And what do you ask in return, Justin? Or are you doing this out of the goodness of your heart?"

"Ah," he commented, smiling in open delight. "You're far more astute than I gave you credit for. Possibly you might have noticed an undercurrent of . . . contention between dear old Ry and me." He stood and walked forward until he was staring down at her. "Ryan's always managed to best me in just about everything. He holds his liquor better than I, rides and wenches with equal expertise, and so forth." Justin balanced a hand on the back of her chair and lifted her chin with the other. "*You,* my dear, are my chance to beat him in an area of which he is supremely confident. He wants you—I want to take you from him. It's very simple!"

"And if I don't agree? Ryan has already assured me he can handle the constable. Why should I exchange your company for his? What if I exposed you as Charles's murderer?"

A cold, sinister light shone from the pale eyes. He considered her questions and answered them in order. "If you don't agree, I'll turn your privateering commission over to Higgins. As for coming over to me, I think you bear Ryan a measure of ill will and would enjoy denting his pride as much as I." The smile on his lips was mirthless, menacing. "Lastly, if you dared to accuse me, who would believe you?"

Cat recognized the truth. He had shocked her with the news that he possessed the paper that could lead to her death. It was the one crime of which no one, including Ryan, could absolve her. In the eyes of the English colonial government she was an enemy. Her stomach lurched and her shoulders slumped defeatedly.

Justin's cold fingers again gripped her chin, forcing her head up. "You needn't worry about my demands. Though Ryan and I are rivals, our tastes run to different paths." His fingers dug cruelly into her flesh. "How shall I phrase it for your tender ears . . . I prefer the exquisite pleasure only a man can provide." Cat's shocked expression brought mocking laughter from his throat. "Oh, I've disillusioned you. Such a naïve little bitch!"

There was no way to escape this madness! Her thoughts tumbled over one another in helpless confusion. Finally she calmed, and considered all the aspects of the offer. Justin had released her, allowing her a few moments to consider. She would be free of Ryan's domination, without endangering herself, or submitting to Justin. When he was otherwise occupied, she could search for and destroy the incriminating document he held.

Suddenly she pictured Ryan, thwarted by her supposed choice of Justin over him. It would serve him right! Let him brood and gnash his teeth because she'd deserted him!

"I can see you've accepted the inevitable, Catherine. Beneath that guileless exterior beats the heart of a born survivor. If not my ardor, you at least have my admiration." He offered her his hand and helped her to rise. "I think we'll get along splendidly. You need only appear fascinated by my wit and charm and we'll both thrive on Ryan's misfortune!" He walked her to the door, brought her fingers to his cold lips, and told her he would be expecting her in the library within minutes. "I'll leave by Ryan's room and occupy the dolt guarding your door. Follow me in three minutes."

Downstairs in the library, Ryan sat behind the desk, idly reviewing a file of deeds that now belonged to him. He'd had no idea the lands were so extensive. Charles had always been a spendthrift, satisfying his slightest whims and indulging Ryan, but the worth of the estate had to be in the hundreds of thousands of pounds! As his only heir, Ryan inherited everything.

Ryan had come across the deed to Canterbury Hill, the rolling, forested estate that sat on a high bluff above the upper Hudson. It rightfully belonged to Catherine, and as soon as the will was officially read, he planned to deed it to her. Perhaps then she would realize how highly he valued her. He thought about the passionate encounter in the wee hours of the morning and a smile touched his mouth. When the girl allowed herself free rein, she was a tigress, as passionate a partner and as beautiful as any he'd experienced. Once she had accepted the fact that he wanted her at his side, she would settle in.

The constable arrived to interrupt Ryan's pleasant reverie, still brushing at the biscuit crumbs that littered his dark coat. Ryan had already warned the Frenchman that the meeting would be limited to the four and when Justin arrived, followed a minute later by Cat, the group was complete. Ryan watched her enter, eyes demurely lowered and took note of the simple, almost girlish style of dress. He mentally decided to send for the French seamstress when all this business was behind them. Too much of Cat's lovely, supple charms were hidden by the gown. He was proud of her beauty and vain enough to want to display her to the best advantage. He found himself wishing she'd arrived before Justin and Higgins. He'd had so much to do this morning he hadn't had a chance to tell her how much the night had meant.

Cat refused to look up from a spot on the rug, directly in front of her. She was aware of Ryan's studied gaze and twisted restlessly under the close scrutiny. The devil was preening his feathers over her surrender during the night! All the Nicholls wealth now belonged to him and he had probably already considered showering her with gifts as a token of esteem for the use of her body. For a moment she was happy about the turn of events, couldn't wait to see the stunned expression spread over his features when he realized she'd spurned him.

The constable positioned himself by the fireplace, one hand resting on the mantel, the other clamped on the lapel of his coat. He cleared his throat officiously. "We are here to determine if the young lady present is at fault in the death of Sir Charles Nicholls." He turned to glance down at Cat, who was seated demurely in the same chair she had occupied the previous night. "Mistress Devlan, it's been noted that you bore Sir Charles a degree of hatred for his alleged part in your father's death. Is this so?"

"It is," she acknowledged truthfully. The doltish constable harumphed sagely, as though he'd made an important discovery. "But not alleged, Constable."

"Ma'am?"

"His part in my father's *murder* was factual, not alleged, as you stated."

Higgins drew a deep breath and glowered in a comically forbidding manner. "You speak ill of the departed, Mistress! Sir Charles was a respected member of the community. He is not here to defend his honor."

Justin chose that moment to interject his defense of Cat. Her fingers were tightly clenched, whitening at the knuckles, and in another moment she would have exploded in a furious tirade. "Really, this has gone far enough! Ryan, you know Catherine well enough to realize this is all nonsense. Your very silence is an indictment of guilt!" Ryan tensed, his jaw flexing in an effort to remain calm. Before he could reply, Justin rushed on.

"For your information, Constable, I saw Sir Charles alive, *after* Mistress Devlan left the library!"

The declaration was greeted by stunned silence. Cat studied him, amused by the sham of righteous indignation. She hadn't been told what story he would concoct and was curious to hear what followed. Higgins was clearly flabbergasted by the turn of events and Ryan's gaze went from Justin to her and back to Justin as he puzzled over the truth of the defensive statement.

"If I'd thought this farce would have continued till now, I'd have spoken sooner. My intent was to save the girl from additional distress." He cast a sympathetic glance her way, continuing with a talented display of feigned disgust. "I happened to be in the hall when the poor girl ran from the library. She was in a state of terror, her bodice ripped, the imprint of fingers reddening at her throat. She even seemed frightened of me until I calmed her and she wept out the truth of what Charles had attempted to do."

Cat picked up her cue from the ingenious lies and paled, raising a trembling hand to shield her eyes. Her attitude was a perfect representation of assaulted innocence, though a degree of it was very real as she recalled the maniacal, crazed lust in Charles's face.

"As I comforted her, I caught a glimpse of Nicholls by the open door of this room. His face was a mask of rage, mottled an angry, frustrated red. When he saw me with her, he quickly withdrew and slammed the door. I helped the poor, shaken girl to her room and sent a servant to fetch Charles." He paused and glared at Ryan as though he represented his uncle. "He was my host, but someone had to call him to account for what he tried." The constable stared at him with a dull, open-mouthed expression. "Ryan knows the rest. Jethro found the body. I know not who struck Charles Nicholls down, but I vouch for the girl's innocence!"

Higgins was clearly at a loss. Despite the young innocence of the girl, he'd been satisfied to have such a convenient scapegoat to tie up the case. Now he had his work cut out for him. Who among the guests, many of whom had already left the area, could have been the culprit? He silently cursed de Rysfield's revealing alibi. He turned to Ryan, seeking his assistance. "Master Nicholls, you know this man. Have you any reason to doubt he speaks the truth?"

Ryan was mystified. If it *was* the truth, why hadn't he heard of it before now, why had Justin and Catherine both remained silent? Still, the night had been hectic and tense; it was possible. On the road, she had insisted his uncle had assaulted her. He had meant to allow the inquiry to proceed long enough to satisfy Higgin's official sense of duty and then intervene. Now he put one question to Cat. "Do you agree with this tale of Justin's?"

"It's no tale—if not for Justin, I'm sure Charles would have followed me to my room and . . ." Her voice faltered convincingly, her eyes damp and wide with remembered fright. She appeared increasingly agitated. "I had nowhere to turn—it . . . it was a nightmare!" Her fingers dabbed at a tear on the corner of her eyes.

"Is that why you ran?"

Ryan's voice sounded coldly disbelieving to her ears. Her head came up and she glanced from Higgins to Ryan. "I was hysterical—after the guests left, I knew he would try again, until he . . . succeeded. It was so humiliating . . . I had no one to defend me! He was master of everything and everyone at Seahaven."

Ryan smirked, noting that Higgins appeared stricken with sympathy. He was suddenly eager to have done with it all. There were some very important questions he wanted answered, without the audience of Justin and Higgins. "Constable, don't you agree that we've struck on the truth? I don't think it does my late uncle's memory any good to seek further. He had his faults, as we all do. Please continue to follow any leads and keep me informed of your progress." His tone was one of dismissal.

Higgins cleared his throat for the tenth time. It was a most annoying habit. "All the evidence points to that conclusion, sir. Rest assured I'll do my best to find the scoundrel!" He asked Ryan if he could question the guests who still remained and received permission. Finally, he bowed, including all three in the courtesy, and bid them a good day.

Ryan's eyes, as cold and black as the night, gleamed with menacing challenge as he ordered Justin to leave the room. "Find something to occupy your time for a while. The lady and I have something to discuss."

"Now, see here—if you intend to browbeat the girl, she's suffered enough already."

"I asked you politely enough, Justin. Now, get out!" He made a motion as if to rise and de Rysfield began to back toward the door. He'd experienced Ryan's anger before and wisely decided to retreat.

"Wait." Cat stood up, smoothing the wrinkles from her dress. "No one has asked me *my* opinion." Both men stared at her as though she had suddenly materialized from thin air. She glanced at Ryan, her expression haughty and disdainful. "I don't *choose* to stay, therefore I will not."

A touch of confusion flared in Ryan's eyes before he gave vent to his rising fury. His gaze never left her face as he ordered Justin to leave for a third and final time. "I wouldn't try my temper further, if I were you," he warned.

Justin assured Cat he'd be close at hand if she needed him. Neither of the two heard the door close behind him. They were too involved in a battle of wills, each glaring at the other and refusing to back down.

"I suppose you have a plausible explanation why you never told me of Justin's assistance last night." His voice had the lightest touch of sarcasm that revealed his suspicions of the story. His even teeth flashed white in a mocking grin as he added, "I'm waiting with bated breath!"

Cat's back was stiffened by indignant fury. "I owe you no explanations," she snapped. "As usual, you were too concerned with your own feelings to care about what took place. I'm sure if Charles had succeeded in raping me, you would have laid the blame for it entirely on me!" Her hands rested at her waist as she continued to upbraid him. "You don't own me, you're not my father or my husband, thank God! Justin was good enough to come to my aid and has my gratitude. His kindness is a refreshing change from your selfish, arrogant demands—he, at least, treats me like a lady!"

Ryan couldn't believe the change in her attitude. Last night she'd been soft and loving and now . . . now, suddenly she hated him! His wounded pride made him forget the plans he'd made to care for her and fulfill any whim she might have. Without delving into the reasons for the change, he allowed his bitter hurt to command his tongue.

"Justin always was a bad judge of character. He couldn't recognize a lady if he fell over one." His gaze raked over her face and figure, silently calling himself every kind of fool imaginable. "That idiot's been taken in by your act of injured innocence." Ryan remembered that day in Tortuga when he'd blundered in on her, and cursed the motives that had sent him chasing off after Briar. *"As I was,"* he added, wanting to hurt her as much as she'd hurt him. Until now, he hadn't realized how much a part of him she'd become. The red-haired witch had somehow enchanted him, cast such a subtle alluring spell he'd become blinded to her true nature. "I suppose he's even offered to 'save' you from me."

Cat was incensed by the cruel mockery. The scoundrel ravaged her, kept her a virtual prisoner to his whims and then had the gall to claim *she'd* beguiled *him,* that she'd lured him against his will! She smiled, hoping her reply would sting his conceit to the quick. "As a matter of fact, he has. And I was overjoyed to accept the chance to escape your high-handed domination! We will be leaving immediately; I'll send for my things."

For a brief eternity that lasted seconds, Ryan was blinded by rage and a strong desire to strike the smug contentment from her beautiful face. Seizing command of his temper, he searched for a way to strike her with words that would hurt more than a physical blow.

"I hope poor Justin's aware he's taking possession of secondhand goods."

"I doubt he considers his luck poor. If not for your brutal lust, I'd still be a virgin!"

Ryan bowed mockingly. "I can't really accept the credit for that *honor,* m'lady! You were born to be bedded, a trait you share with your sister. I merely plucked a flower that was ready to blossom. If not I . . ." He let the implication dangle in the tense air of the room. His bold, angular features were rigid with contempt. "I dislike following where others have trod. Justin apparently has no such qualms. Do wish him my best, though I fear he'll need more than good wishes before you've finished with him!"

Still seething with fury at his ruthless, cavalier attitude, Cat managed to maintain an air of cool, unruffled hauteur. "Justin has no need of your sympathy or good wishes." She tossed back her head and smiled wickedly. "After all, he'll have me!" She gathered her skirts to one side and swept past him, only to be brought up short as his fingers closed cruelly on her arm.

"You may find yourself regretting this decision. Don't come crawling back to me. I told you *I* don't want used goods!" Ryan spit out the words through clenched teeth.

"Never!" Cat flung back the retort with equal violence. "Should I find myself abandoned in the streets, I would not crawl lower to seek your help!" For an endless moment they glared at each other, her wide, amethyst eyes answering his narrowed, coal-black gaze. Finally Ryan released his grip on her arm and stalked to the terrace windows, refusing to acknowledge her presence until the door slammed violently after her.

Chapter Eight

The house Justin had rented for his stay in Bath Town was isolated from the rest of the community. It lay on a wooded plot of land west of town. Now, with a blizzard raging through the area, it seemed even more cut off from the rest of the world.

Seated by the window of her room, Cat sighed heavily with boredom as she gazed at the swirling snow. The light of the late afternoon sun was fading and nothing was visible beyond the frosted, windblown branches that tapped a beat against her window. The rest of the trees, the small, untended garden, even the slaves' quarters were hidden by the wind-buffeted snow drifts. Despite a roaring fire, the room was damp and chill and Cat finally rose from her perch on the window seat to seek the warmth of a seat by the fire. She found herself nervously looking for something, anything to occupy herself. A half-worked sampler lay on the small table next to the chair and she picked it up, idly stabbing the needle in and out.

She'd been with Justin over three weeks now, three long and dreary weeks with nothing to do. This storm was just the latest of many that had battered the coastline. Even nature seemed to join in the effort to keep her confined and fatigued from lack of exercise. True to his promise, Justin had left her alone. She rarely saw him except at dinner. He seemed to have no problems keeping busy. At night she would lie awake, tossing restlessly in the large, canopied bed, just barely aware that the root of her sleeplessness lay in the sensual demands of her body, in feelings that had lain dormant until Ryan's own demands had awakened them.

After a few minutes, Cat impatiently tossed the work aside. Her grandmother had insisted she learn to embroider, but she'd never become accomplished with the needle. She rose now and paced the room. If the weather kept her a prisoner one more day, she would go mad! Her irritation increased as she thought of Will. In the time that she'd been here, she'd seen him only once, and then by accident.

The first week of her stay Justin had insisted she send for the seamstress and enlarge her wardrobe. He planned to show her off at the round of winter festivities. "Make them daring," he'd insisted. He wanted to twist the knife of jealousy deeper into Ryan's heart. She'd jumped at the chance but managed to persuade him to let her ride to Madame Courais's small shop near the Inn of the Three Eagles on Chester Lane. As the carriage rattled down the cobbled street, she chanced to see Will entering the inn. She dared not call out to him because the driver might report the contact to Justin. At the shop she had dismissed the carriage, ordering the driver to return in three hours. It would allow her plenty of time to be fitted, make her selections, and still manage to see Will. By now he must be mad with worry.

Inside the small, cluttered shop, Madame had greeted her like an old friend. "My dear, so much has happened since we last talked," she chattered in French. "You must fill me in on *all* the details!" The plump, still pretty older woman was a born gossip and seemed to have adopted Cat. There were no other customers in the shop and she insisted Cat share refreshments with her before they began the fittings.

Clarise Courais clapped her hands, summoning a petite dark-haired servant to fetch them tea. The girl gave a quick curtsey, hurrying off to the kitchen at the back of the shop. Clarise chattered on for minutes before Cat could break into the conversation and enlist the woman's aid in contacting Will.

"Madame . . . may I call you Clarise?" The Frenchwoman nodded, beaming at the prospect of a close friendship with a compatriot. "Clarise, I know you miss France as much as I do." The woman agreed, extolling the virtues of her native land, marking the lack of them in this new country. When Cat confided the secret of her commission, Clarise's brown eyes widened with a measure of surprise and then dawning admiration. Cat was pleased with the reaction, knowing she had discovered an ally she could call upon in an emergency. Her visits to the shop would be taken as innocent fittings and yet she could maintain contact with Will.

"You have my word, I will not divulge your secret, *chérie!*" Clarise fairly glowed with the possession of Cat's trust and confidence. "These *Americains,* they are great fools, their boorish behavior exceeded only by that of their English cousins! But of course my loyalty is pledged to France and Louis. How can I help you, *ma petite?*"

Cat quickly explained about Will and his presence at the nearby inn. "There is already so much gossip milling about me that I dare not seek him openly. Could you send your girl to fetch him here? It is of the utmost importance!"

"Oh, *ce n'est rien,*" the seamstress chuckled in a low, throaty tone. "It is nothing, what you ask of me! I will send Marie at once." Cat quickly described Will, assuring Clarise that little Marie would not be able to miss his huge, raw-boned frame. The girl was instantly dispatched with a severe warning that she would be dismissed if she didn't guard her tongue.

While they waited for Will and Marie, Cat sipped at her tea and filled Clarise in on the first-hand details of Charles's murder and her reasons for leaving Seahaven. "Until I locate that document," she explained solemnly, "Justin has the power of life and death over me. I must see it consumed in flames before I'm free to leave."

"And Monsieur Nicholls, the nephew . . . was there not an attraction between you? Could *he* not help you to retrieve this dangerous paper?"

"No!" Cat's face had set stubbornly at the suggestion. "There never was anything between us but a constant battle of wills. He meant to subdue me as though I were a prize mare he had bought. He mustn't know any of this, Clarise. I trust you to keep silent!"

The woman patted Cat's hand in a consoling gesture. "I think there is more there than you will admit to yourself, *petite*. That man"—she rolled her eyes heavenward in Gallic appreciation—"that man is *formidable*, one in a thousand. If only he were French!"

Cat was a trifle irked by the woman's appreciation of Ryan, "If you knew him as I do, you'd not be so entranced," she said spitefully. "Believe me, you——" her comments were interrupted by Marie's return.

"The gentleman is in the rear dressing room, Madame," she said timidly, disappearing as silently as she'd appeared.

Cat threw Clarise a grateful smile and followed her down a dark hallway to the rear. Clarise left her at the entrance to the dressing room and when Cat parted the drapes, she found Will standing uneasily amidst the laces and satins that littered the small, mirrored cubicle. His big, burly shoulders stood out against the backdrop of bright silks and brocades. "Will, oh, Will!" she cried out, throwing her arms around his neck.

Will hugged her close for minutes before he roughly pulled her arms away, and set her back to assure himself she was unharmed and then exploded with a roaring tirade of reproach. "Do you know how worried I was—d'you have any idea what you put me through? Lord, girl, I knew you was alive when y'left Seahaven but who's this other bloke, de Rysfield? I didn't know what to think when y' didn't show up at the inn!" He continued his barrage of questions, while Cat sheepishly waited for a pause to explain her actions. Finally some of the frustrated anger and worry eased from his craggy features. His huge paw of a hand settled on her shoulder, impelling her to be seated.

Cat stared up at him, regretting the worry she'd caused. From her youth, he'd always been there to save her from everything that threatened, clucking like a mother hen over every problem. She'd almost taken him for granted. "I had no time to contact you, Will, I swear! Everything was so chaotic following Nicholls's death." Slowly, she detailed everything that had taken place since that night, explaining Justin's hold over her, stressing the importance of finding and destroying the French document. Apparently, her escapades were the talk of the small community, filtering down even to the barmaids and mariners who frequented the taproom of the inn, for Will knew the general details of the scandal at Seahaven.

Will studied the problem for moments, then shook his head, disagreeing with her intention to stay and find the document. "You're wrong, Cat. We should leave *now*—to hell with that accursed commission! Even if he called the law down on ye, we'd be gone afore they took to lookin' for ye!" Once again he recognized that Devlan stubbornness on her face.

"Cat, the men are gettin' restless—they been waitin' three weeks now. We'll end up with a bleedin' mutiny 'fore long!" His own expression mirrored her stubbornly set features.

"No, Will, I want to try! Give me until the end of the month. If I need your help, I'll send a message through Clarise." Cat rose on tiptoe, pressing a light kiss against his rough cheek. "Don't worry, you old seadog! I promise not to take any chances. Soon enough we'll be sailing away in the *Falcon,* you'll see!"

Will grumbled, but as usual couldn't find it within himself to refuse her anything. "Aye, I'll keep the men busy wi' repairs, but mind ye girl—ye only have a little o'er two weeks till the month's up. Paper or not, I'll break down de Rysfield's door and carry ye off o'er m'shoulder!" Cat hugged him, her eyes moist from a rush of affection for the dear, simple man who asked so little and gave so much.

Cat had returned from the fitting elated and more hopeful than ever that she would succeed in extricating herself from Justin's hold. Each day when he was absent or occupied, she searched the rooms of the house, prying open cabinets and drawers for the elusive paper that represented her freedom.

Without her knowledge, Will had made up his mind to confront Ryan. He rode out to Seahaven one day and blustered his way past the butler and into the library, where Ryan sat behind a desk piled with estate papers.

Ryan started when he looked up to see the huge, imposing figure glowering from the doorway. The butler stood behind Will, ineffectively trying to pull him back. "That will be all, Marcus," Ryan directed, noting that the stranger dwarfed the old servant and looked as though he could have squashed him like a fly with one swipe of his bearlike paws. Amusement was hidden beneath his detached, pensive expression. "I assume you have a reason for barging in unannounced?"

"I come to see you, 'bout Cat—Catherine Devlan." Will explained his relationship to Cat and implied that Ryan was at fault for her present predicament. "I want to know what you're doin' 'bout her and this de Rysfield bloke."

Ryan had listened quietly, measuring this giant advocate of Catherine's. Cat, he'd called her. Somehow it fit the sensual, feline aura she projected. He turned the name over and over in his mind, savoring the sound.

"I don't see that I have any responsibility for Cath—

Cat's present arrangements. She left here of her own free will. Though I don't approve of her choice of bed partners, it's of little concern to me what her problems are." The disclaimer sounded cold and harsh, even to his own ears. It was the bitterness that still ground his heart like broken shards of glass that brought the denial of feeling to his lips. He'd tried to put her from his thoughts, immersing himself in the care of Seahaven and the other holdings his uncle had bequeathed him, but she haunted him still, a vision of flame-touched gold tresses and milk-white flesh that teased him from a distance. Now he rose and came around the desk to face this Will Foster.

"I consider myself lucky to be rid of Catherine Devlan. Now you'd best leave before my temper is unleashed. Don't forget you're on Nicholls land." He turned to ring for Carlin and found Will's hand clutching his arm. The grip felt like a vise had closed on his muscles.

"Cat wouldna' fallen into the man's trap if you wasn't so high-handed and lordly, bringin' her here like you done!"

"Trap?"

"That wretch is holdin' somethin' over her head, a paper that could hang her. She's too damn stubborn fer her own good." Will paused, grimacing in disgust. "A lot like you, I might add. Cat won't leave till she gets it back."

"You expect me to believe that!" Ryan's laughter was mocking. "Go find another to test your stories on, for I haven't the time or the inclination to listen further. Now loosen your grip and follow your nose out of here!"

The two glared at each other, both bitter and frustrated, but for different reasons. Finally Will let go of Ryan's arm with a disgusted shove. He turned to go, pausing to unleash his thoughts.

"I guess I thought you had more guts than y'do, Nicholls. Once you took 'er when she didn't have no one to protect 'er. Now you could do right by 'er but you're too damn proud!" He glared at Ryan, then spit at his feet and whirled to stomp away. "A pox on your devil pride!"

Ryan stared after the departing giant who was so

loyal to Cat, glowering as the library reverberated with the slam of the door. The man was as accomplished a liar as his mistress! Foster had the gall to try and lure *him* into rescuing the fair maiden from the dragon! Well, Justin was no dragon, only a foppish version of a man, and Cat—he had come to think of her by that name—Cat was no innocent maid. She had claws, that one did, and the ability to land, like her namesake, on her feet. He'd be damned if he'd involve himself with her again. The very idea of "a paper that could hang her" was ludicrous! Disgruntled and indignant, Ryan slammed himself into the desk chair, opening the brandy decanter on the desk to pour himself a liberal dose and toss it down his throat. Cat Devlan, he thought broodingly, was as helpless as a tigress on the hunt.

When the foul weather had settled over the area, Cat had been unable to venture out to see Will. Clarise had come to the house for the final fittings and now an assortment of beautifully made, daringly low-cut gowns hung in lovely splendor in the wardrobe. Cat studied the dresses, stroking the velvets and satins with a sense of longing. At least a ball would break the monotony!

A soft rap sounded at her door and as Cat opened her mouth to ask who it was, the door swung open. Justin stood there, a bottle of champagne in one hand, two glasses in the other, a congenial smile on his face. His brocade dressing gown gracefully draped his slender figure, and he ignored her surprise, easing the door shut with his foot before crossing the room to the fireplace and placing the bottle and glasses on the table.

As Cat shut the wardrobe and faced her visitor, he smiled again and popped the cork from the wine. "I came to apologize for your boredom, my dear. Not only has the weather kept you in, I've been delinquent in my duties as your host." He gestured with the champagne, poured a small amount in one glass, and tasted it. "An excellent year . . . truly excellent! The French have a way with the grape, but then you must know that." For a moment he turned his back, filling both glasses. His hand, hidden from Cat's view, dropped a crystalline powder into one glass. It dissolved instantly, to take on the effervescent golden glow of the wine. To the naked eye, there was no difference in the glass that Justin held out as an offering to Cat.

Cat crossed the room, her satin nightgown covered by a demure velvet wrapper. She was totally relaxed and appreciative of his efforts. Had she not known of his sexual inclinations, she would have looked upon his late visit with more alarm. Yet she felt safe from his attentions, and accepted the proffered glass with a welcoming, almost eager smile. It would pass the time, at least. Perhaps she could pry information more easily from an inebriated Justin than from a sober one.

"Your apologies, though unnecessary, are as welcome as you are!" Cat sipped at the bubbly wine, noting with satisfaction that Justin disposed of his quickly and reached for the bottle again. At that rate, he'd soon be an easy mark for a few well-placed inquiries, and in the cold light of morning might not even remember what he'd divulged. His face was already a bit flushed, his fair complexion tinged with a telltale red. She had the distinct feeling he'd already been drinking before joining her.

This time he proposed a toast, raising his glass high. "To our mutual enmity for the Nicholls family!" Their glasses clinked together, and the delicate, long-stemmed crystal rang. The fire popped and crackled as Justin used the poker to stir the logs, scenting the room with the sweet, heavy odor of pine. Cat sank into one of the fireside chairs, relaxed and warm, sipping the last of her wine. Justin noted her empty glass and graciously refilled it, once more turning his back for the briefest moment. A flick of his wrist and another portion of powder dissolved within the golden liquid.

"It's a shame about the snow," Cat commented lightly, swirling the glass in one hand, watching as the bubbles floated to the surface and the firelight flickered amber through the wine. "I had so looked forward to appearing at your side at one of the winter balls, to seeing Ryan's face twist with impotent rage." Her laughter tinkled from her throat, as liquid as the golden champagne in her half-filled glass. She felt decidedly languid and easy, unaware of Justin's thoughts behind the smiling mask of flushed, fever-bright features.

Justin answered her, his voice oddly vague and distant. "Yes, it's a shame, dear Catherine, but we'll yet have our revenge on Master Ryan. It appears we both have rather tenacious, vengeful natures. See how long it took to take care of Charles!"

Cat blinked several times to clear her vision. She seemed to see Justin through a haze. She'd only had a glass and a half of champagne, and yet her head felt so light.

". . . you must miss his attentions on a cold night such as this," Justin was saying. "Ryan's body *is* superb, and I would imagine him to be a master of the senses. Come, admit it to a friend," he coaxed in a sly, soothing tone. "You miss the touch of his hands on your skin, the demands he made of you!" He leaned forward, anticipating her reply, noting the heavy-lidded, violet gaze. She appeared vaguely apprehensive at the direction of his questions and he eased off a bit, until the drug could take full effect.

"You must have been quite a sight on the deck of your own ship, attired as a pirate captain, leading your men into battle. I admire your spirit. I really would love to see you that way." He poured himself a third glass, offering to fill hers.

Cat declined the offer, aware that with each passing moment she felt more entangled in a web of illusion. The room swam until she closed her eyes, the heat of the fire scorching her skin until she felt as though the flames surrounded her. One clear thought echoed in her mind—the paper, she had to locate the paper! How could she phrase it . . . "Justin, I . . . I hope you placed the commission in a safe place. Should anyone find——"

Justin interrupted her, his voice like a shout. Her eyes flew open to find him leaning over her like a vulture eyeing its prey, his face only inches from her own. "No need to worry, my little privateer. I've been discreet. *No one,"* he emphasized with a wicked grin, "could find it by chance!" His hands dropped from the chair-wings to fall on her shoulders, as the guise of friendly interest dropped from his face, revealing a malicious leer. His fingers closed like talons, biting through the material of her gown as he pulled her to her feet.

Through the mists fogging her drug-deadened mind, Cat realized her danger. She willed her limbs to struggle. It seemed that all her senses but a portion of her thoughts were numbed. Tears trickled from her eyes as she collapsed, unable to stand, and felt him lift her into his arms. Her hands pushed feebly at his chest, as ineffectual as the frantic beating of a butterfly's wings against the web of a spider. His cruel, inhuman laughter pounded at her aching temples.

Justin deposited the girl on the bed, stepping back to disrobe. A look of terror sharpened her beautiful features, her softly pouting lips forming a silent scream of protest. His pale, hairless body was almost feminine in its delicate grace. He moved slowly, the wine warming his blood, as he drew out his pleasure. The thought of using the helpless girl, of degrading what had belonged to Ryan, was his supreme motive. He almost wished he'd been less liberal with the drug. Cat lay sprawled before him, her fingers and hands moving restlessly in an attempt to move herself. His enjoyment would have increased had she been more aware of his actions, if she could have struggled to escape what he'd planned.

Cat's eyes were wide with terror. They seemed trapped, the only animate feature of her tranquilized body; pools of lavender that rebelled against the inevitable violation by Justin's perverted, animal instincts. Some distant, lucid portion of her brain mocked her as she compared the effete leering creature that was Justin with Ryan's darkly tanned, boldly masculine body. Her pride had cast her this lot, had made her turn from the caresses of a real man to this callous, twisted caricature of one. He loomed over her, his hands huge and distorted as they reached to tear at her clothing until she lay exposed amidst the torn velvet and satin.

Justin pulled Cat up until she was seated limply at the edge of the bed, stationing himself before her dazed face. His fingers twisted cruelly in the curls at the back of her head, his expression full of disgust for her sex. "Gullible bitch," he screamed, "no wonder Ryan found you such an easy mark!" His fingers twisted mercilessly once more, slowly, relentlessly pushing her head to his loins.

Something snapped in Cat's head. From a deep wellspring of strength, she summoned her slack muscles. Her hands clawed at him, scratching deep scarlet furrows in the smooth, chalky flesh of his belly. The rebellion was brief, serving only to incite Justin's passion for domination. He pulled her head sharply back, slamming his hand across her soft, tender mouth. The force of the open-handed blow rocked her, a scream escaped her bleeding lips, cut off sharply as his sweaty palm closed over her mouth. The brief resistance was over, replaced by hopeless misery.

Justin jerked her forward again, forcing her head down. She had no alternative but to accept him, though she gagged and waves of nausea washed over her, setting her skin crawling with repulsion. Throughout the whole sordid ordeal, he screamed abuse, his weak, high voice taunting her with crude insults. After an endless, humiliating eternity he drew back, shoving her away. Her mind reeled with shock, an edge of numbing relief deadening the ache of her bruised lips. She buried her face in the covers, her breath ragged sobs that tore from a dry throat.

A moment later she recoiled as his hand touched her shoulder, grasping it tightly. His other hand seized her hip and in an instant he'd flipped her on to her stomach, pulling her to her knees. She might as well have been a rag doll for all the ease with which he controlled her. Cat's hands clawed at the covers of the bed, tears blinding her.

Without pausing, Justin parted the firm, ivory flesh

of her buttocks, fingers digging sharply into her skin, and plunged forward to bury himself in her exhausted, shattered body. His insane, lust-crazed laughter melded with the agonized, convulsive screams that racked Cat in shuddering spasms. Mercifully, the pain receded as she slipped into a black void, floating away to a mist-shrouded haven where Justin's cruelty could not reach her. She collapsed, unconscious, still at the mercy of his maniacal lust.

Cat moaned softly, awakening from a suffocating depth of humiliation. Despair and heartache would come later. Every fiber of muscle in her entire body ached, her lips were raw and dry, smeared with blood from Justin's blow. She hesitated to open her eyes, terrified that he still hovered near, waiting to torture her again. When she eased her swollen eyes open, the room was dark and still, with only the crackling of the fire to break the silence. She gazed listlessly at the elegant furnishings of the room that had become her torture chamber, shrinking from the memories of Justin's loathsome perversions. She reached a shaking hand for the crimson velvet draping the corners of the canopied bed, seeking to pull herself erect. Pain radiated from her lower body, sweeping upward until she paled and fell back. Deep gulping breaths helped to alleviate some of the pain, but the throbbing of her torn body continued. She had no idea of the time. She moved again, knowing she had to get away before the madman returned. Clenching her teeth she inched forward, stopping each time she felt faint, then moving again until she grasped the newel post of the bed. She glanced back to see a trail of blood staining the sheets. The sight of her own blood terrified her anew and she began to sob, as much from the animal degradation of the attack as the continuous assault of pain.

Once her tears had ceased, she grew calmer. The effects of the drug were still with her and as she attempted to stand, the room blurred. But for the support of the solid oak bedpost, she would have crumpled helplessly to the floor. Cat willed herself to move across the room to the wardrobe. Progress was agonizingly slow, step by faltering step, each movement jarring her abused limbs. Along the way she clutched at objects, pausing once before the full-length mirror next to the dresser. The girl who stared back from the mirror was a stranger, a wild-eyed child with tangled hair who reflected none of Cat Devlan's cool assurance or spirit. The change frightened her more than she could admit and she hurried past as fast as her weak legs could carry her.

She dressed warmly, covering the bruises that were beginning to darken on her pale skin. A cream wool dress would be protection against the blizzard that still raged beyond the window. She slipped on her riding boots, frowning at their short length. They'd be little enough help in deep drifts of snow. Finally she had her fur-edged woolen cloak and muff in hand and quickly sneaked into the hall. The house was deathly quiet and still, the servants long since asleep, their master probably insensible in his bed. She paused by Justin's door, a brief flicker of fury almost tempting her to enter, to find a weapon and strike him while he slept off the effects of the alcohol and his sated lust. But caution and remembered terror made her continue on, tiptoeing down the stairs until she reached the kitchens.

There she located the door by memory, for the room was as dark as the rest of the house. She drew her cloak close about her, thrust one hand into the muff, and valiantly raised her chin. She faced a long, arduous walk to Clarise's shop, a strenuous journey in fair weather, but nearly impossible in the strong, icy Atlantic winds and snow. The thought of what lay behind her propelled her trembling hand to the bolt securing the heavy back door. It gave, creaking drily, and she paused a moment, afraid the servants who slept nearby would awaken and call Justin. The house stayed silent, mocking her racing heart. The door swung inward, blasted by gusts of wind. Bracing herself, she pulled the hood forward and tucked both hands in the fur of the muff.

Within minutes Cat was chilled and soaked. Her

dress dragged soddenly about her feet, impeding her progress through the knee-high drifts. Gusts of wind slammed at her from two directions; icy crystals of snow stung her face, blinding her with their force. The night was black, and the huge mounds of snow were piled high on either side of the road. Luckily a wagon or carriage had recently traveled it. The tracks marked her way, which otherwise would have been indistinguishable from the white-frosted landscape. She was numb and chilled to the bone after fifteen minutes. Only the knowledge that she would perish if she stopped kept her going when her dazed mind began to wander.

She would later look back on that blind, despairing flight through icy wind and blasts of snow as a feat of pure willpower. Time and time again she slipped, stumbling to the ice-covered ground, only to drag herself up and trudge forward. Finally, after almost an hour's exposure, she recognized the small, painted sign of a needle and thread over Clarise's shop. Cat collapsed at the door, pounding her frozen hand against it with the last ounce of strength in her aching, chilled body.

At last, endless minutes later, a light shone in the back of the shop and a face peered curiously through the panes of glass, rubbing a clear spot in the frost that coated them. Clarise saw only a huddled form fallen at her door and quickly drew it open, calling excitedly to Marie to help her. Together they managed to pull the snow-crusted, limp body into the warmth of the shop. Marie had all she could do to force the door closed again against the blizzard's tempest winds.

"Jesu Marie," Clarise cried, as she turned the figure over and recognized Cat's face, icy white, tinged with red. The seamstress whirled to shout an order to Marie, sending the girl scurrying for blankets and warm water. Meanwhile she cradled Cat against her, plump face frowning as she felt Cat's forehead. To Cat, the heat of the little shop seemed like an inferno. Her body shook yet beads of sweat poured from her forehead. The ache from the brutal attack receded as she slipped into delirium, calling Will's name over and over in a pleading whimper. Through the heat that seemed to radiate in waves before her glazed eyes, she vaguely saw Clarise, gently bathing her forehead with a warm cloth. Despite the warmth of the three blankets thrown over her, she trembled and shook in the throes of a raging fever, her resistance lowered by the exposure. From a great distance she heard the sympathy in the older woman's voice as she attempted to soothe her, telling her that Marie had gone for Will, that everything would be all right.

Cat must have lapsed into unconsciousness, for when she opened her eyes, she lay in a warm bed, dressed in a flannel nightgown. Will leaned over her, his rough, plain-hewn features twisted with worry and concern. "Thank "God," he exclaimed, as he saw that she recognized him. She could swear that a veil of tears misted his tired, brown eyes.

"Will," she whispered, clutching his hand. "Will, we *must* get away. I . . . I ran from . . . him. He . . ." Her eyes closed. She was unable to tell anyone what had happened. Not even Will, who was the dearest friend she had. In a measure of self-protection, the memory receded into the dark recesses of her mind, the terrifying details hazy and blurred. "Will, we have to make for the *Falcon, tonight!*" Her fingers tightened their grip on his hand as hysteria raised the pitch of her voice.

"Easy, lass, easy," Will soothed. "You're in no shape to be traipsin' off in a blizzard like this! How you made it this far on your own two feet's beyond me." His free hand touched her forehead, tenderly sweeping back the damp, rust-colored tendrils that framed the pale face. "Y'll rest, lass," he ordered paternally. "I've arrangements to be makin'. My promise—we'll be on our way 'fore the first light o'dawn. Not soon enough, if y' ask me," he added, frowning deeply at the sight of her cut, swollen lip. A pale, reddish bruise was beginning to appear on her cheekbone. The answer seemed to satisfy her, for almost as he finished, she drifted off into an exhausted sleep.

Will went about his business during the night, while

Cat slept on, Clarise at her side. At dawn the Frenchwoman woke her, helping her to sip a cup of warm broth before urging her into warm clothing. From somewhere in her vast stock of clothing, Clarise produced warm breeches and leggings that fit Cat perfectly. Her friend had worked through the night altering the clothing to Cat's diminutive size. Cat impulsively hugged Clarise, saddened at leaving behind a woman who was so sweet and loyal.

"What can I say, Clarise?" she asked. "Without your help, I'd have died out there!"

"You've been a refreshing breath of air for a homesick Parisian, *ma petite,*" the woman answered lightly. She gestured to her well-padded figure. "I am past my prime, but the blood still warms with old, fond memories. You remind me of my youth, for I, too, was wild and full of life." For a moment her gaze was distant and melancholy, but she seemed to shake off the sadness and shook her head in mock dismay. "Your friend will be back soon —that giant protector of yours will bite off my head if I do not have you ready to leave!"

Soon Cat was dressed in the breeches and a warm, woolen shirt. Clarise added a black knit cap and heavy cloak and stood back to admire her handiwork. *"Eh, voilà!"* she exclaimed. "No one would take you for the young girl who entered my shop. The disguise, it is perfect! Monsieur Will assured me your ship is anchored in a cove just south of town. By wagon, you will be exposed to the weather only a short time. Otherwise, I would put my foot down"—she stomped her small, plump foot in comical emphasis—"and that big bear could bluster and fuss until Heaven turned upside down before I would let you venture out!" Her gaze was fondly maternal as she adjusted the cap to cover one of Cat's reddish curls.

Minutes later the "big bear" returned. Will's face creased in a frown as he noted Cat's somewhat wobbly stance. "Catch your death o' cold, Catherine Anne Devlan, and I'll not forgive you," he growled. He turned to Clarise and brought her hand to his lips in a rare display of gallantry. "I owes you a debt o' gratitude, Madame." Cat noticed a look pass between the two that was warm and friendly, and a touch conspiratorial. She made a mental note to question Will later. He'd been up to something, for it couldn't have taken all night to arrange for a wagon and horses.

Now, though, she was eager to be away, to escape the terrible memories of this place. She would put it all behind her once she was safely aboard the *Falcon*. It seemed like an eternity since she'd sailed aboard her ship, a lifetime ago when she was naïve and carefree. Clarise saw them to the alley behind the shop where the wagon stood. Cat hugged her close, unable to voice her appreciation. The snow had lightened, drifting lazily down from the gray, cloudy sky in large, heavy flakes. The air was still bitterly cold and the seamstress retreated to her doorway, huddling just out of the chill breeze. She waved once as the wagon started off, blowing a kiss to the two before she wisely retreated into the shop.

The wheels of the borrowed wagon crunched over the frozen layers of ice and snow. Cat snuggled close to Will, and managed to keep her trembling under control to lessen Will's worry. She'd already caused him enough trouble. They took the road west out of town. A small path trailed off to the south and the cove where the *Falcon* lay at anchor. Her first sight of the proud, old brig, its topmast frosted with snow and shrouded in morning mist, tugged at her heart. She was home at last, for nothing could hurt her when she was once again in command of her ship. Will drew the wagon to a halt near the shore, jumping down to light a lantern. He swung it in a half-arc three times, signaling the watch to send the gig ashore.

A half-hour later, Cat stood at the wheel on the brig's sterncastle. She had briefly greeted the crew, issuing orders to sail with the tide. Will would see that they were carried out. Though fatigue threatened to overcome her and the ache had returned anew, she remained topside for an additional quarter hour, contentedly watching the efficiency of the seasoned crewmen as they scaled the iced ratlines to unfurl the mainsails. The ship creaked and groaned as the sails filled, its movements slow and ponderous at first, then increasingly light and graceful as she responded.

Cat and Will had discussed their plans on the trip from town. They would set a course for New York, sail up the Hudson, and she would rest at a deserted Canterbury Hill while Will took the *Falcon* downriver for refitting and provisions. Tortuga was lost to her. Without the safety of having destroyed that infernal commission, she faced the danger of being captured by an English or American ship. There was no doubt in her mind that Justin would immediately turn the document over to the magistrate as soon as he discovered her missing.

No, she had to make a clean break with the colonies. Will had mentioned that many of the Brethren of the Coast had deserted the Trade Islands and the Main for the Red Sea and Madagascar. Some had returned wealthy, boasting of the easy pickings. They not only preyed upon the ships of the English East Indies Company but those of the Mogul of India. The idea fascinated Cat, especially the description of the tropical weather. She'd had enough of snow and ice to last her a lifetime! Madagascar it would be—the decision warmed her frozen body more than the heavy garments that covered her slender figure.

Chapter Nine

Ryan arrived at Canterbury Hill on a cold, clear January morning, almost two weeks after Cat's disappearance. As he cantered along the wild overgrown road leading to the house, he wondered to himself whether he would find her here or whether the long journey would be in vain. She had to be here! Madame Courais had refused to confide the reason for her flight except to add a disparaging comment that Cat had plenty of reason to leave, and that if he wanted answers he should call on Justin de Rysfield.

He'd done just that, visiting the man at the inn, where he'd taken rooms the day after the fire that destroyed his rented home. Justin had been no help, insisting cryptically that he knew nothing of Cat's whereabouts, implying for reasons that he failed to justify that Cat was somehow responsible for attempting to murder him in the set blaze that had consumed the house during the night. Before he left Justin's rooms, Ryan wanted to wipe the floor with the scoundrel's face. He refused to answer any of Ryan's questions, especially the one concerning the alleged threat he held over Cat's head. "She left you of her own volition," Justin had insisted with a sneer. "Don't try to make excuses for her reasons." He had shrugged carelessly and added with a yawn, "The girl's unstable—I wouldn't let it worry you, old man, just be thankful she's left the area."

Ryan had stomped from the room lest he give vent to his fury and throttle Justin. After a half hour in the taproom, he'd managed to figure out which direction Cat must have gone. Of course that giant of hers must have helped, perhaps even fetched her ship. Returning to Seahaven, he'd packed a light bag, leaving instructions for the staff before he set out on the stallion. The journey had worn him down and taken longer than usual because of the weather. Only when he'd reached the boundaries of New York had the ice and snow disappeared. The area had missed the series of storms that had kept the Carolinas locked in the grip of bitter winter weather.

Now he approached the house, his fine leather saddlebags containing the deed to the estate. He meant to hand it over as an offer of peace, should he have the fortune to find her. In the month Cat had spent with Justin, Ryan had come to realize just what she meant to him. Despite her wild, mercurial temperament, she was a woman of fiery passion and lovely beyond belief. No woman had ever spurned him as she had, and it only served to fuel his desire to regain possession of her. In the short time that she'd been his, the little enchantress with the flame curls and wide, innocent violet eyes had settled under his skin. He wanted her, and was determined that she should be his and his alone. If she wasn't here, he would search the country, if need be, until he found her again.

Despite his preoccupation, Ryan was unable to miss the needless neglect of the huge estate. His uncle had done nothing to maintain the house or keep its elegant lines clear of an overgrowth of ivy and shrubbery. Why, he puzzled silently. If Charles had been so intent on wresting the property from Brian Devlan, why had he let it go to a state of near ruin? Questions buzzed at his mind as he drew the spirited mount to a halt before the main entrance. The estate would have made a lovely summer retreat, an escape from the sweltering heat of mid-July in the south. Ryan had visited here only once, a year after his uncle had acquired the land. He'd been on leave from school and was unaware of who the former owner had been. The tasteful furnishings had been left untouched, for Charles had oddly refused to invest a pound in the house.

Using his key, Ryan unlocked the ornate wrought-iron gate that enclosed the door to the entrance hall. Its hinges creaked from lack of use. Within, he unlocked the heavy mahogany double doors, his heart beating with anticipation as they swung inward. The long, wide hallway was bathed in the dim light that filtered from a vaulted skylight set into the second-story ceiling. Dust motes floated through the stuffy, damp air of the long-sealed room. Cobwebs stretched across every corner, elaborate creations of many years standing. The white sheets that protected the furnishings had turned a dirty gray with the passing of time.

As he walked slowly forward, Ryan's feet created tiny clouds of dust that slowly settled with his passing. Clearly no one had trod these halls for a good many years, possibly since his long-ago visit. His stomach dropped with a sudden nameless despondency. Either he had guessed wrong or she had come and gone already.

He turned to enter a room he remembered as one of the drawing rooms. It was the same as the rest of the house, shrouded in dust and disuse. Light entered the room through one of the front, ceiling-high windows whose draperies hung askew. A musty smell of decay permeated the air. Across the room, above the wide, elaborate fireplace, hung a covered painting. Ryan moved to it, drawing the cover away. Yes, now he remembered it. The portrait of a blonde beauty that had enchanted him once.

The painting was untouched by the mold and decay

of the house. The oil sparkled as clean and pure as the day it had been painted. The woman gazed down at him, as lovely and patrician as the first time he'd looked on her. He stepped forward, examining it closer. The artist had been skilled, capturing the light, sweet smile of the gently bred young woman. This, then, was Brian Devlan's wife, the former mistress of this domain and the mother of Briar and Cat.

Ryan was startled to discover the family resemblance. Christine Devlan had bequeathed her beauty to Briar, though the younger daughter seemed to lack the common sense to handle her looks. He saw Cat only in the clear, gray-violet eyes that gazed down on him. That gaze was somehow sad, as though she had guessed at the future that lay ahead for her loved ones and was powerless to alter it. Cat's eyes were more expressive, blazing with fire, smoldering and smoky with resentment, and bold, yet innocent. He sighed, wondering what this gentle-eyed woman would think of his quest for her wild-eyed, hot-blooded daughter.

Ryan had almost given up hope, but he decided to check the upper floor. He quietly made his way up the long center staircase, his fingers touching the layered dust and withdrawing in disgust. He would see that the place was renovated, for it rankled his fastidious nature to see its beauty lost from sight. At the top of the stairs he paused, trying to remember the plan of the upper story. By instinct he headed for the main bedchamber, the one his uncle had used.

The door swung open without a sound and Ryan stepped into the large, well-lit room. The drapes were open and his pulse raced faster as he realized the covers over the furniture had been recently disturbed. He searched the room, his glance taking in a small pile of clothing that lay on the floor by the right side of the bed. The bed itself was huge, canopied in embroidered velvet, its hangings drawn. It lay on a raised dais. Ryan approached, his breath held until he reached out to gently draw the velvet to one side.

Cat lay sleeping in the bed that had belonged to her parents, the bed in which she'd been born, secure in the knowledge that she was safe, here of all places. Her hair framed her tranquil face in a halo of rusty waves, her mouth pouting in sleep, thick golden lashes dusting her cheeks. Ryan started as though he had seen a vision. He felt a twist of remembered passion, and something else—a wild flood of relief that he had found her! She stirred a moment as though she were aware of his observation, then snuggled lower beneath the covers until only the tops of her creamy, bare shoulders were visible.

Ryan let the curtains fall together and stepped quietly down from the dais. Within minutes he had stripped his clothes away, to join her beneath the coverlet. Desire stirred him, but more than that—he wanted to hold her close, to feel that satin skin against his own again, to assure himself he wasn't dreaming. The sweet ache urged him to hurry, and moments later he drew back the drapery and gently raised the satin coverlet to slide beneath.

Cat was dreaming, a vaguely happy dream of contentment and more, of warm, strong arms that held her protectively, warding off some evil threat that loomed in the mists at the dream's edge. She stretched her muscles, the dream slowly receding, replaced by the reality of Ryan's arms surrounding her. His face lay on the pillow next to hers, his expression benign and self-satisfied. "You! How did you . . ." she exclaimed in a startled, resentful tone.

"Find you," Ryan finished her sentence, a lazy, contented smile spreading across his long, sensual mouth. His fingers softly stroked her smooth, silken back. "I merely employed my God-given wits and deduced that you would seek sanctuary here. You'd forgotten I had the key, my love." His mouth moved to her throat, his lips teasing the soft, tender skin.

"Don't!" Cat struggled to evade the kisses of his gently encroaching lips, adding indignantly, "and don't call me your love, either—I never was and never will be!"

"Don't what?" came Ryan's hoarsely whispered reply. "Don't touch your satin skin... don't caress the warm softness of your gentle curves ... don't kiss lips that were made to be kissed? I can no more resist all that than I can stop time from flowing forward. You don't mean it, even now your resistance is ebbing. You've missed me as much as I have you!"

"Stop it!" Cat was close to tears, for her body *was* responding to the lean, hard muscles pressing against her. She shivered, recalling her last encounter with a man, or so-called man. She equated Justin's brutal attack with Ryan's increasingly insistent caresses. She couldn't let him touch her, use her! Her mind rebelled against what her body craved.

Ryan's lazy smile vanished, replaced by a mocking sneer. "I can't touch you—yet you welcomed Justin between those long, silken legs! You have odd tastes if you prefer that poppinjay!" His fingers closed cruelly on her arms, forcing her back into the soft down mattress. "Why," he demanded resentfully, "why must I always take what you willingly give to others? Am I so repulsive, such an inept, bungling lover that you fight me time and again?" His eyes darkened to cold, hard flints. "So be it then. I want you and I intend to have you, Cat Devlan. Fight me if you will—perhaps it's the only way I can enjoy you!" His mouth fell on hers, his tongue a relentless weapon that plunged within. She struggled wildly against the pressing, suffocating weight of his body.

Cat's mind screamed in hysterical rebellion. She was transported to another time when Justin's rough, unmerciful hands had subjected her to his unspeakable depravities. She cringed from hands that seemed to be everywhere at once, seeking, harshly attempting to reaffirm possession of her. His fingers tangled in the cascade of copper curls, trapping her beneath him, urging her head up to respond to his kisses. Thwarted by what seemed like a rejection of him, Ryan was intent on taking his pleasure, sure that she would eventually be swept along on the tide of passion. As his hand moved down her back to stroke her rounded buttocks, Cat exploded in a renewed struggle, screaming in terrified confusion as Ryan's hands once more became Justin's. She kicked and pounded against his chest, a wounded, wild creature that fought its hunter.

The desperation in Cat's struggles reached Ryan. She'd fought him before, but never so violently, as though she faced a demon. He caught the arms that flailed randomly, holding her until the resistance seeped away. She shook with the aftereffects of the terror that had seized her. Ryan peered down at her, easing his grip to tenderly sweep the tangled tendrils of gold away from her face. She flinched, staring up with wide, smokey eyes that failed to recognize him. He moved a hand to touch her again, to soothe away the fright, and she seemed ready to bolt. "Cat . . . what is it, love?"

The heavy fringe of lashes descended, fluttering several times in confusion before her eyes focused on his concerned expression. She tilted her head, puzzled to find him there when it was Justin whose hands . . . No, Justin was in Bath Town, she had left the devil behind her when she ran.

Ryan saw the change come over her and breathed easier. His ardor and demands were left behind as he sat up to lean back against the bedframe. This had something to do with Justin and he swore to find out what within the next half-hour. Gently, he offered a hand to help her rise, waiting patiently until she showed enough trust to accept. She, too, used the frame for support, though she pulled the cover beneath her arms to cover her breasts and warily stayed an arm's length away from him.

"Tell me what happened," Ryan asked in a tone that requested instead of commanded. "It was Justin you saw, instead of me, wasn't it?"

Cat caught her lip with her teeth, staring down at the strong, tanned hands that lay near hers. She nodded, too embarrassed to look him in the eyes. The hands moved, one of them lifted her chin with the gentlest of motions until their eyes met.

"What on God's earth did he do to you?"

Cat trembled on the brink of confiding in Ryan. No, she couldn't! She jerked away from him, her hair veiling her shaking shoulders as she sobbed into her hands. The sobs were dry, tortured sounds, for tears would not come. "I can't," she cried out in a tormented voice. "I can't repeat what he . . . what——"

"Why didn't you come to me?" Ryan broke in.

"You?" Her head rose and one shaking hand shoved the tangles away from eyes that were reproachful and still glazed bright with shame. "You told me *not* to come back. I remember something about secondhand goods."

The words Ryan had said in a moment of hurt and disillusionment came back to haunt him. "You must have known I didn't mean it. Lord, Cat—you were a different person that morning in the library. Your moods change with the directions of the wind. I never know what to expect!"

To Cat, it sounded like a description of his own changeable character. How could he accuse her of being capricious when he'd abandoned her so soon after they'd made love? She stubbornly refused to give ground, her mouth pouting as she sullenly accused him of other charges. "I'm sure you must have known what he was like when I left. How amused you must have been——"

Her bitter taunt was cut off by Ryan. He caught her wrist, pulling her close. "I can only imagine what he did, from your reaction. As long as I've known Justin, I've never heard of any cruelty or odd behavior until now. He must've been drunk."

"Oh, he was drinking, we both shared wine from the same bottle. His clever surprise came in the drug he slipped into my glass. He had to before he . . ." Her head dropped, the cascade of copper hiding her features once more. "What does it matter?" she whispered softly in despair.

Ryan swore silently. The girl who sat next to him, whose arm he still gripped, seemed altogether different from the spitting wildcat he'd come to respect and admire. She was vulnerable now, humbled by whatever that blind fool Justin had done to her. He wished now that he'd followed his impulse and crushed the worm where he'd stood. Ryan suddenly remembered the fire that had totally consumed Justin's house the night Cat had fled. "Did you get back at him by setting the fire?" Someone had set the blaze, thrown rocks through the windows in the servants' quarters as a warning and vanished in the night.

Cat's head rose sharply, her tone puzzled. "Fire?" Someone had burned Justin's house? Then it all fell into place, Will's long absence that night, the look that had passed between Clarise and Will. Will had killed two birds with one stone. He had avenged her for Justin's brutal attack and at the same time assured himself that the paper that threatened her was destroyed. She wished she had thought of it before Justin had abused her.

"No, I didn't," she admitted truthfully. "Was he killed?" She held her breath, wondering if the mad, depraved satyr had been caught in the blazing inferno.

Ryan shook his head. "The servants warned him. Lord, Cat, when I heard about it, I thought you'd been . . .

"Cat." The word was spoken as a soft caress as he released her arm. She looked up through the veil of silken tresses. Ryan smiled disarmingly. "Come home with me. I won't let anyone hurt you, you'll have nothing but pleasurable pursuits to fill your time. Anything you desire is yours." His smile deepened, revealing a flash of white teeth. The strong cleft in his chin again drew Cat's fascinated attention.

Cat had to resist the urge to touch his face. No, she yielded too easily, too quickly to this tall, handsome man who had burst into her life. It was obvious he meant to woo her, to carry her home like a prize he'd won. He'd offered her everything but marriage, the one thing that would have made her follow even if he'd been a penniless nobody. She was to become his mistress, then, an ornament to dazzle his friends and warm his bed and then— and then be discarded when a different woman came along to draw his attention. She mentally shook herself, resisting the warm, coaxing tone. What was it he was saying, something about Canterbury Hill?

". . . the deed is below, in my saddle bags. I want you to have it back. By right it belongs to you and Briar. You needn't worry about the state of the house, I'll have the whole place redone. There's plenty of money for Briar and the child, too. I don't want you to have any worries." He lightly massaged the back of her slender neck, his gaze never leaving her perfect features. Even now the sweet ache was returning. Cat little realized her ability to enchant. The gold-fringed, amethyst eyes were enough to set a man's blood racing in his veins. He'd seen them spit violet fury but now they were soft and dark as a warm Caribbean night, regarding him with a puzzled skepticism.

Cat sighed as his fingers magically caressed the tight knot of tension from her neck muscles. Will would be returning soon; he was due back by nightfall. She had no intention of going with Ryan. He possessed too much power, power to sway her with a gentle word or touch. He had given her the deed to her beloved home, a gesture he'd made freely, without her request. Her betraying body ached to feel the long, lean length of him against her, to carry a memory across the world with her, for once she set foot on the *Falcon,* she would never see him again.

Ryan became aware of a sudden pliancy in Cat's body. A soft smile lit her features. A thrill of victory overcame his usually cautious nature. Had he not been intoxicated with the closeness, the warm, sweet scent of her, he might have questioned the sudden relaxation more closely. Her arms crept timidly about his neck, her eyes closing as she tilted her head back for his kiss, lips slightly parted in sensual surrender. He was drunk with the feel of her yielding, slowly savoring the moment as he bent his head to taste the offering of her softly pouting mouth. A low groan escaped him as she melted into his arms, ardently returning the kiss.

Cat's body slipped lower and Ryan settled, half covering it with his. He took one of her small hands in his, guiding it to him, tensing with pleasure as, hesitantly at first, then with growing confidence, she caressed and fondled him until he felt huge within her fragile grasp.

A steadily increasing drumbeat thrummed within him. The two rolled in the softness of the bed. Breathless minutes passed as Ryan explored every inch of her supple body, his pride soaring like an eagle as she moaned with pleasure.

Still gentle in his urgency, Ryan moved between her legs. He stared for a moment, stunned by the display of natural beauty that awaited him. She tossed her head on the pillow, eyes half-closed. The delicate, patrician features, firm, high breasts, softly rounded hips—all belonged to him at this moment. She was ready, softly calling his name, and Ryan could delay no longer. He sank into her, fitting himself gently to the warmth that welcomed his trespass. Cat's hips wriggled in a delicious, tantalizing way that left him breathless. He built a steady rhythm with his hips, then bent his head to suckle one rosy nipple, teasing it til she moaned aloud, then switching his attentions to the other.

Cat cried out, her hips arching to meet his deep thrusts until a warm tingle began in her toes, spreading upward to center at the junction of her white thighs. A low scream that was hardly recognizable as her own voice broke the silence of the room as the sound of waves crashed in her ears, setting her adrift in a deep wash of passionate release. From a distance, she heard Ryan softly call her name, then a triumphant, low shout as he, too, joined her in a rapturous release.

Ryan collapsed at Cat's side, his desire ebbing, replaced by a strange, new tenderness for the breathless beauty who had surrendered to him. *This* was the response he'd fantasized those many sleepless nights. Quiet contentment settled over him as he gathered her posessively in his arms. Her eyes were closed, her breathing slow and even, and he took advantage of the time to study her. Cat was curled snugly against his chest, her hand draped over his waist. Her ivory skin was winter pale now, the light, golden blush of summer's tan fading. A hint of rose touched her cheeks, emphasizing their upward slant. Her straight, fine-boned nose perched above a rosebud mouth that pouted delicately, begging to be kissed, even in repose. Yet for all her alluring features, she possessed the air of a waif, and deep within himself Ryan felt a stirring of protectiveness that was alien to him. She had no one, save that huge bear of a man who had come to plead her cause that day. Knowing what he did now, he found himself wishing he'd listened more closely.

Cat stretched, nuzzling Ryan's shoulder with her cheek. Her eyes remained shut, though a tiny smile curved her lips. Ryan would never admit it aloud, but at that moment, he came as close to love as he ever had. The sleeping girl touched something within him; he could almost believe he would marry her if she made it a condition of coming home with him. Somehow the idea wasn't as distressing as it should have been. He was twenty-eight, master of a large plantation now. He'd sown his wild oats and was growing tired of the inane, tedious chatter of girls like Marian.

For the first time he considered the thought of an heir. What wild, spirited sons he could breed with this copper-haired minx! The thought was so appealing he lowered his head and placed a tender kiss on the tip of her nose. She wrinkled it with a pert motion but failed to awaken. He would see how they adjusted to each other before he was bold enough to make the suggestion. His lips touched the soft, velvet skin of her throat. Her earlier response had almost destroyed his doubts but he now sought to assure himself that it was not a temporary surrender. Slowly, he brought her awake with the touch of his lips and light demanding strokes of his fingers. She finally opened her eyes, warm and aroused, smiling indulgently as she stretched against him.

This time the union left no doubt in Ryan's mind. Once she was aware of his intent, she offered herself to him, blossoming under him, unselfishly giving of herself until they fused into one being, bent on releasing the mutual passions they experienced. This time it was Ryan who easily sank into a deep, restful slumber.

Cat waited until her breathing returned to normal. She had allowed herself free rein, knowing she would soon be gone from Ryan's side. She would carry the memories of this time with her as long as she lived. She glanced down at his peaceful features, her heart twisting with a tug of feeling. She didn't want to leave him, wanted nothing more than to stay in the safety of his arms and continue the delightful idyl.

Still, she knew she had to escape her strange dependence on him, the helpless feeling that made her want to bury her head against his shoulder when anything threatened her. How he would laugh if she admitted that! She could picture the quick flash of cynical amusement that would light his black eyes. Cat, independent, willful, unmanageable Cat Devlan, docile and subdued in the throes of love! The idea brought an amused glint to her eyes. She had to leave *now,* before he awakened and used his overwhelming physical strength to stop her from fleeing.

She couldn't stay to become a helpless pawn in his hands. Leaving assured her a chance to maintain her independence, a chance for a life of her own, free and untethered by emotional ties to anyone. If only . . . Why couldn't he have once mentioned marriage? Wasn't she his social equal, well able to assume a position as mistress of Seahaven? Hadn't he found her a fascinating bed partner?

What reason made him wary of legal ties? Cat felt a brief touch of bitterness, recalling his doubt when she had denied guilt in his uncle's murder. Possibly *that* had colored his decision. After all, one might keep a mistress who possessed a wild and disreputable past, but marry her—sire children by her? Cat shook her head sadly, shedding a single tear for what might have been. Carefully she eased herself from the bed. Ryan tossed restlessly for a moment, then settled under the warmth of the covers.

She found her clothing and was dressed within minutes. Will wouldn't be back until late but she would have to wait in the cave. It was too dangerous to stay here. She hesitated wondering if she should leave a note. But what would she say? *Sorry, Ryan, even though I'm falling in love . . .* or *Goodbye, darling, it was never meant to be?* No, it was ridiculous, there was nothing she could say to explain. She would never see him again—what difference did it make what he thought of her leaving? He would probably curse and storm for a while and then forget her.

Before she left the room, Cat parted the curtains of the bed to stare down at Ryan's sleeping face. She studied each strong, bold feature, memorizing them to carry in her heart. She had to tense her fingers to keep from reaching out to touch the tangle of ebony curls. No, she dared not even touch him in farewell, for if he awakened, she was lost. The curtains dropped, obscuring his face from view, and she whirled to race from the room before the tears that hovered on the edge of her eyelids could fall.

Above deck the wind howled through the rigging and rain still lashed the windows of the cabin like glass needles. The *Falcon* had rounded the Cape of Good Hope and an icy chill pervaded the room, unrelieved by a small brazier filled with glowing coals. Will sat on the edge of the bunk, staring down at Cat as she tossed in restless exhaustion, her thin, delicate hand lost within his large one. On the plank flooring lay a pile of discarded sheets, darkened and stained with the blood she had lost. Jonathan Wiley, the old gray sailor who served as the ship's medical officer, stood at the desk, rinsing his hands in a basin of water.

Will cleared his throat to catching Doc Wiley's attention and indicated the cupboard across from the desk. "You'll find brandy and glasses there," he said in a hushed tone. Slowly he withdrew Cat's hand from his and laid it at her side, drawing the coverlet beneath her chin. She moaned in her sleep but didn't waken, and Will cautiously eased his weight from the bed to join the older man in a drink. He desperately needed one and knew Wiley would also, after their long vigil with Cat. "How far along was she?" he asked as Wiley handed him a glass brimming with the liquor.

Doc glanced at Cat, her face pale and strained, and shook his head. "Hard to tell, Foster, I'd venture not more'n a month, mebbe' six weeks. She was lucky, though. Further along she'd a had more pain and . . . complications." He paused and tossed the brandy down his throat. "Ahh, that felt good!" He indicated the bottle and added, "Mind if I indulge? Rarely see stuff this good." It had been a long two hours. "She'll be fine in a couple o' weeks, though she must stay abed. Seen rest work more healin' than medicine." He pointed to a small, dark green bottle. "She may need another dose." He glanced over at the sleeping girl and scratched at his stubbly beard. "Don't mind tellin' you, Will Foster, that was one hell of a shock, findin' our darin' cap'n's a frail woman!" He began to pack his supplies into a satchel, preparatory to leaving.

"You'll be rememberin' your vow of silence, Wiley. I'd not take kindly to hearin' you spilled the secret whilst in your cups!" Glancing at Will's imposing size and the frown on his face, Wiley quickly reassured him.

"If the tale's repeated, it won't be by my lips, you can rest assured o' that!" He grinned, a lopsided, near toothless grin, and glanced down at the knife handle protruding from Will's boots. "I've no desire to feel that wicked blade between me shoulders, mate."

Will quietly closed the door on the man and stretched his muscles wearily. Nothing in all his long years had ever affected him so as the sight of Cat, blanching a ghostly white and clutching her belly in pain. She had collapsed in his arms, wracked by waves of severe cramps. It had been his decision to call Wiley and risk revealing her secret. Looking down at her wan, weary features, he knew it had been his only choice. She'd lost a great deal of blood, and for all he knew would have died without Wiley's care.

His mouth hardened with disgust as he thought of the man whose selfish desires had caused Cat so much pain and grief. Ryan Nicholls, a man who knew not that Cat had carried his seed and who most likely wouldn't have cared had he known.

Cat loved him, that much had become evident since they had sailed from the Atlantic coastline over five weeks before. Her pride had never allowed her to admit it, not even to him, but on the voyage that took them toward their destination, she had seemed to languish. Her appetite had diminished, her interest in everyday happenings almost becoming nonexistent, until finally she had lost the babe she had been unaware that she even carried. At least the man was left behind. With any luck, she would never come into contact with his arrogance again. Perhaps the shock of losing the child would sever any ties that still bound her to Ryan. He, who never prayed, now closed his eyes in silent prayer that it was so.

A sound drew his attention. Cat had awakened and stared at him from sunken eyes, still a lovely violet but lined and smudged by deep purple, seeming too large for the thin, tired face. "Will . . . how tired you must be," she said in a weak whisper.

He was at her side immediately and she shifted, pain flickering across her features, to allow him room to sit beside her. "I'm fit as a fiddle, sweetheart. It's you I'm worried about. How d'you feel now?"

Cat smiled weakly, an effort that sapped her strength. The light in the room was dim and she tried hard to concentrate on Will's dear features. "I'm just tired and sore. I . . . I lost a baby, didn't I, Will?" He sadly nodded his head. She turned her face to the wall, tears squeezing forth from tightly shut eyes.

"Don't try an' talk, Cat. Doc said you must rest. We'll be in Madagascar soon and we'll lay up for a while—we've plenty o' money until you're well again. Just think of the warm sunshine, child." He leaned forward, kissed her cheek, and rose.

Cat turned quickly to face him. Her eyes were liquid

jewels, amethysts asparkle in a setting of white pearl. "Wait! I need to talk, Will. *Please,* stay." He sat once more at her side and she grasped his hand tightly.

"Will, what's wrong with me? For all that's happened because of Ryan—God in Heaven help me," she cried, her eyes desperate. "I *still* want him! I only know his touch made me warm and alive. Will, I never felt that way before." It was as though she had returned to her childhood and sought the help he had always been able to give her. Her expression pleaded, beseeched him to help her understand the emotions tearing at her heart and soul.

Will shook his head, overcome by melancholy. He'd watched Cat grow from a child to a lovely young girl but now she was a woman, a confused woman who sought his advice in an area of which he had little experience. What could he tell her to ease the pain within her, a pain that had little to do with the loss of the child? "Love is something I know nothing of, Catherine. I've never had the pleasure or the time to indulge in it. It's a crusty old bachelor you've asked and I don't know what to tell you. You're a woman of strong feelin's and you set your heart on Nicholls. If I'm not mistaken, 'e reminds you of your father. Dev had the same way with your mum. Nicholls just wasn't ready to settle in, lovey. You'll forget all about 'im within the year, mark my words it you don't!"

The tears had ceased to flow. Cat drew as much comfort from Will's wisdom as she could. Perhaps she should have stayed in France, accepted one of Grandmère's matches. Wouldn't it have been better to marry without love than to taste its sweetness and be forever parched and thirsty for its loss? Will, dear Will, still watched her, the same, warm paternal glint in his brown eyes. How selfish she was in dwelling on herself only to distress this old friend! She forced a smile to her lips and held out her arms to hug him.

"You're right, as always, Will. The past we'll leave behind and look to the future. Now please, you're exhausted and I *am* tired, go and rest." She kissed his cheek and was rewarded by the easing of his worried expression.

"I won't be far if you need me, sweet. Thing's'll look better by mornin'tide, they always do!" He tucked the covers beneath her chin once again and snuffed the wick of the lantern, leaving only the bright moonlight to stream through the windows.

As the door closed on Will, Cat turned to the wall, the moonlight silvering the tears she had saved until he left. She vowed to guard her heart well in the future. No other would find the hidden key to its now locked portals.

Part Two
Madagascar, 1720

Chapter Ten

The island of St. Mary shone in the sapphire setting of the Indian Ocean like a small emerald. Thirteen miles off the eastern coast of its mother island of Madagascar, this lush, deeply forested tropical isle was now Cat Devlan's home. By curious coincidence, she had purchased the fortified home built by Captain Kidd during his sojourn in the tropics. Though Kidd had long since departed, his home still graced the steep, verdant hills of St. Mary; and Cat found it a welcome retreat as well as a perfect base for her operations.

She had also bought a small house on the outskirts of the English settlement of Fort St. David. The outpost was a garrison and trading post for the English East Indies Company and lay on the eastern edge of India known as the Coromandel Coast. There goods were stored and readied for shipment to England. The Indians, unimpressed by the quality of English imports, had insisted on advance payments in gold bullion for their products. These payments arrived twice a year and were also stored at the warehouses until transferred to the Mogul's treasury. There were three such factor houses or factories on the Coromandel alone. Others lined the entire coast of the subcontinent. The ships headed for the posts were ripe for the attacks of pirates who had transferred their operations from the Spanish Main.

Cat had more or less retired from active participation in the forays of the two ships she now owned. She was secretly the head of a pirate consortium, the mastermind behind a wild, motley group of international rogues who plundered the ships of the East Indies and the Red Sea. They brought their captured bounty to the wharves known as Shelley's Landing at the harbor of St. Mary to be stored in Cat's warehouses until sold or bartered for trade goods. Will Foster now commanded the *Falcon;* Cat's partner Sean Rafferty was in charge of the other ship, the frigate *Spirit*. Aside from Will, Sean was the only person aware of her dual role as patron-factor to the pirates and as the demure, reclusive "widow" of one imaginary Carleton Barbour. The cover allowed her to move within the small groups of Europeans at the trading posts and easily gather information regarding trade routes and cargoes of the merchant ships. This knowledge relayed to Sean and Will, allowed them a measure of success that had heretofore been unknown among the wide-ranging Red Sea marauders.

Now Cat strolled the gardens behind her home with her chief source of information, her fiancé, George Pembroke. George was a councilor at Fort St. David, where they had met. She'd been daydreaming and gave herself a shake, apologizing to her companion with a pretty smile. "I'm sorry, dear, what was it you were saying? I'm afraid I was off in my own dream world." She flashed an amethyst gaze at him from beneath a fan of dark gold lashes.

George shook his head, dazzled anew by the beauty of his fiancée. Each time he saw her, his thoughts whirled with a passion he had long believed to be dead. The reality of attracting and holding the interest of such a young, lovely girl was a constant source of amazement to him. Though he was well settled financially, she'd been left a fortune by her late husband and had no need of his support. He had finally decided it was his distinguished, mature appearance that drew her attention. She had come to love him for the security and protection he offered. Whatever appeal the match held, he thanked God every night that she was to be his. "My sweet, I was again urging you to pack your belongings and move from this island, this disreputable place, and settle permanently at the Fort." He paused and took both her hands into his, bringing them to his lips and placing a soft kiss on her upturned palms. "It does your fair reputation no earthly good to live in a place frequented by rough, vulgar rascals. For that matter," he added peevishly, "it hardly helps my own good name to be seen visiting St. Mary. Why, I fear for your safety even more than for your good and gentle name!" George was ridden with worry, too, lest the Company should hear of his visits. His manner softened as Cat stared up at him from beneath the wide brim of her straw sun hat. She was a vision in pale yellow, a gossamer dress of lawn ruffles; and, as usual, he could tell she would get her way.

"George," she said in a soft, soothing tone of light reproach. "You *know* I'm perfectly safe! I was against coming to this isle when Carleton first suggested it, but I've come to love its seclusion and beauty." In the deep, blue green forest at the edge of the clearing, an owl hooted. Around them a wild profusion of striking flowers filled the air with heavy fragrances. She paused and picked a brilliant red-orange hibiscus blossom, tucking it at her temple. "The breezes are soft and gentle here, George; I'm surrounded by nature at its most glorious. Soon enough I'll have to leave for the heat of India. Surely you'd not force me to do so before I'm ready?"

Her fiancé relented as always. George was a child in her hands, a piece of malleable clay that she shaped and toyed with at will. He had probably known before he asked her that she would not leave the island, and now he seemed to accept her lie at face value. Deftly she turned the conversation toward her objective. "Darling, are you still troubled by those wily pirate devils? Have any more merchantmen been attacked?" She reached up to smooth the wrinkles formed by his frown. "You grow more somber with worry each time I see you."

"Aye, it seems to increase with every passing week. These sea-rovers are brazen in their plunderings! But don't worry your pretty head, my dearest, I've redoubled my efforts to stop them; indeed, I must, for the home office is in fine pother over the loss of goods. I either stop them, once and for all, or face losing my position and disgrace." His pallid complexion was mottled red by the sun, his pendulant jowls quivering with pleasure as he gazed at her concerned expression. "Just this week, I devised a plan. Would you care to hear it?"

Cat's eyes were aglow with amusement, which her vain fiancé mistook for admiration. He led her toward a garden seat of bamboo and when they were seated, began his proud recital of the plan.

"I've outfitted the *Queen's Rose* with twice her former firepower. The word's been put out on the waterfront that she's heavily laden for her homeward journey. Bejeweled gifts for the King from the Mogul, silks and satins and gold from Madagascar. Catherine, no pirate worth his salt will be able to resist the bounty she carries! We'll have her on alert and those scurvy seadogs won't escape this time!" He straightened his back, sucking in his slight paunch and waited vainly for her appreciation of his cunning. It came, as expected.

"Oh, George," Cat cried, her wide, violet eyes gazing at him in apparent esteem. "Surely you'll catch them this time! How ever did you think of such a plan?" She touched his arm, her face a mask of awe and admiration. "The Company will surely offer you a post of higher responsibility following your success—I'm so proud of you! I shall say a prayer for the success of the plan."

The gullible old fool preened like a peacock under the spell of her enchanting flattery. "It has yet to succeed, my sweet, but I foresee no reason for failure. Those damn rogues'll plead for mercy 'fore I'm done with them!"

Cat could barely restrain her contempt. The fussy, swaggering man before her was old enough to be her father. If he'd had any brains beneath his blustering, vainglorious exterior, he would realize she used him for her own ends, that she could never love such a posturing, conceited dolt. She had long ago decided to use men to her advantage, for if she didn't, she'd be taken advantage of herself. The only man on earth she trusted was Will. Even Sean Rafferty was suspect, despite their close friendship.

Her native houseboy, Coco, appeared suddenly before them. "Lunch is ready, Missy," he said, with a short, deferential bow. He bobbed his head and withdrew as silently as he had come.

"Y'see, my dear," George exclaimed with an exasperated glare at the retreating figure. "You're a white woman, alone on this island except for these natives. They're sneaky, I tell you! I worry about you coming to harm. Only a step removed from savages, they are!"

"Don't fuss so, darling," Cat pleaded, linking her arm in his and leaning lightly against him. "I *am* stubborn when I make up my mind! Now let's enjoy our meal; I know you must be back aboard your ship soon." They strolled through the garden toward the house, their heads bent together in low conversation.

Several hours later Cat stood at the edge of the fortifications surrounding her home. She smiled and waved gaily at George as he rode away in her carriage, bound for the harbor of St. Mary. When the vehicle was far enough down the road, the smile faded and she sighed heavily. She climbed down the steps wearily and made her way across the courtyard to the house. These visits with George were essential to maintain the valuable relationship, but they bored her so; she always felt the need to escape to her room and rest afterward. She sometimes wondered if Will and Sean knew how much effort it took to smile and coddle the old goat!

Entering her room, she found her maid, Rovani, placing freshly washed clothing in her wardrobe. Sean had been responsible for bringing Rovani and all the other servants to work at the house. The girl was a Moriandria who spoke little English and only a few words of French. She had resisted all Cat's efforts to teach her either language. Rovani had an exotic cast to her face, inherited from some Arab trader who had dealt with her tribe in the distant past. The dark, slanted eyes always seemed to bear a sullen resentment toward Cat. Several times Cat had tried to break through the barrier the girl had erected around herself, but to no avail. She had finally given up, and the two coexisted with few exchanges other than simple orders from Cat.

"Rovani, I'll rest now," she said, indicating sleep by touching the pillow on her bed. "When I awake, please bring Paddy to me. You may go now." For a brief second, Cat could swear she saw a murderous glare within the slanted eyes, but the flash of fury was gone quickly. The maid's eyes remained lowered and she nodded curtly, closing the chest of clothing and quietly slipping from the room.

Outside, the late afternoon air was cool and refreshing. A gentle rain fell, its sound soothing and restful as Cat lay down for her nap. She tossed uncomfortably for a few minutes, wondering if she had misread the reaction to her orders. The girl had no reason to harbor any ill will for her, unless . . . unless Rovani was in love with Sean. Cat had never considered the girl's possible affection for him. Certainly she seemed more alive and eager to please when he appeared. It was a possibility she would have to look into, something else to discuss with her partner when he returned from his latest voyage.

Sean. Cat lay in the half light of late afternoon, remembering the first time she had seen him. It had rained that day too, a different rain from the gentle drizzle of today. She had just purchased the house and surrounding property. The *Falcon* had brought them to Madagascar in late March, with nearly a month to pass before the humid, rainy season ended. From the first moment she saw the house, she had fallen in love with it, taken by its sturdy English architecture, standing in intriguing contrast to the dark, heavy growth of the tropical rain forest. Compared to the frigid climate they had left behind in America, the warm, temperate air was a blessing and the island abounded in natural richness. Tall pines and sago palms surrounded the fortified house and grounds; fragrant, exotic blooms grew profusely in a wild tangle of vibrant colors, fresh mangoes, coconuts, and other delicious fruits grew in an abundance.

She and Will settled into the house, making do with native help hired from the small town at the harbor of St. Mary. The rogues who inhabited the waterfront and wharves assured Will that the cool, dry season was almost upon them and Cat spent most of the first month just settling in and recovering her health following the miscarriage.

One day, a particularly humid, steamy afternoon, she wandered from the house to catch what little breeze existed. Adopting the wisdom of the native girls who worked at the house, she dressed in a cool, silken sari, similar to those worn on the Indian mainland. Since the sun beat down through a haze of cloud, she covered her head with the silk for protection from the intense heat. Though Will had warned her not to venture far from the house, the woods past the clearing seemed so cool and invitingly shady, she threw caution aside and hurried toward them. She meant to keep the house in view, in the event that she should meet any of the natives who were reported to live in the hills.

Entranced by the bright blossoms of poinsettia shrubs and the variety of orchids that grew wild and free, she wandered deeper into the forest. The sound of rushing water caught her ear and she sought its source, carefully picking her way through the dense, verdant underbrush.

Suddenly she stumbled upon a scene of such sylvan

beauty that her breath was momentarily taken away. A rocky promontory jutted abruptly toward the sky, its sharp edges softened by lush green foliage. From its peak a small waterfall cascaded into a wide pool. The water foamed and frothed at the base, rippling away to quiet stillness at the farthest edge, forming a small stream that slowly meandered down the mountainside. She had seen such cascades on Madagascar but she had little realized that one lay within her reach. Colorful tropical birds flitted among the low branches of the trees and above, the sky seemed cut off by the vast canopy of the forest. It was a perfect spot, a secluded place she might seek in moments of distress, and she vowed to return again to this secret retreat beneath the trees.

She threw herself down by the pool's edge, delighting in the cool grass beneath her. She lay there, musing as she stared into the water, absently gazing at her reflection. Lost in unbidden remembrances of Ryan, she took no notice of the sudden change of weather. A brisk wind had begun to stir the trees but even the sound of its keening in the branches overhead escaped her. She dipped her fingers in the water, playfully catching a handful of the cool liquid in her cupped palm and letting it trickle out.

Suddenly, as the water smoothed to a mirror surface once more, she became aware of a horrifying reflection in the water. Beside her own mirrored expression of rapidly dawning terror, another joined, a hideous apparition with distorted features. She rolled to her back, her fingers covering her mouth as her eyes widened at the nightmare sight confronting her. A half-naked savage, darkly tanned and sinewy, towered over her, his face obscured by a gruesome carved mask, a spear held in one hand, his other reaching down toward her. The wind had risen to a feverish pitch. Her hair whipped across her face, blocking the vision for a second before his fingers closed hard around her wrist and pulled. Cat's reasoning returned and she struggled, twisting wildly in an attempt to escape.

Her strength, fueled by terror, was nothing against his muscular vitality and she was drawn helplessly to her feet.

Suddenly the storm broke. A gale force wind slammed against the two as a torrential rain drenched them. In a breath's time Cat was soaked, the silken sari affording no protection against the buffeting winds and downpour. It clung to her body, outlining every rounded curve, every detail as though she wore nothing. Tears mixed with the rain streaming down her face as she tried to break and run. The man said nothing, easily picking her up and ignoring her desperate attempts to struggle away. He thrust the spear into the wet ground, trotting off with Cat encased in his strong arms as though he carried a feather comforter. The winds continued to slam at them in gusts. Cat had kept her eyes tightly shut, her sobs lost in the gale, remembering too late her promise to keep within safe range of the house.

The native carried her toward the waterfall and suddenly the rain no longer beat against her face in sheets of water. He knelt, placing her on the ground. Cat saw that he had found the shelter of a cave.

Outside its entrance, the wind howled, and the roaring of the waterfall blended with the tropical deluge. The man went to the cave opening and stood there, staring out at the storm. Cat opened both eyes, searching the cave for another means of escape. It was small and rocky, darkened at the rear, and her heart sank in despair as she realized her tall, muscular captor blocked the only exit. He lounged casually against the entrance, his stance suggesting a panther at rest. Cat bit her lip, brushing damp bronze curls away from her eyes and face. She had to find some way to defend herself. A sharp piece of rock shaped like a spear head lay near her outstretched hand. She seized it, hiding it quickly behind her as the native turned and stalked toward her, pausing at her side with long legs astride. In a sudden movement he squatted, hunkering down on his haunches beside her. She recoiled, inching back as far as the rocky wall allowed. He maintained the same position for minutes, studying her from behind the horrible mask. Her hand closed tightly on her weapon, ready to strike if he moved.

After what seemed to Cat to be an eternity, the man reached up and drew the mask from his face. Cat's eyes widened with shock. He was a white man, his eyes a brilliant blue beneath sun-whitened blond brows, his hair a damp tangle of gold. He grinned at her, a deep dimple creasing one cheek, for all the world acting as though he had not just scared her to death.

"Who—who are you?" she managed to stutter.

"And might I not ask the same, m'lady," he replied in a lilting Irish brogue. "I took you for one of the mermaids the Moriandrias believe in. Indeed, I thought to me'self, Sean, m'boy, . . . Sean Rafferty, that's m'name . . . you've come upon one o' them lovely ladies of the water. Now, I must admit, it's not an everyday occurrence to find a lovely bit o' red-haired mermaid like yourself all stretched out cozylike by a waterfall!"

The man oozed charm and his almost comical explanation eased Cat's anxiety. Her expression lost some of its distrust and a tiny smile began to break through.

"By the Saints, Mary and Joseph," Sean exclaimed. "You're a goddess when laughter touches them rosebud lips!" He peered closer, cocking his head to one side. "You wouldn't be Irish by any chance? No," he answered himself before she could reply, "no, I ain't died an' gone to Heaven yet. That'd be too much to expect!" Again he flashed his engaging grin.

Cat rose to a sitting position, quickly covering her outlined breasts with the edging of silk she had worn over her hair. Her fingers still clutched the rock, hidden beneath the material, for though he appeared charming and rather harmless, so had Ryan Nicholls when first she set eyes on him. "I'm half-English, half-French," she admitted. "My name is Catherine Devlan. I've just bought the house beyond the clearing." She tendered a bit more of a smile, hoping she could keep the conversation light and easy. His gaze had briefly swept her figure, taking in every detail revealed by the clinging gown.

"Well, Devlan is it," he answered with a nod. "That could well be transplanted Irish—you've the look of Ireland about you! What on earth's a woman like yourself doin' here? St. Mary's attracted all manner of scoundrels. Indeed, we're awash with a rogues' gallery of stout thieves and piraters. Surely you'll not have me believin' you've come to join our buccaneer society?"

Something about his easy, relaxed manner welcomed Cat's confidence. She turned her head to one side, studying his open, rascally expression, and decided impulsively that she could use him. He had the look of a seafaring man, a man who would stay cool in the face of enemy fire. "You haven't told me why you're dressed as you are. Perhaps if you confide in me, I might do the same."

"Fair enough, lady o' the lake!" Sean quickly explained that he had plied the waters of the Indian Ocean under a variety of pirate captains, including the illustrious Kidd, now deceased. Three years before he had rescued the wife of the chief of the Moriandria tribe from almost certain death at the hands of the raiding Sakalavas of Madagascar. The tribe had adopted him and when the old chief died, he became the new headman of the village. "Sort a' fell into it, y'might say," he explained. "Might call me semiretired; mostly I lay back and let them bring me food and drink."

Cat laughed at the tale's end, amused by the hint of boredom that crossed his angular features as he described his life of leisure. She knew that most of the rogues who chose a pirate's life did so for the adventure as much as the profit. It seemed the Irishman could be ripe for an invitation to join her.

"Well, Sean, I admit you scared me half to death." She smiled warmly, already forgiving him the fright. He settled back while he talked and now sat cross-legged, his chin resting on his hands as he gazed down at her with a lopsided half-smile. He leaned forward a bit, his bright blue eyes atwinkle with a touch of mischief as he listened.

"I've a proposition to make to you," she declared, startling as he grinned at the statement and made a move toward her. His eyes had flared with blue fire, instant ardor transforming his features. The ardor was stilled a moment later as she brought her sharp rock into view. "Keep your place, Sean Rafferty, that's not what I meant," she threatened, waiting until he settled back with a resigned sigh.

Sean's good humor was infectious. "You've an Irish lass's temper, too," he commented. She released her held breath and relaxed once more.

"Have you ever heard of Brian Devlan? He commanded the *Devil's Revenge* out of New York. They called him the Red Devil."

"Aye, he's known among the island men. He was hanged over ten years ago though; one o' me mates saw him swing."

A flicker of remembered pain passed quickly over Cat's face. "He was my father. I sailed with him many a time." Her head was bowed with sadness for a moment, then she lifted it to gaze into his eyes, defiance blazing forth. "I've got the heritage, I've got the skill and my own ship. I intend to have my share of the riches being plundered here. Join my crew, Sean Rafferty. You don't seem the sort to while away your hours in idle boredom. I promise you a fair share of the bounty."

Sean was taken aback by the offer, for he'd never chanced to meet a lady pirate before nor been offered such a tempting proposition. His eyes narrowed in contemplation, one hand rubbing at the light blond stubble on his chin. He finally decided the challenge alone was worth it and agreed.

Cat beamed happily at the thought of adding an able-bodied fighting man to her crew. Will would be able to keep him in line. Possibly, if they captured a prize worth keeping, she could put Sean in command of the second ship. Her mind buzzed with eager plans. Outside the cave, the rain ceased as suddenly as it came. She watched Sean rise, admiring the leanly muscled, spare torso as he stretched and offered her his hand to help her rise.

Preoccupied with exciting plans for the future, Cat missed the gleam of cunning in the blue eyes that gazed down at her. She accepted his help and rose, to find herself captured within the steel bands of his arms. Struggling indignantly, she threw back her head, spitting fury at the outrage. He seemed to enjoy her struggles, deep laughter rumbling from his chest as she glared in helpless rage. His mouth lowered to hers, surprisingly gentle and searching. She struggled a moment longer, relaxing slowly under the soft pressure. It had been three months since she'd felt the touch of a man and despite her vow of abstinence following her heartbreak with Ryan, a tiny twinge of desire twisted deep within her. Any moment she expected his hands to sweep over her, for she had no means of defense against his strength, but he merely continued to hold her close and softly kiss her. Finally he broke the embrace, freeing her to gently adjust the silk across her breasts.

"I could take you, lass," he assured her. "There's nothin' but that bit o' silk between us, but in my vain, Irish way, I'm as stubborn as a mule. I prefer you willing and warm. Someday, perhaps instead of my share of booty, I'll claim your treasures instead." He added warmly, the same crooked smile lighting his face, "But *you'll* have to choose when." He made a small bow, somehow looking regal in his near-naked state. A sudden thought brought a deep frown to his face. "You're not already bound to any, by chance? Dolt that I am, I hadn't thought . . . Well, I'm handy with a cutlass if need be."

Cat was stunned by her release. She had already resigned herself to her fate, and the shock of finding herself free and unmolested but for the sweet, brief kiss made her like him all the more. She invited him back to the house, arriving just as Will returned from a trip to the waterfront.

Now, she drifted off to sleep, warmed by the memory of the meeting. Almost two years had passed and true to his claim, Sean had never again tried to force her into his arms. As he predicted, she'd come to him, eased by six months of close companionship and success of the *Falcon.* He had proved to be one of the best of her men, equal only to Will, and when they'd captured one of the Mogul's frigates bound for Mecca nine months ago, he'd become her captain.

Though Cat still kept her heart ensheathed in an icy barrier to protect her from hurt, she had come close to loving Sean. He was a friend as well as a lover, a teasing companion to lighten her mood when she found herself depressed, a wild rover whose sense of free spirit seemed a near perfect match for hers. Occasionally she would withdraw from him, seeking solitude when the hurtful, depressing memories of Ryan returned. Sean had always seemed to sense the mood and let her be until it lifted, as it always did.

One day, shortly after he had been made captain of the *Spirit,* Sean came to her with a little blond-haired boy in his arms. The child was a toddler, not more than a year and a half old. He had glanced up at her, a shy version of Sean's impish grin lighting his tiny features. Cat instantly fell in love with the boy and when Sean requested her help in raising him, with no questions asked, she could not have refused the appeal in exchange for the plundered treasures of all the ships on the ocean. Padrail was his given name but all who came under the little boy's mischievous spell called him Paddy. He resided down the hall from Cat's room, in a nursery of his own. Rovani cared for him, in addition to her few duties as Cat's maid, and the two seemed to enjoy each other's company immensely.

When Cat awoke from her nap, she felt refreshed and renewed. Beyond the doors leading to the garden terrace, the last vestiges of a glorious sunset had faded to streaks of pastel pink and gold. It was close to twilight, Cat's favorite time of the day on the island. She opened the doors wide, allowing the heavy, sweet scent of mimosa and bougainvillea to waft into the room, and then strolled to her desk and seated herself to reread the last letter from Briar. She smiled again at her sister's description of two-year-old Brian's latest antics. She could easily picture him, for Paddy was about the same age. Brian had a last name now. Grandmère St. Marin had arranged a match for Briar. The kind and gentle Pierre Bornait loved them both and had made no inquiries concerning the boy's paternal heritage.

Suddenly, without warning, Cat felt the tip of a blade at her back. She stiffened, turning her head slightly to see a tall shadow, just barely visible in the growing darkness of the room. Careful not to jostle the wickedly sharp tip of the weapon, she inquired what the intruder wanted with her.

"Something only you can give me, m'lady. I mean to have you. Rise and face me!" Her heart raced wildly, but she rose to face the intruder, whose features were still concealed by shadow. His extended rapier pointed at the soft white skin of her breasts, and his intentions became clearer as he moved into the light of the single candle, flickering on the desk. He smiled a disarmingly wicked grin as his gaze swept over her. The blade tip flickered carefully, severing the satin ribbon that tied her gold silk wrap. It fell open to reveal a yellow chemise whose gossamer material did little to conceal her charms.

"Breathtaking," he whispered, as his free hand reached out to trace the soft swell of her breasts. It moved lower, across the flatness of her belly, then returned to grasp the ribbons fastening the chemise across her breasts. Slowly, drawing out his pleasure, he tugged at each bow until the undergarment lay open, exposing the treasures it had veiled. The blade was lowered to his side as his left hand reached out to slide down her back and come to rest at her waist, then clattered to the floor as she was pulled into his arms with rough urgency and his lips sought the tender, satin skin of her throat.

Cat smiled, her eyes heavy with anticipation as her arms crept around his neck. "Truly, you're a madman,

Sean Rafferty! Why I continue to suffer your antics I cannot understand!"

"Because," he grinned, pausing to emphasize each word with a soft kiss, "you . . . have . . . cravings . . . only . . . I . . . can . . . satisfy! All Irishmen are mad, my love. We suffer a common malady that only the touch of a beautiful woman can cure. Come," he added, bending to sweep her into his arms, "come and help me cure my latest lapse!"

Cat's laughter rippled through the room as she cuddled against his chest. He carried her to the bed, laying her there and beginning to impatiently tear at his own clothing. She watched him and their eyes locked in the beginnings of a mutual fever. Finally he lay beside her, his fingers urgently exploring the familiar sweetness of her body. Cat felt her senses sharpen to a razor's edge. Sean's hands played them as though they were the strings of a finely tuned instrument. He was a tender, yet demanding lover, and the attentions he paid her sent tongues of wildfire leaping through her body. In the months that they had spent together, he had taught her to please him and she did so now, openly, boldly, without shame. The passion Ryan had awakened was now full blown and freely given.

Afterward, they lay contentedly together, wrapped in each other's arms. While they rested, Cat informed him of her visit from George and the information she had gleaned. "I could scarcely contain my laughter when he described how the rogues would plead for mercy when he caught them!" Cat exclaimed with a giggle. She bounced to an upright position, playfully tugging the gold curls on Sean's darkly tanned chest. "Well, don't keep me in suspense, how did the latest foray go?"

Sean caught her hand, bringing it to his lips to kiss her fingertips. "We are now richer to the tune of twenty thousand pounds, my lovely wench. Without harm to a single manjack, I might add!" Cat bubbled over with excitement, casting herself into his arms and hugging him. She lay there, giggling as he regaled her with the story.

"She hove to with barely a fight, lass." He had left the humiliated captain and crew trussed up like chickens on the deck and set the frigate adrift. "Ah, the curses that rang down upon my head, lovey! I deserve an extra divvy of spoils just for the risk to my immortal soul," he joked.

Cat joined in the teasing mood. "Your immortal soul is long past recall, you Gaelic scoundrel! We will divide as usual." She gazed warmly at him through the heavy fringe of gold lashes dusting her cheeks. "Besides, you have already claimed a fitting reward." Her mouth formed a delicate pout when he failed to answer. "Have you not?" she insisted petulantly.

"Indeed I have, Cat." he finally replied in a low whisper against her lips. "But I would claim a rematch, for it seemed as though you enjoyed yourself more than I," he continued to tease. "Such a wildcat you've become lately. Between my duties aboard the *Spirit* and my efforts here, I'm fair worn to a frazzle! I think I deserve a rest from one post or the other! Which would you suggest I give up?" His nonchalant tone of light banter drew a quick response from the girl at his side.

"Choose the one that pleasures you best," Cat retorted smugly, well aware which it would be.

Sean buried his head against the silky, fragrant mass of apricot curls, his voice a warm breath against her ear. "It seems I have no choice," he quipped dryly, nuzzling her neck and running a hand along her thigh. "I'd rather face a thousand guns on the open seas than turn my back on your claws, little tigress." His lips found hers and gently pried them open. "It is clear where my duty lies." Two strong, broad-fingered hands cupped the back of her head, fusing her lips to his in a rebirth of desire.

Engrossed in each other, neither Cat nor Sean heard the soft knock at the door or saw Rovani's white, shocked face as she poked her head around it and saw their bodies fused in passion. She glared daggers at the couple, silently withdrawing before they discovered her presence. It was just one more affront to her pride, one more to add to a long list of grievances.

She had been happy until the white woman came. All her sorrows could be traced to the red-haired witch who had stolen her man. The woman had woven an enchantment, a spell that had captured Sean. He had ended his loving relationship with Rovani and brought her to the house to serve the witch, coldly warning her to keep silent. The worst cut of all had been the usurping of her rights to her own child, the small boy whose hand she now held. She had watched the woman play with her son, watched as his affections turned away as his father's had done.

Now she returned the boy to the nursery, laying him down for a nap and hugging him close before she left to seek her own small room. She would rid herself of the sorceress; in some way she would regain the love of her man and the child she had borne him. Nothing, she vowed silently, nothing would stand in her way!

Chapter Eleven

On a warm, summer's eve in late June, Cat and George strolled through the parade grounds at Fort St. David. Following an urgent message from him, she'd set sail from St. Mary within hours. As they walked, she plied him with sharp, incisive questions. His desperately scrawled note had mentioned only that he'd received orders from the council of directors in London to the effect that they were sending someone to oversee his position as local councilor. The Company's stockholders were up in arms over the lowered dividends during the past year. George had already received orders to deal with the loss of revenues due to the pirate ships in the area.

Cat, too, was anxious, though for an entirely different set of reasons. "George, darling, please contain yourself," she insisted in a soothing tone. Her arm was linked with his and she could feel the disgusting tremble of his slack, flabby muscles beneath her fingers. His overwrought, shaken nerves were a tangible force she had to deal with before she could sort out the details of this new threat to her operations.

She purposely kept her tone confident and light. "They can't blame you—you've done everything possible to stop these raids. This man they've sent can do nothing beyond what's already been tried. Believe me, George," she added convincingly, already planning to step up her attacks on shipping, "he will look ridiculous for his efforts. Only when he fails, will the council realize what a difficult task you've had!"

George was sweating in the cool night air. He grasped at the straws of comfort, readily accepting her assurances. It wasn't so much his position with the Company that worried him as the threat to the lucrative private trade he'd set up in his years as a Company official. Three of his own ships plied the waters between India and China. They were profitable ships that had somehow been lucky enough to escape these devil marauders. The Company frowned on private trade, though they were unable to stop it. He could just imagine some fool tying him in with the pirates. He had a vision of being sent back to London to stand trial for piracy himself.

"Of course you're right, m'dear—hadn't thought of it in that light!" He gathered her into his arms, touching her forehead in a dry, paternal kiss. "Thank God you came so quickly; I'd have continued to brood needlessly." Again he reminded himself how lucky he was.

Cat smiled, gently extricating herself from his embrace. An appearance of calm concealed her agitation. What kind of person were they sending? George had been easy to control. Because he trusted her he shared his problems with her. She knew when an important shipment was due in or outbound, for he would worry over the ship's safety until it arrived. There were few that made port without coming to terms with one or the other of her ships.

She silently berated herself now. She should have forseen that the Company would take more stringent measures. Certainly anyone they sent would be more effective than poor, foolish George. She had to know more about this expected official. If she had the time to plan, George would retain his position. "How much time have you before he is due to arrive?" she asked.

"The letter was sent on the *Castor,* a fortnight before he was due to depart London. From what I understand, this Nicholls fellow should arrive any day now."

"Nicholls?" A deep sense of dread settled over Cat. No, she thought, she was being silly. The name was common enough, there must be many who shared it with Ryan.

"Yes, dear," George affirmed. "Never heard of the man, m'self. I gather he's not an employee, though. Letter mentioned something about a stockholder. Probably how the blighter got the Council to send him. Worried 'bout his damn profits, no doubt! Full name's Ryan Nicholls, if I remember correctly." When utter silence greeted his explanation, he peered through the fading twilight trying to discern his fiancée's expression. "Catherine . . . is something wrong, darling?"

Again silence. Cat's entire body was stiff with shock. If George had shouted, she wouldn't have heard him. Her first blind impulse was to run, to seek the haven of her island home. There was no way she could face Ryan; never in her wildest dreams had she expected to see him again. What odd twist of fate had decreed that they would meet, halfway around the world?

Two years, happy, productive years, seemed to dissolve in a wisp of fog and it was as though she'd stepped into the past. The vision of Ryan's lean, hawklike features, the coal-black, mocking eyes set beneath bold, black-winged brows, the cynical, commanding lips that had so often spoken cruel taunts, all the hurtful memories came flooding back to open a wound in her heart. She grew dizzy at the thought of the intoxicating, sensual effect he'd had on her.

"Catherine!" George's sharp exclamation of concern intruded on the dreamlike trance.

Cat shook herself, suddenly aware that she owed

him an explanation for her strange behavior. Blinking hard to shake away the feeling of unreality, she raised a trembling hand to her temples, her thoughts racing ahead for an excuse. "George, I didn't want to add to your worries, but I haven't felt well lately." The lie sounded convincing, even to her own ears. "I've been so upset ever since I received your note that I haven't been able to sleep. I'm sure it's that and nothing more. Perhaps it might be best if I retired early tonight."

George silently cursed himself. "I'd no idea—Lord, what a fool I've been, burdening you with my problems! I'll not discuss them further." His arm curled protectively around her shoulders and he mistook her sigh of relief for one of contentment. He led her back to the small, single-story house she owned, seeing her safely inside before he bid her a good night's rest.

"Rest tomorrow, my love," he ordered gently. "If you still feel ill, I'll have the Company surgeon take a look at you. It might even be best if you returned home."

Again Cat suffered the light, dry touch of his lips and from somewhere amidst her dazed, preoccupied thoughts, she managed to raise a brief, reassuring smile.

Sleep eluded her that night. Again and again, she examined her feelings in an attempt to understand the mad rush of physical and emotional sensations that had assailed her since she'd learned of Ryan's imminent arrival. How could he come back into her life when she'd put him out of her mind? She hadn't forgotten him, but had merely buried the hurt and pain deep inside. Facing her was one of the most difficult decisions of her life. Should she stay and risk falling under his influence again or run while she had the chance, before it was too late to escape?

Fool, she named herself, over and over. She was a woman now, with her own life to live. To him she was probably nothing more than a dim, elusive memory, *if* he remembered her at all. Cat finally decided to stay. It was necessary to protect her ventures, she reasoned. She had to consider Will and Sean, not only herself. She had to know what changes Ryan meant to institute.

In the morning Cat bathed and donned a cool dress of damescene linen. Here, in the company of the very proper and decorous English, she was forced to follow the dictates of polite fashion and wear hot, tight-fitting gowns or risk scandalizing the tight-knit group. Such rigid adherence to custom was just another reason she would sail for St. Mary's the moment she was free. The cool, light saris she wore at home were far more suited to the climate. She was just finishing breakfast when her maid returned to say that George was waiting for her in the drawing room.

Cat was surprised. He had told her to rest and here he was. She drank the last of her tea and quickly checked her appearance in the mirror. Perhaps there'd been some new development, she thought. A wicked grin appeared on her face. Wouldn't it be a lark if Ryan's ship had been attacked by pirates! If she'd had time, she would have arranged such a fine welcome herself. She left her room, heading for the drawing room, and recognized George's rambling pattern of speech as she approached. She wondered briefly who had accompanied him on such an early visit and steeled herself to face the unexpected guests.

Cat had a moment to study the three people in her drawing room before George caught sight of her. A tall, dark-haired man was politely listening to George relate the story of his many trials and tribulations. A well-dressed blonde was seated in one of the brocade chairs, attentively listening to the discussion.

Cat felt her heart cease beating for a moment. Despite the two years that had passed, she recognized Ryan immediately. Though his back was to the door, she would have known his lean, elegantly attired figure in a crowd of a thousand similarly dressed men. George peered past him now, his facing lighting with a welcoming smile as he saw her. He excused himself to come to her side and escort her into the room.

"Catherine, dear, you seem much recovered—you

must have rested well last night! Come," he said proudly, anxious to show her off. "Come and greet our new arrivals."

Ryan turned with a polite smile. George had spent the better part of an hour boring them with the details of his strenuous efforts to control the plundering of the local pirates, and extolling the virtues of his fiancée. Ryan expected to find a dowdy widow in her forties, and his smile froze in place as he recognized Cat.

She was more beautiful than he remembered, more perfect than the visions that had haunted his bittersweet dreams long after she'd disappeared. His face whitened beneath its dark tan as she held out her hand to George, smiling with sweet devotion into the older man's eyes. It was no wonder that Pembroke had rattled on about her charms. By God, though, what was she doing here, of all places, and engaged to marry the crusty, jowled fool that was George Pembroke?

With a skill of long standing. Ryan quickly regained control of his composure, remembering that his own fiancée was seated nearby.

Alicia Crowley was the only daughter of Peter, Lord Avery. The earl was an old friend of his uncle's and when he'd reached London, Ryan had made a point of calling on him and his family. It was a pleasant surprise to find that Alicia had grown into such a delicate beauty. She'd just come out into London society; and although many had sought her hand, she'd quickly set her sights on him. A month after he'd arrived, their betrothal was announced at a lavish ball held at the Crowley's London townhouse. When Alicia discovered his plans for the trip to India and realized how long he might be gone, she'd insisted on coming along. After much coaxing on her part, and a display of tears, she managed to convince her father to relent and give his permission. Now she noted, with that instinctive second sight of fiancées, that his face had an odd cast and she rose to join him, slipping her arm possessively into the crook of his.

When George made the introductions, Cat smiled

brilliantly, though her eyes remained cool and distant. Neither George nor Alicia could have guessed that their respective partners-to-be had a shared past, especially such an intimate one. Ryan bowed over her extended hand, raising a dark brow in mockery at her presentation as the widow of Carleton Barbour, and complimented George on his good fortune. Cat's eyes glittered like icy amethysts when the clinging blonde at his side was introduced as Ryan's future bride.

Cat decided to draw Alicia to one side and interrogate her casually. She was avidly curious to know more about their relationship. She caught the girl's arm and guided her to the settee. "I'm sure you two men have business matters to discuss," she said with an innocent laugh. "I simply *must* find out the latest fashions in London! We're so isolated here, you know." Ryan was the only one to doubt her genial solicitude but he was drawn to the other side of the room for another boring recital of George's problems as councilor.

Through the heavy veil of her lashes, Cat saw Ryan glance uneasily in their direction. She smiled, pleased that he'd guessed her motives and was helpless to stop her. Intermingled with her curiosity concerning the latest fashions in Europe were tactfully proposed inquiries about Alicia's wedding gown and the forthcoming nuptials. Once started on her favorite subject, Alicia proved to be a fountain of information, overflowing with more details than Cat had originally requested. It seemed the engagement had been a whirlwind affair. If Cat had taken an instant dislike to the petite blonde on sight, she developed a fullblown hatred for the pretentiously spoiled girl when she was forced to listen to a drawn-out, nauseating account of how "dear, sweet Ryan just came along and swept me off my feet!" If Cat had known the truth, that Alicia had stalked Ryan with all the wily cunning of a cat in pursuit of its dinner, she might have been spared some of the resentment that built within her.

When the unwelcome visit ended at last, Cat had dutifully promised to call on Alicia, once she was settled in the house Ryan had rented for her and her chaperone. Ryan bowed politely, telling Cat and George that they would more than likely see a great deal of them in the coming months. "Believe me, I'll be looking forward to our meetings," he added with a sly, measured glance at Cat. She ignored the insinuation, keeping a bright smile on her face until the door had closed on them. George remained behind, eager to find out her opinion of the impression he'd made on Ryan.

Cat was unable to keep the irritation from her voice. "George, I thought you told me to rest today," she snapped. "I *was* feeling better—but to put up with guests when you know I haven't felt well—really, I don't know what you were thinking of!"

George was crushed by her display of temper. Cat had never been anything but sweet and gentle. She truly must be feeling ill, he thought guiltily. " 'Fraid I forgot in all the excitement, Catherine dear. Do forgive me! I insist you go and rest now—we'll talk later." He touched her forehead with his lips and hurried away before she grew more irritable.

If she hadn't been so upset at Ryan's arrival, Cat might have felt a touch guilty over her treatment of George. As it was, she was irked at his appearance with the two people she least wanted to see and little concerned with his feelings. She wanted only to seek the quiet and privacy of her room.

Once George was gone and she was alone in her bedroom, Cat threw herself on the bed. As much as he'd claimed he wanted her, Ryan had warned that he wasn't ready for marriage to anyone, yet he'd blithely become engaged to that simpering blonde bitch after an acquaintance of only one month! It made it only too clear what he'd thought of Cat.

Now she had one more evening of mental torture to look forward to, thanks to George. She could have kicked him when he'd suggested a small dinner party at his house to welcome them properly. The fool was attempting to curry Ryan's favor and she would be forced to play hostess for the affair. She tossed, now, flipping over onto her back as she imagined delightful tortures for Ryan and his empty-headed fiancée. After the first naked shock crossed his face, he'd seemed to recover, reflecting a cool, aloof distance for the remainder of the visit. Her pride had been thoroughly trampled in the dust when Ryan smiled at Alicia and courteously offered her his arm as they left. He'd never treated *her* so tenderly!

The following night at George's turned out to be as miserable as Cat had predicted. George was unusually attentive to Alicia for obvious reasons and Cat was forced to deal civilly with Ryan. Captain Perry, the garrison commander and his pale, pretty wife Anne had joined them and Cat managed to stay close enough to one of them that Ryan could only make polite, dry conversation. She had come to the dinner party armed with an intention not to allow him to browbeat her.

After dinner, the men retired to George's library for brandy and cigars, while the ladies stayed to gossip around the table. By then, Cat's nerves had been wound into knots, though she found that the after-dinner cordial somewhat alleviated a coming headache.

With little prompting from Anne and Cat, Alicia chattered of endless, boring details of the gay life in London and her expectations of life in America. When she mentioned that Ryan owned a lovely estate in upper New York that they would use as a summer home, Cat experienced an intense desire to rake her nails over the bitch's creamy complexion. Alicia and Ryan living in *her* home—the thought infuriated her so, she was tempted to blurt out the truth about her previous relationship with Ryan. That would serve the high-bred slut right! With a great deal of self-control, Cat restrained the urge and excused herself from the table.

In the tiny English country-style garden that lay behind the house Cat sought refuge. She strolled through the beds of columbine and pinks, noting their parched, bedraggled state and feeling a definite kinship with them. If she'd thought ahead, she would have lied and pleaded a headache and avoided this irritation.

A full moon shone above in a clear, star-studded sky. Cat stared up at the blue-velvet heavens, picking out the constellation Orion. On another clear night long ago her father had explained the myth of Orion and Diana.

Suddenly, from close behind her, came a voice as familiar to her as her own. "Star-gazing, Cat?" Ryan's hands settled on her shoulders and he slowly pulled her around to face him. "I thought I saw you come out here. What's wrong, love, aren't you and Alicia getting along well? You do have some things in common, you know." In the moonlight, his face was all sharp angles and shadows, and though his tone seemed light and teasing, his expression appeared brooding.

"We've nothing *important* in common," Cat replied spitefully, with a casual shrug of her shoulders. "Oh . . . excuse me," she added with an overdramatic, feigned apology, "you meant yourself, didn't you? I'm afraid we didn't even discuss you. She did mention something about a summer home on the Hudson, though."

Ryan's fingers tightened almost imperceptibly on the bare skin of her shoulders. She wore a pale, cream-colored evening gown trimmed in black lace that clung to her body like a second skin. In the moonlight she gave the appearance of a nude statue, a perfect sculpture in marble. He toyed absently with the lace. His voice showed no reaction to her cutting remarks when he answered. "You've grown impossibly lovely, kitten. Far more beautiful than I remember."

"Remember?" Cat's laughter was icy in the night air. "I'm surprised you remember me at all," she went on with a cool smile. "I'd almost forgotten you completely."

Ryan stepped closer and the smell of George's excellent brandy drifted to Cat. "Still an accomplished liar, my love. You haven't forgotten and neither have I. Why did you run from me that day—or was it yourself you were afraid of?"

Despite the warmth of the night, Cat's hands felt like icicles in a winter storm. She reached up to push at his hands and free herself. "You haven't changed one bit, Ryan Nicholls, except to become more presumptuous and conceited! The period of my life when you were vain enough to think you owned me is over, it's nothing but a vague, unhappy memory. If you don't mind, I don't see any reason to discuss it. And, if you persist, I'll return to the house!"

Ryan smiled, devilishly handsome in the moonlight. He, too, had spent much of a long, sleepless night dwelling on the time they'd spent together. He recalled the pain of his wounded pride and the frantic, unsuccessful search for her after he'd discovered her missing. By some odd decree of fate, they'd come together again and he had no desire to let her get away a second time. His hand rose, his fingertips tracing a path from her temple to the soft curve of her lips.

"Don't!" Cat recoiled from the yearning caress as she would from the sting of a poisonous snake. She took a step backward, her face pale and defiant in the golden glow of the full moon.

" 'Don't,' " Ryan echoed in a mocking, incredulous tone. "And what is there to stop me, pray tell?"

"I—I'll scream," Cat threatened, sure that she was on firm ground. "How would you explain that to George or that simpering, empty-headed bitch you're engaged to?"

A deep arrogant chuckle rumbled from his throat. "George! Do you think I give a damn what that old goat thinks? Considering I was sent to save the old fool's neck, I doubt he'd object. As for Alicia——" His mouth curled in a sardonic smile. "Alicia is a very realistic young woman. She decided she wanted me and has gotten her way. She'll do nothing to risk my anger—at least until the vows have been said."

He was menacing once more, a reincarnation of the old Ryan. "So you see, there's nothing to keep me from reaching out"—he did so as he spoke—"and taking you into my arms to reassure myself I'm not dreaming." His mouth descended on hers, stifling her quick exclamation of protest. With that first contact, they were swept back in time.

Cat struggled vainly as the key that only Ryan held twisted in the lock of her buried emotions, releasing feelings that she'd denied for nearly two years. She battled within herself, hating him enough to kill, wanting him enough to die for. Still, she struggled, attempting to break free before it was too late. It wasn't supposed to happen like this, she thought as a tingle of desire washed over her. She had triumphed over her weakness for him, defeated the strange power he held over her, and now with the touch of his hands on her body, of his lips against hers, she again became slave to his mastery. His long, nimble fingers ran freely across her skin, tangling in her hair, sweeping across her breasts. They tugged at the low-cut, lace-trimmed bodice until his hands caressed her naked breasts.

Ryan's arm encircled Cat's narrow waist, pressing her against him until they blended into one shape in the shadows of the garden. His head bent, lips playing across the satiny skin of her breasts, and Cat moaned in feeble protest, as much a victim of her own passion as his compelling need to possess her again. Realizing the danger of her position, she made a valiant effort to break free, straining to redeem the shattered remnants of her pride and dignity. Suddenly she was free. Ryan too had realized that the time and place was wrong and had checked the wild surge of desire that had made him want to take her here, to throw her down among the garden flowers and end the longing of two years.

Cat turned away to straighten her disheveled clothing. Her cheeks burned with shame and tears threatened to fall at any second. With the realization that she was still enslaved by the undeniable attraction between them, despondency settled over her like a black, suffocating cloak. She would never be free of him and never happy with what he had to offer her. Because she loved him, she would not accept a position as his mistress, could not put herself in the position of being the woman he kept for his enjoyment while he shared his name with Alicia. She was growing more confused by the minute. She didn't love Sean and yet she'd so easily slipped into becoming his mistress.

"I knew it—your body never lies, Cat." Ryan stared down at her, disconcerted by the soft, resentful pout and stubbornly lowered gaze. In a tone of command he told her he would call on her the next day, that they would take up where they'd left off.

Thick, heavy lashes swept back, revealing wide, dark violet eyes that snapped with defiance. Before she could open her mouth to refuse, Ryan interceded. "I wouldn't consider disobeying, love. Should I find you uncooperative, I wouldn't hesitate to inform poor George about our past. You know me well enough to realize I'd do it."

It was true. Ryan was ruthless and would do as he threatened. He hadn't changed in that respect. She bit back a curse that tempted her tongue and sullenly agreed, allowing him the liberty of one last kiss before she caught her skirts to one side and swept past him to hurry along the garden path to the safety of the house.

In the morning, Ryan prepared for his rendezvous with mixed anticipation and remorse. He'd allowed the dormant wound of his pride to break open and had handled her wrongly. Her beauty, her defiance, and her own fierce pride aroused an arrogance in him when he'd meant to have her by tenderness and gentle words. He decided to apologize when he arrived at the house.

He left early for the appointment, arriving almost a half-hour before he'd promised. The house had a closed, shuttered look. When no one answered his repeated knocking, he cursed and stalked away from the house to make his way to the commander's quarters. Upon his arrival, Anne Perry gently informed him that Cat had been taken ill and had sailed for Madagascar on the morning tide. Ryan called on a deep wellspring of willpower to control his fury and politely thanked the woman for her trouble.

Once again the girl had danced away, just when she'd been so tantalizingly within reach. It was enough to drive him mad! That night he drank himself to sleep, trying to forget the fickle bitch who teased a fire in his loins then flitted away, leaving the fire to consume and lick at the walls of his heart. Past midnight he staggered to bed, roundly cursing all women for faithless whores.

Two endlessly boring months followed Cat's flight homeward. Ryan's temper grew touchy and the slightest aggravation sent him into a fury. He threw himself into his work, hiring men to spy at the local ports and report anyone who inquired about Company shipments. When nothing of importance came to his attention, he left a disgruntled Alicia in Anne Perry's care and spent a month touring the countryside, visiting various Hindu and Moslem principalities. Every ruler had the same complaint—his shipping was being preyed upon by pirates. All of them seemed to blame the English for attracting the marauders to the area. Some talked of arming their vessels more heavily in the future.

Despite the official nature of his visits, Ryan was able to enjoy a few weeks of hunting in the Hindustan. He had quickly become friends with a young Maratha prince named Rajir Singh. The dark, slender heir to the throne of Kohlapur had taken to him immediately, perhaps recognizing a fellow sensualist.

The time Ryan spent in Kohlapur was relaxing and enjoyable. There were tiger hunts, festivals, revels by night with a few of Rajir's generously offered concubines, and every conceivable type of entertainment to dazzle the American guest.

Rajir was very proud of the cheetahs his father had imported from Africa. He took Ryan on several hunts to show him the skill of the sleek, spotted hunters. The animals were hooded like falcons, wearing coats of bright crimson velvet. Carried to the hunting site on bullock carts, they were released when a herd of black buck were sighted. The hoods were whipped off, and the deadly killers released to bound from the carts toward their prey. Moments later a buck would startle and separate from the herd, scenting the danger and desperately attempting to escape. Inevitably he was brought down, held by the throat until the cheetah's keepers arrived. The well-trained cat would retire a few feet, awaiting the wooden spoonful of warm blood that was his reward, returning quietly to the cart, his black lips still wet with crimson blood.

Ryan enjoyed Rajir's hospitality for a fortnight, though his friend urged him to stay indefinitely. He wanted to return and check on his progress with the pirates, and promised Rajir that he would come again as soon as possible. With regret Rajir saw his friend safely to the borders of Kohlapur.

Chapter Twelve

A dusky rose blush suffused Cat's clear, ivory complexion. The warmth that always enveloped her when Sean had teased her to fulfillment left her skin glowing and her senses atingle. She stretched contentedly, burrowing against the hard, tanned length of his body. Sean lay back, a pillow propped beneath his head, a cocky, smug grin stretching his lips across strong, white teeth.

"I must congratulate m'self, Cathy darlin'! You've the rosy glow of a very satisfied wench."

Cat blushed at the comment, a half-smile touching her mouth. "Your conceit outweighs your talents," she teased in return. She *did* feel decidedly wanton on this lazy, cool afternoon. It had taken her a while to relax and conquer her apprehension following her meeting with Ryan.

Sean had just returned from another successful foray, capturing a Mogul galleon bound on a pilgrimage to Mecca. The ship had been a storehouse of jewels and gold and also carried several of the Mogul's concubines. Upon transfer of the treasure to the *Spirit,* Sean had allowed the ship to proceed on her holy voyage. Cat and Sean had just spent an hour playing with Paddy, allowing the toddler to run and frolic until Sean had grinned at Cat over his son's head and wryly suggested they retire to her room for play of a different sort.

Sean rose up now, sitting cross-legged and reaching for one of the long, thin cigars he smoked. He lit it, glancing down through the haze of blue-gray smoke at the girl who stretched languidly by his side. Cat was a sensual vision, at ease amidst the tangled covers, her wild copper hair spread across the pillow like a sheer veil. He'd done a great deal of meditating on this last voyage. His feelings for Cat had deepened within the past year. The idea of life without her seemed meaningless and empty.

It was more than just a feeling of lust that bound him to her, for others had satisfied the urgings of his loins. It was her keen, sharp wit and free, untamed spirit that held his interest so. Cat and he were kindred spirits, members of a breed who were meant to be as free as the wind.

Drawing a deep breath, he asked the question that had been plaguing him ever since his return to the island. "Cat, what would ye think a' marryin'?" He blew a ring of smoke into the air, casually watching with an air of tranquil contemplation as it disintegrated while his heart raced oddly within his chest. He read Cat's reaction in her shocked expression; and before she could reply negatively, he hurried to explain his thoughts. "It's not a bad idea, girl. We like the same things; I raise your spirits and keep a merry smile on them sweet lips!" He reached out to touch her shoulder, his fingers sliding lightly across her breasts in a longing caress. "We come together like lightnin' n' thunder, love," he added with a sleepy-eyed grin.

Cat was stunned by the sudden unexpected offer. Sean had never indicated that he entertained such serious ideas, and had seemed perfectly happy with their arrangement. Now, as she considered the proposal, she found herself balking, rebelling at the thought of being tied permanently to one man, subject to him by solemn vows. It was true—they got along famously, with hardly ever a quarrel to disturb their close friendship. She suddenly became aware that she considered him a friend but her feelings didn't extend deeply enough to include love. Marriage was a frightening proposition; she had wanted it only once in her life—with Ryan. Now, even if it meant an end to their casual, relaxed relationship, she couldn't bring herself to agree to Sean's proposal.

Cat reached for her silk wrapper and slowly drew it on, her expression troubled and pensive. Finally, when she'd decided that honesty would be the best method of handling Sean's feelings, she replied in a gentle voice, "In my own way I care for you, for the devil-may-care rogue who swaggers into my bed from time to time, for the rascal who commands the *Spirit* so well; but I'm not ready to wed anyone." She leaned closer, her eyes wide in an effort to communicate what she felt. "Not anyone," she emphasized.

Sean reacted with more emotion than he had wanted to show. For the first time since they'd become lovers, his temper flared as jealousy clutched at his heart. "If it was that bloke you're always moonin' o'er, you'd a' already jumped up t'find a priest," he snapped. He glared at her, resenting his unknown rival. She'd come back from India all in a fluster a couple of months back, and he'd managed to wheedle the admission out of her that her old love had appeared out of the blue to upset her. He'd managed to glean from the few thoughts she'd shared that the man was as selfish as they come, and the thought of marrying Cat had never entered his head. Just as quickly as his anger had flared, it died. He couldn't stay angry at her for long when she gazed at him with such a soft, wounded expression. He smiled and held out his arms and as she cuddled against him, the tension seemed to drain away.

"Well, nothin' ventured . . ." he quipped in a light, bantering tone. The cigar drooped casually from a corner of his mouth, and his easy manner hid a sharp pang of disappointment that twisted in his belly. "You'll tell me if y'feel a change a heart, lass?"

"Of course I——" Cat's relieved reply was cut off by a sharp rap at the door. As she turned to stare, wondering who would dare to interrupt them, Ryan burst into the room.

The smile died on Ryan's face as he saw Cat lying close to Sean's chest, her loosely tied wrapper revealing a tempting display of ivory breast. Her face reflected his own shock and growing fury. The past few weeks the thought of her had become an obsession. Cat's face seemed to float before him by day, he dreamed of holding her in his arms by night until he finally came to a decision.

Irritable and peevish, he had instigated an argument with Alicia, pushing her to the point of calling off the engagement and heading home to London to weep on her father's shoulder. The day after she left, Ryan had taken passage on a schooner bound for Madagascar, determined to vanquish the devil pride in both of them that had kept them apart for so long. He meant to persuade her to break off with George; the old fool was as wrong for her as Alicia had been for him. He'd be gentle this time, wooing her with words instead of arrogant embraces.

Now all his good intentions fled. Ryan forgot that he'd lost her long ago, that he'd intruded on her privacy, as a righteous blaze of red-hot fury consumed him. He bowed low in a mocking gesture. "My pardons, Cat. Had I known you were busy cuckolding poor George, I'd have picked a more opportune time to call. Pray, continue your pleasures, I'll not disturb you and your lover a moment longer!" He scowled blackly at Sean as though he wished to slice his throat.

Sean knew at once that the intruder was none other than Ryan Nicholls. He grinned, considerably amused that the selfish bastard had been dealt the shock of finding Cat in bed with another. It might open the devil's eyes a bit! The amusement infuriated Ryan further and he took a step forward with a low growl.

Cat quickly recovered from her initial shock, her own temper rising on the crest of a storm of indignation. She bounced to her knees and jumped up, careening around the end of the bed to face Ryan. She was furious and embarrassed. She too had noted Sean's impudent expression, and it only added fuel to her fiery temper.

"You've no right being here," she shouted angrily. "I'll not stand for you barging in, acting as though you owned this house and me along with it!" She crossed her arms beneath her breasts. "And I might add, 'poor George' has no need of your defense—you weren't so concerned with his feelings when *you* were after me!" She and Ryan glowered across the length of the room. "If you were vile enough to tell him, he'd not believe you anyway." She pointed to the door and ordered, "Get out!"

The two men stared, both awed by the tangle-haired, wild-eyed virago. When Ryan insolently refused to budge, Cat squealed in outrage and whirled to enlist Sean's aid.

"Do something, Rafferty," she demanded. "Don't just sit there like a great, grinning ape—make him leave, *now!*"

Sean sealed his own fate by laughing in genuine amusement. "I'm hardly in the position to fight a duel, m'love." He glanced significantly at his nude body, only his lap covered by the bedsheets. "I think our uninvited guest will leave soon enough—unless he'd care to stay and witness our lovemaking!" His blue eyes crinkled merrily with continued good humor.

"Your current lover has more sense than you do, madam. I'd be more than happy to take my leave!" Ryan's eyes were blacker and more coldly menacing than she had ever seen them, but Cat refused to back down, continuing to glare defiantly until he wheeled and stalked from the room, slamming the door behind him.

Once Ryan was gone, Cat turned the full force of her considerable fury on Sean. "You can get out, too," she screamed, infuriated by the fact that he'd done nothing to help her and had in fact treated the entire incident as a joke. Irate tears cascaded down her cheeks and her voice shook as she added, "Go—and don't bother coming back!"

Sean shook his head in resignation, climbing from the bed to find his clothes and dress. Cat threw herself on the bed, sobbing into her pillow as she gave vent to her temper. Finally the door closed a second time, though a great deal more quietly than in Ryan's furious exit, and Cat was left alone with her fury.

Men, she thought savagely. They were all alike—peremptory, vain, and selfish creatures who thought only of their own pleasures. The gall of Ryan, blustering into her home as though she were a possession he'd temporarily misplaced! He acted as though he'd caught her cheating on him! And Sean, that devil's imp—should she ever need to rely on him for assistance, he'd be as much help as a limp rag. Thank God she'd had the sense to refuse his proposal!

When Ryan slammed from the house, he had mounted his horse and whipped the animal to a gallop, racing down the rough trail that led to Shelley's Landing. He had come expecting to stay indefinitely and the ship he'd arrived on had already taken on stores and sailed for Madagascar. He swore an oath as he realized he'd have to take a room at the noisy waterfront tavern that served as an inn.

Several ill-kempt ruffians lounged at the door of *The Merry Widow,* blocking the doorway. They moved only after Ryan fixed them with such a murderous glare that they skulked off down the wharf. Inside, the taproom was dark and crowded with a variety of rogues and low-life renegades in various stages of intoxication. A buxom, black-haired serving wench spied him immediately and impatiently brushed away the pawing hands of a dark, bearded blackguard, to hurry over to him. Above the noise of drunken chanting and slurred calls for more rum, she smiled suggestively and sidled close, her heavy, pendulous breasts threatening to overflow a daringly low-cut blouse.

The girl's eyes glowed with lusty appreciation of Ryan's clean, strikingly attractive figure. She was used to the loud, rum-swilling seadogs who made the tavern their headquarters between voyages. "La, sir—we don't get no swells in 'ere," she exclaimed, leading him away to a corner table before the other serving girl could get her hands on him. "Come away, 'fore them dirty drunkards rub against them fancy duds."

Ryan threw himself in a seat, his ears deaf to the brazen appeal in the girl's low, throaty voice. He was in no mood to wench, for his mind still reeled from the shock of discovering Cat in bed with her lover. The bitch, he thought miserably. From the first, he hadn't been able to understand what attraction George held for her. Why tie herself to a man old enough to be her father? He snapped an order and dismissed the girl, hardly noticing her sullen pout before returning to his brooding thoughts.

Cat's last name now was Barbour. What was it George had told him—that she'd been left a wealthy widow? Another mysterious lie, but why? Apparently the girl he'd known in the Colonies had changed drastically, had become jaded enough to betroth herself to one man and play him the fool with another. Rafferty, that was what she'd called that impudent blond rascal. At least he was young enough for her; for what reason did she need George? He turned the thought over and over in his mind.

There were so many unanswered questions. She certainly had income, but from where? The answers seemed to be just out of reach, floating tantalizingly at the edge of his mind. Suddenly he remembered her ship, a brigantine called the *Black Falcon*, and everything clicked, coming together like the pieces of a puzzle. There were only a few elusive pieces missing. When the barmaid returned, his manner had changed. He smiled, his gaze sweeping appreciatively over her voluptuous figure as he asked her to join him. She cooed with delight, quickly sliding next to him. She posed artfully, her large, plump breasts appearing like an offering of two ripe melons.

"Cor', but y' scared me afore, sir! A great ol' glower ye did gi' me." She smiled coyly, arching her head to one side to gaze at him with bold, appraising eyes. Her hand slipped to his knee as she leaned against him, her fingers slyly insinuating their way up his thigh. When Ryan asked her name, she told him it was Mary. "Jus' like the virgin saint," she giggled with a sly wink. "Used t'be one meself!"

"And which might that be, sweetheart," Ryan laughed sardonically, "a virgin or saint?" A moment later she joined in his laughter and then accepted his offer to share the brandy. She tossed a glassful down her throat without a blink and held the glass out for a refill. Ryan obliged, sliding an arm around her shoulders. She grinned up at him and wiggled suggestively against his chest. "You seem a bright flower in these drab surroundings, Mary. I vow you'd know more than anyone here about who comes and goes. Tell me, sweet, have you ever chanced to hear of a brig called the *Black Falcon?"*

"Course I 'ave—'asn't everyun'? Ye must a' come from a far place, sir. The *Falcon*'s men get rum-soaked 'ere whene'er they be in port." She nuzzled his throat with her cheek, more interested in his hard, lean body than his inquiries. "They don't anchor 'er in the 'arbor, though. Seems t'me there's a cove o'er near Kidd's ol' place—the one owned by tha' red'eaded Barbour woman."

Ryan absently touched his lips to her forehead, vaguely noting the overly sweet fragrance that clung to her. Her hands became bolder, as his mind raced to consider the implications of what she'd unwittingly revealed. Cat was wealthy, Cat still had the *Falcon,* and Cat was engaged to a man whose position could be very helpful to someone engaged in piracy.

When he returned to the Fort, he had to find out about George Pembroke's private trade. If none of his ships had been attacked, he'd know for sure Cat was involved. He doubted if the blustering idiot was even aware that Cat used him. Though she was a bitch, he didn't want to see her caught and tried for piracy, merely stopped.

Mary's breath was warm against his ear as she whispered a lewd suggestion and giggled. Her hands were in his lap, fondling him with an eagerness that elicited a twinge of desire within him. The short, plump vixen was hardly a substitute for Cat, but she'd been helpful and could be useful in the future. Across the room three men had begun a fight over the other serving girl, and Mary took advantage of the moment to grab Ryan's hand and lead him through the taproom and up a short flight of stairs.

The room she led him to was hardly more than a cubbyhole, furnished only with a table, washbowl, and a narrow, lumpy bed. Even by the dim light of one candle, the bed linen appeared used and rumpled. Ryan told her to go below and fetch clean linens and another bottle.

When she returned, she changed the bedding in a wink, quickly stripping her clothes away to reveal her plump white body. In a few years, Mary would run to fat but now her pale, still-firm flesh was soft to sink into. The liquor was having a warming effect on Ryan and he lay back, allowing the girl to pull off his clothes and attend him.

Mary couldn't have been more than sixteen, but with her experience at the inn, she was more adept and experienced than many older whores he'd had. Her knowing hands quickly brought a response from him and she threw herself into the play with a gusto that surprised and pleased him. Massaging and stroking him until his fury with Cat receded from his conscious mind, she giggled incessantly until he rolled her over and penetrated her pliant softness. The liquor had its desired effect, transforming Mary's vaguely pretty features into a bewitching image of Cat. He closed his eyes, taking his enjoyment on the tavern wench and fantasizing that it was Cat who twisted with such willing abandon beneath him.

When they'd finished, the girl lay exhausted and sated at his side. He urged more drink on her, waiting until the strong brandy loosened her tongue. By the time he'd finished questioning her, Ryan knew as much as the barmaid about "the Barbour woman and 'er lover, Rafferty."

In the morning Ryan took his leave of a petulant, slightly hungover Mary, promising her that he'd look her up if he chanced to return. She never inquired what business he'd been about, hardly remembered the questions he'd skillfully put to her, and bade him a regretful farewell, pocketing the gold coins he left with her.

Cat rose early that same morning, surprised that Sean was missing. In her anger she'd ordered him out but really hadn't thought he would go. Still, she was angry enough to feel she was justified. It would do him good to stay away for a while. He'd most likely taken himself off to the forest and the Moriandrias.

Cat's temper seldom reached the breaking point these days, but when it did, it lasted long enough for all in her way to take shelter until it passed. Even poor Will suffered the brunt of her disfavor. She went to his room to question him about the *Falcon*'s next trip. Still preoccupied, she knocked lightly and entered without thinking, only to discover Will laboring atop their native cook, Dali. The woman's sarong was shoved up above her waist and she displayed no shame, merely hiding her head and giggling. Cat's mouth formed a round O of shock. Will paused only a moment before continuing, stating in a calm, offhand manner, "If it's not tha' important, lass, I'll catch ye in an hour or so!"

Cat had withdrawn, appalled at having blundered in on such an intimate scene. Strangely, she felt abandoned, almost as though her best friend had deserted her. Later she realized she'd been unfair to expect Will to lead a celibate's life. After all, he was a man, with a man's needs. She'd just never thought of him that way, perhaps because he'd been discreet enough to keep it hidden from her. It had been like walking in on her father and finding him making love to a strange woman. She forgave Will because there was nothing for her to forgive.

Still, when Will found her later as he'd promised,

there was a distance between them that hadn't existed before. Cat was embarrassed, though Will seemed to have dismissed the episode with a shrug of his huge shoulders. A naïve part of her had been shocked awake and though she really didn't wish to, Cat subconsciously lumped him together in a wide, encompassing category of *men,* those irritating but necessary creatures set upon the earth to plague women.

Sean was missing for some time following the incident with Ryan. No one seemed sure where he'd gone, though Rovani went about with a smug, contented look instead of her usually dour expression.

According to the last information that George had unwittingly revealed, a large shipment of gold bullion was due at Fort St. David in August, probably about the middle of the month. With the gold seized, the Company would be in the embarrassing position of being unable to pay for its exports. There would be havoc at the warehouse, along with a panic in London when the Council of Directors were assailed by irate stockholders. This particular foray was to be Cat's personal vengeance for Ryan's high-handed, blundering interference in her life. He'd been sent to deal with or control the pirates and so far, to her knowledge, he'd met with very little success.

George had mentioned that a few independent marauders had been trapped and sent to England for trial, but that had no effect on her operations. She knew the men for fools, eager for riches but too stupid to take precautions. While Sean was absent, she planned to take the *Spirit* out, with Will to help her. It had been a while since she'd commanded her own ship and a keen excitement seized her at the thought of striking a direct blow at Ryan's pride.

On the morning of August fourteenth, Cat stood at the helm of the *Spirit*. None of her crew suspected her identity, for she'd taken great pains to disguise herself. The root of a forest plant stained her fair skin a dark, swarthy color. Her bright mass of curls was hidden beneath a dazzling white turban. A white silk shirt, several sizes too large, and a long, red brocade waistcoat covered the all too obvious curves of her breasts and hips. Comfortable, soft leather breeches tucked into knee-high boots completed the outfit. A scarlet sash crossed her breast, a wicked brace of pistols tucked carefully within. The silver scabbard of her rapier hung on a narrow leather belt at her waist.

Though she'd inspected the frigate after her capture, Cat had never sailed aboard her. The voyage had been smooth as silk thus far. Considerably longer and heavier than the *Falcon,* the *Spirit* was better equipped for fighting. Her gun decks were located high above the waterline, and the main decks had been cleared of nonessentials to allow for hand-to-hand combat. Instead of a sterncastle, the frigate sported a quarter gallery, a small, enclosed cabin area in her stern. Though not as swift as the brigantine, she could stand and face the fire of the largest ships the Company could arm. Her thirty guns, located on two decks, could cripple a lesser target that failed to heed the call to surrender.

In most cases, the only need was for a warning salvo fired across the quarry's bow. Should that fail to stop the ship, a second salvo was aimed at the mainmast sails. The men who sailed for the Company were anything but foolish. To give up one's life protecting the ship's cargo was foolhardy, to say the least.

Cat paced the deck with anxious strides, pausing now and then to lean over the taffrail and sight the horizon with her glass, double-checking to make sure the lookout hadn't missed the expected merchantman. She might be a frigate, but was more likely a bark, well armed with a full complement of seasoned crewmen aboard. Cat had full confidence in her crew. They'd all been handpicked by Sean. Some of them were a bit rough around the edges but she could trust in Will's burly, imposing strength to keep them in line.

The day was hot and cloudy, with a following sea helping the ship to make headway. The sails were drawn full, speeding the frigate along at a fast clip. The Dutch colony of Ceylon was thirty leagues to the southwest and soon they should cross the merchantman's course.

Suddenly sails were sighted. The lookout's cry echoed among the crew and all scurried about in last-minute preparations for action. The Company ship *was* a bark, and she appeared to have seen the threat the *Spirit* posed and responded by unfurling full sails in an attempt to outrun the pirate vessel.

Will swung the wheel hard to port, gaining on their prey until the *Spirit* was within hailing distance. He turned the wheel over to his second in command and joined Cat at the rail, winking before he cupped his hands to shout an order to surrender. His big, booming voice carried well across the water. "Company don't make no allowance for widows an' little 'uns," he claimed, adding a heavy threat to the challenge. No answer came back across the blue-green chop of the waves. Will gave them a second chance, repeating his command to surrender or face a volley of fire. Still there was silence, broken only by the call of seabirds wheeling overhead. Will turned to Cat, shaking his head. "Don't like it—them fools got a reason for stallin'!"

Suddenly all hell broke loose. A rain of gun fire assaulted the frigate's crew and everyone dived for cover. The bark had men stationed in the shrouds, sharpshooters armed with muskets. From high in the topmast, the lookout shouted that he'd sighted two more ships heading toward the *Spirit*. "Frigates they be," he yelled. A moment later he gave a bloodcurdling scream as a musket ball tore into his chest and he fell, his body tumbling over and over until it smashed to the deck. The man at the helm was hit and fell across the wheel. Will was busy shouting orders for defense and Cat scrambled along the deck to reach the helm.

They had to get out before the two Company escorts closed on them. Attacking the bark had been child's play but the *Spirit* would be powerless if caught between its fire and the cannon of the two approaching frigates. It meant only one thing—they'd be forced to surrender and face deportation to England and the gallows. With a strength fueled by desperation, Cat seized the huge wheel and strained to pull it hard to port. Their only chance was a swift retreat. Will already had the crew returning fire, keeping the enemy at bay while they made their escape. The escorts gained steadily.

Cat strained at the wheel with all of her strength, calling for Will. He turned and ran toward her, reaching her side just as a ball from one of the more skilled pistol shots grazed her left shoulder. The pain was blinding and only her tight grasp on the huge wheel kept her on her feet. Will cursed at the sight of blood staining her arm, easing her down to the deck and calling for the medical officer. Doc Wiley hurried over from the side of a fallen crewman. He was the doctor who knew Cat's secret, the man who had cared for her on the voyage from America. He helped her to her feet, assisting her down the companionway to the quarter gallery.

Once the door was shut and she'd collapsed in the small alcove bunk, Cat was able to give in to the tears she'd restrained above deck. There was a roar of cannonfire and the *Spirit* shuddered with a hit on her bow. Cat tried to rise, worrying over Will, but Doc insisted she lie back. "You're in no shape t'go walkin' about," he warned. Cat was forced to agree as a wave of weakness washed over her.

Wiley's skilled fingers cut away the blood-soaked silk, exposing the torn white flesh of her upper shoulder. The ball had gone deeply, leaving a two-inch furrow that pulsed with seeping blood. He warned her to grit her teeth as he used a metal probe to check the extent of damage. It was, as he thought, a flesh wound, but a vein had been nicked. He had to stop the bleeding or she'd rapidly weaken. With quick efficiency, he bound the arm with a strip of torn silk, urging her to lie back and rest.

The old man hurried about with youthful strides, fetching a small brazier filled with coals. Within minutes he had a blazing fire going. When it died out, the coals glowed red-hot and he placed a short metal poker amongst them to heat. He pulled a short twist of leather from his bag of supplies, explaining to Cat what he had to do. She was to bite down hard on the leather, concentrating on it while he seared the wound closed. Cat's face was pale beneath the tan-colored stain, but she nodded and urged him to hurry.

Wiley tested the poker several times before he was satisfied. His expression was sympathetic as he bent and patted her hand. "It'll only be a second, lass. I've kept your secret these two years—if y'can refrain from screamin' it'll remain a secret."

Cat closed her eyes against the sight of the white-hot poker, her teeth clamped on the leather bit until they ached. She tensed against the pain, bit down harder as the too sweet odor of burning flesh, her flesh, filled the air and the poker sizzled against her torn flesh with a sickening sound. He only held it there long enough to sear the wound and keep it from becoming infected, but to Cat it was an endless, excruciating eternity. Her body jerked with unbearable pain, her tightly closed eyes blinded by an explosion of stars. She fainted then, and the doctor's gentle fingers bound the wound with strips of clean linen.

Doc Wiley stayed close by, keeping an eye on Cat's pulse and heartbeat. She'd lost a great deal of blood. An inch closer and the ball would have smashed into bone. There was still noise and confusion on the main deck and the ship groaned, speeding along. He could only guess that they were making a safe retreat. For the girl's sake, for all their sakes, he hoped so. Even now he could imagine the rough feel of a hempen rope about his neck.

Chapter Thirteen

Cat lay abed for days after her return. The voyage had ended in a narrow escape from capture. She was weak as a kitten, her shoulder sore and tightly bandaged. She'd lost a great deal of blood before Doc Wiley had been able to stem the bleeding. Will had carried her off the *Spirit,* grumbling about her reckless nature. She'd been forced to listen to the tirade until he had her safely back at the house.

A week later Cat insisted on getting up. Will fussed, warning her she'd never be able to use the arm if she didn't allow it to heal properly. She'd shrugged off the exaggeration, aware that forced bedrest would do her spirits more harm. The first day she puttered about the garden for several hours, returning to her room when her strength began to flag. Each succeeding day she was up and about for longer periods, until at last she could stay on her feet for as long as she wished without tiring.

Finally, when the wound was no more than a nuisance, a dull ache that twinged occasionally, she considered herself recovered. She visited the nursery that day, stricken by guilt for her neglect of the little boy Sean had entrusted to her care. During her recovery, Rovani had spent more and more time with the child, keeping him busy and occupied with play. When Cat appeared at the door, Paddy saw her immediately. Pulling himself impatiently from Rovani's arms, he toddled over to Cat as fast as his wobbly legs could carry him. She hugged him close, unable to lift and swing him about as she had in the past.

Still holding the boy, who chattered baby talk into her ear, Cat glanced up to find Rovani glaring resentfully once more. Puzzled and angry, Cat snapped at her, wanting to know the reason for her dislike. The girl's dark oval face took on a shuttered, sullen expression and she shook her head, indicating she was unable to understand.

With Paddy tugging at her hand, Cat dismissed Rovani, making a mental note to question Sean when he returned about this petulant resentment in the servant girl. With a sudden desire to escape the house, Cat decided to take Paddy down to the waterfront. It would give her a change of scenery, allow her to check on the warehouse, and provide a pleasant excursion for the child.

When he heard of it, Will insisted on coming along. "Them roughs at Shelley's Landin' don't know ye for a fellow pirateer, girl—even your own men don't. They sees a pretty woman alone, no tellin' what might happen!" The two argued back and forth, each stubbornly insisting he was right. In the middle of the brief argument, Cat happened to glance out the terrace door of the drawing room, to see Sean merrily rambling toward the house from the direction of the forest. She pointed him out to Will.

"You see, I'll have my escort. Sean's back! I have a great deal to discuss with him anyway, so *he* can accompany us to the wharves."

Will was still a touch disgruntled but as long as she had protection, that was what mattered. The girl took too many damn risks as it was. He shuddered to think what would have happened if the stray ball had hit a vital part of her body. Following a grunt of approval, he grudgingly added a comment that she was too damn stubborn for her own good.

"You never told Dev that," Cat pouted.

"Oh, he was a stubborn 'un, too," he admitted. "But 'e was a man, sweetheart, able to wriggle out a' trouble if need be!"

Cat raised herself on tiptoe, planting a kiss on his cheek and tugging at his sideburns. "I can too! Now be off with you, I must catch Sean." She smiled reassuringly and turned to hurry to the terrace and hail the returning prodigal.

Minutes later, Sean stood on the terrace, grinning his familiar, crooked smile as though he'd been absent for an afternoon instead of a fortnight without word. "What's new, love?" he asked, reaching out to pull her against his bare chest. He wore only breeches and was tanned several shades darker by the tropical sun. It took him several seconds to realize that Cat lay stiffly in his arms, that there was resentment smoldering in the violet eyes that stared up at him. "I thought after you'd had time to consider, I'd be welcomed back wi' open arms, lass. Ye can't still be mad at me!" His head lowered, his lips touching hers in a yearning kiss. Still there was no reaction and he raised his head to reveal a puzzled frown. "Still in a fuss, are ye?"

"Where were you for so long?" Cat demanded. "*I* had to take the *Spirit* out when you disappeared. For all you cared, I could be dead now!" She pulled away, wincing as his arm bumped her shoulder, glaring up at him. "I'll carry a scar now because you deserted me!"

Sean's expression was half-concern, half-irritation. She appeared well enough, though she'd hinted at a wound. Cat Devlan was pure woman, through and through, as exasperating as she was beautiful. He smiled charmingly, drawing her gently into his arms again. "Ah, but it's a wicked wench ye are, blamin' poor old Sean for all your troubles! I'd not a' been gone, if ye hadn't tossed me out on my ear. All's well though, I'm here t'set your mind at ease!"

Cat slowly lost her irritation. It seemed he could always charm her out of a sulk. "Right now you can ease my mind by getting dressed. I was just about to take your son out for the afternoon. You, my devil-may-care wanderer, are requisitioned to act as our protector!"

"Not wi'out a kiss—a proper one, mind you! Otherways I ain't goin' nowhere." He raised a blond brow in a droll challenge that drew her laughter. She nestled close, lifting her face and he kissed the bright smile she gave him. The kiss was a hungering caress that begged for deeper involvement. After a few breathless moments, Cat pulled away.

"No, you don't, you rascal!" A blush tinted her cheeks a dusky rose as she raised a trembling hand to secure a curl that had tumbled to her shoulders. "One kiss you asked for. It's been so long since Paddy's seen you, he'll forget who his father is!" Her sparkling eyes promised to resume their reunion later.

"All right, darlin', you ever know the way to twist a man's heartstrings! I'll go change. Get the lad and meet me out front." She smiled contentedly as his strong, gentle hands turned her toward the door, sending her on her way with a playful pat on her derriere.

The three made a charming picture, strolling down the wharf at Shelley's Landing. The man, darkly tanned and handsome in his rakish, blond way; the child, held high in his father's arms, a darker version of his sire; and the woman, her bright, copper-gold curls covered by a white straw hat, her willowy figure in sea-green watered silk that seemed to float with every graceful motion. Cat's hand was tucked within Sean's as they walked, their heads bent close together in mutual enjoyment of Paddy's mischevious squirmings.

So involved were they with the pleasant, cool afternoon and the bright chatter of the child that neither Cat nor Sean took notice of the solitary figure who lounged against one of the pilings, a wide-brimmed hat slouched down over his face, his rough, worn clothing indistinguishable from that of any other seafarer who frequented the port. The man raised his head after they passed, coal-black eyes glacial with sullen, wounded resentment. He tensed, a muscle ticking furiously in his jaw as a joyful peal of feminine laughter drifted back to him, then he rose with an abrupt, angry jerk to stalk down the wharf toward the waterfront tavern. He glanced back once, when he'd reached the entrance to the taproom, swearing an oath as he witnessed the close, intimate look that passed between Cat and Rafferty as he handed the youngster to her and held open the door to one of the warehouses.

Inside The Merry Widow, it seemed that the same noisy crowd littered the room, unchanged since Ryan's last visit. He swept off his hat, heading across the room to one of the more secluded tables. He slammed his tall, muscular body onto the bench, calling for a bottle of wine. Almost instantly, Mary appeared before him, smiling breathlessly before she threw her arms around his neck and cast her plump, voluptuous body onto his lap.

"You came back, lovey," she cried, burrowing against his chest, her fingers twining in the black curls at the nape of his neck.

Ryan was in no mood for Mary's overzealous affections. He pulled her clinging hands away, roughly settling her on the seat next to himself. "I called for a bottle, girl. Unless I'm mistaken, you're here to serve," he growled rudely, his scowl deepening at the hurt pout that settled over her ripe, red lips. The expression annoyed him, for there was only one woman he knew of who could wear it without seeming like a spoiled child. Cat. Cat, the enchantress, Cat, the passionate bitch—Cat, the mistress of that devil, Rafferty and the mother of his bastard.

"Are you deaf, girl? Move," he roared. Mary rose quickly, stunned at the change in him, running off to do his bidding before the tears that threatened could course down her cheeks.

Ryan cursed silently to himself. There was no need

to take out his anger on a poor girl whose only fault was her free and easy attitude toward men. His fingers curled tightly, itching to twine around Cat's slender, white throat, to squeeze until the last breath was gone from her beautiful, wanton body. This was the woman to whom he would have offered his name, the woman who had bewitched him so much that he'd imagined her bearing his children, the woman who had run from him and yet so quickly offered herself to another. She must have taken up with the scoundrel immediately, for the child appeared to be almost two years old. Jealousy snaked around his heart and coiled like a venomous snake.

When Mary returned, she placed the wine hesitantly on the table, intimidated by the black, dour cast of his face. She timidly reached out to touch his arm, fairly jumping from her skin when he turned sharply and glared at her with a murderous glower. She inched backward, enthralled by fright, but Ryan's arm shot out and he grasped her wrist.

"Nay, Mary, it's not you I imagine throttling! Forgive my black mood, girl, and join me. I've a need for light and merry company." Her hesitant smile warmed to a saucy grin as she forgave him the short display of temper and settled happily next to him, her fleshy, half-exposed breasts threatening to overspill the loose gathers of her blouse as she bounced enthusiastically into his arms. Anticipation hardened her prominent nipples, thrusting them against the thin cotton material.

During the hour and a half that followed, Ryan proceeded to get roaring drunk. He joined in the bawdy song a seaman started, fondled Mary's thigh, ordered drinks all around, and somehow managed to stagger up the stairs to the wench's loft.

To Mary's indignant frustration, Ryan's tipsy, fumbling attempts to bed her came to nought. Over and over, he referred to her as Cat, damning her wide violet eyes, naming her a faithless, copper-haired witch, even while his fingers were buried in Mary's rich black tangles. Finally she turned her back on him, her brown eyes insulted and resentful of the strange hold this violet-eyed Cat seemed to have on her tall, dashing patron.

The evening following her delightful excursion to the Landing, Cat was seated before her mirror, idly brushing the tangles from her long mane of curls. A slight smile curved the fine lines of her lips. The whole day had been a pleasure. Sean had overwhelmed Paddy with fatherly affection, and the awe in the child's eyes had been rewarding. At the warehouse, they'd set him down to play amidst some bolts of silk and satin while Sean fetched Red Winsor. Red was a retired sailor, with a neat, precise mind and a penchant for numbers. Without consulting his books, he had rattled off an astounding list of the assets stored in the building, easily converting the goods into their monetary value.

Red had finished the inventory with a self-satisfied smile and a deferential tip of his cap to Sean. He was under the mistaken impression that the husky blond pirate was his boss, that Cat was merely a friend of Sean's and Will's. It bothered her that she was unable to deal openly with the men she controlled, but if they knew a mere woman was behind the well-planned raids and final distribution of the plunder, they would surely mutiny.

The day had ended with an intimate candlelit dinner and an even more intimate interlude beneath the satin coverlet of Cat's bed. Sean had taken her slowly, deliberately, toward satisfaction, his skillful caresses making up for his absence.

A gentle breeze drifted into the room from the terrace. The nightblooming flowers wafted a musky, sensual scent into the air.

Sean was to join her again, for it seemed his desire for her had increased in the fortnight's parting. Cat had insisted he leave her for a while, to give her time to bathe and freshen herself. The rascal had decided to stroll the gardens, promising her with a comically solemn vow that he would return with an armload of exotic blossoms to bedeck her bare, velvety skin.

Cat suddenly sensed a presence in the room. The fine blonde hairs at the nape of her neck bristled with instinctive warning. She whirled, surveying the entire chamber and finding nothing amiss. Shaking her head, she chided herself for the mistaken impression and resumed her brushing. A sound broke the silence, a soft shuffle that was over as quickly as it had occurred. Again she glanced about, but there was nothing to explain the vague sense of alarm that had set her on edge.

Her lips pursed. It must be Sean, she thought, playing at his impish games again. She smiled as she faced the mirror once more, recalling the time he'd held her captive at the point of his rapier.

Cat concentrated on her reflection, tugging at a snarled curl at her crown. Suddenly a second figure appeared in the mirror, and a silver flash of steel arched downward. Only her quick, reflexive action saved Cat's life. She dropped to the floor, whirling to find Rovani looming over her, exotic, slanted eyes bright with a fanatical gleam of hatred, a long, wicked knife grasped tightly in a hand that already plunged in a second murderous attempt. Cat screamed, rolling to one side, and the blade missed again, this time by mere inches. The end of the bed was at Cat's left; she was hemmed in, unable to scramble away. She faced death in the triumphant glare of Rovani's merciless, maddened eyes. In a moment it would be over.

With a slow, sure deliberation that came from having cornered her enemy, the girl raised her hand high in the air. Cat closed her eyes, weakness washing over her. There was no time to question why, and she prayed instead that the pain would be over quickly. Then she heard a low, shocked curse and the sounds of a struggle, opening her eyes to see Sean, his face a mask of fury, easily wrest the knife from the slender, dark hand, savagely twisting Rovani's wrist to propel her backward.

She landed in a tangled heap of limbs. A cursory glance assured Sean that Cat was shaken but unharmed. He turned to vent his rage on the sobbing native girl, his large, strong hands fastening on the thin, flowered material that wound around her body in the native style of dress. It ripped as he roughly pulled her to her feet. She wobbled in front of him, sobbing a bitter plea in her own language.

Cat watched, sick and unable to move, as his hand swung back, then came forward with tremendous force to connect with the girl's cheek in an audible crack. She was thrown violently to one side by the blow, held up only by Sean's grip on her clothing. He shook her as though she were a doll, righting her almost limp body to prepare another torturous slap. The girl seemed stoic in her acceptance, her heavy ebony hair framing cheeks that were smeared with her own blood.

Cat scrambled to her feet, unable to bear witness to further abuse. She grabbed Sean's arm, felt the tensed, bunched cords of his muscles, and screamed to him to stop. He faced her a moment, unable to recognize her through the red haze of his rage. Cat screamed his name and he seemed to shake himself, returning to reality, loosening his grip on the girl with an exclamation of disgust. Rovani fell to the floor, gazing up at him with an incredible look of adoration. She glanced once at Cat, seeming to hate her all the more for her intercession.

Sean shouted at Rovani in the same, odd-sounding language and she obeyed him instantly, using a chair to pull herself to her feet. Her face was already beginning to swell from the brutal blow he had dealt her. She hurried away without a backward glance.

Cat dropped to the edge of the bed, her eyes wide with horror, her hands stretched over her mouth, breasts rising and falling with each panting breath. Sean's feet appeared before her and she slowly raised her head to find him staring down at her, his arms dangling at his sides, a dull, red flush suffusing his features.

"Why?" Cat could think of nothing but the simple, one-word question.

Sean turned away, stalking to the terrace to stare out into the darkness. "She resents ye," he answered as simply. "She hates ye'r guts," he amended a second later. He slowly turned to face her. "She has her reasons. Rovani and I were lovers for five years—until ye came, lass." His face was torn by desperation.

"I never wanted to touch her after that first time I saw ye by the water. Y'looked like a fair, golden goddess, y'did." He seemed overcome by self-disgust. "Oh, I were patient—sensed you'd shy like a frighted filly if ye was handled careless. I bided m'time till ye trusted me, till ye couldna' resist m'buffoonery, m'wild Irish charm!" His laughter was mirthless, mocking his cynical confession.

Cat stared in stunned silence, seeing Sean as he really was for the first time. A blindfold had dropped from her eyes, revealing his true face. His good nature, his teasing, it had all been a calculated trap from the beginning. It was a different style of seduction from Ryan's outright demands or even Justin's use of drugs, but it all came down to the same lust. She felt used again, disillusioned when she had just begun to trust. A sudden, horrifying thought struck her.

"Paddy—he's her son, too, isn't he?" Guilty silence greeted her question. Cat's voice rose with a hysterical pitch. "Isn't he, you bastard!" Sean nodded, stepping towards her, halting as he saw the stricken look in her eyes. "No wonder she hates me! She thinks I lured you away—that I tried to take her child too! Oh God, Sean," she sobbed, "how *could* you do it?" Tears cascaded down her cheeks, falling unnoticed on her clenched hands.

Cat's throat ached with a tight knot of misery, her belly churning with nausea. She held nothing against Rovani. In her place she might have done the same. She was as much to blame as Sean. She should have noted the boy's resemblance to his mother, should have connected Rovani's antagonism with its source and would have if she hadn't been so blindly involved in her own happiness.

"What are you going to do?"

"What can I do? The harm's been done," Sean answered, knowing he'd lost Cat for good. What he wanted most in the world was no longer within his reach.

"Get out—and don't come back this time," Cat commanded in a dull, halting monotone. "Take the boy and his mother back to the forest. They belong together." She rose, her fingers clutching the bed hangings for support. "Paddy needs you. Rovani needs you." Her eyes were shards of deep violet ice as she emphasized her last statement. *"I don't."*

For a long eternity of seconds the two stared at each other. Sean wrestled with his desires and what little conscience he had, turning on his heel to stride away into the night. Cat stared after him, seized by shuddering, wracking sobs. She flung herself face down on the bed, weeping until there were no more tears left, until her eyes were puffed and swollen, then she fell into a restless, exhausted sleep riddled by nightmares.

The next morning, Sean, Rovani, and the boy were gone. Will took one look at Cat's swollen, purple-smudged eyes and knew what had happened. He'd noted the child's resemblance to the native girl and said nothing, sure that it was none of his business. Now he wished he had. He extended his arms and Cat came into them, sobbing against him. His large, roughened hands stroked her fair hair until she had calmed enough to blurt out the whole miserable story.

Again, there were no wise words of comfort he could offer her. It was something Cat had to deal with herself.

Chapter Fourteen

The *Falcon* swept through the golden moonlight, her sails billowing with the brisk night winds, only the night watch and the helmsman topside. The crew rested below deck to the gentle, steady rhythm of the strong current that carried them east toward their goal. On the morrow they would seek their quarry, the merchantman *Caliope,* bound from China along the Malabar Coast to Bombay. Black waves, gilded by the moon's glow, lapped the hull in the wake of the two-masted brig.

A dim light shone beneath the door of the captain's cabin. A single lantern, burning low, flickered on the weathered oaken desk. Cat leaned back in her chair, eyes closed as she rested briefly. She was tense with excitement, unable to grasp elusive sleep. By her calculations, unless the whims of nature had altered her course, the *Caliope* should sail across their path about thirty leagues south of Bombay. The *Falcon* was primed for action, all her guns cleaned and set, lines and rigging checked for strength, and spare ammunition covered with canvas, ready to be wet down in case of fire. She could almost smell the acrid scent of gunpowder, hear the roar as the cannon exploded.

This time there would be no retreat, Cat vowed, still smarting from the near capture of the *Spirit*. Ryan had outwitted her on that one, but she'd learned her lesson well, and still carried a half-healed wound to remind her. This time the *Spirit* followed and would cut off the escort that was sure to shadow the Company ship. If George had supplied accurate information (something she had come to question lately), the treasures carried by their prey were worth a king's ransom, enough for her to quit the trade and leave the area for good. She had a longing to see France again, to gaze upon the estate where she had lived with her grandmother, and to see Briar and her child. Perhaps she would settle there. The gentle, rolling countryside where her ancestors had lived seemed to be the only place she could safely call home.

The soft roll of the ship lulled Cat into memories of her life in France. She recalled a story Grandmère had once told her, a tale that had been meant to instill a sense of heritage in Cat.

An ancestress, the first of a line of Catherines, had caught the king's notice, ensnaring him with her gentle blonde beauty. Though she held his heart, his marriage to a princess of Spain had been arranged and settled. She had traded high, that first Catherine, granting the king her most prized possessions: her virginity and her devoted loyalty. The birth of a son had been celebrated with the awarding of an elegant chateau on the Loire, a vast, towering edifice of gold-veined white marble, designed to acknowledge the royal pride, if not to confer legitimacy on its issue. The son was given a dukedom and later distinguished himself in the service of his half-brother, the royal heir. Cat could still remember the pride in the sparkling eyes of the aristocratic old woman. Though Cat had always considered the story a fabrication for her benefit, there *had* been a dukedom in the family, passing out of Marguerite's line to a male cousin.

There was no doubt that her long-ago ancestress had loved and loved well. A bitter, cynical smile settled on Cat's lips. Love was something that seemed to exist only in fairy tales. There were few marriages that held it; in fact, the devotion shared by her own parents was something of a mystery to her. Christine and Brian Devlin had been opposites, she gentle and quiet, he bold and audacious. Cat had loved once, not wisely, and all it had brought had been pain and heartache. Perhaps it was her choice of men, but then—had the choice really been hers? Love had been thrust upon her, like a sudden, savage storm on the sea, boldly overwhelming her senses until somehow the lust and passion had receded, replaced by a warm need to care. Ryan had never realized her love, had never seemed to look further than her face and body, probably would have taken advantage of her weakness had he known. Still, she could no more command herself to cease caring than she could stop her heart from beating.

For a second she indulged in a heartbeat of self-pity. Why couldn't he just once have said, "I need you, Cat . . . I love you!" Her eyes flew open in anger at the useless direction of her thoughts. *She* was the cause of her own torment. If for some reason she could not inspire him to love her or if he lacked the capacity to feel the emotion, why did she continue to dwell on it? With a heavy sigh, she dismissed the ache within, banishing it from her thoughts to turn her attention to the map that lay on the desk. She should try to rest again. All her senses had to be sharp for the coming day.

The map was an excellent chart of the waters they now sailed. She had chanced to find a crusty old salt, retired from the sea and residing at Shelley's Landing. The man existed on rum, lived for nothing else, and when she'd discovered he'd spent his life as a cartographer, charting the local waters for Kidd and his cohorts, she'd settled a bargain with him.

Burke was brought to live at the house, given his daily portion of rum and fed and clothed well in exchange for his work. In the mornings the old man would remain sober, calling on an unbelievable memory to draw precise, accurate charts of the areas she requested. His afternoons were spent in the garden, swilling his beloved rum and crooning snatches of bawdy sea chanteys. It had worked to their mutual advantage; and thus far, Burke's memory had proved infallible.

A twinge of pain from her wound finally made Cat seek a few hours' rest before dawn. She would not be in peak physical condition should she need to defend herself, yet her confidence in the next day's action was so great that the thought caused her only a moment's unease. Just one more foray and she would leave this tropical paradise that had brought her financial independence. Just one more, she thought, as sleep finally overcame her.

Cat overslept the next morning, waking to the sounds of her crew bustling overhead. She jumped up from the bunk, hurrying to the cabin windows to check the weather. The sky was a hazy blue, overcast with a pale, reddish cloud cover. She didn't like the looks of it—a red sky meant the possibility of a quick squall, or worse, in these parts, a monsoon. It was the one variable she couldn't have predicted or altered.

With a great deal of haste, Cat dressed, binding her sore shoulder tightly with strips of linen before donning her disguise and checking it in the mirror. The stain—she'd almost forgotten it! Her appearance above deck with a pale complexion would have aroused suspicion among the men. Only when the turban was wound at the right angle, covering the telltale gold curls, did she venture from the cabin.

On deck, the day watch had assumed duty. Jon Pike, a trusted crewman from the old days in Tortuga, stood at the wheel, barking orders to the crew to look lively. When he noticed his captain's approach, his hand rose to touch his cap in a respectful salute.

"Mornin', sir!"

It never failed to amaze Cat that she succeeded in her masquerade. She had striven to give the appearance of a loner, a laconic, seldom friendly commander, removed from the ship's company. She lowered her voice when forced to issue a direct order, for it was the only feature she had difficulty disguising. Pike squinted at the sky, shaking his head and commenting, "Bad sign, sir— ne'er seen a red sky t'fail yet. 'Fraid we're bound for a bad 'un!"

Cat nodded her agreement, unrolling the chart to assure herself they held a true course. Satisfied, she clapped Pike on the back, ordering him to hold her steady before the slight wind that had risen. "I'll be in my cabin, should you need me," she added huskily.

During the night, the *Spirit* had swept due east and would lie in wait along the Malabar, concealed in a cove until the *Caliope* sailed past. Will would swing the frigate out and sail south to intercept the escort and cut her off while the *Falcon* sought the unprotected merchantman.

In the early afternoon, Cat went above deck and took a position at the starboard bowrail, leaning over it as she scanned the water. Cat almost scented the prey across the wide expanse of dark, bottle green sea, even before she sighted the ship or the lookout shouted from his perch high in the main topmast shrouds. They were far enough back to avoid detection except by the sharpest of lookouts aboard the *Caliope.*

The order went out to trim the sail. Cat wanted to lie back until she was sure Will had enough time to encounter the escort. A strong, gusty wind had risen from the southeast and she prayed silently that he wouldn't have trouble with the weather. Pike bellowed and some of the men scrambled aloft, letting out more sail to take advantage of the wind. He steered her several degrees to port and the sails caught, billowing taut and speeding the vessel toward the coastline.

Under Pike's skillful handling, the *Falcon* blazed a trail of foamy froth as she cut the waves in pursuit of the barkentine. Like a sleek, well-muscled tiger, the brig responded, swiftly gaining on her unsuspecting quarry. As in the past, her lightning speed was the *Falcon*'s greatest asset. As she closed in, activity aboard the trade vessel quickened to a frenzy when the captain recognized the red flag whipping from the *Falcon*'s main royal mast. The challenge had been issued and he could either surrender or fight. The brig was too fast to outrun and the Company vessel's captain had every reason to believe his escort would soon appear to trounce the audacious pirates. He made preparations to defend until help arrived.

The flag of the British East Indies Company still flew from the *Caliope*. The *Falcon* sped closer and a warning shot was fired over the merchantman's bow, the gunners standing ready to twirl their slow-burning wicks and set off succeeding volleys of fire if there was no sign of surrender. Pistols and muskets were handy, a vast array of boarding axes and pikes, and all manner of cutlery designed to wound the defenders.

Cat whirled from her post at the starboard rail, nodding to Pike. He brought the wheel sharply to starboard and the ship groaned and creaked as she turned across the wind, heading for the trader's stern. Grappling hooks and nets were made ready.

At a signal from Cat, the gunners twirled the wicks until the wind set them glowing a bright red-orange. The cannon roared in succession, erupting with fiery charges as the acrid smell of gunpowder filled the air. In the heavy pitch of the waves, only two hits were scored. One burst near the fore gun deck with only fragmentary damage but the other slammed into the fore topsail, snapping the mast and sending it crashing to the merchantman's deck.

The *Caliope* carried few cannon and those few now blossomed with a return of fire. Her angle was bad, for the *Falcon* was still off her stern and the firepower had no effect at all. Cat heard a curse and a shouted order to the bark's helmsman to swing her to port. She laughed, ordering Pike to stay steady with the turn.

Pistol shots were exchanged as the *Falcon* hove close to her opponent's beam, grappling nets at the ready. The two ships groaned as their hulls scraped together and the hooks were cast, catching well in the bark's shrouds. A cry went up from the pirates, a bloodthirsty yell, as they began to swing across and board the prize. Though the *Caliope*'s crew kept a steady hail of small arms fire aimed at the boarders, there were few casualties, and the marauders swarmed like locusts over the deck.

To the south, there was still no sign of the escort. The pale, sweating captain of the vessel shouted an order to defend at all costs. Now it was all hand-to-hand combat, with boarding axes and pikes, knives and pistols. Cutlasses sliced the air in silver flashes, parried and thrust, sank into limbs and torsos and withdrew dripping scarlet. The incredulous, agonized moans of the dying blended with the keening winds that wailed a death song through the shrouds and rigging of the beleaguered ship. Overhead, clouds scudded in the heavy winds; to the southeast the mists of a rapidly approaching squall hazed the horizon a dull, dirty gray.

Cat leapt to the nets connecting the two ships, gracefully landing on the *Caliope*'s sterncastle deck. All around her men battled and she was soon engaged defending herself against a hulking seaman who'd spotted her approach. Though the man towered over her by a foot, he was clumsy and no match for her agile moves. Every time he lunged, she was one step ahead of him and easily parried the strong thrusts of his cutlass with her lighter rapier. Suddenly she stumbled, tumbling off balance as her feet struck a coil of rope. The man jeered, his sharp blade poised to plunge into her body. She rolled in a quicksilver movement and his cutlass splintered the deck where she had lain. He gave a grunt of surprise as her weapon found his unprotected side and plunged through his ribs to enter his heart.

Cat took great gulps of sea air, her heart racing at the close call. She gathered her wits about her and in a moment was on her feet, lithe, feline steps carrying her towards another defender, a man whose broad shoulders and erect carriage seemed familiar. As if he sensed her approach, he wheeled to face the threat at his back. She was face-to-face with Ryan! His scowl was fierce and he lifted his rapier ready to strike in defense.

Cat was faced with an impossible dilemma. If Ryan possessed the greater skill, she would die beneath his weapon. Yet if she managed to best him, could she send her blade plunging into his heart?

She had no time to consider. Ryan circled her, testing her position with a narrow, measuring gaze. She had a slight advantage, for he stood at the edge of the steps leading to the gun deck and could be forced down, while she could fight from higher ground. Her legs were planted astride, her body balanced gracefully on the balls of her feet as she waited for the first thrust. Ryan was totally taken in by her disguise and eager to strike down one of the enemy who had foiled his plans.

Behind them, all around them, men fought while curses filled the air and blood puddled and ran on the decks. Ryan moved, adjusting his balance and then his powerful right arm lunged forward, aimed at his opponent's shoulder. The man was slight and Ryan was confident he would finish him off in minutes. Surprisingly, the slender, swarthy pirate easily sidestepped the thrust, parrying and bringing his own rapier up to nick at Ryan's forearm. The tip of the weapon sliced his black velvet coat, cut through the silk shirt beneath, and scratched his skin before he was able to recover from his own thrust.

Ryan's eyes narrowed further, a new measure of respect for the man's skill alerting him to the shocking fact that *he* could possibly lose the match. His greater strength and height seemed his only advantages, and he put them to full use now, aggressively keeping the scoundrel on the move defending feints and thrusts from every angle and direction. The man parried each move but his strength seemed to falter after minutes of the steady, offensive attack, his breath coming more raggedly with each defensive movement.

Below them on the main deck, Cat's men were beating down the defenders. Within minutes the *Caliope* would be another in their long list of prizes. Pike drew his cutlass from the belly of a dying sailor, turning to catch sight of his captain, stalked by a tall, muscular man in gentleman's attire. He bellowed an order to secure the ship, racing toward the stern to aid his leader.

One tilt of the *Caliope*'s hull as she smashed against the *Falcon* was Cat's undoing. She was slammed against the stern rail, landing hard against her left shoulder. Her rapier dropped to the deck as she grabbed her shoulder, swallowing hard at the throbbing pain that sent blood trickling down her arm. Until now she'd held her own against Ryan's steady, ruthless attack, but it was over. She leaned against the railing, paralyzed as she watched Ryan close in for the kill, fully aware that she was at his mercy and he was still unaware of her identity.

The tip of his blade was a bare five inches from her heart, the muscles of his arm were tensed to lunge. Cat had closed her eyes, willing the pain to cease, willing herself to feel nothing when the cold steel entered her body. He was a blade length away when she opened them again, afraid, yet stoic in the face of inevitable death. She could not, would not cry out who she was.

Ryan's victorious sneer faded as the weakened pirate stared at him. There could never be another pair of eyes the same shade of misty violet as those that stared up at him. A shock of recognition went through him, stopping his rapier seconds away from her death. As he paused, Pike charged him from behind. Cat's eyes widened as she saw the cutlass lift to strike at Ryan's back. From each side, two more of her crew closed in; like wolves scenting prey, they raised their weapons in unison.

"No!" Cat shouted, stopping her men in their tracks. Her voice was low and throaty with the pain of her reopened wound. The men paused, chagrined at the captain's show of mercy for a man who would have killed him minutes before. Cat retrieved her rapier and pressed a hand against her wound to stem the flow of blood that threatened to weaken her.

Ryan, hopelessly outnumbered, grudgingly dropped his weapon to the deck. If he hadn't been so stunned to discover his opponent was Cat, shocked by her near death at his hands, they'd never have caught him off guard. Cat, only her eyes familiar in the darkened mask of her face, ordered her men to take him to the *Falcon's* cabin.

"Tie him well, Pike. Leave no loose bonds or you'll answer to me!" Cat refused to look at him; it was as though she'd dismissed him from her thoughts. Ryan was roughly hustled to the nets and dragged to the pirate ship.

Ryan's black eyes had been a mixture of anger and resentment when her men dragged him away. Cat pushed the thought away, concentrating on staying afoot until she saw that the ship had been secured and its bounty transferred to the *Falcon*'s hold, refusing to give in to the pain in her aching shoulder until she made the safety of her cabin. It wouldn't do to faint in front of her crew. Sounds of revelry floated up from the lower deck as the pirates broke the seals on bales of silks and casks of wine, plunging their axes into wooden chests and generally rifling the contents of the merchantman's hold. She issued orders to see that the wounded were cared for, and, with a great deal of difficulty, managed to climb the nets and make it to the deck of her own ship.

Pike was at the wheel when she arrived. She asked him to take over and see that the men controlled their jubilance until they were under way and headed for home. The storm that had been brewing all day was fast approaching and the ship's rigging had to be secured before they were blown inland and foundered in the shallows of the coast. They would cut loose the *Caliope* and try to outrun the gale.

When she wearily opened her cabin door, Cat found Ryan firmly trussed and bound to the large desk chair, his handsome features a brooding mask of ill humor and frustration. The sight of him, helpless before *her* for once, brought a cheerful smile to her lips. It left quickly on the wings of the growl of fury he emitted.

"Playing pirate again?" Ryan couldn't keep the acid sarcasm from his voice. He was seething, infuriated and embarrassed that he hadn't been able to recognize his former mistress as his nimble-footed opponent.

"I wasn't playing, Ryan. Considering that you're the

one who's trussed like a chicken awaiting the axe, I should think you'd realize I'm deadly serious." She moved across the room, drawing her pistols from the scarlet sash and carefully laying them aside. The turban came off next and the flood of heavy copper curls fell in waves past her shoulders. She totally ignored Ryan, wiping the stain from her face and unbuckling the scabbard with quiet efficiency. Before she laid it down, she withdrew the rapier and held it to the light in contemplation. It had served her in good stead today.

Cat moved across the room toward Ryan, a self-satisfied expression masking the pain that continued to sap at her strength. Ryan warily watched her approach, keeping an eye on the hand that held the sharp weapon. She paused a foot away from him, raising the rapier like a dagger. As it plunged downward, Ryan shut his eyes tight but there was no sudden explosion of blinding pain. He opened one eye, then the other. Cat was perched on the desk, calmly studying his features while the rapier quivered in the leather seat, a mere hair's breadth from his most valuable, personal possessions.

"I dare you to move, Nicholls," she threatened with a pleased grin that showed a rare glimpse of her dimples. "I've been waiting for this moment for a long time. Go ahead, darling, breath too hard and you'll qualify as one of the Mogul's eunuchs!"

Ryan paled slightly beneath his dark tan, cocking an eyebrow as he tried to fathom her sincerity. He didn't truly believe her, but considering what was at stake, he wasn't taking any chances. He held his breath uncomfortably for a moment and then gave a half-hearted laugh. "Ah, Cat . . . you wouldn't do it! Too many wenches would mourn the loss—including you. Now be a good girl and put your toy away!"

Cat felt a strong desire to carry through with her threat and geld him. With one flick of her wrist she could divide his manhood into separate but equal parts, and he dared to laugh. Worse, the crowing cock claimed she would suffer as much as he! Suddenly she joined in his laughter, stopping just as suddenly as blood trickled down her arm again. She released the rapier, holding her wound with the free hand.

Ryan frowned as he noticed the dark crimson stain spreading across her shoulder. "What the hell," he cursed. He hadn't touched her with his blade!

Cat stood, swaying as her stomach churned and nausea threatened her. It took all of her effort to carefully retrieve the rapier and toss it on the desk.

"Cat, cut me loose—for God's sake girl, d'you want to bleed to death!"

Cat stared distrustfully, catching her bottom lip between her teeth as she turned to measure the steps to the door. She was growing weaker by the minute. . . . If she could just reach it and unbolt the latch to call for help. But she couldn't do that either—her hair was down, the stain had been wiped away—whoever answered her call would know her secret! Her arm throbbed, hanging heavy and useless at her side. She had no choice—in minutes she might pass out and continue to bleed and Ryan wouldn't be able to help. With a great deal of effort, she drew a knife from its sheath in her boot and sliced at the ropes that bound him. She had difficulty, for her men had followed her orders explicitly.

Ryan jumped up, impatiently thrusting the frayed, cut rope ends aside, grabbing for the knife as it fell from her slack wrist and casting it carelessly on the desk. Cat stared at it, dazed and unable to focus. Her eyes met his in a silent plea and closed as she slumped unconscious into his arms. He lifted her easily, carrying her to the bed to lay her carefully upon it.

Cat was unaware of Ryan's touch as he gently pulled the clotted silk away from her wound. He swore an oath as he caught sight of the gash from a healing wound that had broken open. It marred the flawless, ivory flesh in a seam that would later leave a scar. He'd find out later how she came by it; now he had to clean and bind it to stem the flow of blood that still oozed from it. Long, quick strides carried him to the desk and he returned with the knife blade, using it to slice away her waistcoat and shirt. The shirt was quickly torn into strips and dipped into a basin of clear, cool water that lay on a nearby table.

After he'd cleaned the wound of blood, Ryan bound it tightly. From the looks of it, she'd been wounded by a pistol ball. He shook his head at the wild impetuous nature that had led her into such danger. Her lovely, heart-shaped face was pale as alabaster. Lying there without her usual rebellious expression, she seemed like a fair angel in distress. Unaware of his ministrations, she moved restlessly and then lay quiet once again. He cut away the breeches and boots, covering her with a blanket and moving away to study her from a distance.

Outside, rain had begun to lash at the windows and the squall that had been approaching all day was suddenly upon the ship, tossing the brig from side to side as huge walls of water crashed against her hull. Ryan made sure Cat was secure in the bed and strolled about the room, familiarizing himself with its contents. In a cabinet on the wall, he found a bottle of brandy, and helped himself to a drink. It sank to the pit of his stomach, easing the tension that had been with him most of the day. He found few personal belongings, just some clothing in a chest beneath the windows. For almost an hour he sat at the desk, alternately listening to the violence of the raging storm and watching Cat.

She seemed more rested now, her breathing even and her coloring close to normal. By the disguise she'd adopted, he surmised that none of her crew of ruffians was aware that a woman led them. By God, he knew her well and he'd been fooled! Since he was technically her prisoner, aboard her ship, he could only guess that his plan had failed. She must have learned a lesson from her abortive attack on one of the Company's ships several weeks ago and cut off the escort. Perhaps that was when she'd been wounded.

Ryan had no idea of the time. It had been early afternoon when the attack came and by now it must be close to four, possibly five o'clock. Outside the sky was so black and chaotic, it could have been midnight. He yawned, suddenly deciding he could use a bit of rest himself. The door was still bolted from the inside and he walked over to test the lock's strength, finding it adequate to hold back Cat's men should they become curious about their captain's absence. He stripped off his shirt and breeches, grinning wryly at the tear in his sleeve where Cat had nicked him. She was damned good with the blade, better than most men he'd come up against. She might have even bested him if the wound hadn't distracted her. Thank God he'd recognized her in time! It was well that it had turned out as it had—neither one of them wished for the other's death. He knew by the way she'd shouted to her men when they'd closed in on him.

When he stood naked before the bed, he stretched his tired muscles and carefully lifted the cover to join her. Before he closed his eyes, he laid a hand on her forehead, testing her for a fever from the wound, thankful that her temples felt cool and dry. She shifted at the light touch and snuggled lower under the blanket. A damp chill had invaded the room and the warmth of her slender body as he lay close soon eased Ryan into a restful sleep.

Sometime in the evening. Cat opened her eyes to a dark cabin. The lantern had burned low enough to flicker out. She was disoriented for a moment until she realized she was safely aboard the *Falcon* and her dreams of defeat before Ryan had been just that—dreams. She touched her shoulder, finding it carefully bound and aching only slightly. Then she remembered—she'd almost fainted and Ryan had insisted she let him help.

Her senses were rapidly returning to normal. She made a move to rise and fill the lantern when a strong firm hand closed on her thigh. It took her only a second to realize that the warmth that had kept her so cozy while she slept had come from Ryan. He lay next to her in the darkness, as naked as she.

Lord, she thought in a panic—what had she let herself in for when she'd loosed him? Ignoring the fact that he'd helped her when she'd desperately needed it, she was seized by an irrational fear. He could do as he pleased with her—even hold her at knife point, forcing the crew to obey him or else! She struggled, clawing at the fingers that gripped her, trying to scramble out of the bed and find the desk. Her rapier lay somewhere there, and at least she could hold him at bay.

"Damn it, Cat, stop fighting," Ryan demanded angrily. He could feel the desperation in her squirming attempts to evade him. "You'll break open the wound again!" His fingers closed on her arms, forcing her back onto the soft down mattress. He did nothing, except hold there until the fight drained from her.

"What do you intend to do?" Cat inquired, her voice a sullen whisper in the darkness.

Ryan was incensed by the implication in her tone. "For a start, I thought I'd rape you, seeing how weak you are," he snapped sarcastically. The storm still tossed the vessel but a strong wind occasionally swept the cloud cover away from a full, golden moon. Now, moonbeams flitted over the bed, settling briefly on her face to reveal its stubborn, rebellious set.

"Jesus, Cat," Ryan swore softly, "I'm not the monster you take me for. I don't need relief so badly I want you bleeding all over me!" His fingers eased their tight grip and she sighed, remaining at his side but stiffly drawing away from contact with the warm, hard length of his body. Still, he could feel the slight trembling of her body underneath the covers. "What're you scared of?" His voice had a sly edge to it as he continued, "Afraid I can't resist taking advantage of the situation?" He turned on his side, presenting his back to her and smiling at the trap he was laying. "And I thought you'd grown into a mature woman of the world. Seems I was wrong, though. Still can't admit it when you need a man—can you?"

"Ooh, you black-eyed devil," Cat growled through clenched teeth. "I can well admit it, *if* I feel any desire—which I don't! I'm not the wide-eyed child you took advantage of two years ago." Silence greeted the declaration, then a slyly planned snicker that challenged her claims.

Her hand whistled through the dark, landing open-palmed on the broad, muscled back next to her.

"Turn around, if you're going to make insinuations," Cat ordered furiously. Ryan complied, shifting his weight and facing her once more.

"I think you're all bluff, little girl. A brave face that covers a quivering spirit!" Thoroughly enjoying himself Ryan refused to let go of his game until he had produced the desired results. "A man must take you or you can't be aroused," he asserted. "If you had to reach out and caress or kiss me of your own accord, you couldn't bring yourself to do so." Ryan's face was lit by the moon and beamed with smug confidence. "Could you?"

"Of course I could—I told you I just don't care to!"

"Of course."

"Damn your black heart, Ryan Nicholls!" Cat was growing more exasperated by the minute. Though he couldn't see them, her gold-fringed eyes were narrowed with antagonism as she was forced to defend herself. He was truly *the* most aggravating man she'd ever met! She was just furious enough to show him how wrong he could be.

The tension and stiffness drained from her body as Cat considered her plan of attack. Her hand reached out to flatten against his chest, sinuously stroking upward through the dark, crisp curls to slide to his nape. Her long, slender fingers played through his hair, gently urging his head down to hers. Soft lips parted to meet his, and the tip of her tongue teased him, darting in and out of his mouth. Against her will, Cat felt her belly lurch with a deep stab of desire and pressed closer, the pink-rose peaks of her nipples flaming as they brushed against his chest.

Ryan made no move to embrace her and lay almost passively enjoying her aggressive behavior. She'd expected him to come alive and take command and when he failed to do so, she broke the intimate contact and drew back. He could almost see the soft, puzzled pouting of her lower lip through the darkness.

"There, I told you," Cat declared.

"Told me what, my sweet? I felt nothing but the

light touch of a butterfly's wings against my lips. Really, Cat—if that's *all* you've learned!"

Cat took the bait, stifling an urge to strangle him. She'd been affected by the close contact. Why hadn't he? Her pride was wounded and she dismissed the aching of her shoulder to launch herself at him in a wildcat attack that would leave nothing to chance.

Ryan rolled with her, found her soft breasts delightfully pressed against his chest as her fingernails dug into his back and her lips found his mouth. His long arms wound around her narrow waist, one hand stroking up her sleek, velvety back, the other moving lower to caress the smooth, rounded curves of her buttocks. Somewhere in the passionate blend of intimacies they exchanged, he took command and Cat gracefully yielded to him, her body pliantly molding itself to his until she lost sight of the beginnings of desire and gazed down a long, dark tunnel toward its goal.

The storm was Cat's emotional partner. Lightning struck silver over the black, boiling sea and she felt a jagged flash of passion. The wind howled in the rigging and she moaned her pleasure in the same desperate tone. And finally, when she could no longer bear the exquisite, agonizing sensations that ran riot over her entire body, she exploded with a scream of ecstasy that was made mute by a sharp staccato of thunder.

The explosion of release that Cat experienced then was the first of several that night. Once the first tendering of themselves had been made, the two lovers reveled in the privacy of the darkened cabin. Several hours after midnight, Ryan rose to light the lantern, insisting he must see as well as feel her flawless skin and gently rounded contours.

In the soft glow of light, Ryan worshipped at the altar of her body, making his devotions to her softly scented, ivory flesh. She unfolded like a blossom seeking the sun's warmth, leaving all modesty behind. Ryan's fingers struck magic chords within her until she was assailed by flaming arrows of desire that pricked her senses, leaving tiny brands as they extinguished, only to flame to life at another pulse point. He left no sense untouched until she was assaulted by the sight, the touch, the sound of his lovemaking. In turn, Cat insisted he lie back while she ministered to him.

Even while Cat caressed and kissed the length of his lean, darkly tanned body, Ryan knew jealousy, felt it gnaw at his soul. As each artful touch brought him nearer to the edge of passion, his thoughts whirled with doubt and distrust. From whom did she learn to please a man? Which lover had taught her such tantalizing skills? Or had she acquired a bit of experience from each of the scoundrels she'd allowed into her bed? With an imagination fueled by envy, he envisioned a legion of lovers, each more licentious than the previous. Finally, though, the haunting vision paled and was thrust away as powerful waves of shock seized him, jolting his entire being with the pure intense pleasure of release.

Cat stretched back on the bed, a contented smile on her face as she listened to Ryan's ragged, impassioned breathing returning to normal. She had proudly employed every artifice Sean had shown her and added a few imaginative twists of her own devising to elicit the savage response from Ryan. Despite the pleasure it had given him, he would undoubtedly be furious if he realized who had been her teacher. She wondered briefly whether he would merely accept her attentions or question her about her change in attitude. She turned to face him, greeted by a scowl.

"You've grown by leaps and bounds, my little seductress," Ryan snapped. "I'd never know you for the shy, modest virgin of two years ago! What a difference the passage of time can make." He was unable to suppress the biting sarcasm that had returned with his renewed jealousy. Certainly she hadn't been bound to him by spoken vows, but from the moment he'd subdued her sweet-scented, virginal body that day in Tortuga, she'd been his. He'd introduced her to the delights of the flesh; it rankled his pride that others had taught her the finer points of pleasure.

Cat's answer was a resigned sigh. It would have been

too much to expect that he'd have accepted her ministrations at face value. His resentment drew an irritated retort from her. "Did you expect me to lie still and quiver timidly at your touch? In all honesty, Ryan, admit that you haven't led a celibate life since we parted! I could better believe the sun won't rise at dawn than to envision you chaste and unsatisfied until we came together again. I never expected to see you again. Should I have entered a convent?"

"Of course I've had my share of wenches—what man wouldn't?" Ryan defended himself. "Don't forget you're the one who left me, though. It didn't take you long to find a lover—or breed his bastard, for that matter! Wouldn't he marry you, or did that interfere with your plans for George?"

Cat was astounded by Ryan's knowledge of Paddy, wounded by his unfair accusation that she had borne a child out of wedlock. A quick denial sprung to her lips. No, she thought peevishly, let him think Paddy was hers if he was such a blind, stubborn fool! If he paused to count on the fingers God had given him, he'd realize the boy couldn't be hers. It was just like Ryan to jump to the worst conclusion!

"The child is none of your business," she answered without committing herself, "and neither is my life for the past two years. If you'd care to detail all of your affairs, I might follow suit. Otherwise, I think we should drop the subject." She glared stubborn defiance and twitched her nose in disdain before scrambling over his legs and climbing from the bed.

Ryan watched Cat move about the room, searching through the chest below the window until she found what she was looking for, the same gold wrapper she'd worn the day he'd found her with Rafferty. Her movements were abrupt and angry as she jerked it on and belted it tightly at her waist. Next she took a clean glass from the cupboard and went to the desk to pour herself a glass of brandy. She surprised him by motioning to the bottle and suggesting he join her.

"You're welcome to share a glass," she said, grinning wickedly as she added, "Consider it partial payment for your services!"

Ryan swung his long legs out of bed and reached for his breeches. This was a new Cat—much more assured and confident. Perhaps it came from the security of being aboard her own ship, a call away from her crew. He stood and bowed. "I assure you the pleasure was mine, m'lady," he quipped. "You did say partial, though—am I to assume I have a further reward in store for acting as your stud?"

Cat relaxed in the huge desk chair, hugging her knees to her chest. She cocked her head to one side, still amused as she studied him. "Yes. I'm planning on dropping you ashore in the morning—all in one piece, of course. By rights, I should maroon you naked on a narrow spit of deserted isle!"

"I see—I'm to be grateful for your generosity. Suppose, love, just for the sake of theory, that the dawning sun finds the *Falcon* facing a fully armed Company ship—what then?" He tossed down the brandy and poured another glassful.

"There isn't a prayer, darling. The escort you're referring to has been thoroughly trounced by now. My frigate cut her off even before we attacked the *Caliope*." Cat's expression was cheerfully smug.

"I have to admit you've covered yourself well." Ryan leaned against the desk, staring down into her eyes. "Are you so very sure which ship was the vanquished and which the victor? Since we've been cut off by the storm, we won't really know until morning, will we?" Cat's face lost some of its confidence and Ryan smiled to himself at the seed of doubt he'd planted.

Cat hadn't even considered the idea of Will failing. Now, she caught her bottom lip between two, pearly teeth as she pondered his fate. As Ryan said, they wouldn't know until the morning sun lit the sky.

Chapter Fifteen

The morning following the *Falcon*'s capture of the prize, *Caliope*, she became a captive herself. First, the ocean was her captor, for the raging storm had passed late in the hours before dawn, leaving the brig becalmed on a sea as tranquil as a country pond. The storm had swept to the northeast, taking every breath of air with it.

Cat hadn't slept at all when she appeared on the main deck with Ryan at her side. Luckily she'd had spare clothing in the window chest. Ryan had ruined her disguise when he'd tended to her wound the previous afternoon. She looked the part of the captain once more. If any of the crew were puzzled that the prisoner had spent the night in their leader's cabin and now appeared free and at ease instead of bound, they kept it to themselves.

The lack of any breeze to speed them on their way set Cat on edge. Floating along, moved only by currents, they were a sitting duck for anyone with an armed galley. Granted, there were few in use these days, but still enough existed so that the thought was unnerving. Above them not a cloud existed to provide shelter from the sweltering heat of the sun. Cat paced the deck of the sterncastle, while Ryan lounged against the taffrail and smiled at her increasing agitation.

"Won't do any good to wear down the planks, Cat," he commented wryly. "You may control the ship, but never the weather." His smile widened to a grin. "Don't you wish you had a little of last night's moaning winds at your fingertips?"

It was clear what he referred to, and Cat stopped beside him restraining herself from slapping the smug mockery from his face. Instead she leaned close and snapped, "Remember whose ship you're on, Ryan Nicholls. I'll have you chained and thrown in the hold if you can't control your snide remarks!"

Ryan held up his hands in mock chagrin. "My lips are sealed, sweet captain! Though I'm sure you'd have a time controlling these rascals of yours if I reached out and tugged at that turban. Imagine their shock when those long silky curls tumbled to your shoulders!"

Cat stepped back, wary of his threat. It appeared she'd have to put up with his railery for the time being. She couldn't wait for the first wind to rise so that she could put him ashore.

There was a sudden shout from above. "Galley off the starboard bow, Cap'n—she's headed our way!"

Cat felt her heart lurch with panic. She whirled and ran to the bow, Ryan sauntering casually in her wake. Sure enough, a three-masted galley crawled steadily toward them, her two banks of oars dipping and rising in a smooth rhythm. The ship wasn't heavily armed and was smaller than the *Falcon,* but her threat lay not in size but in ability to maneuver. She was still far enough away to prepare some kind of a defense. Cat turned to shout an order to Pike, and Ryan's hand closed on her arm.

"Don't bother," he said quietly. "If you think they'll row within range of your guns, you're a fool. They can stand off the bow and blast us with a broadside and you couldn't do a thing in retaliation."

"Are you mad?" Cat pulled away and faced him in-
ignantly. "You think I'd just give up my ship—surren-
er to God knows who without a fight?"

"I'm suggesting you haven't a choice unless you say a
uick prayer for a gale wind to come up within five min-
tes and it's answered immediately. You don't have a
hance in hell of getting away unscathed—they have the
dvantage of mobility, in case you hadn't noticed." A bat-
e raged on her face. She wanted to damn him for a liar
nd let the cannon blaze, and yet she realized the truth.
'at Devlan was all fire and fight and it went against
er character to give in so easily.

Ryan wet his forefinger and held it up, testing for
vind. "You haven't been praying," he said with a laugh
hat dwindled as his expression grew serious. "Tell your
nen there's to be no resistance." He shaded his eyes
gainst the sun's glare and gazed across the calm blue wa-
ers at the fast approaching ship. "She looks to be French-
nade, but if I'm not mistaken, that's a Hindu flag she's
lying."

Again he took hold of her, this time gripping both
rms in an attempt to impress her with their position.
'Listen, love, if they're Indian, the odds are they'll not
ake kindly to pirates. You won't like what I'm going to
ell you but it's for your own good. If you've any dresses
elow, put one on. When they board, I'll claim I'm the
aptain. They'll go a lot easier on you if they think you're
captive I picked up off a prize."

"But——"

"But nothing, Cat," Ryan interrupted impatiently,
iving her a shake. "For once in your life, listen to me! It's
ver with the *Falcon*. Once we're taken prisoner the
rew'll find out you're a woman anyway."

Cat wanted to refuse just because it was something
e insisted on, but he was right. Without a wind they were
ost, and she was in danger as the captain. She couldn't
elp wishing Will were here—he'd know exactly what to do.

"You haven't much time."

"Oh, all right," she answered in grudging agreement.

"Come with me and I'll tell Pike." At the helm, she ordered a stunned Pike to offer no resistance to a boarding party. Already the galley had come within firing distance and as they spoke, a warning shot splashed over the bow. Cat called another seaman over to the wheel and told Pike to follow her below.

In the cabin she revealed the truth to him. Ryan leaned against the desk, his arms crossed as he watched with a bemused expression. Cat unwound the turban, letting her silken copper curls wave over her shoulders. A quick scrub with a damp cloth exposed her creamy complexion. Pike stared, unable to believe he'd followed a woman and never known it.

"We can't escape, Jon. Unless by a miracle, Will shows up with the *Spirit,* we're as good as captive now." She begrudgingly introduced Ryan, telling Pike he'd be taking over as captain. The man had absorbed three successive shocks and it took a short while for him to recover.

"Aye, Cap'n, sir—er—ma'am, I'll handle the men, but ye'r sure ye wants this fella' takin' o'er? It don't have t'be that way." He was resentful of accepting Ryan's commands when they'd captured him only the day before.

"It's best that way. I appreciate your loyalty, Pike. If we come out of this with our skins, you'll be rewarded for it. Now please see to the men and introduce—Captain Nicholls." The tall, thin pirate saluted and gestured to Ryan to follow him topside.

Ryan paused a moment, wanting to assure himself Cat would follow the rest of his plan. She ignored him, going to the chest below the window and carelessly tossing aside clothing until she found a dress. She held it to the light, frowning at the idea of giving up her ship, at the frustration of surrendering her beloved *Falcon* without even a chance of defense. Her shoulders slumped defeatedly and Ryan, reluctant to irritate her further, quietly left to join Pike on deck.

The galley ceased firing when there was no move to

defend the brig. She moved alongside and a grappling net was cast, hooking the two ships together. A row of scarlet-uniformed soldiers aimed muskets at the *Falcon*'s crew while their captain and his officers boarded the ship. Ryan ordered the men to lay down their weapons, and while there were a few disgruntled curses, all obeyed.

The Indian captain accepted the ship's surrender from Ryan and the two moved to the stern to talk at the rail. Meanwhile the pirates were herded together and ordered to transfer to the galley. They shuffled along, openly surly and resentful of their fate, but urged on by the sharp tips of the enemy soldiers' pikes.

When Ryan knocked and opened the cabin door, a different Cat greeted him. She had removed all traces of her disguise and sat meekly in the desk chair. He entered with the Indian captain in tow, winking at her before he made a show of describing her as his latest prize. Cat glared at him, drawing on her very real well of resentment to appear as sullen as a true captive would be. The captain smiled, baring dazzling white teeth in a dark, swarthy face.

Ryan walked over to Cat, reaching down to pull her to her feet, his arm possessively encircling her waist. She tried to struggle away, for the whole idea of playacting for the benefit of her real captor was disagreeable. Ryan laughed, easily subduing her struggles and dragging her along toward the door.

"You see what a wildcat I've captured," he commented and Cat kicked his shin, eliciting a growl of displeasure and an attempted cuff. The Indian stepped between them and took Cat's arm, gesturing to an accompanying soldier to take Ryan to the other ship. Ryan objected, roughly shoving the soldier away, only to be clubbed with the butt of a pike when he turned to retrieve Cat. Cat tensed, unable to move to help him in the horrible melodrama they played out, forced to watch as more soldiers clattered down the companionway at their captain's call and dragged Ryan away. She turned back to the Indian to find a chilling leer on his face as he studied her figure. Cursing silently, she damned the weather, Ryan's plans, and the openly grinning Indian in quick succession.

Surprising her, he made no attempt to take advantage of the privacy of the cabin. She'd already had a horrid, vivid image of a quick, savage rape and she sighed with relief when he merely urged her toward the companionway and the deck above.

A skeleton crew of Indian soldiers was left aboard the *Falcon* with orders to bring her into port when the winds allowed. Cat's crew were tied and thrust into the small area in the galley that served as the ship's hold. Ryan was thrown in with them though Cat was allowed to stay on deck at the captain's side. She watched morosely as the *Falcon* became increasingly smaller, until at last her ship was nothing but a speck on the horizon.

After a few attempts at conversation, which Cat stubbornly ignored, the captain left her to herself. The ship skimmed along, propelled by the power of slaves' muscles, making good time until the winds finally rose and the sails were hoisted. Almost at dusk the galley arrived in a small, dirty seaport on the Malabar Coast. The captives were hustled off the ship and on to quickly procured horse carts for a journey inland.

Cat still had no idea where her captors came from or where they were headed. She refused to ask the captain, remaining stubbornly silent instead. She was unbelievably tired, and ached with every jostle of the cart. The soldiers were mounted on horses and she almost envied them the smoother ride, for they were following a road that wound through foothills toward a purple range of mountains in the distance. The captain had ordered her wrists tied in front of her when they'd left the ship, explaining with a toothy, apologetic smile that he must see that *all* the captives reached their destination. The procession of carts and their mounted escorts stopped close to midnight at a caravansary, one of the elaborate hostels that a past Mogul emperor had erected for travelers. Cat had fallen into an exhausted sleep and was carried into a chamber to spend the night and scarcely remembered her arrival when she was awakened before dawn to continue the journey.

The Indian commander took pity on her the next day and allowed her a mount, though her hands remained tied. It was a much more comfortable method of travel and she fared better that day. Occasionally she had a glimpse of Ryan and the others, but for the most part she was kept separated from them.

They traveled high into the mountain range, sometimes on a road so rough, it was only a path through steep canyons with towering, jagged granite cliffs to shadow their passing. On the fifth day they passed into the arid flatlands known as the Deccan. The captain had volunteered the information that they were headed for the Hindustan, ruled over by the great Maharaja of Kohlapur. It was he who would decide their ultimate destiny. The rakish Indian offered her the solace that her beauty would save her from the fate that awaited the crew of the captured brig. It only served to increase her worry. What was the mysterious fate the men were to be dealt? With each cantering step of her mount's hooves that brought them closer to the "justice" of Kohlapur's ruler, Cat felt guiltier and more anxious.

The escorted captives passed through villages and farmland until they came to a large city. This was the capital of Kohlapur, an enchanting city of sprawling streets and houses washed in shades of blue, white, and red, lying on a slight rise of hills above a clear lake of crystal waters. Banyan trees provided shade from the tropical heat and lush green vines covered the sides of the houses, adding even more color to the surroundings. It seemed out of place in the flatlands that they had traveled through since leaving the mountains. The procession skirted the town, heading for the royal palace.

The palace itself was magnificent, sprawling over acres of wooded, terraced grounds. It was domed in the Moslem style, though Kohlapur was and always had been a stronghold of one of the oldest lines of Maratha Hindu princes. The structure was immense, as though it had been carved from a single chunk of pale pink marble.

Cat had only a glimpse of the grounds as the prisoners were taken toward the back of the palace and the carts were drawn up in a courtyard before the soldier's compound. She was immediately hustled off into a side entrance and saw no more of Ryan and the *Falcon*'s crewmen. The captain, who'd informed her his name was Rhan Cita, hurried her along so fast she was unable to question him about their destination. They went through what seemed to be a hundred hallways, all laid out in a twisting maze that grew more confusing as they moved deeper into the recesses of the palace. Guards, attired in uniforms so colorful they were almost gaudy, were stationed at every doorway they passed. All the doors looked the same to Cat, as she breathlessly tried to keep up with her captor's pace. Finally he stopped before one, and at a sharp command, the guard swung it open.

She found herself in a small, decorative chamber that seemed to be an anteroom for a court reception hall. Rhan Cita impatiently herded her toward a cushioned alcove and told her to be seated until she was summoned to the royal presence. The room was as luxuriously furnished as the rest of the palace; though in her present state of exhaustion, Cat was unable to appreciate its splendor. Worn and weary from the grueling, overland journey, despairing of Ryan's fate, she slumped on the cushions with defeat etching tired lines in her face. She was far too tired to worry over her own future, and cared little what happened to her.

It was almost a half-hour before the captain returned. Again he dragged her along, entering the main chamber by a side door. Latticed windows shed light on a milling crowd of dignitaries and courtiers. To her right, on a raised dais of white marble, under a tented awning of white and gold-striped silk, sat the short, squat omnipotent ruler of Kohlapur, the Maharaja Shah Anan. His gross bulk was covered in the finest brocade, his slack, flabby body threatening to overspill the jewel-encrusted gold throne. His dark, jaded eyes peered cynically from folds of wrinkled fat.

Cat, pulled roughly along by the ropes that tied her wrists, was only too aware of the curious, brazen stares of the men in the room. After five days' travel with little sleep, she thought miserably that if her safety depended on her beauty, Shah Anan would be hard put to find it beneath the layers of dust that covered her. She was dumped unceremoniously before the dais, ordered to bow low until His Royal Majesty deigned to look upon her face. A rapid flurry of Hindustani floated over her head and a blush spread across her face as she managed to grasp that her attributes were being discussed as one might at an action of horses. The captain ordered her to rise and turn for the benefit of the Maharaja.

Though Cat kept her gaze lowered, she had several glimpses of the man who would decide her fate. This was the heir to the great Shivaji, the ruler of the Hindustan, a pompous cynic who would have been nothing had he not been born on the right side of the covers of a royal bed. The old goat licked his dry lips and made a comment that sent the fawning assembly into gales of laughter. Cat could only imagine what it was and her temper took a quick rise until she remembered the hopelessness of her position. The Indian maharajas were the ultimate source of justice or injustice. She must not in any way offend him, though she seethed indignantly at the continuing appraisal and ribald comments that were bandied about.

Shah Anan croaked a command to Rhan Cita in a dry, reedy voice that seemed out of place coming from his huge body, and she was dragged off again. Perhaps that was to be her punishment, she thought irritably, to be dragged eternally from one place to another. Once out of the chamber, the captain slowed his pace and was good enough to explain that she would be quartered in the harem of His Royal Highness, Prince Rajir. Cat frowned at the idea. She demanded some word of her men and Ryan, but Rhan Cita fell silent, warning her solemnly that it was not her place to question what went on in the palace. He added, "A woman is an ornament to delight the eye of man, but should remain silent or she loses her value." It was hardly advice that sat well with someone as spirited as Cat Devlan.

Chapter Sixteen

The royal harem was quartered in a secluded palace, connected to Shah Anan's monumental edifice by a well-guarded passageway over a half-mile in length. Rajir's smaller group of concubines also resided there, though they were awarded a mere wing of the huge white marble building.

The architecture was magnificent, a combination of Moslem arabesque and Hindu simplicity. There were towering colonnades and lattice-screened balconies, golden fountains that shimmered in the midday sun, terraced gardens with fruit trees and an endless sea of colorful blossoms, lounges and game rooms, sunken baths of Persian tile inlaid with precious lapis lazuli and luxurious, well-cushioned rest chambers draped with gossamer hangings. In essence, it was an opulent prison, an isolated paradise on earth for those who had found favor in the eyes of the maharaja and his son.

The security of the harem was maintained by a complex system of guards. Well-armed troops were deployed about the perimeter of the palace, a ring of foot soldiers keeping watch on the grounds. Within, eunuchs were stationed along the halls, and armed women, huge amazons with heavy, muscular bodies, stood as the ultimate deterrent to anyone mad enough to seek entrance to the *zenana.*

Cat lounged in one of the rest chambers, reclining on a bed of silken cushions, staring absently at the jewel-encrusted ceiling that simulated a star-studded night sky. She counted the diamonds and sapphires for the hundredth time since she'd arrived over a month ago. A Nubian slave stood by the bed, ready to satisfy any whim she might have, be it a desire for iced sherbet or a scented bath and massage of perfumed oils.

Sighing heavily, she flipped over onto her stomach. Each day was the same in this strange world occupied only by women. The others here were an odd assortment of almost every faith and nationality, and all seemed to find the cloistered, leisurely life very pleasurable. They spent their days playing at games of backgammon or chess, whiling away the time with idle pursuits, experimenting with fashions, bathing and being massaged, perfumed and pampered, only to rise the next morning for the same routine. Shah Anan was old and grossly fat, so near impotence that he seldom requested the services of either wives or concubines. There was a titilating rumor amongst the women of Rajir's harem that many of the Maharaja's hundreds of concubines found physical pleasure with each other.

The prince and heir made excellent use of his forty concubines and two wives. He was young and virile, with seemingly boundless energy. He managed to keep each woman content and occupied, sometimes calling for several in a day. Cat had never seen him, for he always sent for the chosen one instead of visiting the harem himself.

Françoise, a voluptuous, dark-eyed blonde from Paris, was his current favorite. She would strut proudly upon returning from a visit with the prince, displaying the latest bauble he'd given her and boasting that Rajir thought her the most beautiful of all. The other girls hated her; she had no friends among any of them. From the first time she and Cat laid eyes on each other, there was mutual antagonism. The blonde's eyes would narrow to wicked slits when she passed Cat in one of the many chambers of the harem, and she occasionally made a snide comment.

One day Cat had been bathing with some of the other girls. She lay back in one of the sunken baths, relaxing in the warm, scented water, her eyes closed while rose petals floating on the surface gently caressed her skin in passing. The other girls spoke in soft whispers and every now and then there was the sound of a splash as one slipped into the silken waters. Suddenly there was silence and Cat opened her eyes to find Françoise standing above her, brazenly studying every feature of Cat's slim, ivory body, until her gaze settled on the thin scar that marked the smooth flesh of Cat's left shoulder. She smiled with delight, seizing an opportunity to taunt the only girl she considered lovely enough to be a threat.

"You aren't worthy of my master," she sneered. "It's no wonder that he hasn't bothered with you. The sight of your ugly scar would make him ill." The three other concubines stared in fascination, sure that the smug, blonde bitch had met her match in the copper-haired newcomer.

Cat stared up at the girl, who was bedecked in her finest gown for a connubial visit with Rajir. A flicker of irritation shadowed her eyes but she failed to react to the unnecessary slight. She sighed, rose calmly from the water like Aphrodite from the sea, and climbed the steps to allow the attendant to wrap her in a silken sheet, before sauntering over to Françoise, who openly gloated in triumph.

Cat addressed the girl in French. "I can tell by your speech you were raised in the gutters of Paris. If Rajir hadn't purchased you, even now you'd be walking the streets offering your overblown charms for a sou! Now, get out of my way, whore." The others were unable to grasp the language but they knew how insulting Cat's remarks were when they saw the stupid, gaping expression on Françoise's face. Cat smiled, acknowledging her appreciative audience, and passed her enemy, neatly hooking her foot around the girl's ankle to send her plummeting ungracefully into the water, amidst a round of appreciative shrieks. The blonde came up sputtering furiously, looking like a drowned rat, her seductive, revealing costume ruined and plastered to her plump, ripe figure. Cat turned and strolled out, ignoring the string of obscene Gallic curses that rained down on her head.

From that day forward, the two were openly confirmed enemies and Cat became the champion of the other girls. She alone had little to fear from Françoise's influence with Rajir. She'd had no word of Ryan since the time she'd been dragged off to the harem. At first she'd worried that because of her he'd been tortured and thrown into a dank dungeon somewhere in the palace. None of the girls had heard any rumors about an Englishman. She'd questioned almost all of them when they returned from their visits with the prince. Finally, she'd managed to cease worrying. He was an official of the Company. That alone should have secured his safety.

Cat had become very friendly with a girl named Indirah, a sloe-eyed beauty who had been the favorite until Françoise had been purchased at the local slave auction. Indirah, of all Rajir's concubines, was truly in love with him. She was a shy girl whose principal charm lay, not in her dark, petite delicacy, but in the sweetness of her personality. Following Cat's altercation with Françoise, Indirah had timidly approached her, thanking her for the moment of pleasure. Since then, they'd spent hours each day together. Indirah delighted in passing the time by showing Cat the use of various cosmetics that were compounded in the harem. There was collyrium, a black substance used to line the eyelids and emphasize their shape. Pastes and powders smoothed over the face brought color to pale cheeks. Many of the girls were Moslem and dipped their fingers in henna, while Indirah, as a Hindu, stained the parting of her waist-length, black hair a bright vermillion. A few used the betel leaf to redden the lips and scent the breath with its sweetness. There were endless costumes of silks and satins to try on and every conceivable type of jewelry, from earrings and jewel-encrusted gold armbands to anklets of beaten silver and ropes of precious pearls.

Now, Indirah poked her head through the arched doorway of Cat's room, her eyes bright and glowing with excitement above the sheer, silvery veil that hid the rest of her face. She wore a short bodice of gold material, her midriff bare and slim above a skirt of gold studded with pearls. She called her friend's name in a soft, musical tone, unwilling to awaken her if she were resting. Indirah had some very good news for Cat, something that would repay the beautiful, flame-haired foreigner for her kindness and friendship.

Cat smiled a welcome. She rose and sat cross-legged so that the girl could sit next to her. She knew Indirah must have just returned from a visit with Rajir. Happiness stained her cheeks with color and lightened her step. Cat couldn't understand the prince's preference for the overripe blonde when this delicate, almond-eyed wisp of a girl adored him so. Among the many blondes, brunettes, and redheads in all shapes and sizes in his harem, Indirah stood out like a fragile, creamy rose in a garden of more common blossoms.

The girl unfastened her veil and dropped it to smile at Cat. Her teeth were small, perfect pearls, set off by her reddened lips. "I have news of the man you seek, my friend. I have seen him with my own eyes!"

Cat was stunned. Thank God he was safe, was her first thought. But how would Indirah have seen him? Surely he was being held prisoner somewhere. A flood of questions tripped off Cat's tongue as she grasped her friend's arm. It was the first heartening news she'd had.

Indirah's tinkle of laughter blended with the sound of the tiny bells on a golden belt around her waist. She patted Cat's pale hand that clutched at her so anxiously. "He was with Rajir today. They are great friends, my master and the one who is sleek as a black leopard. I recognized him immediately. He was here last summer, when I . . . when Rajir still found me fair above all others." The last statement was tinged with sadness.

Cat was thoroughly confused. Ryan had been here, in Kohlapur, before? Her thoughts tumbled back in time to the *Falcon,* five weeks before. The colorful uniforms of the Maharaja's armed guards were distinctive; if he'd been here before, Ryan surely would have known who their captors were and yet he'd cautioned her to keep quiet and let him talk to the captain of the Indian vessel.

Suddenly it was all crystal clear. Ryan had meant to teach her a lesson, to let her worry and fret over his safety, isolated and powerless to escape the seclusion of the harem. And all the while he'd been free to hunt with Rajir, free to come and go at will. Undoubtedly the generosity of the royal prince had extended to keeping Ryan's sensual appetites well fed, too. She could hardly picture him maintaining a monkish abstinence for a month!

Indirah seemed to be unaware of her friend's sudden quiet. She bubbled happily, relating the best part of her news. "Rajir has had a change of heart! I have the fortune to find favor in his eyes once again—and best of all, Catherine, Françoise no longer enchants him!" Cat raised her head, still preoccupied with her thoughts, but happy for Indirah's sake. The girl chattered on, describing how she had danced for the prince and Ryan; how, afterward, Rajir had offered Françoise to Ryan and then swept her up to carry her to his bedchamber and renew their love.

"And what was the whore's reaction?" Cat's voice was cold and infuriated.

Until now, Indirah had thought Cat was only concerned for the welfare of someone who'd been captured with her. Now she realized it went much deeper. She hesitated to describe any more of what had taken place. "They—they've been together many times in the past weeks. The yellow-haired one would admit to no one that she was losing the prince's affections."

Cat cursed silently, withdrawing her hand to clench it in her lap. The position he'd placed her in was galling. She knew how his mind worked. Ryan would have his pleasure and let *her* stew until she was so bored, she'd be grateful to see him again. She was a captive in a prison, well fed and luxuriously clothed but a captive nonetheless. He was attempting to humble her, to bend her spirit to whatever whims he might have. Her mouth tightened into a rebellious line. She'd be damned if she'd let him succeed! The scheming devil—she'd pay him back if it meant waiting a year or a lifetime!

"He asked about you and I told him you seemed content." She reached out to touch Cat, a puzzled look in her dark eyes. "Was I wrong to say it—are you not content here?"

"As content as a caged bird can be," Cat answered grudgingly. "Ryan knows me well enough. I'm sure your claim surprised him. You answered well, little Indirah!" Let the scoundrel think his plans had failed. Indirah knew nothing of the constant battle of wills between the man called Ryan and the violet-eyed girl beside her, but she recognized the resentful determination in Cat's eyes and felt a brief flare of pity for Rajir's friend. Now Catherine was the prisoner, but Indirah wisely guessed that sometime in the future their positions would be reversed.

A heavy, overpowering scent of musk washed into the room. Both Cat and Indirah noticed it and turned to find Françoise lounging at the door, her face as sly and smug as a mouse that has outwitted the trap and stolen the bait. A new jewel dangled on a golden chain between her large, fleshy breasts, a sapphire the size of a robin's egg. From the smirk on her face, it was clear who'd given it to her. "I had no idea you once belonged to my new lover," she cooed in a tone of triumph. "It's no wonder he decided to put you away here and request a *real* woman!" Her dark brown eyes were narrowed and gleeful.

"How brave you are from the safety of the door," Cat responded in a honeyed tone. "I doubt you have the courage to enter and repeat that to my face."

Indirah watched the two size each other up. The French bitch was taller and heavier but Catherine was quick and agile. Without a doubt, it was her friend who would win, for there was a dark, vengeful fury seething beneath her cool exterior. She would have to put a stop to it before they came to blows, though she would have loved to have seen Françoise crying for mercy. The whore would use her nails in an attempt to ruin Cat's beautiful face, and *that* she would not stand for.

"Leave now," Indirah commanded, rising with a new air of authority, "or Rajir will hear of your behavior within the hour!"

Françoise stared at the petite Indian girl as though she'd suddenly gone mad. A mocking sneer began to form on her face; it faded as she considered her somewhat shaky position. When she'd been the favorite, she'd abused her position a bit. Now this simpering idiot had replaced her, and the thought of being subjected to Rajir's displeasure was sobering. "I don't care to dirty my hands with you," she snapped, whirling to stalk to her own quarters.

Indirah turned to Cat, pleased with her first taste of renewed authority, unprepared for the anger in her friend's expression. "I needed no help," Cat declared vehemently. "The bitch deserves to have her hair pulled out by the roots!"

Gently, Indirah touched Cat's shoulder. "There are other means of revenge, Catherine. She has already lost ground and has no one here to call friend. Believe me, everything will improve now. The day will be a brighter one tomorrow. Perhaps this man of yours will send for you, *then* you will have revenge on Françoise."

God forbid, thought Cat, alternating between a desire never to set eyes on him again and a stubborn will to devise a plan to get back at him.

The next day was a dull repetition of the past weeks. Cat slept late, soaked in the baths, was given a relaxing massage with oil of jasmine, and dabbled in her wardrobe of silks and satins for the tenth time. She finally selected a bodice of rainbow-hued silk that exposed the creamy, satin skin of her midriff above a matching skirt that showed just the slightest view of a slender, neatly turned ankle. The outfit had a pale green, gossamer veil that floated around Cat's burnished locks, secured by a simple, golden circlet. A pair of velvet slippers with a tiny gold bell at the tip of each matched the outfit. When she was finished, she twirled in front of a mirror, drawing a short veil across the lower half of her face.

Cat hardly recognized herself. Somehow she'd been integrated into the exotic, oriental atmosphere of the harem and found herself almost indistinguishable from the other girls. The woman who peered mysteriously from the reflection seemed an Eastern enchantress, more seductive for the filmy veil that hid her expression from view. Her eyes were wide and looked smoky gray, lined with black to the edges.

Beneath the veil, Cat's rosebud mouth twitched with irritation. What was the use of dressing so beautifully when no one saw her? She experienced the frustration of the European mind in the mysterious, unfathomable East. None of the other girls were unhappy, and yet their only reason for living was to be ornaments to enhance and gratify their master Rajir. They were as much his property as the jewels he handed out so freely.

Bored and disgruntled, Cat decided to seek the cool air of the gardens. She made her way through a labyrinth of halls to a lattice-screened terrace and peered outside, hoping she would be able to enjoy the fresh air in privacy. In her present frame of mind, she would make poor company for anyone.

The gardens of the harem were a masterpiece of planning. Peacocks sauntered beneath cool shade trees, preening in full splendor even when no one was present to watch. Terraces in tiers filled a huge courtyard. Banks of colorful blossoms scented the air and delighted the eye with a rainbow of colors. Cat strolled along the tiled paths, stopping to pick an orange-gold rosebud, wandering until she found herself by a huge marble fountain.

Rose water cascaded from a central font, forming waterfalls that splashed and gurgled as the water flashed golden in the last rays of the setting sun.

Cat perched on the fountain's edge, dipping her hand into the cool waters. The fragrance of crushed rose petals seemed to surround her, soothing her irritation away, replacing it with tranquility. She thought of Will again, as she had so many times since her capture. Poor Will, he was forever doomed to watch helplessly as she fell into a series of scrapes. How ironic it was that the attack on the *Caliope* was to have been their last brush with danger. If fate hadn't intervened, she'd now be in France.

Suddenly a pair of low, intimate voices penetrated her meditations. She glanced up to see Indirah stroll toward the fountain, her arm linked with that of a young man of striking, darkly handsome features. Their heads were bent together in tender conversation as they approached and Cat blushed, embarrassed to intrude on the private scene. This had to be Rajir Singh, for he was the only man besides his father who could enter the secluded world of the harem.

Indirah's voice was as bright as the half-hidden smile beneath her veil as she saw Cat and called out to her. She grasped her hand, drawing her forward to present her to the prince. "My lord, this is Catherine, the girl I mentioned. Is she not as lovely as I said?" Secure in Rajir's love once more, Indirah was as proud of Cat's slender, bright beauty as she was of her own.

Rajir's voice was low and melodious, his English clipped and sharp. Confidence born of royal breeding marked his every movement. He studied her from head to toe before announcing his agreement. "You have excellent judgment, my dove. If your friend is as loyal as she is beautiful, you have indeed made a fair choice of companions." He faced her, his mellow, dark brown eyes warm with appreciation. Cat felt slightly uncomfortable under the scrutiny, and started as his hand moved to tug the veil from her features. "Ah . . ." he said. "My friend Ryan also is to be complimented for his excellent taste."

He walked around her, surveying her figure from every vantage point.

Cat refused to allow her annoyance to surface. She maintained a cool mien during the entire inspection. If she had stood on the block of a slave auction, she couldn't have felt more nakedly exposed or evaluated. Ryan seemed to have found his indentical twin as far as arrogance and conceit were concerned, she thought. Both men exuded a confident, raw sense of power. Cat was sure Rajir could be just as ruthless as Ryan when thwarted; perhaps even more so, because of his powers as prince. Finally he completed the inspection and stood facing her once more.

"You are truly a fair flower. I question Ryan's wisdom in restraining himself though. To allow such rare beauty to be seen only by the flowers of the garden is a waste I find intolerable!" He smiled, his teeth flashing white against his olive skin, dismissing Cat with a regal nod as he took Indirah's arm once more and strolled down another pathway.

Her rising anger at the cavalier treatment that reminded her so much of Ryan spoiled the garden's beauty for Cat. The sunlight faded as she hurried toward her chamber, irate thoughts buzzing like a swarm of angry bees within her head. In her room, she paced back and forth by the bed, railing against the odd twist of destiny that had imprisoned her here. After almost an hour of pacing she had calmed enough to join the others for the evening meal. Indirah found her there and excitedly pulled her to one side.

"I told you today would be as bright as gold," the girl whispered excitedly. "My master commands us to join him in a meal at the palace. Your Ryan will be there too!"

Cat wasn't impressed. *"And,* I suppose, Françoise! You may send my regrets, Indirah. I don't intend to go."

Indirah was horror stricken. "Rajir *commands,* Catherine! You dare not refuse or the earth will surely tremble with his righteous fury. Please do not risk incurring his anger! Come—let us go and freshen ourselves. Even to be a few minutes late would greatly offend His Highness."

Cat found herself swept along by the insistent, diminutive girl. They bathed and Indirah hurried the slaves who massaged them with scented oil of jasmine until they both glowed and a cloud of fragrance wafted forth with every movement. The royal favorite left to see to her wardrobe and then returned to supervise Cat's attire.

Almost an hour after Indirah found Cat, they were ready. Cat revolved slowly as Indirah scrutinized every line of the outfit, finally issuing her approval with a soft sigh. "Praise be to Shiva," she exclaimed, delighted with the effect. "You are the very image of Uma, the goddess of light and beauty!" Cat's slender, willowy figure was covered by a sheer bodice and skirt in cloth of gold. In the light of the mirror's reflection, she shimmered with a golden aura. Bands of engraved gold circled her arms, delicate earrings in the shape of the sacred lotus blossom dangled from her ears, thin gold anklets jangled as she moved. Even her thick, curling locks appeared burnished beneath a thin, gauzy veil.

Indirah stepped up, dabbing perfume at Cat's temples and throat until the sensual fragrance blossomed and filled the air. Cat faced the mirror, drawing the short veil across her face. The effect was breathtaking. Once again she was a different person, an exotic, oriental incarnation. She smiled beneath the veil, oddly curious to see the effect on Ryan. At least she faced him with a full arsenal of feminine weapons.

A half-hour later, Cat and Indirah had traversed the passage to the palace and stood poised at the entrance to Rajir's apartments. On the way, Indirah had instructed her on the proper etiquette before the prince. She was to bow low, rising only on command, remain veiled, and speak only when addressed. The concubine had finished her instructions with a giggle as she confided a secret. Rajir meant to surprise Ryan with Cat's presence, since his friend had seen fit to ignore her for so long. "My lord was well taken with your beauty, Catherine. Were you not so dear to me, I would be jealous!" Cat diplomatically failed to inform her that nothing could draw her to the prince, for it would be a repetition of another Ryan.

A guard swung the wide doors open, announcing their entrance. The room was long and lavishly decorated, its walls covered by hangings that vividly depicted men and women coupling in every conceivable manner. The ceiling was an arched vault of marble, intricately carved with lotus blossoms. A *musnud,* the richly draped dais of Indian royalty, was the focal point of the room. Upon it sat the prince, reclining on a silken divan. Ryan lounged on a similar one a foot lower. Female slaves surrounded them. A girl stood on either side of the *musnud,* cooling the air with huge fans of peacock feathers. Several others were ranged about the steps of the dais, one girl, a dark African, played at the strings of a sitar and another balanced a tray of confections, offering them to the two men.

The two veiled girls approached the dais and a wide smile broke over Rajir's face. Unlike his father, who had been known in his younger days for his ruthless, cold nature, Rajir was an incurable romantic. He was anxious to see Ryan's face when he realized who it was that accompanied Indirah. The two women bowed in unison and the prince impatiently bade them rise and ascend the dais. A slight arching of a bold black brow evidenced Ryan's interest as Indirah left Cat's side and took Rajir's extended hand to join him on the divan.

Ryan stared at the girl who stood before him. It was obvious from the prince's complacent grin that she was meant for him. The French girl, Françoise, was a dull, insipid shadow who paled in comparison with this offering. The girl's gaze was modestly cast down, her features, except for a lovely fringe of dusky gold lashes, were covered by a tantalizing wisp of veil. Just a hint of peachy color showed on the girl's fair cheeks. There was a faint feeling of familiarity about the slender, gold-sheathed figure. A glow of appreciation came into his dark eyes. Rajir certainly had excellent taste in the women he chose for his harem.

To his left, Rajir waited with anticipation. "She is yours, my good friend." Impatience added a biting edge to his tone as he added, "You have never been so reticent before, why do you hesitate? Unveil the bounty set before thee!"

You did not refuse a command of His Royal Higness, Rajir Singh, even if he regarded you as a friend and boon companion. Not that Ryan had even considered refusing. His dawdling was due to an esthetic appreciation of the veiled beauty. The mystery of what temptations lay beneath that gauzy covering was alluring, whetting his appetite for what he knew would be a memorable evening. He smiled, more to himself than at the tranquil, submissive harem girl.

Cat was still in the harem. He could picture her raging fury at being penned in. No, Cat would never offer herself with the gracious deference of this one. She'd spit an angry retort, cursing his arrogance as she had so many times in the past. If ever there was a perfect woman on earth, he was sure she would have Cat's face and the sweetness of the passive girl who stood as still as a golden statue in front of him. He reached out, his long, darkly tanned fingers a prominent contrast to the creamy gold of the veil as he tugged it away.

Cat was thrilled that Ryan had failed to recognize her. Dressed in borrowed plumes, she was a different person. The docile act had succeeded in fooling him. She had carefully taken a peek at him through the fringe of her lashes. He seemed more than well. The month's sunlight hours had deepened his tan to a rich bronze. He was dressed like Rajir, in a brocade coat whose russet hue complemented his coloring. The sharp, bold features were already flushed with amorous shading, his large, expressive eyes heavy and langorous with sensual anticipation. The veil covering her face dropped, fluttering to the floor as gracefully as a butterfly in flight.

Ryan sucked in his breath. It was Cat who stood so calmly before him, more strikingly beautiful than he'd ever seen her. Rajir broke into laughter, a good-natured sound that mocked his friend's surprise.

"You see, Ryan—is my offering not a reflection of my high esteem for you? Surely you've had second thoughts; to keep such a jewel hidden is a sacrilege. She is like the pearl—more lustrous when worn!" As he spoke, his fingers caressed Indirah's knee. Clearly he was well pleased with his amusing charade and in an amorous mood himself.

Ryan grinned sheepishly, nodding his agreement. Only his eyes reflected his true feelings and they were turned away from Rajir. They were forbidding; frigid, sullen coals burning out of place in the mask of congeniality that had covered his shock. They threatened Cat as his hand shot out to close on her wrist and pull her on to his lap. Defiance blazed briefly in the violet eyes until she was forced to meekly lower her gaze. Ryan's arm banded her waist, his fingers casually fondling her breast through the thin material. She wriggled uncomfortably, unable to escape the visible mauling, for the prince was smiling with benevolent pride in his matchmaking. "How wise you are, Rajir. There are times we need to be reminded of the value of our possessions. You have my gratitude for arranging it so."

The gall of the strutting peacock, Cat thought furiously. She bristled at the word possession, longed to turn and rake his face with her nails. She was trapped, suddenly frightened of the show of solicitude that covered his intentions. Beyond the pounding of her heartbeat, she distantly heard Rajir order that the meal be served. She was aware of nothing but Ryan's hands running freely over her. Involved with his own amour, Rajir was unaware of her discomfort.

Ryan had temporarily shelved his irritation and was enjoying the prospect of carrying Cat off to his rooms. He tugged eagerly at the veil still covering her glorious hair, impatient to run his fingers through the silken, copper waves. Her soft skin was sweetly scented, luring him to touch its satiny texture. She stiffened, taking advantage of Rajir's preoccupation with a giggling Indirah to attempt to claw his hand away from her waist.

"Now, now, my lustrous pearl . . ." he whispered in a warm, caressing tone. "You wouldn't want me to offend Rajir's generosity by complaining!" His fingers wound in her curls, painfully forcing her head around until she faced him. His eyes lost their benign glow, naked desire mating with resentment to breed an ominous glare that predicted he would have his way, regardless of her feelings. Her hands pushed ineffectually at his chest, pinned uselessly between their bodies as his arms closed the short space between them and his lips mastered her mouth, forcing it open to submit to the bold entry of his tongue.

Cat shrank from Ryan, twisting to escape the assault on her senses. Even as she struggled to fight off the embrace that held her captive, she found herself molded to his body. For a moment she melted against his hard, muscular chest. He sensed her yielding, his lips forming a smile against her throat with a conceit that dampened the thaw like the bite of a cold winter wind. Ryan always had his way. He only had to touch her to renew his claims of dominance. She went limp in his arms, willing herself to feel nothing. It was her only weapon, the only thing that could pierce the elation that was surely pulsing through him.

Ryan cursed silently, feeling both resistance and response drain from Cat's body. He set her back from him, glowering at the masquerade of cold, unyielding martyrdom. The food had arrived and was placed before them on small tables. Rajir broke his embrace with his concubine, glancing over to Ryan to see how he fared. Ryan was forced to calm his ire once again, but he was more determined than ever to vanquish the spirit that had temporarily won a small battle over his own will. The smile he gave Cat was cold and relentless.

"Be a good girl and follow little Indirah's lead," he said mockingly, gesturing to the girl who delighted in placing tempting morsels of roast duck between her royal lover's lips. "Show Rajir that Western women can be as sweet and affable." The comment was a command, not a statement.

A tart, caustic retort flew to Cat's tongue and she was forced to catch her lip between her teeth to refrain from spitting a refusal at him. He guessed at her thoughts and grinned, his fingers brazenly stroking her inner thighs through the thin skirt. Unable to stop him, she shifted and reached for a piece of meat, roughly thrusting it into his mouth. He reacted quickly, grabbing her hand and squeezing her wrist until she winced with pain. In what looked like a gentle lover's whisper, he warned her to behave. To her chagrin, he calmly chewed the food and pulled her fingers to his lips to lick the taste of the meat from them in a taunt at her helplessness.

A set of golden jeweled chalices filled with a dark, heady wine sat on the table. Ryan reached past Cat to grasp the stem of one and offer it to her. She pursed her lips in a stubborn line and his fingers tightened on the tender flesh of her thigh in an indisputable message to drink. She hesitated a moment before taking the goblet and swallowing a tiny sip. Ryan frowned, his hand leaving her thigh to grasp her shoulder. He took the wine from her and pulled her back until she lay cradled in his arms, then brought it to her lips, forcing her to gulp it quickly or choke. She struggled weakly against his iron grip, swallowing until the cup was empty. A trace of the dark ruby liquid trickled from the corner of her mouth and down the alabaster skin of her throat. Ryan tossed the chalice to the table and bent his head to her throat, his lips following the sweet trail of wine until his tongue found its source and dipped to drink in the last vestiges of the spirits.

Cat's senses reeled, as much from the intoxicating wine as from Ryan's sensual attack. This time she had no will to resist the caresses of his hands or the powerful, driving force of his tongue as it invaded her mouth. Her arms crept around his neck, urging him on, and she cared not a whit if he felt he'd won. She moaned softly when he broke the passionate kiss and raised his head to address Rajir.

"M'lord, I beg your indulgence, but I'm swept by a desire to seek another kind of nourishment. By your leave, I'll retire to my rooms."

Cat was unaware of the look that passed between the two men. Her face was buried against Ryan's chest. Rajir glanced at her, noting the soft yielding in her manner as she clung to Ryan. Her face, in profile, was a perfect cameo that reflected her own impatience to be gone from prying eyes. The dark eyes of the prince were envious, even though he had the lovely Indirah at his side. Ryan's face was flushed with desire and a touch of pride as he stroked the girl's silken curls. Rajir gave his leave with an indulgent smile tinged with jealousy as Ryan stood and carried the girl across the room with long, confident strides that were so characteristic of him.

A moment later he dismissed the servants with a clap of his bejeweled hands, turning to Indirah to assault her with more intense ardor then he'd ever felt. She responded, molding her body to his, unaware that his fervent passions had been stirred by a fantasy of his friend possessing and mastering Cat's beautiful, supple body.

Ryan carried Cat down a long hallway toward his rooms. She stubbornly refused to look around, warring within herself. There was no doubt his virile strength had affected her, but what of her pride, what about her resolution to revenge herself for his callous treatment over the past month? She knew they passed through a door and suddenly she was dumped negligently on a soft bed of velvet cushions.

If Ryan had controlled his irritation with her manipulating and complimented her on her appearance, or even admitted he'd missed her, Cat would have been lost. As it was, he stared down at her with an expression of exalted judgment that brought all her resentment boiling to the surface. "What an artful bitch you've become," he sneered. "I was fooled by your little charade, but it seems you haven't learned anything from the harem girls but their manner of dress." He sighed with emphasis as he added dryly, "It appears I still have my work cut out for me."

Cat forgot the twist of desire that had brought her close to an acquiescent surrender and was instantly sobered by the sharp, biting comments. She scrambled off the bed, jumping to her feet with eyes that blazed violet fury. "You dirty, conniving, selfish bastard!" She advanced on him step by step, her hands balanced at her waist as she burst forth with a long string of epithets, switching to rapid French when she ran out of English expletives.

Ryan calmly crossed his arms, waiting until the tirade of verbal abuse wound down and she sputtered to a stop, glaring with helpless frustration at his patient expression. "If you're quite through, you can oblige me by stripping off your clothes and lying down."

Her mouth rounded to an indignant, shocked O, then snapped shut as she swept past him, headed for the door. She was stopped in midstride as Ryan's arms circled her waist from behind and he picked her up, ignoring her shriek of outraged protest and the backward kicks she aimed at his shins. "I'd rather bed the entire palace guard than you!" she screamed as he dumped her sprawling on the bed once more, adding a punishing smack on her derriere. She rolled to her back, ready to curse him again.

What Ryan said next in a cold, menacing threat sobered her rage as though he'd doused her with a bucket of icy water. "That can be arranged quickly enough, though after the tenth or so I think you'd lose track!" He smiled, but his eyes were somber enough so that she was unable to decide whether he'd carry through with such a horrid idea.

"All right, you'll have your way as usual!" Cat rose stiffly, her face closed and sullen as she stood and gestured to him to take her place on the bed. Pretending he wasn't in the room, she quickly pulled at the fastenings of her bodice and tugged it off, throwing it carelessly on the bed beside him. Her breasts stood full and firm, creamy white and tempting him with each further movement to undress. The long skirt followed and she stood before him, proud and straight despite his keen appraisal of her nude body.

In a low tone that was husky with urgent desire, Ryan ordered her to lie next to him. Her mouth twitched rebelliously but she obeyed, lying stiffly at his side, stubbornly refusing to unbend for an instant. He rolled over, his fingers lightly tracing the outline of her waist and hips, and the rough, gold-threaded brocade of his coat brushed her nipples, teasing them to life despite her vow to remain impassive and unmoved. His knee brushed against hers, raising to prod her thighs apart.

Cat directed her attention on the satin striped awning hanging above the bed, counting the tiny stripes to keep her mind occupied and insensitive to his attentions. She was only partially successful as his skilled touch began to elicit a reaction from her and a tingling spread over her skin wherever his hands caressed the firm, supple flesh. She ground her teeth together, tensing her muscles to repel the traitorous surrender of her will to his domination. It seemed he was everywhere at once, his fingers massaging the smooth skin of her inner thighs, his lips drawing a nipple into his mouth, to flick at it with his tongue until she moved uncomfortably, losing a battle with herself to resist him. He sensed her restlessness and increased the tempo of his stroking until the tenseness slowly left her body. Her eyes fluttered open, already glazed with the beginnings of passion, temporarily losing their resentment as her arms crept around his neck and she lifted her head, offering her rosebud mouth for his kiss.

Then Cat pulled back, the tiniest pout pushing out her lower lip. "It's not fair—you haven't taken off *your* clothes." She tugged at the coat, but his hand closed over hers and she glanced up with surprise to find him grinning, his dark eyes black with an overspill of passion.

"Not important," he said in a whisper against her throat. "I want you *now!*" He reached down and freed himself, rolling on top of her with an urgency that swept her along. Her breath came harder as he moved over her, her thighs parting to accommodate him. She gave a sharp gasp as he entered her and began to move. It had been over a month since their passionate lovemaking aboard the *Falcon,* a month without the sight of a man until this evening and she was ready for him almost at the first driving plunge between her passion-spread thighs. He fell forward, one hand under her neck to capture her wildly twisting head and bring the sweet taste of her lips to his, his other hand roughly fondling a breast. She was a wild thing beneath him, as eager for release as he, clawing at his back like a frenzied jungle cat, moaning his name softly as her desires swept to a fever pitch. Only one thing could cure the fever's heat and it came, an explosive of release of frustrated, built-up passions that brought a tearing scream from her throat. He continued the thrusting of his hips until she shivered under the assault of a second, gentler explosion that sent her body arching against his, aching with intense ripples of pleasure that swept her from head to toe. It was a while before her breath came evenly and Ryan held her close the entire time, his lips brushing the soft silk of her hair as she lay against him.

A while later Ryan rose and gently laid her aside. She looked sleepy and content, stretched across the satin sheets like a lovely sea-nymph, her hair a blaze of autumnal color surrounding the perfect, heart-shaped face. Her eyes half-opened, questioning his leaving. Ryan crossed the room to fetch a bottle of wine and glasses. As he walked, he stripped his clothes away and glanced back to assure himself she was still there. Silently, he called himself a fool for depriving himself of her company for so long on a mere whim of teaching her a lesson. He was naked when he returned, a bronzed, muscular giant who smiled down at her. He offered her a hand to pull her up and gave her one of the glasses of wine. He was far from satisfied. They had a long night ahead and he toasted it, raising his glass with a warm, glowing smile.

Chapter Seventeen

The market place of Shah Anan's capital lay at the center of the city, like the hub of a great wheel. It sprawled in a circle, surrounding a small oasis of cool shade trees, the streets leading up to it teeming with an overflow of busy shoppers. The sights, sounds, and scents of the bazaar were a feast for the senses.

The lusty cries of vendors hawking their wares rose above the clamor of the crowds that pressed together in a shifting sea of humanity. Children squalled, begging their mothers to stop for a treat. A businesslike auctioneer called out the attributes of his latest shipment of slaves in a cold, impersonal inventory.

The stalls and shopfronts were a riot of color, hung with awnings of gaudy reds, peacock blues, and garish yellows. The goods were displayed to their best advantage, tempting passing browsers to touch and test their quality. Silks and satins, damasks and damascene linens, all in rainbow hues of pastels and pure, vibrant shades, were carefully draped to catch the eye. One stall peddled confections, almond and honey candies in crystalline flower shapes. Another sold spices and herbs that filled the air with pungent odors. The smell of onions battled with nutmeg; spicy peppers, chutney, and curry won over cinnamon and allspice. From still another open shop that sold perfumed oils, the fragrances of attar of roses, jasmine, and musk wafted forth. Strips of sandalwood burned in a censer, spreading its sweet fragrance throughout the bazaar.

It was a pageant, a dramatic spectacle meant to entertain as much as to barter and sell goods. The shoppers were a potpourri of Kohlapur's citizens. The illustrious rubbed elbows with the notorious, the splendidly attired nobles of the court brushed by shabbily dressed farmers in from the countryside. Street urchins in tatters lurched against the wealthy, groveling in apology before scrambling away into the crowd, a stolen purse jingling in small, dirty fingers.

In the midst of this crush, no one took notice of a tall, broad-shouldered man dressed in a long, voluminous robe. A hood covered his features, hiding them in shadow. His long strides were quick and purposeful as he headed for an alley that led off the marketplace.

The congestion of the street lessened as he reached the corner of an alley known as the Way of Suffering. This section of the city was reserved for beggars, for the halt and lame who had no other place. The man paused, studying the pathetic figures that lined the alley. Some had limbs missing, their worn garments limply draped where arms and legs should be. One stood out like a beacon on a dark night. His body was thin and wasted, a light cotton robe hung loosely over his bony frame, but there was a proud, aristocratic strength in his back as he sat cross-legged before a crumbling dwelling.

This was Fateh Jai, and Will Foster had come searching for him. As he approached the blind man, Will was surprised by the dry, crackling voice that greeted him before he had a chance to speak.

"Thou art blessed, stranger," intoned Fateh Jai, stretching out his palm to receive the coins that jingled in Will's cupped hand. "Vishnu favors those who remember the less fortunate. Kalkin, who is yet to come, will surely bless thee."

In the shelter of his hood, Will smiled sardonically. It wasn't heaven's blessings he sought from this poor blind soul; he needed a very earthly favor. The alley was almost deserted now except for the forlorn row of beggars lining each side of it. The nearest was well out of hearing range when Will squatted next to Fateh Jai.

"Thou seekest something, stranger," the blind beggar said, more as a statement of fact than a question. His keen, sharp hearing had become his eyes. By the sound of his approach, he judged the man to be tall and strong, most likely a European.

"I was told y'could help me, Fateh Jai. Ali Ben Kabran spoke highly of ye." The slave trader came frequently to Kohlapur, as he did to the other native states. Will had met him over a year before on the Malabar Coast and had been lucky enough to run into the wily, sharp-eyed Arab here.

Will could hear the amusement in Fateh's whispery tone, almost see the thin smile in the shadow of his hood. "If Ali sent thee, I welcome thee as a friend. Any help I might be able to give would depend on the nature of the request." A good-natured laugh softened the sardonic statement that followed. "If it is a guide thou needest to view our fair capital, I would be of little use!"

Will lowered his voice and cautiously leaned closer. "I've a friend who's bein' held in the harem. I was told if anyun' could arrange an escape, it's be ye, Fateh Jai."

Silence followed the dangerous request. It was well known what fate lay in store for those who failed in such an audacious undertaking. The blind man thrust out his hand, searching for Will's arm. He found it, using the well-muscled limb for support as he rose to his feet. "Such things are better said in privacy, friend of Ali Ben Kabran." With a gracious gesture he indicated the poor, dilapidated building before which he begged. "Humble as it may be, thou art welcome."

It was dark inside and Will was asked to wait by the door. The beggar made his way across the room with sure, steady steps, locating a seldom needed tallow candle. When it was lit, the feeble glow revealed the austere, monkish cell that Fateh Jai called home. A small wooden cot lay in one corner, covered by straw and a light, worn blanket. A chest stood against the opposite wall and a table and two chairs were the only other furnishings.

The blind man felt for the high back of one of the chairs, drawing it away from the table for Will. "Pray be seated, friend." A cloth-wrapped package lay on the table and he felt for it, unwrapped it to reveal several saffron rice cakes. "This simple food is all I can offer; thou wouldst honor me by sharing it."

There was no way for Will to refuse the offer, though he felt guilty for taking the poor man's food. He vowed silently to pay him well for his help. "Honor's mine," he insisted, breaking one of the cakes into uneven pieces and handing the larger portion to his host.

"Tell me thy name, my friend, and the events that led thee to my door."

Will had been told that Fateh Jai could be trusted. He proceeded to explain how the *Falcon* had been captured and how he had searched for weeks until he found where Cat had been taken. "I seen her ridin' a few times. Veiled she was, but I'd know that girl if she was covered from head to toe!"

The blind man nodded. "And so I am to help rescue the girl. The fates have sent thee to the right person, Will Foster; I owe nothing to the fat bull who squats on the throne of Kohlapur. It will take time, but we will free thy captive friend."

"I know the risks, friend," Will replied, "but rest assured I'll make it well worth your trouble. Name a price; it's yours, no matter how high ye sets it!" For the first time in weeks, Will felt a glimmer of hope.

"Gold will be required for bribes, but I will not accept a rupee for my help. Indulge an old man with an hour of thy time—that is all I ask." Fateh Jai proceeded to tell why he would risk the danger without profit to himself.

"The world was mine when I was young. My parents indulged their only son, allowing me free rein to do as I pleased. I was a sensualist, a hedonist with a poetic soul. The rising sun brought words of praise to my lips; I saw beauty in the very air I breathed—everything shimmered with a golden glow. I was strong and straight, vain about my looks, proud in the love of the most beautiful girl in the Hindustan." Fateh Jai's voice vibrated with emotion, growing younger with each succeeding memory of his youth. "Farah was her name. She possessed an excellent lineage, as long and proud as that of my own family. We were to be wed in her fifteenth year, on the celebration day of her birth." The old man smiled at the memory. "I have written many odes to her beauty and still do so in the late hours of the night. Would thou care to hear the latest?"

Will was a stout-hearted Englishman, unfamiliar with the fine arts of poetry or music. Still, he found himself fascinated by the man's tale, by the pain and still-fresh ache reflected in his voice. "That I would, Fateh Jai," he answered.

The old man nodded, pleased that his visitor was so patient. He cleared his throat, his tone changing to reflect the love he had felt for his long-ago fiancée.

She was my beloved; revered in my sight,
She was the earth, from whose fertile soil all abundance springs,
She was the wind, the sweet breath of air that eludes capture,
She was the light, the bright rays of the sun, the mellow glow of the moon,
She was my beloved; she is gone.

She is the moist earth that welcomes the velvet jasmine petals,
She is the wind that gently caresses these sunken cheeks,
She is the light that shines in these poor shriveled sockets,
She is my beloved.

Will no longer thought of Fateh Jai as a poor, blind beggar when the man finished his ode to a lost love. He was no judge of poetry, but the man seated across from him seemed rich in dignity, wealthy in the sweet, clear memories of his youth. A strong curiosity about the fate of the beautiful Farah seized him. "Ah, but that was lovely, m'friend," he commented. "Tell me if y'would—what happened to the girl that ye lost her?"

Fateh Jai rose, moving around the table to touch Will's shoulder. "Thou art not so rough a man as thou would like to believe, Will Foster!" He turned and walked to the door, his blind gaze turned to the fading light. "As I said, we were soon to be wed. Shah Anan was the heir to the throne in those days. Ruthless, cold, grasping, he seized whatever he wanted, wherever he went. He chanced to see her one day in her father's garden as he and some of the royal guard passed by. She was veiled, of course, but Farah's beauty was impossible to hide. Inquiries were made and he discovered she was to be mine." The old man laughed bitterly, turning to face Will. "He made an offer of marriage but she refused. In spiteful, imperial fury, he ordered her brought to the palace, forcing himself on her. Still she refused, for it was me she loved. He set out to teach her a lesson."

Will stared, shaking his head at the arrogance of the man who now ruled the country. "And that was . . ." he prompted.

"Patience, my friend, the tale is almost at an end. *I* was the lesson. I was seized from my home, carted away despite the pleas of my distraught parents, and brought to the palace. The prince ordered a wedding feast, decking my Farah in jewels and silks. Her vows were said under duress, for he threatened her with my death if she did not agree to marry him. At the celebration that followed, he had me dragged before her stunned eyes and I was blinded with white-hot pokers." The skeletal hand rose, tugging at his hood. It fell back to reveal his face in the light. His sockets were empty, black, hollow rings surrounded by scarred, wrinkled skin. The flesh of his face was stretched tight across his facial bones, giving the appearance of a breathing, parchment-covered skull, a parody of what had once been a handsome face. He replaced the hood, adding, "Shocking, is it not? *This* was Shah Anan's revenge. My crime was not in loving the girl he had chosen, but in being loved by her."

Will felt his belly churn as he imagined the pain. "Lord, what a devil's spawn he must be! Good God," he exclaimed a moment later, "and Cat's in his harem!"

Fateh Jai held up his hand. "Have no fear—he is beyond the ability to harm any more women. He grows more corpulent and gross with every passing day. The girl is safe enough until we free her."

Will breathed a heavy sigh of relief. "And Farah . . . she's dead now?"

"Yes," the old man admitted with a sad whisper of a sigh. "She died nine months later, giving birth to her son. I am told Rajir has her features. Thanks be to Vishnu that he failed to inherit his father's cruelty! Now thou must realize why I will help. My reward will be to know thy friend is free."

With gratitude choking his speech, Will rose and grasped Fateh Jai's hand in friendship. "Ye must let me do somethin'," he insisted. "Y'need food, clothin' . . . someun' to help ye."

"I have all I desire," he answered with a smile. "My needs are few and simple. There are friends if I need assistance. It must be dark, my friend. Return at dawn and we will have our plan." He walked to the door with Will, dismissing the thanks he offered again, listening as Will's footsteps receded and silence returned to the room once more.

The following day, unaware that Fateh Jai's plan for her escape was already under way, Cat rode with Indirah to the palace arena in a *howdah,* an elaborately decorated, cushioned platform that perched atop the broad back of an elephant like a ship on the rolling seas. They joined a procession of nobles and courtiers, some riding magnificent Arabian steeds, some carried along in palanquins, relaxing while servants jogged the mile from the palace.

The arena was huge, almost two hundred yards long, one hundred and fifty wide, with blue-washed walls that rose twenty feet to the grandstands. The Maharaja's pavilion was located midway down the length of the arena, an elegant, shaded dais that provided ample room for the royal party and the retinue of favored concubines. The prince was seated on a throne just slightly lower than his father's, Ryan in a place of honor at his side. Indirah perched on velvet cushions at her master's feet, Cat next to her at Ryan's knees. The royal party had been the last to enter, the crowd standing in the public area bowing low until their ruler was seated. Shah Anan's dark, cynical eyes, lost in folds of wrinkled fat, signaled the captain of the guard to begin the festivities.

A parade led by the royal elephants wound around the arena. The huge mammals were gilded in intricate designs, stained with bright vermillion, their broad backs covered by scarlet silk. They lumbered past, two abreast, in step to the heavy, resounding beat of a drum. The mahouts took them through a series of kneeling bows before the pavilion, then herded them past with a prod of the ankus. Scarlet-liveried servants marched on either side, carrying banners of silk with the royal insignia embroidered in gold. Black, white, and dun Arabian horses pranced in spirited pairs, the uniforms of their riders matching the mount's coloring. It was a splendid, colorful start for the day's festivities. Gladiators followed, clad only in loincloths, their well-muscled bodies shining with perfumed oils. They marched in unison with long, powerful strides. Later, their fingers would be fitted with needle-sharp metal tips, and they would fight, with a passionate abandon induced by imbibing liquid opium.

When the last of the parade wound through the gate at the end of the arena, a hushed, expectant silence hung over the excited crowd, broken only by the cries of vendors peddling refreshments.

Gates were opened at opposite ends of the arena and two huge bull elephants were led forth. It took three skilled trainers to handle each animal, for they were crazed with musth, a condition resembling the rutting season, brought on by a special diet. The sound of their frenzied trumpeting vibrated in the air.

The two were almost perfectly matched in size, massive behemoths whose sharpened tusks were sprinkled with gold dust that sparkled in the midday sun. A cheer went up from the crowd as the mammals scented each other and were loosed to charge down the arena toward each other, their huge legs shaking the ground with each thundering step. They met almost halfway, crashing into each other like two Goliaths. The larger of the two scored a hit with his tusks and the populace screamed their approval as blood dripped from his opponent's dark gray hide. The victor trumpeted proudly, continuing to jostle and charge, swinging his heavy, ponderous trunk. The fight was finished.

Rajir leaned down to ask Cat's opinion of the match as the two elephants were herded off through the gates. He had come to admire her in the past weeks. She failed to fit the timid, subserviant pattern of Eastern women and he found the difference refreshingly enchanting. If not for his friendship with Ryan, he'd have moved to make her his. Loyalty was the only thing that held his growing desire in check. He could see her smile through the sheer white veil as she answered that she was far more accustomed to the battle of men than beasts. Cat was attired in pure white today, veiled from head to toe in shimmering silk, only her bright, gold-fringed eyes clearly visible.

Ryan glowered at the low exchange between the prince and Cat. Nothing was working out as he'd planned.

Rajir was bewitched by Cat and had used his power to see that she was extended every comfort. If she wanted to ride, Rajir rode with her. She was even allowed to ride alone except for a small escort of troops. Ryan didn't like it, but there was little he could do. Shah Anan was the ultimate power in the small country and as his heir, Rajir exercised almost as much power. Ryan had warned his friend that Cat couldn't be trusted, that she would attempt an escape on one of those seemingly innocent rides.

Directly across from the royal pavilion, the beggar Fateh Jai sat with a large man whose features were concealed by his hooded robe. In the row below them, a man turned, then jostled his companion with an elbow. "You came to see the sights, eh, Fateh Jai?" His friend turned to glance at the blind man and joined in the ribald laughter that broke out among the nearby spectators.

"There are times when the blind see more than the sighted, my observant friend," Fateh Jai remarked in a tranquil tone of acceptance. He and Will were here not to enjoy the games of the arena, but for Will to study the pavilion and its occupants. The plans for Cat's escape were proceeding smoothly thus far. Ali Ben Kabran had been enlisted to help, at a high cost, for despite his friendship with both Will and Fateh Jai, his head would be forfeit if he was caught.

The plan was for the slave trader to appear before the prince in an anteroom of the harem palace, to offer several girls he'd recently acquired. At the end of today's performance, when the royal party made its exit, a street urchin named Gabel would accost Cat, begging for alms as a cover while he thrust a note into her hand, warning her to be ready for Kabran's visit. Will had assured the blind man that Cat was quick enough to cover the exchange. In some way she'd be disguised among the rejected slave girls and in that way escape the confines of the harem. Kabran had his entourage of slaves and servants ready to leave at a moment's notice. There was always the chance of a slipup, and if his visit was connected to the missing girl, he wanted to be well out of harm's way.

A short battle between two water buffaloes followed. It was more humorous than gory, with the animals butting against each other until they were unconscious. Finally the gladiators were brought out, two at each end of the arena and a pair in front of the royal stands. Cat was unable to share Indirah's enjoyment as the men stalked each other, circling for advantage, each man's hands extended like animal claws, ready to slice at the adversary. In a moment the first blood had been drawn, a wicked scratch over one man's right eye. At the other end of the arena the spectators were shouting encouragement to their favorites as the fighting became progressively more savage. Cat turned her head away, glancing at Rajir to find an excited gleam of blood lust in his eyes.

Strong brown fingers settled on her shoulder and her eyes met Ryan's. His expression was impassive but he seemed to empathize with her reaction. Over the past weeks he'd become jealous; Cat had taken advantage of Rajir's interest to goad him into it. She was sure he thought it was well hidden, but it was quite evident in his eyes, in the possessive touch of his hands, in his tense, surly manner. She'd thought long and hard to find a suitable vengeance for his arrogant treatment of her.

Indirah had told her a great deal about Rajir's past. He had a favorite half-brother, Jahkrishna, the son of one of Shah Anan's concubines. Jahkrishna had listened to his mother's jealous relatives and tried to wrest control of the throne from his father. The attempted coup was put down with little bloodshed, though Rajir had been forced to watch while his older brother was beheaded. He blamed his father for the boy's envy and insecurity. Almost ten years had passed since Jahkrishna's death and Rajir had become fanatical about illegitimacy. Only his two wives had borne children; the concubines all used varied methods to keep from becoming pregnant.

If Rajir thought she was going to bear Ryan's child,

she might be able to sway him. If not for his loyalty to Ryan, she knew he would have already moved to add her to his harem. A week ago he'd made her a gift of a beautiful, spirited Arabian mare, and there'd been other indications of his favor. Cat could shed a few tears, perhaps threaten to harm herself if Ryan wouldn't marry her. It was well worth the try. Ryan deserved to suffer, and it was the only way she could get back at him. In the length of time they'd known each other, he'd never offered to marry her—and yet he'd become betrothed to that vacuous bitch Alicia in less than a month's time!

There were plans under study in other minds during the gladiator matches. Ryan was contemplating Cat's future, trying to decide whether he should take her back to the Fort soon. With her ship gone, she was no longer in the pirate trade. That had been his goal, and he'd achieved it. Of course he still knew nothing of the frigate she'd mentioned. It could be a threat, but without the information Cat received from George, a very minor one. Still, he was a little wary of allowing her to leave the harem. Within it she was virtually his prisoner, under his control as long as they stayed. If they left Kohlapur, she'd be more difficult to handle. The thought of marrying her poked at the edges of his mind. After all, a woman was subservient to her husband's will, actually a possession. Yet if he suggested it and she refused . . . a fleeting smile crossed his lips as he considered asking Rajir to arrange it. If they were married here, she'd have no choice in the matter. He could just imagine her reaction. She'd scream and rant, and all for nought. The idea was becoming more enticing with each passing minute.

The games were coming to an end. In their opium-induced states of frenzy, the pairs of gladiators at the far ends of the arena had torn each other to shreds. There were no victors, yet they fought on until attendants came to drag them away. The two in front of the pavilion were thought to have given a better performance. The taller of the two blinded his opponent and continued the merciless savagery until Shah Anan signaled an end to it. The victor wavered on his feet before the maharaja, bowing respectfully before he stood tall for the accolades of the roaring crowds. Later he would be rewarded for his prowess, but now he needed assistance just to stumble off the field of battle.

Cat had refused to watch any of the fights, though she noticed Indirah felt no such qualms. The party of dignitaries and nobles in the pavilion rose as trumpets pronounced the end of the games and Shah Anan stood to leave. His son followed with Indirah, and Ryan took Cat's arm to lead her out to the waiting howdah.

In the hallway leading to the outside of the arena, a small boy in tattered, worn clothing broke through the line of royal guards that cordoned off the crowds. Cat was startled as the urchin headed directly for her, grasped her hand, and pleaded in a singsong wail. Though he spoke in Hindu, it was obvious he was begging for alms. A guard trudged forward, hefting his sharp pike with a threatening motion. The boy seemed so pitifully desperate that Cat turned and appealed to Ryan. He dug a few gold coins from his coat and tossed them to the lad, who grinned impishly and bobbed several times in a bow, then clutched Cat's hand and gallantly kissed it. He was gone in a flash of dirty gray rags as he effortlessly avoided the guard's cuff and vanished into the crowd.

Ryan took Cat's arm once more. They proceeded past the staring mobs of people and down the stairs into the bright sunlight. He failed to note that her right hand was tightly closed in a fist, carefully concealing the paper the little beggar boy had thrust into her hand.

Chapter Eighteen

When she'd reached the privacy of her room at the palace Cat carefully withdrew the crumpled piece of paper she'd thrust into her bodice for safekeeping. Her heart pounded as she smoothed at the wrinkles with a trembling hand and read the short, cheery note in Will's almost illegible scrawl. She was to be out of the harem within a week, helped to escape her prison by the visit of a slave trader named Kabran. The only thing she was expected to do was to be present when the man showed his sampling of new slaves for the prince's approval. That would be easy enough to arrange—Indirah had already mentioned a slave showing in the huge anteroom of the harem palace. At the time Cat had listened halfheartedly, her mind occupied with the note the beggar boy had shoved into her hand.

Now she held the paper to a candle flame, watching as the evidence of her desire to escape turned into a small mound of gray-black ashes. Her mood had been light and cheerful upon leaving the arena. Just the thought of her ultimate revenge on Ryan for his domineering treatment had brightened her outlook. This sudden news wouldn't change her plans in the least; it only meant that she had less time to influence Rajir. In fact, the more she thought, the more enchanted she became with the idea of wedding Ryan, only to desert him within a few days, to disappear from his life and strike a double blow at his self-possessed pride.

The next morning she asked Indirah to send a note to the prince, asking if she could ride. She knew he would jump at the chance to accompany her. Indirah was happy enough to do it—she thought nothing of the rides Cat shared with her lover, and she herself had no inclination to have anything to do with jogging along on the back of a horse, no matter how beautiful the steed. She thought it odd that Western women would enjoy such a strenuous exercise—a quiet stroll in the gardens was more to her liking.

Within an hour, Cat and Rajir were riding the hills above the city, with a suitable escort of guards protecting the royal heir from a discreet distance. Rajir mentioned that Ryan was in the city for the day to look over a shipment of horses that had just arrived. He was doing the prince a favor by weeding out the undesirable mounts. "He seemed to have no objections to our ride, my dear. I sometimes wonder about Ryan's intentions toward you. My friend has fallen under your enchanting spell, yet he resists the inevitable—he is as much a subject of his obstinate pride as you are." They had cantered the horses to a lovely, grassy stretch of land above the lake, with a view of the city as well as the magnificent palace. Rajir slowed his spirited stallion to a walk and gestured to a tree-shaded spot. "Would you care to rest a while? Surely it will be a relief from this glaring sun."

Cat agreed; it would provide a perfect spot for her to bewail her distress over her "pregnancy" and Ryan's callous treatment. "How thoughtful you are, Your Highness," she replied, reining her mare to a halt. Rajir caught her as she slipped gracefully from the beautiful sidesaddle he'd given her. He held her a moment longer than necessary and she blushed modestly and lowered her gaze as he studied her features. "You're far too kind to me . . . ." An artful flicker of despair shadowed her lovely features as she glanced away, then stared up into his eyes. "As kind as Ryan is cruel!" He released her, tucking her slim arm into his as he walked her over to the shade of two banyan trees whose graceful boughs bent together as though they were lovers touching.

"You have known him a long time, Catherine. I would think by now you would be used to his attempts to subdue you. He has already conquered your delightful body; he seeks something more, and hides his true needs with bold demands." Cat leaned against one of the trees with a dejected attitude.

"And what are his true needs, m'lord? If you know them, pray tell me, for I have never seen beyond his arrogant use of my unwilling body. Has he a master plan to woo me by threats and brute force?" Her voice was a soft, puzzled plea and, as it was meant to, touched Rajir's sentimental heart. He reached forward and pulled at the fastening of her veil, revealing the innocent bewilderment in her expression.

Rajir stared at her pouting bottom lip, tempted to kiss her. He restrained his desire, reminding himself she belonged to a friend, and instead tried to explain his impression of Ryan's feelings. "Even a prince can be wrong, but I think he wants you to admit that he is the only one for you. There is a strong fascination in Westerners that I admit puzzles me—this need to be tied to one person. It has nothing to do with the physical." He took her hand and placed it across his heart. "It is here. He wants your love but goes about it in the wrong manner. Give him time, little one; he will realize it himself."

"Time! We've known each other for years, and he's always treated me this way." Ready to throw out the bait, Cat experienced an odd twinge of guilt, until she remembered Ryan's past arrogance. "I'm running out of time, it's too late even. . . ." Cat imagined herself pregnant and abandoned, and it brought an immediate impressive rush of tears to her eyes. She hesitated deliberately, waiting for his curiosity to goad him into prying her secret out of her. Tears rolled down her cheeks as she squeezed her eyes shut.

"Why is it too late?" Rajir studied the delicate features that were swept by misery, and guessed at its cause. "You are carrying his child!"

Two slender hands rose to cover her face as Cat nodded and sobbed. With a sense of detachment, she watched her own performance and applauded the perfect portrayal of wounded innocence. Even now she imagined she heard Ryan raging against Rajir's decree that he marry her.

With almost brotherly affection, he pulled her against his chest to let her cry, patting her back in comfort. "You have no reason to be sad. Ryan will surely marry you and give the child a name."

"I don't want to . . . to get married—at least not to *him,*" Cat stammered between sobs. Knowing Rajir's intense dislike of illegitimacy, she cast the final temptation. "He won't marry me anyway—he's too stubborn to be forced into anything."

Rajir was growing increasingly distressed. Friend or not, he would insist that there be a ceremony. "You have nothing to worry about. Dry your eyes, Catherine. Whether either of you wants to wed is unimportant. The child you carry must have his father's name." His tone had become an imperial command. Cat allowed herself a tiny smile against his chest, before drawing back to confront him with her fears. Her eyes were wide with fright. "Even if he did marry me—he'd blame me! He'll be ten times worse than he was. I know he'll find some way to make me suffer!" She trembled against his chest and looked down in despair, adding a desolate sigh.

"I will see to the arrangements. By this time tomorrow, the two of you will be as one. Tremble and weep no more, for I will see to it that he treats you with the proper respect due the mother of his child!" He raised her chin and wiped a tear away, to be rewarded by a brilliant, trusting smile. "Now we must return—I will need to send for one of your Christian reverends. Put all worry aside, for it will do the child no good."

Cat smiled tremulously, sending aloft a thankful prayer that she'd been able to carry it off. It fluttered heavenward on the wings of a second prayer that the escape would go as planned. She would hate to face Rajir's wrath when he discovered she wasn't pregnant and, worse, had manipulated him in her plans.

The next evening a small wedding ceremony was held in the antechamber of Rajir's apartments. A sullen, white-lipped Ryan stood next to Cat, painfully gripping her small hand in his as they repeated the words that made them man and wife.

Cat was attired in a silken sari whose pale peach color complemented the heavy fall of copper curls that lay across her shoulders. A hastily recruited minister of the Church of England officiated, peering through his wire spectacles with the pinched expression of a true ascetic as his wavering voice intoned the solemn, binding vows.

Ryan answered in a cold, clipped tone that echoed in the long hall, while Cat replied with a soft assurance that came from Rajir's beaming approval. He was seated on his divan, Indirah at his side, and benevolently gave his blessing when the ceremony ended.

Despite the constraint he was under to "treat his wife with due respect," Ryan managed to impart his mood to Cat when he embraced her to seal their vows with a kiss. His arms banded her body like iron bars, crushing her as his mouth slammed against hers, bruising her tender lips and forcing them to part and submit to the punishing intrusion of his tongue. She couldn't struggle; she could barely breathe. When he released her she would have stumbled backward if he hadn't caught her arm.

Ryan was the epitome of gentlemanly courtesy as he

thanked the minister and marched Cat up the steps to the dais. "Was everything done to your approval, Your Highness?" Ryan asked politely.

"You are angry now, Ryan, but when you hold your child in your arms and know that he is protected, you will thank me for my interference!" He turned to Indirah and told her to escort Cat to Ryan's chambers to prepare for the wedding night. "Stay and share a toast with me, my friend," he asked Ryan, smiling as he watched the two women leave the room. "You are a most fortunate man, Ryan Nicholls. You have yet to realize that many men will envy you for what is yours." Ryan growled a noncommital reply that managed to dispute Rajir's claim without insulting him.

A lovely slave girl appeared with a flagon of wine, bowing as she offered them each a golden goblet and filled it to the brim.

Ryan accepted the toast to a happy married life, staring broodingly down the length of the hall toward the door through which his wife and her friend had vanished. "My problems are only beginning, Rajir. Now that I've got her—I've got to keep her." His lips twisted in a wry grin as the wine warmed him and improved his view of the evening's happening.

When Rajir approached him the previous evening, the arrangements had already been made. Rajir broke the news with gentle firmness, and Ryan was well aware that he would have no choice but to comply. Despite the fact that he'd been dwelling on the very same idea, it galled him that she'd connived and deceived Rajir in order to force the marriage. There was no doubt in his mind that she'd lied about a child. If he'd really wanted out, he'd only have had to insist that the royal physician examine Cat.

Ryan accepted another glass of wine, smiling to himself over Rajir's injunction to treat his bride with gentleness. There were other ways to make her realize what she'd bargained for when she'd hatched her little plans for him. Now he rose and excused himself. "We'll settle in soon enough, Rajir. I'll just have to get over the feeling I'm one of those black bucks your cheetahs run down so easily!" He grinned and held out his hand to the prince. "You'll forgive me if I'm anxious to join my bride!"

Rajir sighed happily, glad that his friend had accepted the wedding with such grace. "Tonight is only the first of many nights of splendor, Ryan. Treat her tenderly and she will respond like a flower to the warmth of the sun. Go now, I know how you must feel!"

When Ryan entered his room, it was dimly lit, with a candle glowing on either side of the bed. The sheer hangings were drawn; through the gauzy material he could just discern Cat's figure. Indirah had discreetly made an early exit after helping Cat into a silken gown whose sides were split and tied with lace bows, revealing a tempting display of rounded breast and thigh.

Cat kept her gaze lowered, concentrating on her serenely folded hands as Ryan swept aside the draped hanging and stared down at her. The tiniest hint of a smug smile touched the corners of her mouth. She'd succeeded in trapping him into a marriage he never would have proposed, and there was nothing he could do to her without invoking the Prince's wrath.

"You're very well satisfied with yourself tonight, aren't you, darling?" The bland question contained an underlying menace that made Cat glance up hesitantly as Ryan settled on the bed. He reached for one of her hands and held it captive within his grasp, observing her with a penetrating gaze and a smile that had nothing to do with amusement. She had the distinct feeling she was a butterfly that he meant to imprison in a glass dome. She suddenly felt the snare she'd set settling over her own fragile neck. When she attempted to draw her hand away, she found it was impossible. His fingers squeezed until she winced from the pain. "Rajir——"

"Rajir will do *nothing!* He might use his influence to ask me to be lenient toward you, but a wife belongs to her husband; more so in the Orient than Europe." He eased his tight grip but still held her hand. "Why so silent,

Cat? I would think you'd be overjoyed this evening. All your schemes turned out as you'd planned—or have they?" He shoved her hands away and rose, beginning to take his clothes off.

Cat stared down at her hands again, twisting them nervously together as her confidence drained away, leaving a chill, knotted feeling in the pit of her stomach. She'd never considered that aspect of marriage—she'd been too concerned with the contentment of forcing Ryan to do something against *his* will for once. She was growing increasingly apprehensive, considering a frantic attempt to bolt from the room. Even as she thought of it, she dismissed the idea. Ryan would only delight in having her dragged back and still would do as he pleased.

Minutes later the bed sank under his weight. Cat slipped lower and closed her eyes, her face white and devoid of any expression. Ryan made no move to touch her and after a few minutes, she slowly opened her eyes to find him studying her with a scornful stare. "You can relax, sweetheart. I have no intention of making use of your body tonight or any other night until *I* choose. I dislike the idea of having anyone, even as beautiful as you, forced down my throat like a dose of medicine. Leaves a bad taste in my mouth." He grinned, enjoying the blush of humiliation that colored her complexion. "In the morning, back you go to the harem. Consider it a token of my husbandly affections that I don't embarrass you by banishing you tonight! Now, if you don't mind I'd like to get some rest. It's been a long and trying day." Ryan turned his back on her, smiling at the chagrined expression that crossed her delicate features.

Long after she heard Ryan's breathing become even and rhythmic, Cat huddled on her side of the bed, infuriated by his insulting treatment. Let him send for her three days from now, and he'd be the one who was humiliated. It wasn't an everyday occurence for a bride of less than a week to run away from her husband. She bit her lip, glaring at his broad, muscled back. *She'd* have the last laugh on the high and mighty Sir Ryan Nicholls!

True to his word, the first thing Ryan did upon rising the next morning was to ring for a servant and have her escorted back to her room in the harem. Indirah seemed more embarrassed then Cat herself. She was used to his whims by now, she explained to the concubine with a resigned air. Why should the simple repeating of vows change either of them?

Two days later the slave trader appeared at the palace gates with a bevy of well-covered slave girls for the prince to consider. A captain of the guard led him to the harem anteroom, sending a servant to make the prince aware of the dealer's appearance. Under the watchful eye of the head eunuch, a man of height and imposing girth, Ali Ben Kabran herded his offerings together and gave last-minute instructions to the girls to cease the giggling and stand tall and straight. "You'll be treated like queens," he growled, positioning them like merchandise to create the best impression, continuing to snap orders until they all stood with perfect posture, in a neat line awaiting the royal prince's judgment.

Beneath the hood of his caftan, the wily trader studied the room. His eyes were dark and shrewd beneath black brushes of eyebrows, eyes that peered past his eagle nose with a cynical suspicion of the world around him. At the moment he was counting the exits to the room, as a precaution should his plan fail. Unless the prince dawdled, the showing shouldn't take more than a half-hour. If the girl was able to stay back when the others left, he had enough time to disguise her well enough to blend with his girls.

Suddenly the prince and his party arrived. The royal heir took a seat on a divan, his favorite by his feet and a second girl whom Ali Ben Kabran recognized by the bright, red-gold curls that peeked from beneath her veil. This was the one he'd come for. He uttered a silent prayer to Allah that she was sharp enough to carry through without giving him away.

The half-hour seemed like an entire day. Hidden beneath her veil, Cat bit her lip, impatient with Rajir's attention to detail as he ordered each of the eleven girls disrobed and studied them for any blemishes that might mar their skin, listened to the sound of their voices, watched them walk around the room. Finally, after what seemed like an eternity, he selected two, patting Indirah's dark, glossy hair as she admired his choices and the way he haggled with the Arab. At last Ali Ben Kabran threw up his hands in defeat, agreeing to the prince's price, mumbling under his breath at the shrewdness of Kohlapur's future leader.

Rajir laughed. The trader's flattery was part of the ritual he'd known since boyhood. He rose and told him to see the eunuch for payment and drew his two companions to their feet. The two girls he'd purchased were separated from the others and led off to the inner recesses of the harem, while Kabran busily gathered the rejected girls into a group. At the door, Cat paused, whispering a plea to Rajir. He smiled and nodded, seeing no harm in allowing her to speak with one of the girls who had recently been captured on a French vessel. He gathered Indirah's hand into his and strolled away, headed for the gardens.

Cat approached Kabran, asking him in a loud voice if she might speak to the girl known as Mariette. They exchanged a look and he nodded, sweeping down in a bow as he indicated the girl. Excusing himself, he joined the head eunuch to receive the agreed-upon payment. It left Cat alone in the room with the nine slave girls long enough to become one with them. By the time Ali Ben Kabran returned, there were ten quiet slave girls awaiting his orders. The eunuch, was busy defending himself against Kabran's insistent claims that he'd been shorted on the last purchase, failed to note any difference in the group.

The slave trader shouting to the girls to move, herding them out the door while he continued to haggle and insist he was right. Only when the beleaguered servant showed them to the exit, did Kabran give in, admitting with a sigh to Allah that he could be wrong, though it so rarely happened.

Outside, the girls were hastily ordered into a wagon. As the group passed the gates of the palace, the Arab said a prayer of thanks and urged the driver to speed toward the city's edge as fast as the horses could gallop.

The rest of Kabran's assembly of slaves and servants had been waiting for three hours, packed and ready to set off across the flat expanse of the Deccan for the mountain range that hugged the coastline. Cat was allowed a brief, joyful reunion with Will before they were parted by a nervous Ali Ben Kabran. He insisted that they'd have plenty of time to talk once *he* no longer faced the danger of Prince Rajir's rage.

Despite the cumbersome wagons and pack animals, the caravan of Ali Ben Kabran's entourage wound through the steep mountains and passes with record speed, arriving on the seacoast south of Bombay in two days. The Arab accepted Will's thanks, along with a second payment of gold that somehow eased his conscience and nerves. He was in quite a jovial mood when he left them at the dock where the *Spirit* lay at anchor and wished them godspeed before hustling his troupe further north toward Kashmir.

The anchor was weighed and the sails unfurled immediately. Within a half-hour of their arrival, the frigate was on the open seas headed home for St. Mary's. In her small cabin, a jubilant Cat contained her exuberance long enough to give her guardian the details of her captivity. Somehow she failed to mention that she was now a married woman whose husband, even as they talked, might be discovering her disappearance.

When the servant he'd sent to fetch Cat returned with a ridiculous claim that he couldn't find her anywhere in the harem, Ryan stared at him in disbelief. The man shook like a leaf, anticipating his fate when the startling news reached the royal notice. Sending the man ahead to announce him, Ryan called on Rajir, surprising him in the middle of a fitting for a new hunting outfit.

When he heard the story from the servant's trembling lips, Rajir turned red and ordered an immediate search. Within minutes the palace was in an uproar, with servants bustling up and down the halls, all looking for the missing girl.

When no news turned up, Rajir and Ryan closeted themselves together to discuss what would be done. Rajir's embarrassment was extreme. He had no idea how she could have escaped. Escape had been tried several times before, but no one had ever disappeared without a trace!

"I know where she's headed, anyway," Ryan said glumly. Suddenly he remembered the *Falcon*. He asked his friend what had been done with the brig.

"She's still at anchor at Jahalla," Rajir replied with a puzzled look.

"If you'll let me take her out . . . Wait—I haven't got a crew!" Ryan cursed and began to pace the room. Cat was further away with every passing moment. If he wasn't able to catch her on the island, there'd be no way to know which direction she'd take.

"A crew is no problem, my friend. If you think you can find your wife, by all means, take the ship and pick men from the dungeons. We've any number of able-bodied seamen captured from vessels or bought at the slave auctions that you can use as a crew. I'll promise them their freedom at the end of your voyage in exchange for their efforts."

Hope brought a grateful grin to Ryan's face. Within an hour, Ryan and the men he'd chosen were outfitted with sturdy mounts and provisions for the ride to the coast. If Will Foster had masterminded the escape—and Ryan would wager his eyeteeth it had to have been Cat's old guardian—more than likely the frigate was secured in a safe anchorage somewhere along the rugged, uneven coastline to the west. There were a thousand secluded spots to conceal a ship, but he refused to worry about finding it.

She had a head start, and it would have been close to impossible to locate them before the frigate was able to set sail.

It wasn't a chase, though he was racing against time. With fair winds, the *Falcon* could reach St. Mary's a day or two after her. It would be enough time to surprise her while she was still preparing to leave for unknown parts. She was smart enough to know the island was the first spot he'd head for, though she'd have no way of guessing how much time she had to spare.

Rajir saw to it that Ryan had everything he needed to be successful. He called in the young captain who'd captured the brig and ordered him to accompany Ryan and the crewmen with a mounted escort. Rhan Cita was under royal command to requisition stores for the *Falcon* from the warehouse in Jahalla and see to it that Ryan had no problems with local officials.

Rajir dismissed the captain with an order to prepare his men to leave at once. When they were alone, he put his hand on his friend's broad shoulder. "You will let me know the outcome, Ryan. I will not rest until I know how this was allowed to happen." His skin was still mottled with anger at the serious breach of security. It would not go unpunished, for as soon as Ryan was on his way, Rajir planned to send for the head eunuch. He'd have the incompetent fool on his knees begging for mercy if a proper explanation was not produced. Now it was the middle of the night and he was weary, unable to coordinate his thoughts and discover what defenses had slipped.

"If I don't hit foul weather, I should be able to catch up with her within ten days." Ryan's smile was bitter and cynical. "Hardly seems like a match made in heaven, eh, Rajir? My loving bride of four days disappears without a trace. By rights, I should beat her until she's blue!"

"But you won't, my poor friend. Whether you admit it or not, it is not just your pride that is wounded. You are bound to her by more than the contention that exists between the two of you." He walked Ryan to the door and added, "A spirited mare will ever resist rough handling, yet a gentle touch will work wonders to calm her!" He paused at the door to bid farewell. "My own anger is not directed at Catherine. She took flight, as any captive bird would do to regain its freedom. My shame is that the invulnerability of my harem has been shattered. I shall not rest until I know a recurrence can never be possible. Now, may the gods bless your quest and grant you fair weather!" He accepted Ryan's thanks and took his hand in friendship, watching as he strode away and calling out a last word of advice. "A gentle touch, Ryan, remember!"

Ryan noted the advice and turned to wave. He was in no mood to be gentle or forgiving. Outside the men were mounted, ready to set off. Rhan Cita saluted respectfully and ordered his escort to move out as Ryan mounted his stallion and took the reins from the waiting servant. They would ride through the night, stopping briefly to water the horses. Within two days, they should reach the seaport of Jahalla, and would sail as soon as Rhan Cita had secured the proper provisions for the trip.

Across the flatlands and into the range of steep, savage mountains, the party of twenty-four crewmen and its mounted escort galloped a night and a day, following the hard pace set by their black-haired leader. They made excellent time, arriving in Jahalla by noon, the second day. Within two hours the brig was readied for sea, and swept at full sail out of the small harbor on a strong west wind.

The trip was uneventful and it seemed Rajir's prayers had been heard for they had brisk, southerly winds during the entire voyage and were able to make the trip from the west coast to St. Mary's in nine days. On one of his previous trips to the island, Ryan had scouted the cove where Cat always anchored the *Falcon*. The inlet wasn't large enough or deep enough for the frigate to enter so he planned to anchor the brig there. He was at the starboard bow when they passed Shelley's Landing and saw two frigates and several other ships of various sizes in the harbor. Either of the two frigates could be hers. A triumphant smile crossed his face as he thought of confronting her.

Without a doubt, the deceitful little minx had led him on her last merry chase. She must have known of the plans for her escape ahead of time, and yet she couldn't resist a final, spiteful revenge by contriving to force their marriage. He was determined to make her see what a disastrous mistake she'd made, even if he'd willingly accepted the idea of the marriage. Once she realized that he controlled her destiny and not the opposite, he could afford to be more lenient with her. Until that time, he would rule her with an iron hand, stilling any and all resistance until she became pliant and malleable.

It was late afternoon when the *Falcon* dropped anchor in the cove. The ship was secured when Ryan called all the hands together. They'd all been captives for longer than they cared to remember and had been grateful when promised their freedom in return for manning the brig. Now Ryan told them he appreciated the hard work that had brought the *Falcon* in to anchorage at her destination with such speed. "You're all free men now, but I've a proposal for you. Stay on as my crew and I'll pay a fair wage. All I ask is an honest day's work." To a man they agreed, grinning at the sudden change in their fortunes.

Ryan pulled one man aside, a gray-haired, sturdy sailor who seemed masterful enough to control the others. He asked him to take charge while he was ashore. When he returned, the men were free to head for the local tavern.

One of the men rowed Ryan to the beach. He made his way up the rough overgrown trail that meandered through the steep, wooded hillside toward the house. If he'd stayed on the main trail, Ryan would have saved himself trouble by coming upon the unprotected rear of the house. As it happened, he took a fork that led off to the right and ended up on the main road that wound to the house from Shelley's Landing.

Though he'd come alone, Ryan had wisely tucked a brace of pistols into his belt. Behind the tall timber fortifications, Cat thought she was safe enough, but he had no way of predicting her reaction when he appeared before the gates and demanded entrance.

As he approached the palisade he could just see the red tiled roof of the house over the tips of the sharp tree trunks that formed a fort around the main house. Five cannon poked their long barrels out of their embrasures. Ryan smiled to himself. He knew Cat well enough by now to wager she'd threaten him with a charge of gunfire if he failed to remove himself from her sight. The huge double gate was apparently barred from within. Ryan grabbed a rope dangling from a ship's bell and announced his arrival with a clamorous peal of chimes. He continued to raise a clamorous uproar until a head appeared over the top of the palisade.

Will glanced down at the man who stood before the gates, recognizing the tall, lean figure immediately. It was that blasted Nicholls again! He had a moment to wonder how he'd found them so soon before Ryan looked up with a cool air of nonchalance and inquired after Cat's whereabouts, exactly as though he'd come on a casual social call. The black velvet coat and breeches hung on his lithe frame with a casual elegance few men possessed. He managed to look well dressed without appearing like a dandified fop. Will thought he looked good enough for Cat, if only he weren't so awful contrary. He'd better get rid of him before Cat found out. "Begone, Nicholls," he shouted. "Cat wants nothin' to do with the likes of ye! Ain't ye given her enough grief already?"

"I'll camp beneath the gates if I have to, you doddering old Goliath! Call your mistress now, unless she's afraid to face me!" From the other side of the timber fence came a soft call to Will in a voice that Ryan recognized immediately. Moments later she appeared next to Will, equally astonished and annoyed by his presence.

"Go away! I never want to see you again," she shouted. Ryan could see the furious snap of her eyes even at a distance. He moved back ten paces, sweeping off his black, wide-brimmed hat with an impudent grin before he made a mocking bow.

"I demand entrance, madam. Tell that uncouth bear of yours to open wide the gates or I'll be back with a force to knock them in! *Nothing* will stop me or keep me from what's mine." He couldn't see of course, but he was sure she gave a furious stamp of her foot as her temper rose.

Cat continued to glare down at him, addressing Will with a cold, determined command. "Train the cannon on him, Will. Fire when I tell you. You'll move, Ryan Nicholls, or there'll be pieces of you scattered from here to Kohlapur! I'll give you ten seconds."

Ryan was amused that he'd been able to predict her reactions so well. "Now, Cat," he said patiently. "It's only a matter of time until we're together again, and you well know it. You always choose the hard way. You're forgetting one thing. Now that you're my wife, legally I can break down the gates and drag you out if need be." There was a sudden silence from above, and Ryan crossed his arms patiently while a low conversation ensued between Cat and Will.

"What's he talkin' about, Cat? What's this claim that you're his wife now?"

"He's—he's lying! I told you what a scoundrel he is!" Will stared down at her left hand and the thin gold band that she'd meant to take off. She twisted it nervously, watching as Will shook his head and sighed in disappointment. "All right, the fact that we're married doesn't make him any less of a devil. Will . . ." She had a dawning suspicion that he was about to desert her and aid the enemy. "Will, you—you wouldn't let him in?" Her mouth tightened and she stamped her foot as though that would make him listen.

Will was faced with one of the hardest decisions of his life. The girl was like his own daughter and she'd always looked to him for help. He'd just rescued her from her latest escapade but now that she was older, he couldn't sway her anymore. Always willful, she was now nearly unmanageable, and she needed a stronger hand then his to keep her out of danger. Maybe this fellow Nicholls was the one. She'd be screaming mad, but he finally decided to open the gates. He had one last question to ask. "Whose idea was this marriage of yours? The truth, girl!"

When Cat refused to meet his gaze, Will had his answer. "I'm openin' them gates, lass. If ye're married, you settle it with ye'r husband." He ignored her squealed protest and shocked, betrayed look to turn and descend the steps and lift the bar that locked the double gates.

"I'm glad to see someone has sense here," Ryan greeted Will. He sauntered through the gateway into the courtyard, as confident and at ease as if he was already the master. He looked for Cat, to find her storming down the steps. She flashed a hateful glare that included both men in its wrath and flounced toward the house with a disdainful swish of silk. Ryan calmly let her go, raising a brow as she slammed the front door as hard as she could. He turned to Will with high good humor, commenting dryly, "My wife's temper is something to be reckoned with—but I suppose you know that from past experience!"

Will merely stared, then shook his head at this latest predicament of Cat's—one that even he couldn't pull her out of. "Holy Jesus," he swore, "I knew I was goin' t'regret openin' them damn gates!" Ryan smiled and Will turned on his heel to retire to his room. He had a fine bottle of brandy there for just such instances as this.

Ryan entered the house, *his* house now that Cat's possessions had come to him through marriage. He took a long, leisurely tour of the interior before heading for her room. He was just now beginning to appreciate the prospects of wedded bliss; it was time he made Cat aware of them also.

Chapter Nineteen

During the fortnight following Ryan's appearance at the gates, Cat came to regret her impulsive decision to tie herself to Ryan. Though Will had thought he was doing the right thing in allowing her husband to enter the grounds, she'd refused to speak to him from that day.

Ryan had completely taken over every facet of her life. In quick succession, he arranged for the sale of the warehouse and its contents, the *Spirit,* and finally the house. There wasn't a second that she didn't feel his influence. The *Falcon* was anchored in the cove but the crew he'd hired answered only to Ryan. None of the properties had been sold for what they were worth, for it had not been Ryan's intention to make a profit. He merely meant to show her that all her scheming to get back at him had backfired; that when she thought to entrap him, she'd lost title to everything that had been hers.

One day she'd come downstairs to find him showing the house to a prospective buyer. Mynheer Dieter Feldspak was a fat, bald planter from the Dutch island of Ceylon. When Ryan introduced her, he bowed over her hand, explaining that he was very impressed with her husband's property and had decided to buy. "I vill clear de voods behind de house and plant de fields. Such land should not be vasted!" Cat was tempted to laugh at the pompous little man and his heavily accented English, but restrained herself.

"The house is not for sale, Mynheer. I'm sorry if you've been led to believe it was." She glared at Ryan, defying him to refute her claim. His fingers tightened on her arm in an indisputable warning.

"Don't tease so, darling," he cautioned, turning to smile at the Dutchman. "My wife's sense of humor has turned sour. As I told you, her health is the main reason I'm sacrificing the property at such a low cost. She's been too long in the tropics, away from her family." He lowered his voice as though Cat was an invalid who must be sheltered from the truth. "I'm hoping the change will prove beneficial to her 'condition.' "

Cat's eyes widened with shock. How dare he imply . . . Without saying so, Ryan had managed to hint that she was mentally deranged! Any show of her fury now would merely make the man sympathize with Ryan's "problem."

Ryan took Cat's arm, gently but firmly urging her upstairs. "You know the packing must be supervised, dear. The sooner it's done, the sooner you'll see your family again." He patted her back with solicitous, husbandly affection, and Cat glared murderously with a look that promised she'd have it out with him after Feldspak had departed. Within minutes, Ryan had rejoined the planter, escorting him into the drawing room to make final arrangements for the sale.

Upstairs in her sitting room, Cat threw herself into a chair and sulked. Desperately she tried to think of a way to thwart his plans, rejecting each idea as she considered it. She would burn the damn house and head for the forest to find Sean! No, that wouldn't work. She needed

Sean as much as a second Ryan. It seemed there was no place to turn. Ryan had neatly covered every way of escape. She couldn't even trust Will anymore, for he seemed to have some strange respect for the bonds of holy matrimony. Again she cursed the day she'd come up with the insane idea of wedding Ryan Nicholls. She wasn't even the same old Cat Devlan now. She was Lady Nicholls, a nonentity who had no control over her own destiny.

How could she have ever thought herself in love with him? He was cruel and insensitive, selfish and arrogant and spoiled rotten, to boot. She found it hard to decide whether her days or nights were more miserable. Daily, he found some new way of assuring her that she was nothing but a possession of his. The nights . . . well, there were no more long nights of passionate caresses and spent desires. From the first evening of the day he'd arrived, Ryan had come to her room punctually at the same hour, coldly ordered her to strip, and taken her with no more tenderness than he would a common whore, possibly less. He'd informed her that he would bed her each night until she conceived an heir for him. It reduced her to nothing more than a brood mare. There was no doubt that he received pleasure from possessing her, but he was determined that she should derive nothing from the coupling of their bodies but his spilled seed.

That first night she fought him tooth and nail, leaving bloody scratches and tooth marks on his smooth, muscled flesh, ceasing only when she realized he enjoyed her helpless struggles. From that night on she had willed her self to lie still and passive beneath his cold, unfeeling assault, gaining a smidgeon of pleasure from the glint of frustration in his dark eyes. She merely endured him, allowing him the brief, temporary use of her body while keeping her spirit under leash, and he knew it. At times during the day when she was alone with nothing to occupy her, she would brood over the conflict of their personalities that had brought them to such a state of mutual antagonism. Even though he'd committed himself to vanquishing every ounce of spirit and free will within her, she sensed he was not as happy with his victories as he'd hoped to be.

Downstairs, Ryan was at the door, seeing the new owner of the house out to the courtyard. He told him they'd be packed and out of the house within three days. Feeling he'd shrewdly taken advantage of Ryan's eagerness to sell by striking a low price for the land, the Dutchman was in a congenial mood and expansively assured Ryan he could take longer if necessary. His wife was not due to arrive at Shelley's Landing for another two weeks and he still had servants and workers to hire.

When Ryan closed the front door, he headed back to the drawing room and closed the door, throwing himself wearily into a seat by the terrace doors. He'd accomplished the sale of the last of Cat's properties and yet had a furious tirade to look forward to when she came down. In truth, he really couldn't blame her for feeling frustrated or angry. In her place he'd be more than angry, he'd be out for blood. Without a doubt, he *had* been overbearing and domineering since he'd arrived. But she'd deserved it—or had she? He argued back and forth with his conscience and pride, without realizing it, as confused about their relationship as Cat was.

She'd always set him at odds by fighting him, except for the few times he'd made her admit her needs or tricked her into willingness. *That* was what rankled and pricked at his vanity. He wasn't overly vain but confident enough to know he could attract any woman he set his mind on . . . except Cat. It always came down to the same thing. Cat was different from any of those other women. He wanted her soft, sweet body as he never had another woman's. What was it within him that always set her on the defensive, always ready to spit or curse him as a hound of Hades?

If they met in the drawing room of a fashionable manor house, he would have wooed her until she was his. His mistake had been the wild rush of uncontrollable passion that overcame him that day in Tortuga. If he'd resisted the lusty urges of his body then, perhaps now they'd be loving partners in marriage instead of trapped together in a loveless, spiteful union that made them both equally miserable. Oh, he hid his unhappiness well enough, he thought irritably; his damnable pride wouldn't allow her the satisfaction of knowing it was *her* he wanted, not just a child to inherit his wealth.

He'd laid a fine trap for himself when he'd coldly insisted she breed him an heir! *He* suffered more than she. That first night she was like a wild thing, trying to jerk away from his touch, screaming how much she hated and despised him, glaring her rejection from those wide, beautiful, violet eyes. After that, she'd withdrawn from him, her mind a thousand miles distant while he possessed the shell of her body.

Sometimes he thought that if he could only bring himself to talk to her—to try and explain his feelings but then he faced vulnerability, the possibility of rejection, of seeing mockery enter those brilliant eyes when it was the soft light of love that he wanted—no, *needed*.

Suddenly he was aware of the soft click of the door closing and looked up, startled to find Cat leaning against it. Her face wasn't livid with anger as he'd expected. She studied him almost curiously, her lovely head cocked to one side as though she were trying to penetrate his mind and uncover his thoughts. Out of force of habit, he snapped at her, cursing himself instantly as she winced and her eyes took on that familiar, wounded appeal like the gaze of a lost fawn. "You've come to tell me about my insufferable arrogance again, I suppose," he added, unable to keep his voice clear of the sarcasm that had become so natural.

Cat's reply was a weary sigh. She approached him hesitantly until she stood next to the chair. In a quick, graceful motion, she knelt and touched his hand, gazing beseechingly into his eyes.

Ryan felt his heart twist with a breath of hope. Her manner was so soft and appealing, it seemed almost as though she'd come in answer to his thoughts, as though she knew it was near impossible for him to stop the pattern of angry retribution that drove a wedge deeper between them with each passing day.

"Ryan, I . . ." Cat's voice was shaking as she tried to compose her thoughts. She'd finally come to a decision—one that seemed the only solution to their constant, bickering warfare. "I'm sorry I . . ." She had a difficult time saying the words. She glanced away from his dark, penetrating gaze and bit her lip, finally gazing up again with a desperate plea in her eyes.

"I shouldn't have lied to Rajir and . . . and influenced him to force you . . . to marry me. It was wrong—I only did it because you always have your way. Will accused me once of being too willful; I suppose it's true." She hung her head a moment and then raised it again, surprised by the gentle look in Ryan's eyes. It heartened her and her face brightened a touch. Perhaps he wasn't as selfish as she believed. If she could only make him see! "It was a mistake and I apologize." Ryan's fingers gently covered hers and she puzzled a moment over his abrupt change of attitude before rushing on. "Ryan, please . . . before there's a child and it's too late, can't we have our vows annulled? I don't want to make you miserable; I'll go away and you can forget you ever knew——" She gave a sharp gasp of pain as his fingers suddenly gripped hers in a savage grasp.

Ryan had listened to her stumbling, humble apology with his heart, warming to the vulnerability in the soft, violet gaze, ready to take her into his arms the moment she finished. An annulment! He felt as though she'd stabbed him, experienced a blinding pain from the knife blade of rejection. Forget her? He might as well forget how to breathe! Now he ignored the pain in her eyes, pulling her forward until her face was a few inches from his own.

"Never!" He emphasized the snapped denial. "You've given yourself too much credit, my sweet wife. Rajir insisted I marry you, but do you think anything on God's earth could have forced me to tie myself to you if I'd not wanted it? I didn't believe you were pregnant and

could have insisted on a physical examination if need be, yet none of that was necessary. It gave me control of you at last. You're mine now, till death do us part." He smiled mirthlessly, still gripping her hands. "If you want your freedom—pray for my death!"

Cat recoiled from the horrible statement. She didn't want Ryan dead, all she wanted was to be herself again, to have a measure of the freedom she'd never appreciated before losing it. Tears glazed her eyes, but she willed them not to fall. She would not humble herself more than she already had. There had to be some way to make him lose interest in her. She recalled the night she'd lost the child aboard the *Falcon*. In all the time she'd spent with Sean, she hadn't conceived again. What if she couldn't bear a child—wouldn't that make him leave her and seek another who could give him the heir he wanted?

"What if I don't get pregnant?"

"We haven't tried that long, darling . . . be patient." His voice was falsely tender as his gaze swept over her features and one of his hands rose to stroke her hair.

"I . . . I might not be able to have a child," she admitted. "I lost your baby on the trip here." She grasped at the only straw that might mean her freedom. "It's possible that I can't conceive! What of the heir you want so badly?"

Ryan was shocked to learn of the miscarriage. He imagined her alone on a ship full of men, with no women around to help her when she miscarried. Of course she'd lied to him before—countless times, but there seemed to be a sadness in her voice when she'd said, "I lost your baby. . . ." Suddenly he remembered the little blond boy and the way she'd held him close that day on the pier. "What about Rafferty's bastard? You seem to have forgotten *that* pregnancy easily enough!"

Cat's shoulders slumped defeatedly. He still believed that! Now she was sorry she hadn't denied the claim when he'd made it aboard the *Falcon*. "He isn't mine," she said in a weary whisper. "Paddy is Sean's son by a native girl of St. Mary. I don't know when you saw us together but you couldn't have been that close or you'd have seen the slight slant to his eyes." It was hopeless. Why should he believe her? She hadn't seen Paddy's native heritage herself in all the times she'd been close to him. God, what he must think of her to believe she would give up her own child so easily! "If he was mine, he'd be here now, wouldn't he?"

Ryan didn't answer, but stared at her with a stubborn, unyielding set to his face. He released her hands, rising to his feet to brush past her and stalk to the door. She turned to look at him, grasping the chair for support.

"Only time will tell if you're barren," Ryan snarled viciously. "Until it proves out, expect my visits at the same time each night!" He swung open the door and left, slamming it behind him.

Only when she was sure he was gone and unable to hear her did Cat give in to hopeless tears. She threw her arms on the chair seat and bent her head, weeping out the frustration of her helpless position.

That evening, Ryan was late for his appointment. He stood on the walkway of the fortifications, gazing out into the darkness, brooding over his afternoon quarrel with Cat. He didn't care about her suggestion that she might be incapable of bearing his child. Just the thought of the misery in her face when she'd asked for her freedom made him curse. She'd made him out to be a monster. Perhaps he was, but only when it came to her. Should he agree to an annulment? The thought of a long life together, of facing her hatred every day of his life was defeating in itself. He should free her and find someone who at least accepted his advances with warmth and gentle devotion. What did it matter if he loved the woman? There had been many marriages that turned out well without that fickle emotion! Still, the thought of Cat with another man was galling. For that reason alone he would never let her go.

Suddenly a strange flickering caught his eye, penetrated the shell of brooding that had held him for the past hour. A reddish glow lit the dark, indigo night, from the direction of Shelley's Landing. He shook his head, sure that his mind was playing tricks, but the glow brightened. A shock went through him as he realized the town was burning. He was paralyzed for a moment, unable to move until a surge of apprehension went through him. Someone could have knocked over a lantern in the tavern, some careless drunk—but then again, in an area where certain native tribes still resented the intrusion of Europeans, it could be an uprising.

Ryan bolted down the steps, calling out for Will Foster. He'd seen him earlier, after dinner. His shouts aroused the servants and he grabbed the houseboy named Coco, ordering him to mount the steps to the fortifications and keep a sharp eye out for anyone approaching. Will came running out of the house, and Cat appeared at the door. She wore only a thin wrap, apparently in anticipation of his expected visit.

Ryan ignored Cat for the moment, explaining what he'd seen to Will. The huge man shook his head, cursing disgustedly.

"It's them damn drunks down at the landin'," he exclaimed. "I was down there this afternoon an' they was braggin' after how they went'n stole a girl or two off a tribe on the main island. A couple a' Sarakas, yet!" The tribe he mentioned were aggressive and warlike, prone to attacks even without the instigation of having their women seized. "I told that blasted Jack Finn he'd regret doin' it—now it looks like we'll regret it too." Despite their differences because of Cat, the two were suddenly united in a common cause.

Ryan called another of the boys from the house, instructing him to run down the forest trail and alert the *Falcon* to be ready to set sail. If the natives didn't limit their angry rampage to the Landing, they'd be storming this way soon. The house wasn't that far from the town. It sat on a high hill above the harbor. He swore as he realized their vulnerability. The original owner had built the fortifications only half way around the house. Only the front was protected, for he'd expected that any attack would come from the harbor. Captain Kidd had showered the local natives with cheap presents and had no reason to expect an attack from the unprotected rear of the house. It was terraced, with a small garden that led off to a clearing before the dense underbrush and forest began.

Now Ryan was faced with the impossibility of keeping a hoard of vengeful, screaming natives back from the fortifications with very few able-bodied defenders and still keeping their own escape route clear. If he weren't careful, they could be cut off and surrounded.

Cat approached the two men, her hand clutching the thin wrapper closed with tense, anxious fingers. She'd heard most of the explanation and wondered what Ryan's defenses would be. Coco stood watching from the walkway, shading his eyes to try to see through the darkness. By now the smell of smoke hung in the air, sharp, acrid, and choking. Ryan turned to find her near and snapped an order to get dressed and stay in her room. "I can shoot as well as you," she said defensively, determined to stay no matter what he ordered.

"Listen to the man, Cat. He's your husband, now!" Will shocked her with his support of Ryan. She threw a glare that included both of them in its fury and whirled to enter the house.

Will shrugged as Ryan stared after his wife, commenting, "There's not time now to worry o'er her feelin's. I'll show ye where the guns're kept." Even now they heard the first, sharp cries of the approaching natives, cries that sounded like animals, wounded and stampeding.

In her room, Cat was changing clothes when she heard a sound by the terrace door. She whirled to see a native there, but despite the mask that covered his face, she recognized Sean immediately. She hurried over to him, remembering to pull closed the edge of her wrapper, suddenly modest before the man who had been her lover.

"Aye, it's me, love," he said lightly, removing the mask to smile at her with a familiar expression. "You'll be needin' help, I imagine. Got me own troops out back." He gestured. Beyond him she could see a group of natives, Rovani and her small son among them. The sharp reports of musket fire sounded and Cat whirled, her face torn by concern for the man she supposedly hated.

"Nicholls is here, ain't he?" The flat statement still managed to reveal his envy and jealousy.

Cat turned back to him and nodded. The cries of the raiding Sarakas were closer now and much clearer. Suddenly the hall door slammed open, and Ryan's tall, muscular figure filled the doorway. He took in the scene and a familiar black scowl twisted his features. "What the hell is he doing here?"

Before Cat could answer, Sean stepped forward, glaring. Even he knew it wasn't the time for a confrontation over Cat. "I come t'help," he said contemptuously. "If you're too damn proud t'accept it, stay an' get slaughtered. Ye'll ne'er defend this pile o' wood. They'll burn ye out and cut off any escape. If the *Falcon*'s anchored in the cove, make for her. We can hold 'em back till ye hit the beach."

Cat could see it in Ryan's stubborn expression. He thought they could defend themselves . . . or even if he wasn't sure, he didn't want to owe Sean anything. "Ryan, it's our only chance! Sean's risking his life for us—we've got to go now!" A flicker of indecision passed over his face, and he glowered at Sean again.

"Get started down the trail—I'll find Will and follow," he ordered. There were more shots and he wheeled and ran out. Cat would have gone after him, for she wasn't about to leave without either of them, but Sean guessed her thoughts and grabbed her arm, dragging her out the door to the terrace. The smell of smoke was heavy and choking, hanging in the air like a cloud of blue gray.

Sean shouted orders to his villagers and they spread out, heading for the front of the house. All of them carried spears and were dressed as Sean had been that first day in the forest. She hadn't glimpsed the attackers but they could hardly be any more fierce or frightening than the Moriandrias in their war garb. The smoke was filling her lungs and she began to cough. Through tearing eyes she saw him speak to Rovani. It seemed as though he ordered her to retreat to the forest edge and take Paddy with her. The girl glanced at Cat and whether it was suspicion or loyalty, she shook her head and refused to leave Sean's side, though she stooped to speak to her son in her native tongue. He looked at her, nodded and headed toward the woods.

Sean pointed at the trail and told Cat to get moving. She looked back at the house and he repeated the order. "Damn it girl, I got friends gettin' killed out there. If ye don't go now, ye'r wastin' their lives. Ye don't know what them Sarakas do t'women captives! Now, get!" He gave her a shove in the right direction and she ran, stumbling along in the darkness toward the cove trail.

Footsteps pounded behind her and Cat glanced back, her eyes wild and terrified. She was at the edge of the brush now and low-hanging branches scraped at her as she fled. Her name was called in a low, familiar voice and she paused, panting breathlessly as she brushed the tangles away from her eyes. Ryan and Will caught up with her just as a shrill chorus of chilling cries rent the night air. The Sarakas had broken through the line of defense, and there were natives fighting hand to hand all around the house. The Sarakas carried bows and a hail of arrows was discharged, raining down on the defenders at the terrace.

Cat saw Sean charge one of the Sarakas and pin him to the ground with his spear. The haze of smoke shifted and a woman's scream split the night; Rovani dropped to the ground with an arrow protruding from her breast. Cat caught her fist to her mouth to stifle her own terrified scream at the horrible sight. Ryan grabbed her against his chest, his arms encircling her shivering body. She hid her head against him, shaken and nauseated; but, as an unholy cry sounded a triumphant knell, she pulled back and witnessed a scene she would never forget.

Sean had cradled Rovani in his arms, abandoning his

spear at her side. Even at their distance, he seemed dazed as he rocked her body and clutched her close. A Saraka, a huge towering devil daubbed with gaudy paint, threw back his muscled arm and cast his spear with all his might, plunging it through Sean's broad, unprotected back. A slight breeze drifted the smoke clear and Cat saw it all clearly. Sean bent forward as the sharp lance pierced his body and sank into Rovani's. He collapsed instantly, pinned in death to the body of the girl who had loved him more than life itself.

Will cursed the raiders, including the men who'd started the night's terror with their abduction of the Saraka women. He called to Ryan to get Cat down the trail.

"No—Ryan, I've got to get Paddy!" Cat struggled to break away and Ryan shook her, sensing the hysteria in her trembling body. He glanced back and the battle still waged on, though any moment the Sarakas might overcome their enemies and flood over the area. Time was fast running out.

Cat planted her feet, refusing to budge without the boy. Will cursed again. "I'll get him, just point him out." She did so, and he was able to see the top of the child's curly blond hair at the edge of the forest twenty yards away. He sprinted off, agile and graceful for his size, hugging the woods until he found the lad and swooped him up. The whole rescue took a mere three minutes, though, as Cat watched, it seemed an endless wait. She held out her arms for Paddy but Will barked at her. "I can carry him better 'n ye. Damn it, Nicholls, get her out a' here!"

The trail was steep and rugged. Ryan took off at a run, dragging Cat behind him. It soon became evident that she slowed them down. She wore nothing but the thin silk robe and her bare feet were cut and bleeding. He paused a moment and swept her into his arms, navigating the dark twists with as much care as possible. The foliage grew thinner as they sighted the beach ahead. Behind them, the shouts and cries seemed to be drawing closer. Coco greeted them, pointing across the water to the two longboats that even now rowed through the breakers to pick them up and carry them to the safety of the *Falcon*. In the bright light of the rising moon, her masts and shrouds appeared spectral, tinged with silvery color. Ryan could see the crew scrambling aloft to follow his orders to be ready to sail. He placed Cat on her feet, holding her steady as she wavered. When he was sure she wasn't going to faint, he left her and ran to help pull the boats to shore. There was a fair wind rising, and with a little luck they'd be under way within a half hour.

Chapter Twenty

The Dutch planter Feldspak would never live in the house that had belonged to Cat. When they'd reached the beach of the cove where the *Falcon* lay anchored, Cat had turned for one last look up the hill trail that led to the house. The cries of the defending Moriandrias blended with those of the savage attackers, until the two were indistinguishable. A bright flickering glow of red-orange lit the sky and Cat's vision blurred as tears rolled down her scratched, dirt-smudged face. Sean was there, along with the girl who had loved him so. The same Sean she had damned for a selfish liar had risked his life and orphaned his only child because he had still cared enough to see that she was safe.

When the longboats touched shore, Ryan called to Cat, but she stood still as a statue in the moonlight, her head and shoulders bowed. Ryan ordered Will and the child into the boat and went after her. They were still in danger. No one knew which of the two tribes had triumphed. Any moment he expected to see bloodthirsty

Sarakas come streaming down the hill to overwhelm them.

"Cat . . ." Ryan touched her shoulder, but she seemed unaware of him, and he grabbed her, turning her to face him. Her eyes were wet and wide with shock; even at the close range she seemed puzzled and disoriented. He glanced at the trail and gave her a shake. "Cat—for God's sake, it's me!" She suddenly tensed and tried to break away, all the terror of the past half-hour reflected in her eyes.

"Sean—we can't leave him there—let go of me!"

It was clear to Ryan that she was dazed, wanting to believe Rafferty was alive back there. She struggled wildly, screaming hysterically until he slapped her and the fight went out of her body. She shivered uncontrollably in the thin wrapper, half from the cool night air, half from the residue of shock that left her limbs shaken with weakness. "He's dead, Cat, he and the girl both. And we might join them if we don't get the hell out now!" Cat nodded and bowed her head again, would have fallen if he hadn't caught her to him and picked her up in his arms to carry her to the waiting boat.

Cat seemed to recover somewhat once they were seated and rowing towards the darkened *Falcon*. She still shivered, and Ryan took off his coat to put it around her shoulders. The child, despite the terror that had surrounded him, slept trustingly against Will's chest. When they were halfway to the ship, the sound of war cries came from the beach. Either the Sarakas had defeated the defending Moriandrias or a few of their warriors had seen them make for the beach and followed. They danced about, half-naked in the moonlight, crooning their wild, pagan chants as though it would bring their enemies back to shore for them to slaughter.

Cat would have taken the boy but she was unwilling to wake him, to let him be terrified anew by the wicked cries of the natives who had killed his parents. She said a silent prayer that he was young enough to forget the awful night. That Ryan might object to her rearing Sean's child never entered her mind.

Once they had climbed safely aboard the brig, Cat insisted on taking Paddy from Will, gently cradling him against her breast as she carried him, still sleeping, to the cabin. Will and Ryan stayed topside for a while, to see that the ship was carefully navigated through the deep but narrow channel leading out of the almost hidden cove. For a while it was touch and go, for the channel was usually passable only by the light of day.

When Ryan came below, they were well under way and the course was set for the Coromandel and Fort St. David. They would have been headed there in a few days anyway, but Ryan had never imagined leaving in the dead of night or having to escape the lances of vengeful savages by the skin of his teeth. The cabin was almost dark, lit only by the feeble glow of the low-burning lantern. It was still and quiet and his eyes had to adjust for a moment before he spied Cat in the desk chair and the boy still asleep in her arms. She gazed down at the boy with such loving tenderness that Ryan felt his heart twist with painful envy. It was ridiculous to be jealous of a child. He wasn't really, only of that soft, sweet look. He would have given his eye teeth if just once . . . Well, it was ridiculous to even think of it.

Cat raised her eyes and gestured for him to be silent. She stood and carried the boy to the bed, placing him on the sheets and carefully drawing the covers beneath his little chin. He stirred once and yawned and Cat's hand caressed his forehead until he was quiet and peaceful again. She bent and lightly touched his cheek with a kiss, securing the covers again with a maternal touch.

She turned from the bed to find Ryan seated casually on the edge of the desk, studying her. He motioned with his head, his lips forming the words of a near-silent whisper as he asked her to join him. She approached hesitantly, remembering that he'd been coldly furious with her earlier in the day, then tender and caring when he'd placed his coat around her shaking shoulders on the boat. She wasn't quite sure what to expect when he opened his mouth. When she stood in front of him, he hooked his fingers beneath the collar of her silk wrap and pulled her slowly closer, until their faces were inches apart.

Ryan inched his fingers up the slender column of her neck until they were buried in the silky tangles of thick, coppery curls, tilting her head back and bending his own until their lips met in a bittersweet kiss. It was the first time he'd touched her with gentle yearning since his arrival. He sensed her bewilderment, then her body lost its stiffness and she seemed to melt against him without thinking. Even as her lips parted softly beneath the searching kiss, it struck Ryan that the only time they knew any joy in each other seemed to be when they both put aside thought and gave in to the call of their senses. He was sad and bitter simultaneously, brooding because too many words, too many senseless, ridiculous taunts had been cast from both sides.

For the sweet moments that Ryan held her, all the cruelties of the recent past were swept away. She was cradled in his arms, praying the embrace would never end, that the miserable antagonism that separated them would never intrude again. Her fingers clutched at his broad, muscled back, contracting and kneading like the claws of a contented kitten. His breath was warm, brushing against her ear as he whispered that he needed her.

Suddenly reality did intrude, in the form of a series of whimpering cries from the bed. Cat started, pulling away but Ryan's arm closed around her waist. "You heard what I said . . ." The boy's cries were louder now, plaintive and bewildered as he awoke in a strange place. "I finally admitted it . . . I *do* need you!"

"Ryan, let go!" Cat struggled impatiently to be free. "He's only a baby who's lost and lonely. He needs me, now. If what you said was the truth, we can talk when he's gone to sleep again." She tried to pry his iron grip away from her waist and failed, growing increasingly angry as Paddy's pitiful wails grew even more frantic. "Dear God, Ryan—he lost his parents tonight! How can you be so heartless?"

Suddenly she was free, so suddenly she stumbled

backward a step before regaining her balance. "And you lost a lover and I a rival. It seems we're all bereft tonight," Ryan snapped resentfully. Jealousy was written all over his face and she turned away before he could see that she was torn by indecision. There was no one else to comfort the boy, and yet Ryan had been close to dissolving the enmity that existed between them. She hurried to Paddy's side, drawing him into her arms and picking him up. He quieted instantly, cuddling against her shoulder and sniffling until his tears had ceased. She continued to pat his shoulder, but whirled around at the sound of Ryan's heavy tread toward the door.

"Ryan," Cat called out sharply, and he stopped in midstride. Paddy sensed the tension in her body and raised his head, staring at Ryan's back. "He was *never* your rival!"

Ryan paused only a brief second, then continued to the door without looking back. The resounding slam as he banged the door closed after him was her only answer. Paddy's eyes sought hers, to reassure himself all was well. He saw the tears that welled in the corners of her eyes and with a loud wail, commenced his own fit of weeping anew. It took Cat three-quarters of an hour to calm him again and he would lie down to rest only if she joined him. Cat lay on the bed and held him close until at last his breathing was soft and rhythmic. She was awake for hours afterward, but Ryan failed to return.

Paddy was up with the dawn the next morning, nudging Cat until she woke and rubbed at her eyes to clear them. He beamed his small version of Sean's crooked smile and she hugged him close, thankful that he seemed untouched by last night's horrible chain of events. Later, he would question her about Sean and Rovani, but she would handle his questions as they arose.

When Cat rose and stretched, climbing from the bed, a little shadow mimicked her every movement, following her around the cabin, patiently waiting his turn as Cat stood before the mirror and washed her face and ran a brush through her tangled curls. She glanced down and he held up his arms to her with an appeal she found irresistible. He had all Sean's charm without his father's selfishness or guile. She lifted him and balanced him on one side, letting him peer into the mirror at his reflection. He grinned delightedly at the little blond boy who gazed back at him, watching with fascination as Cat brushed at his unruly gold curls until they gleamed.

There was a knock at the cabin door and a moment later Will poked his head through the opened door, smiling a greeting. He balanced a covered tray on one hand and the tempting aroma of a hot meal wafted from beneath the linen covering the two plates.

Cat let the hungry child squirm out of her arms and run across the room to Will. He placed the tray on the desk and caught Paddy in his arms. To the accompaniment of giggles and shrieks, he swung the boy high in the air and tossed him several times before lowering him to the desk.

"Have you seen Ryan?" Cat wondered where he'd slept. Paddy had pulled off the linen and she hurried over to feed him before he could plunge his little hands into the food.

"Aye," answered Will, glancing up at the ceiling. "He's up on deck, pacin' like a surly bear. Spent the night on a pile a rope, he did." Will shuffled his feet and stared down at the deck. "Look, Cat . . . I know ye'r still mad 'cause I let 'im in that day but I jus' thought, well . . . seein' how you went an' married 'im, I figured the sooner ye made up, the better! I guess it weren't my place t' interfere."

Cat had already forgiven him. She missed the closeness they had always shared and the ability to confide her troubles. "You did what you thought was best for me—as you always have, Will." She smiled at him and carefully wiped at Paddy's mouth with the linen, then glanced upward at the sound of Ryan's heavy, pacing tread above their heads. Remembering how close they'd come to a reconciliation of their differences, she cheered Will a bit by adding, "It just might work out yet!" Paddy had finished most of a full plate of food and now seemed to be searching for something to do. "Can you take Paddy on deck for a while? I've still got to find something to wear. Just keep an eye on him and he'll find something to amuse himself with."

"Sure thing, lass," Will agreed, happy now that they'd settled their differences. "You'll be comin' up soon, ye'r-self?" Cat nodded and he hoisted the boy to his broad shoulders and marched him from the room with a jogging motion that elicited excited squeals from Paddy.

Cat sighed as the door closed and walked over to the chest to see what kind of clothing she could find. The chest contained *all* her clothing now, for everything else had been burnt with the house. Anything she found would be more appropriate than the thin silk wrapper that was torn and dirty from last night's desperate escape through the woods. She knelt and sifted through the contents as she had twice on the day the *Falcon* had been captured.

She finally managed to find a light dress of flowered calico, though its low-cut bodice was a bit daring for the bright light of day. The last time she'd worn it had been at the house, on one of those happy days before she'd found out the disillusioning truth about Sean. She absently clutched it to her breasts, rising to her feet to stare out the windows. It wasn't the brilliant blue of a sky spotted with innocent puffs of cloud that she saw, but a vision of Sean as she'd last seen him, running to Rovani's side to cradle her in his arms and dying himself as a Saraka arrow pierced his body.

Cat was seized by guilt. If it weren't for her, Sean and Rovani would be alive and Paddy would still be in their care. She would try to make it up to the child, to shelter him from further hurt and give him all the love and attention she could. She shook her head, snapping out of the trancelike remembrances to hurry and dress. It was time she faced Ryan, though Heaven only knew she was timid enough to want to postpone any confrontation. She was weary and sad, certainly in no mood to defend herself against an angry Ryan if he was truly as surly as Will had said. What kind of reception would she have this morning? Undoubtedly the night's sleep on a hard, uncomfortable deck accounted for some of his irritability.

When she was dressed, she halfheartedly picked at the plate of still-warm food, abandoning it when her nervous stomach objected. Instead, she hurried to the chest and withdrew a green silk ribbon that matched the green and gold flowers on her gown. In front of the mirror, she brushed the heavy red-gold waves back from her face and tied them with the ribbon, then studied her pale complexion, pinching her cheeks to bring color to them and rubbing at her lips with a forefinger until they glowed a peachy rose. If she had to beard the lion in his den, she might as well look as enticing as possible. It just might distract him enough to keep him from snapping at her.

Above the cabin, Ryan had ceased his pacing and leaned at the rail watching the water. He turned to watch Will and the little boy by the helm. The huge man made a startling contrast to the little toddler as he held him up to the wheel and let him pretend he was actually steering the course of the ship. Though it was irritating to be reminded of Rafferty, the child was so engaging, he couldn't help but feel his attitude soften; and despite his will not to be bothered with Paddy, a smile touched his lips. After all, he thought, the child's father was dead because he'd helped save them. Still, Ryan had no illusions that Rafferty had meant to include him when he'd come to see to Cat's safety. Despite the way he'd cradled the dying native girl, it was clear enough to him that Cat was the real love of Sean's life. Not that he could blame the Irishman; he, too, had fallen under her siren's spell, and it seemed impossible to break away.

When Cat appeared out of the companionway, she failed to see Ryan at first. She only saw the charming picture of Paddy at play and smiled contentedly as she thought of the hours of enjoyment they would share in the future. As she moved to join them, she seemed unaware of the effect she had on the crew. They were all men Ryan had hired and though they'd seen her come aboard last night, it had been a brief glance at best, and in the darkness her beauty had been hidden.

All hands paused in their work to stare at their captain's wife. She looked as though she'd just stepped from a painting, and more than one removed his cap in awe. For the most part, they were Englishmen, far from home and used to the blends of Oriental and dark-skinned women who inhabited her waterfront taverns. This one, with her blaze of copper curls and fair, rosy complexion, her slender figure and a goodly display of high, proud breasts above the lace-trimmed bodice of her gown, reminded them of home and the light-complexioned maidens who inhabited the green, rolling countryside of England.

If Cat was unaware of the disturbance she caused, Ryan was only too aware of it. He frowned, his eyes fixed on the creamy swell of her breasts. They bounced delightfully as she walked over to Will and he felt a surge of fire in his loins. If he felt it, these common, women-starved seamen were doubtlessly arrested with the same drawing desires. He had no wish to repulse a mutiny just because Cat had no conception of how her fetchingly exhibited assets affected men. She was tousling Paddy's curls when he joined them.

Cat was startled as Ryan took her arm and tucked it into the crook of his own. "Madam," he said sternly, "I must talk privately with you." She was literally dragged away from the helm and had to hold tightly to his arm just to keep pace with his long strides. He headed for a secluded spot by the stern shrouds.

"Couldn't you have found a more revealing gown, my dear?" he said ironically. Cat blushed and unconsciously her hand rose to cover the deep, shadowed valley that lay between the half-exposed swells of her creamy breasts. The blush deepened and only served to make her even more appealing. Ryan turned to find several of the crew craning their necks for a view of her. He glared and they quickly caught his silent warning and made a show of returning to their alloted tasks.

"Somehow, you always seem to make me feel like a

strumpet with a penchant for displaying my wares! If you prefer that I change, you have a choice of the torn wrapper I discarded or my disguise of a shirt and breeches. However, either would show considerably more than this dress." Cat's confused embarrassment had given way to growing indignation. How could he imply she was parading herself like a brazen tart? She withdrew her hand and straightened her posture, with the effect that the tantalizing display of décolletage came even more prominently into view.

Ryan growled and stepped to the side so that she was in his shadow and completely hidden from the lusting eyes of his crewmen. "I didn't imply you were flaunting anything, but I think the evidence speaks for itself. As long as you're Lady Catherine Nicholls, you'll behave as a gentlewoman should. Your problem is you've been allowed to run wild and free for too long. It's time you discovered that women don't masquerade in men's breeches and don't involve themselves in dangerous situations. I doubt there're many ladies with a scar from a pistol ball on their shoulders."

"I don't care about being a 'lady.' All the so-called ladies I've ever seen you with have only been high-class whores in disguise, trading their dubious favors for a wedding band instead of a fee! I'll be damned if I'll let you mold me into what you think is 'proper'!" Cat was breathless when she finished, the defiance blazing from her eyes as enchanting as the rise and fall of the charms that had begun the argument.

Ryan's black, disagreeable mood had disappeared, replaced by appreciation of his wife's spirited defense. He amazed himself by admiring her wildcat emotions even while he was committed to a course of subduing them. At the moment, he couldn't give a damn what his men thought. He caught her by surprise, sweeping her into his arms to carry her off to the cabin.

It took Cat a moment to recover. She wanted to die from shame. All the men had paused in their work to watch Ryan and most of them wore smiles that reflected their willingness to trade places with him. It was so obvious what he was doing, she could have screamed a few well-chosen epithets at him, but it would have only added to her own embarrassment. He had a smug, self-satisfied grin on his face and the frantic kicking of her legs seemed to have no effect whatsoever.

"Let me down, you devil's spawn," she whispered through tightly clenched teeth. She knew her face must be beet red and she would have closed her eyes to shut out the curious, prying eyes of all those who watched her helplessness but they were about to pass Will. At least he'd save her, she thought trustingly. "Will, help me—make him put me down!"

Ryan obliged Cat by stopping for Will's answer. "Ye did say ye wanted me t'watch the boy, Cat. I canna' do both at once, lass!" Cat's rosebud mouth formed a perfect O of shock and disappointment as her last line of defense fell. There was no one else to turn to and she closed her eyes tight at the humiliation of being carted off like a whore Ryan had selected for the evening's pleasure.

Ryan easily navigated the stairs leading down to the cabin and kicked open the door like a triumphant Viking returning with his latest prize, striding across the room with that long, confident walk of his until he reached the bed and deposited her with surprising gentleness.

Cat stubbornly refused to open her eyes, though she heard an occasional shuffling sound and Ryan's irritatingly happy whistling. Suddenly the room was quiet and she peeked from beneath a fringe of heavy lashes to find Ryan standing naked by the bedside, his arms casually crossed. If she hadn't been so furious and humiliated, she'd have taken the time to admire his long, lean body, but she shut her eyes tight again and her mouth formed a stubborn, resistant line.

"I saw you peek, Cat—your curiosity has undone you. Now be an obedient wife and sit up and I'll help you out of your dress. We don't want to ruin your only suitable clothing." His voice was so calm and patient it made her angrier than if he'd demanded she strip.

"No!"

"Yes, darling. Or should I just throw up your skirts and take you like a gentleman dallying with a whore?"

Cat's eyes flew open, wide and smoky violet as she stared in shock. "You're no gentleman," she said bitterly, jerking herself erect to do as he bid. "You're a scoundrel, a rogue, a——"

Ryan sat beside her, his fingers carefully working at the row of tiny pearl buttons that fastened the back of the dress. "I know, darling. A devil, a rascal, and countless other vile creatures," he commented with amazingly good grace and patience. In the time they'd been together, she'd called him every name possible. He knew them all by heart and could recite them as well as she could.

"Stop patronizing me," she snapped. "You're all those things and more!" She was gently pushed back until she lay on the bed, and Ryan tugged off first one sleeve, then the other and pulled the bodice down to her waist. Cat's bottom lip pouted more with each tug that stripped her of the dress .All of his movements were careful and precise, which only impressed Cat as cold and calculating, as though he were waging a military campaign to conquer a territory instead of bedding his wife.

Ryan wasn't quite as cool as he appeared. He'd never really had to undress a woman before and after he'd finally managed to draw off the gown without tearing it, there was still a chemise and two ruffled underskirts to tackle. His long run of patience was drawing to an end as he roughly pulled off the last underskirt and placed his fingers at the neck of the sheer chemise to rip it down the front. Cat half-rose, leaning on her elbows to glare at him.

"I thought you weren't going to ruin my clothes!"

Ryan smiled and gave a sigh of relief at having finally reached his objective. Her ivory flesh was smooth and satiny, tempting him to reach out and touch. Not an ounce of fat marred her perfectly proportioned, supple figure. Even in twenty years, Cat would still be a gorgeous creature. "No one will ever miss the chemise but you. I'd prefer to think of you walking around without it anyway." He placed a hand on her shoulder and firmly pushed her back.

Cat popped up again, making an indignant inquiry. "Do you know what those men are thinking? If you're so awfully concerned with convention, how can you expose your wife to those gaping clods?"

Ryan pushed Cat down again, keeping his hand on her shoulder this time. "They're thinking I'm a damn lucky man and I can't say I blame them. As far as exposure, it's the most natural thing in the world for a man to want to possess what you've got to offer—and who better to take advantage of it than your loving husband?" He turned his mind to the task at hand, lifting her a little to shift her to the center of the bed and lying beside her. He balanced himself on one arm, running his fingers lightly down the center of her body from her throat to the silky red curls at the junction of her thighs.

Cat closed her eyes, employing her recent trick of counting to a hundred to avoid being drawn to response against her will. To her consternation and shame, she reached a count of five and her skin tingled as his fingers teased a pattern on the inside of her thighs, rising to explore the warm flesh beneath the curly thatch, firmly pushing her legs apart and holding them in a spread-eagled position. She tried to continue counting and lost track of the numbers, starting over at one just as he shifted his position and knelt between her legs.

This time Cat reached three and stopped, forgetting why she'd wanted to count as Ryan's head lowered and his mouth found her, his tongue as skilled and artful as the hands that rose to caress her breasts. Her mouth twitched with frustration, desire flushing her complexion with warm color as the fire that seemed to radiate from between her thighs spread to every inch of her body. Her eyes were closed, her bottom lip caught between her teeth to bite back a moan of pleasure. She twisted restlessly, the wild mane of flaming curls spread across the pillow. She left her petulance behind, tossed modest caution to the winds. Her left hand covered his as it massaged the firm white mounds of her breasts. She drew her knees up, arching against him, ruled only by an overwhelming, blinding lust to release the torturous build-up of passion that centered beneath Ryan's probing tongue. Her right hand touched the thick black curls and stroked his head, guiding him boldly, aware only that she had to satisfy the urges he had aroused. She was close . . . so close the pleasure was almost an exquisite pain, drawing her along as its helpless victim.

Suddenly Ryan drew back and Cat almost screamed in frustrated fury. With a movement as quick and lithe as a cat, he turned until he was poised over her, facing her feet now, and within seconds his mouth was against her again, his hands cupping her buttocks, his fingers kneading the firm, smooth flesh. Aroused by her wild, sensual abandonment, the shaft of his throbbing organ pointed at her lips like an arrow, straight and true seeking its target. She moaned and her lips parted, needing to accept him and return an equal measure of the pleasure that even now was driving her beyond herself. She heard him groan once, then knew nothing but the rapture that assaulted her as she experienced the ultimate moments of physical ecstasy, divine, eternal moments that seemed to be the incarnation of what God had intended for man and woman.

Cat still twisted restlessly, seeking the last pulsings of sweet pleasure. Enthralled and breathless, she was vaguely aware that Ryan had moved between her thighs. Only when he entered her, with the sensation of a white-hot poker stirring the smouldering embers of desire into leaping flames again, only then did she awake from the tranquil euphoria that had followed the sharp heights of passion.

Ryan was near ecstasy himself, aroused to a degree he'd never thought possible, merely because of her abandoned response. He leaned forward, buried in the heat of her body, whispering her name over and over as his lips sought the satin texture of her skin, caressed her throat, her breasts, and finally, when he felt himself hurling toward a vortex of fulfillment, his mouth covered hers, tasting the sweetness of victory, stifling his hoarse cry of triumph as her arms circled his neck and they fused together into one, heated, passionate being.

When only the tender, aching memory of the encounter was left, they rested, sated bodies slowly reviving. Ryan held her close, nestled against him, still joined to her body by an amazing desire that refused to fade.

Cat rubbed her cheek against the dark, wiry curls that covered Ryan's hard, broad chest, delighting in the rough texture against her skin. If the night of terror had accomplished anything, it seemed that slowly, step by step, she and Ryan were moving closer together. He'd admitted he needed her even if he hadn't said the magic words "I love you." She stretched langorously, wondering with amusement if they would pop apart if she moved too much. Smiling against his chest, she looked up at him with a sense of wonder as she realized that couldn't happen. Even as he returned her smile, he grew tumescent within her, filling the warm space that sheathed him.

Ryan rolled onto his back, his eyelids heavy and languid, half-covering a black gleam of renewed desire. Cat lay on top of him, light as a feather, her nipples hardening into dagger points that stabbed his chest. He seemed to grow effortlessly, just by recalling her wild, sensual pleasure. Her fingers locked together behind his neck and as she aggressively sought his kiss, his own hands grasped the back of her head, crushing handfuls of silken tendrils as his mouth ground against hers. They grew more passionate with each passing moment.

Cat pulled back, breathless and eager, staring at him with those chameleon eyes that now seemed the color of an indigo night. Ryan smiled, anticipating another match to equal what had gone before. Pushing at her shoulders, he directed her to a kneeling position and grasped her wrists against the flatness of his belly, avidly watching her expression as he bucked his hips once and drove sharply upward. Her fingers splayed and trembled, then formed a fist, her mouth pouting as she closed her eyes and concentrated on the feeling. He continued to move, building a slow, steady rhythm until she was breathless again and he could feel an answer within her.

Feeling as though she were a will-less doll that Ryan controlled, Cat allowed him to guide her on another sensual voyage through the silken, stormy waters of passion. He lowered her hands to the mattress, giving her balance and freeing his hands to play with her breasts. The firm, white globes swayed in a tantalizing motion with each jarring thrust of his hips. His fingers stroked her nipples to taut, engorged peaks that ached with every touch.

Cat was swept by strong, primal urges and without realizing it, fell into a rhythm that matched his, revolving her hips to meet each hard drive, moaning as he roughly fondled her breasts. Suddenly the tempo increased. He was pounding at her, driving her insane with the sensations until she arched her back, digging her nails into his sides as wave after wave washed her mind clear of all thought and she became purely physical, carrying her along with him toward fulfillment until the feelings ebbed and she collapsed, falling forward into his arms. The pounding of his racing heart was like a drumbeat against her ear.

Ryan gently rolled Cat to his left, curling his arms around her. Her hand touched his mouth and he kissed her fingers lightly before pressing her back into the bed and tenderly brushing the long tangles away from her face. She was aglow with contentment and his lips touched her temples, her forehead, and finally softly found her mouth in a long, yearning kiss that stirred a sense of pride deep within his soul.

A half-hour later, Cat leaned against the alcove wall, a pillow propped behind her as she watched Ryan move around the room. He walked with the lean grace of an animal, his tall, perfectly proportioned figure darkly anned and virile. When he returned to the bed, he brought er a glass of brandy. She sipped at it, lost in thought nd beginning to bless the sequence of events that had rought about the marriage. He belonged to her now, ven if the future still included a share of stormy battles. hey were both too proud and willful to expect that all ould be serene. The past two hours had made her confi- ent of his fascination with her. He wanted her, needed er, and that would be enough until he could admit to ove.

They toasted each other with the brandy, staring eep into one another's eyes as though seeing each other or the first time. Ryan joined her against the wall, pos- essively draping his arm around her shoulders. "Why is we always waste so much valuable time on words?" he uzzled aloud. "I think I've stumbled on the secret of ontentment. I should never allow you a stitch of clothing cover that magnificent figure, and *never* let you out of ed!"

Cat smiled at the nonsense. "You'd grow tired of me oon enough," she answered. She felt wonderful . . . re- axed and warmed by the liquor, without a care in the orld. Leaning back, she rubbed her head against the rong arm that held her, very much like a contented, pur- ng kitten.

"Never," Ryan insisted. "Possessing you is as nat- ral as breathing in and out. So far I haven't tired of at!" He swallowed the last of his brandy and felt it heat is insides. Now, he felt an aftermath of power, of pride at the passionate wildcat at his side was his and a return strength that made him want to continue their love- aking into the night. His fingers curled and relaxed, roking the velvety skin of her shoulders.

"Ryan?" Cat raised a hand to tug at his fingers.

"Umm . . . yes, love, what's bothering that pretty ead of yours?"

"I was just wondering . . . where do we go from here? it so necessary to go back to the Fort? I really don't care to face George." A tiny frown wrinkled the straight bridge of her nose at the idea of seeing the man who had been her fiancé.

"I'm afraid we must, sweet. Have you forgotten you own a house that has to be sold? Forget about George. He'll not bother you with me about." His fingers rose to smooth away the frown. "Then there's the boy to get settled. I thought Anne Perry would be the perfect one to take him in. She'd give him all the care and attention he needs. Of course we can leave a liberal allowance for his necessities and——"

"Ryan," Cat interrupted his planning in a startled tone. "Surely you're joking!" She faced him with a tingling of apprehension.

"About what?"

"Paddy! He's going with us to America—I won't leave him behind with anyone else!"

"I'm sorry, Cat—it's out of the question. I feel sorry for the lad, but you'll be busy enough with our own children." He lifted her chin with his fingers and touched the corner of her mouth, unaware of the shock he'd dealt her.

Cat knocked his hand away, suddenly seeing a stranger replace the man she loved. "How *can* you suggest — Ryan, he loves me, trusts only me. You can't expect him to lose everything at once! When he realizes Sean will never come back for him again, he'll be terrified."

Ryan's eyes narrowed with cynical appraisal. Of course it had to end. They were on opposite sides once more, at cross-purposes. The idyllic moments they'd spent faded to nothing in comparison with her love for Rafferty's child. He made the mistake of confusing Cat's affection for a homeless orphan and her previous relationship with the boy's father. "I told you it was final. We'll stay long enough to see him settled but he will *not* be going with us!"

"I'll take him and leave you," Cat threatened. Her eyes were wide and beseeching as she trembled on the brink of tears. "You're asking me to make a choice between a helpless baby and you." She reached out and touched the side of his face. "Ryan, I've proved what I feel for you. Paddy's no threat to our relationship." Her long lashes were wet and spiky, framing a violet appeal. "Ryan, please, don't . . . don't do this to me!"

Ryan almost relented. He really had no objection to the boy, but he recalled Rafferty's mocking impudence that day in Cat's room. He remembered the blond pirate running his rough hands over Cat, and a black demon of jealousy hardened his heart to the pleading in her voice. "No. I don't even care to discuss it. As for your threat to leave—you've done it before and I've always found you." He caught her chin in a painful grip, forcing her head up until she stared into his eyes. "You'll never be free of me unless *I* no longer want you—and there's not much chance of that! Now you'd better dress. At least until we reach the Coromandel, the boy's in your care."

Ryan rose and pulled on his clothes with abrupt jerks that revealed his anger. He was aware that she stared at him in numb shock and it infuriated him further, making him feel as though he'd slapped her. Once he had her home at Canterbury Hill and she held her own child in her arms, he was sure she'd forget the little boy. He suddenly realized that he was attempting to convince himself he was justified in parting them. He headed for the door, but one glance backward at her expression assured him Cat would never forget—or forgive him.

Three-quarters of an hour later, Will appeared at the door with Paddy, shuffling his feet as he explained that Ryan had ordered him to bring the boy to her. She seemed subdued and unwilling to meet his eyes. Just from seeing her profile and the swollen, reddened skin beneath her eyes, he was sure that she'd had another run-in with Nicholls. He shook his head, knowing if she wanted to she'd have already confided in him. When Ryan carried her off and they were absent for so long, he'd hoped to see an end to their feuding. He closed the door, frowning over the differences that always set the two at each other's throats.

Almost a fortnight later, they were settled at the

small frame house on the outskirts of the Company's garrison at Fort St. David. It was crowded, for Cat had originally purchased it as a place to stay when she was in the area and had no need for a larger home. Will stayed in one of the servant's rooms and Paddy shared her bedroom. Ryan was surprisingly obliging about sleeping in the small guest room next to it.

He and Cat had resumed the same, distant relationship that had kept them apart on the island, though Ryan's cold, businesslike connubial visits had been postponed because of Paddy's presence. Ryan had assured her they would be resumed immediately when he found the boy a permanent home. Throughout the two-week trip they'd barely spoken. Ryan had warned her to appear congenial above deck, for he had no desire to share his marital problems with others.

Once the servants had been engaged and the house was aired and freshened, he'd made her send a note to Anne Perry, telling her she was back and wished to call on her the next day. Cat complied under duress, having failed miserably to come up with any way to thwart his insensitive decision regarding the child.

Gossip spread quickly in the tiny English community. Within two hours of her note to Anne, George Pembroke appeared at her door, belligerently demanding entrance. Cat and Ryan had been arguing in the drawing room as she made a last effort to persuade him to change his mind. When she heard George was at the door, it occurred to her to refuse to see him. The thought was clearly revealed in her expression and Ryan told the servant to show him in. He smiled, aware that she was already in an irritable mood. He would sit back and watch to see George's attitude and exactly how long Cat's edgy temper would be held in check.

Cat glared at Ryan as he took a seat by the window. The armchair was turned away far enough so that George would more than likely miss his presence. Her head already ached from the argument with Ryan and if she could have avoided seeing George, she would have. The thought of making excuses to the pompous old fogey made her stomach churn with irritation. Ryan had warned her earlier to tell George the truth—that she'd used him for her own reasons and now wanted nothing to do with him. That was true enough, she thought disgustedly as he huffed his way into the room, hurrying over to her with a babble of accusing questions before she could even open her mouth.

"Where on earth have you been? How dare you go off for over three months without a word to me! Damn it, Catherine, d'you know what a fool I looked, unable to explain where my own fiancée disappeared to?" He noticed her calm, reserved expression and paused to catch his breath, staring at her with dawning suspicion. "Y'know Nicholls went off the same time as you. The gossip I've had to face was unbearable!" Cat frowned and looked him over from head to toe with unconcealed contempt. Still, she hesitated to begin the explanation knowing that more trouble was on its way.

"Tell the man, darling. You owe him that much at least." Ryan's cold, commanding voice startled George and he whirled to discover him sitting by the window.

"You!" The ugly suspicions George had harbored solidified at the sight of Ryan, lounging so much at ease in Cat's home. He turned back to Cat and sneered, "Tell me what he's doing here. It's mighty damned odd that he'd turn up the same time as you!"

Cat closed her eyes a minute and sighed, then sank to a chair and began her recital with a calm, even tone. "George, you and I are no longer engaged, but Ryan insisted that I give you an explanation. She raised her head and faced him indifferently. "I don't feel I owe you anything. You used me as a sop to your vanity, as an ornament to show the world you had the ability to attract a younger woman. I, in turn, used you for reasons of my own. Everything you confided in me—the worries, the plans, everything worked to my advantage. It was my ships that attacked and plundered your merchantmen. I'm the pirate you wanted hanged!"

George's face turned a sickly white. He couldn't believe his ears. His fiancée, the sweet, clinging beauty who'd seemed to adore him was admitting to piracy before a Company official and worse, implicating him in her confession! He turned to face Ryan, forgetting his suspicions in a desperate attempt to acquit himself before it was too late. "Nicholls, she's lying—I don't know what she's talking about. I never gave any information away—she's trying to discredit me, God only knows why!"

Ryan stood, almost feeling sorry for the white-faced, trembling old fool. "It's true enough, Pembroke. In case you haven't noticed, the pirate attacks on our vessels have decreased amazingly in the three months that your ex-fiancée has been missing. In that time, there's been no one to pass on the little confidences you so freely devulged. I'm not saying you were aware of it; Cat is an extremely persuasive young woman. Nevertheless you're involved as deeply as she if it all comes to light."

Pembroke's face paled even more as a strangled cry of rage choked his throat. He whirled to Cat, stepping close and raising his hand in a threatening manner. "You whore, I could kill you for what you've done!" His fingers formed a fist and swung back. Before he could carry through, Ryan was at his side in a lightning movement that startled even Cat. He grabbed George's arm and twisted, throwing the older man backward.

"There's only one reason I allowed you in here today, Pembroke. In case you had any thought that you might save your own neck at the expense of Cat's, forget it. I'd never stand for a whisper of gossip about my wife." George took a deep breath, glaring at them both with outraged shock. "As for your 'good name,' I have information in my possession that proves you were involved in shady dealings before Cat ever entered your life! Mention one word of this to anyone and I'll make public your traffic in opium smuggling, the women you abducted from China for sale in India, and various other chicaneries that would bring enough charges to hang you twenty times over. I don't think you'd even make it to England for trial." He walked over to Cat and drew her to her feet at his side, possessively draping his arm around her. "You needn't worry, my dear, I think our friend understands quite clearly what the consequences of a loose tongue would be." He looked up at George and smiled, coldly dismissing him with a black, menacing gaze. "We'll be leaving within a month, Pembroke. In that time, I'd appreciate it if you would stay out of our way." The politely phrased statement was an undeniable command.

There was nothing for George to do but slink away. Ryan had him at every turn, otherwise he'd have tried to find a way to avenge himself. He wheeled and walked off, without a backward glance at the couple. Ryan Nicholls was not the simple dandy he'd taken him for. The frigid arrogance he'd glimpsed in those dark eyes was enough to make George breath a deep sigh of relief that he had escaped well and unharmed when he again stood in the bright midday sun.

The next day Cat called on Anne Perry. Ryan insisted on accompanying her, carrying the child in his arms. Despite the fact that he'd seemed to warm to Paddy and the boy trustingly clung to him as they walked toward the Perry's quarters, he was still adamant about leaving him in the care of the childless couple. Cat had begged him to let her go alone but he seemed to think she would try to dissuade Anne from taking the boy, and insisted on hearing every word of the conversation.

Anne met them at the door, dismissing the houseboy who'd bade them enter. Her plain, gentle features lit with a warm smile of welcome as she embraced Cat. In her late thirties, the wife of the garrison commander had already reconciled herself to her inability to carry a child to term. In her twelve years in India, she'd miscarried seven times. Her strong maternal instincts and sweet, giving nature had made her a favorite with the children who lived at the Fort and the small, homeless urchins who wandered the streets of the nearby town.

"We've missed you so, Catherine. George has been so frightfully worried over you!" No one could call Anne's square, thin face pretty, but her brown eyes were bright buttons that glowed with such concern for those around her that her face shone with inner beauty. She noticed Ryan now and her smile enveloped him in its warmth. "And you're back, Master Nicholls; how nice to see you!" Her gentle hand reached out to touch Paddy's cheek and as he gave her a tentative smile that widened into a grin, an immediate rapport sprang up between the woman and child.

"Come, we'll talk in the drawing room. You must tell me where this sweet little boy came from!" She led them toward the small, neat room set aside for visitors. The quarters the Company provided were small and spare but Anne had managed to make the rooms warm and comfortable. When they were seated, she rang for the houseboy and asked him to bring lemonade for all. "And some of my sugar cookies, too," she added, with a twinkling glance at Paddy. "You'd like a cookie, wouldn't you, dear?"

The boy nodded solemnly, then grinned around the thumb he sucked so industriously. Meanwhile, Cat was searching for the right words to explain the boy's presence. "Anne, I . . ." she paused and glanced at Ryan. "Ryan and I are married. I know how shocking that must sound. George knows. I've explained everything to him."

There was a long pause as Anne digested this sudden turn of events. She smiled, leaning forward to share a confidence. "I never really thought you were meant for him, my dear," she admitted. "It wasn't my place to say." She smiled at Ryan. "But I think you've chosen very well. My heartfelt wishes go out to you both. The captain will be delighted. He never has been fond of poor George!" The mild admission was the closest the gentle-hearted woman could come to a derogatory statement about anyone.

"We're grateful for your felicitations, Anne, but we've a request to make of you." Ryan took the difficult task away from Cat. Even now she looked miserable and on the verge of tears, staring down at her nervously twisting fingers. Anne's little pet dog, Snuffy, a bedraggled, lovable combination of terrier and mongrel that she'd adopted as a starving pup came bounding into the room.

Paddy's eyes widened when he saw the dog, and it was love at first sight. He squirmed out of Ryan's lap, toddling over to reach out and pat at the frisky animal. In seconds they were playmates as the boy sat on the floor and Snuffy frolicked and bounded around him with short, energetic yelps. It even brought a tremulous smile to Cat's pensive features.

The refreshments arrived and Anne saw to it that Paddy was given several of her fresh baked cookies. As wretched as she felt about leaving him, Cat recognized the warm, maternal tenderness in Anne and reconciled herself. If Paddy was able to adjust, there was no doubt that he would receive loving care from Anne and her husband.

Ryan lowered his voice even though the child was thoroughly entranced with the playful little dog. "We'll be leaving soon for the Colonies, Anne. The boy is a recent orphan, the only child of an old friend of Catherine's." Cat looked up at the manner in which he'd phrased her relationship with Sean. "We thought if you'd take him in, he'd be happy here. Of course I'd take care of any expenses. The most important thing is my wife's peace of mind in seeing that he's loved and cared for. If you'd be willing . . ." Ryan wasn't sure where he'd turn if there was some reason she couldn't accept the boy.

Anne's heart went out to Paddy and her sympathetic glance took in Cat's painful silence. There was no need for her to ask why they couldn't keep the child; apparently it had already been discussed and decided. "Of course I will! I'll have to consult with the captain, but he's always yearned for a son." She stared down at Paddy, happily at play with his new friend. "He's *so* sweet, I'm positive Gordon will agree. When he comes home this afternoon, we'll discuss it." She rushed on excitedly, already making plans even though her husband had yet to agree. "Perhaps it would be best if you brought him by every day until he's accustomed to us. Oh, I know the captain will love him on first sight!"

Gordon Perry was as kind as his wife. Cat felt somewhat more at ease now, though she still wished with all her heart that she could keep Paddy with her. All the plans she'd made for him went up in smoke with Anne's acceptance. Still, his welfare was more important than her feelings. The sooner she made a break, the more quickly she could get over the heartache. "Anne, if you can take him this afternoon, we'll let him stay and get to know you. When Gordon comes home, he'll be so charmed by Paddy, it'll be settled for you." Ryan's eyes widened in surprise at the suggestion.

Anne agreed immediately that it was an excellent idea. "You don't think he'll be frightened when you leave?" Cat shook her head and rose to kneel by Paddy's side. She caressed the tousled blond curls and her heart wept as he twisted to gaze up at her with a trusting look. She explained that the nice lady was going to spend the day with him. "I'll be back for you, darling," she assured him.

The older woman sensed her sorrow and hugged her close again, whispering in her ear, "Don't worry, dear—I'll love him as you do!" When the houseboy showed Cat and Ryan to the door, Anne was already engaged in a patient conversation with Paddy, and it seemed as though he barely noted their departure.

At home, Ryan was moved to comfort Cat. During the entire stroll back to the house, she'd been so silent, it unnerved him. "You'll forget, Cat," he said softly, touching her cheek. "Once we're settled at Canterbury Hill and you've a household to run and your own children . . ."

The misery in Cat's gaze called him a liar. "I won't forget—it's like giving up my own child! Ryan, it has *nothing* to do with Sean. He's just a little boy I love. Sean was never really close to him. As much a part of that tribe as Sean was, I always felt he was ashamed that Paddy's mother wasn't white. Rovani loved him, of course, and I . . ." Her voice sounded dull and apathetic, hopeless, as she finished, "I'll always love him." She stared at him with a stricken expression, her eyes shiny with unshed tears, and whirled as he moved to console her, running to her room to hug her misery to herself. She wanted no words of false comfort from a man who heartlessly insisted on separating her from Paddy.

Gordon Perry was as excited as his wife about taking Paddy. During the next four weeks, Paddy visited every day, finally spending several nights and the entire last week at their quarters. He seemed to accept the change with his usual good humor. As long as he felt love, Paddy was a happy, secure child. Though Gordon insisted it wasn't necessary, Ryan left a generous sum of money with him and promised to send more for the boy's care. Without Cat's knowledge, he asked the captain to keep him informed of the boy's progress and anything he might need.

A month after their arrival, Cat said farewell to Paddy. He seemed to understand that she was leaving and hugged her neck with his chubby arms, submitting to the kisses she lavished upon him with a pert wrinkle of his nose, transmitting a message to Ryan that, just between men, women were far too demonstrative.

The *Falcon* sailed south past Ceylon, then set a southwesterly course for the Cape of Good Hope. Within six weeks Cat would be back in America and the mistress of the estate that had belonged to her parents. It seemed to her as she stood at the taffrail and stared pensively across the blue-green waters, that she'd come full circle; she was going home.

Chapter Twenty-one

It had taken Cat a while to settle in at Canterbury Hill. In the six months that they'd been home, she'd had to learn to manage a huge staff of servants and keep the affairs of the large house running smoothly. Ryan had surprised her by having the house refurbished by the time they'd arrived from India. All of the original furnishings had been skillfully copied to the smallest details, and when he'd walked her in the door, it was as though she'd stepped into the past. She almost expected her mother to sweep gracefully down the staircase.

It was spring now, and Cat had much to occupy her time. The gardens were entirely dug up and she was working with the head gardener and his staff of ten to plan orderly divisions of flower beds surrounded by neat bricked walks and lined by decorative shrubs. Twice a week Avery Simons came for her painting lessons. She knew her work was barely passable, yet the dashing young artist who was so popular among the fashionable ladies of the county seemed impressed with her landscapes and constantly encouraged her not to lose heart. He seemed to be more enamored of her, though, than of her struggling attempts to transfer the beauty of the green and awakening countryside to canvas. To date he'd managed to keep a growing ardor in check, contenting himself with flowery compliments to her beauty. Cat was beginning to wonder if she shouldn't discontinue her art work.

There were always social calls to return and balls to attend. The dashing Sir Ryan Nicholls and his beautiful bride were always in demand at the round of seasonal social events. To all outward appearances they were a perfect couple. Ryan's pretense of the attentive, doting husband had fooled everyone. In public he was ever at her side, eliciting envious sighs from less fortunate wives. At home, they rarely even spoke.

She supposed a good deal of the distance between them was as much her fault as his. From the time they'd sailed from India, she'd held herself aloof, blaming him for leaving Paddy behind; though from all accounts, the boy was well and thriving in Anne's loving care. She had to admit Ryan tried to make it up to her, from the redecorating of the house to the courtesy with which he'd treated her on their homecoming. When she'd stubbornly failed to respond to his subtle overtures to call a truce, the rift had widened to a yawning chasm that was almost impossible to bridge; they were little more than polite strangers sharing the same house now.

She still had not conceived, and Cat had her doubts that there would ever be a son to carry on Ryan's name and title. She had submitted to him, and each time he tempted her to forget the grievous differences of the past, she would summon to mind a vision of Paddy's face and any passion that had begun to warm her to him died, replaced by a cold withdrawal of her spirit to a place where he could not reach or hurt her.

His visits were infrequent now, and Cat had a vague suspicion that he had found another source to satisfy his desires. She was ambivalent about the suspicion. Ryan belonged to her and if she knew whom he was seeing, she'd most likely search out the tart and scratch out her deceitful eyes, and yet she knew her rejection was responsible for his wandering. Could she blame any woman for accepting the attentions she spurned? He was an adept lover, relentlessly charming, he seemed to grow more devilishly handsome with each passing day. It was all such an ugly, vicious circle. He'd hurt her, she'd withdrawn; and his turning away now was another painful blow to her feminine pride.

This particular morning, Cat woke with a need to escape the boring duties of the mistress of Canterbury Hill. Warm, spring air and the scent of flowers beckoned to her through the open doors of her balcony. She stretched indolently, deciding the morning was to be hers, to do with as *she* pleased. She was on holiday and the house could go to blazes for all she cared! She rang for her maid, ordered a bath, and a quarter hour later, sat back luxuriating in the warm silken waters as she planned how she'd spend her few precious hours of freedom. There was little chance she'd see Ryan. At times he was gone for days and she would never dare to inquire where he'd spent his time or risk a cold, shuttered glare that mockingly challenged her right to know.

Cat finally decided she'd exercise the spirited bay that Ryan had given her as a homecoming present. A ride over to Darla's would put her in a decent mood and prepare her for Avery's visit in the afternoon. Darla Caswell was the scandal of the county, and that was one of the reasons she was Cat's closest friend. Ryan had mentioned in passing that she wasn't suitable company and that was all it had taken. The girl was slightly older and worldly enough not to bore Cat with talk of babes and weather.

The rumors about her were wild and rampant; before she'd married Burton Caswell, she'd been a whore, an actress, a dirt-poor, ill-bred farm girl. For the most part the tales were all lies concocted by envious "ladies," and Cat dismissed them as nonsense. The women were all afraid of Darla's seductive beauty and brazen, carefree attitude. The single men panted after her now that her aged husband had died and left her wealthy and free; the married men snubbed her publicly but were equally enamored.

Cat defended Darla whenever she had the chance; not that Darla was an angel, but Cat admired her free spirit. The raven-haired beauty with an alabaster complexion and full, pouting red lips had confided to Cat that she'd escaped the desperate poverty of her father's farm to become an actress. She indulged in every pleasure now that she was rich enough to take whomever she pleased into her bed and keep him until *she* decided it was time for a change. Now that Cat lived such a tamed, boring existence, she enjoyed her friend's highly descriptive, entertaining accounts of her lovers.

Cat's humor was high and exuberant as she dressed in a light cotton gown of pale green that matched the budding leaves of the trees. An overskirt of white poplin and a white silk ribbon to tie back her coppery curls made her look as gay and spritely as the springtime weather. Before she left the room, she threw open the door of her dressing room and selected a wide-brimmed white hat to shade her winter-pale complexion from the sun.

With a lighthearted step, she descended the stairs and called to her housekeeper, telling her to arrange a menu for supper and that she would give her approval when she returned. A groom was sent to fetch the mare she'd named Uma, in honor of the golden goddess of the Hindus. Surprisingly, it was Will who brought the mare from the stables. She greeted him with a pleased smile and a hug. She felt guilty, for it seemed that she seldom had time for him now. He was always about somewhere, though occasionally he ran an errand for Ryan in the *Falcon*. She missed their comfortable talks, and as he helped her to mount, she caught his hand and told him they would have to get together soon.

Cat held the spirited animal at a trot until she'd passed the gates of Canterbury and headed north toward Darla's estate. Rather than take the long way around by the main road, she cut across an open field that belonged to a neighbor, letting the frisky mare stretch her legs in a racing gallop. They sped across the green, rolling meadow and an exhilarating sense of freedom set Cat's complexion glowing. How Ryan would frown if he saw her, she thought, and urged the mount forward at an even more reckless pace. She was a picture of wild, free beauty as the wind swept her hair flying in a thick red-gold mane, the thin dress molded to every curve and a dazzling smile betraying her enjoyment.

Finally she slowed the panting animal to a walk as they approached the small estate called Locksley. She couldn't wait to hear of Darla's latest exploits. The last time they talked she'd hinted at a new love who seemed to have surpassed all others in her affections.

She cantered the mare the rest of the way, riding up the long, straight road to Locksley to arrive breathless but refreshed. It was a smaller house than Canterbury Hill—a two-story brick without the larger house's two wings. A groom came running to her as soon as she dismounted. His face colored oddly when she asked if his mistress was at home and he stuttered that she was, before hurrying off to lead Uma toward the stables.

Cat puzzled for a moment over the odd behavior, wondering if Darla was entertaining her latest paramour. She would know soon enough, she thought as she walked up the steps to the front door and lifted the heavy, ornate knocker to announce herself. The Caswell butler, Fitzroy, a stoic old retainer whose wrinkled eyes had seen much and revealed nothing, answered her knock. His expression was stolidly immobile as he informed her that Mistress Caswell was not in. Cat stared at him hesitantly, knowing the groom had just revealed the opposite. He asked if she would care to leave word.

"Just tell her Lady Nicholls stopped by, Fitzroy." He nodded respectfully.

"Very good, m'lady; I shall inform her as soon as she arrives home. Good day, m'lady!" He started to close the door. Cat's voice stopped him.

"Fitzroy . . ." He peered at her inquiringly. "I've just had a long ride and it's dreadfully warm today. I'm sure your mistress wouldn't mind if you fetched me a glass of cool water."

The butler, normally the epitome of civility, hesitated, finally holding the door open for her. Cat entered, trying to puzzle out the several strange occurences in a row. First Darla was home, then she wasn't, and now Fitzhugh displayed an unusual reluctance to admit her.

He asked her to be seated in the entrance hall while he sent a servant for the refreshment. She watched him disappear down the long hallway toward the rear of the house and sat down on a cushioned bench with a weary sigh.

Suddenly from above an unmistakable peal of low, throaty laughter drifted down and Cat smiled. Darla *was* at home, and entertaining as Cat had guessed. The sly minx had warned the servants to admit no one, and Fitzroy had mistakenly included her in the order! Well, she would leave as soon as she'd her drink. It was none of her business what took place here unless Darla chose to confide in her.

There was another laugh, equally unmistakable, and Cat stiffened as a shock went through her entire body. Fitzroy hurried down the hall, a maid following in his wake with the water Cat had requested. Another low rumble of laughter followed and Cat rose, her face pale as snow. Fitzroy seemed shaken for the first time since she'd known him, glancing up at the second-story balcony and then back at her.

Cat was rapidly recovering from the surprise of hearing Ryan's voice. A cold anger possessed her as she accepted the crystal goblet of water and drank, handing it back to Fitzroy before she took a deep breath and brushed passed him, heading up the stairs. With an agility that surprised her, he hurried forward and blocked her path.

"Get out of my way," she warned him in a tight, clipped tone. He hesitated, unable to decide if he dared

lay a hand on her, yet knowing his mistress would be outraged if he allowed her to proceed.

"Please, m'lady—you'd best return home!" Though he towered over her a good six inches, the murderous glare in those wide violet eyes was intimidating, and he docilely stepped aside, watching as she swept up the stairs, pausing for another deep breath before she reached for the door handle.

By the time she swung open the door to Darla's bedroom, Cat was in complete control of her self. She had to see their faces when she discovered them wrapped in each others arms. Beyond the door she heard a low, mumbled exchange and a shocked giggle from Darla. Cat bristled, well aware of Darla's acting abilities—as if anything could shock that two-faced, conniving whore? She'd even had the gall to taunt Cat with a shaded hint of the virility of her newest devoted follower!

The dramatic encounter that followed seemed like a scene from a play about infidelity. Cat flung the door open, and it crashed against the wall with a loud bang, startling the two occupants, who were half dressed and engaged in a very passionate embrace. Ryan pulled his lips away from Darla's fleshy, half-exposed breasts to curse at the interruption. The curse died as it was born. His wife stood in the doorway, her fiery glance taking in every detail of the disheveled bedding, of his clothing discarded on the floor. He still wore breeches, and they even now revealed the waning evidence of the desire that had caused him to half-tear the skimpy, black silk gown from Darla's seductive, voluptuous figure.

Darla brazenly demanded an explanation from Cat. "If you weren't such a cold bitch he'd never have come to me," she sneered cruelly.

Ryan made a disgusted sound, warning Darla to shut her mouth. He reached down to the floor for his shirt, straightening to stare at Cat. She'd ignored Darla as though she didn't exist. He doubted if she'd even heard the taunt. He was disgusted enough without facing the steady glare of those stricken eyes. She hadn't taken her eyes off him the entire time. He stepped forward, trying to think of something, anything to explain.

Cat retreated as Ryan stepped toward her. So far she hadn't said a word. She was deathly afraid that if she opened her mouth a horrible tirade of useless, embittered accusations would roll off her tongue, exposing her to the mockery of her husband and his whore. She permitted herself a bitter, reproachful smile before she called him a hypocrite and added, "Evidently Darla is suitable company for *you!*" Ryan accepted the stinging rebuke that cut deeper than if she'd cursed him with a thousand vile names, watched as she whirled and raced away.

Darla watched him dress, hurrying over to grasp his arm and beg him to stay. "Let her go, darling. What difference does it make? Didn't she make you miserable?" Her voice took on a honeyed tone as she wrapped her arms around his neck and pressed her body against his. Ryan glanced up with a cold, contemptuous glare that made her drop her arms and she stumbled awkwardly backward to sink to the bed. His black, glaring eyes had branded her a simple, ill-bred whore instead of his bewitching mistress. They'd been together over a month, an idyllic four weeks in which time she'd come to need the rough, demanding touch of his strong hands and the feel of his lean hard body dominating her soft flesh. She couldn't let him go—no matter what he thought of her!

"Ryan, darling, please! She knows now, that's the only difference. She doesn't want anything to do with you—especially now. Darling, stay, I'll do anything, anything you want, only don't leave me!" She began to cry. Large tears formed paths through the rice powder and rouge on her face.

Ryan had finished dressing. He had to find Cat before she did something crazy. If she'd screamed at him and gotten rid of some of her rage he'd feel better. Now it was locked inside her, festering. He ignored Darla's maudlin weeping, casting one last disgusted glance at her. How could he have been attracted to *her*, when he had

Cat? He felt as if his eyes had been opened. He'd had to have an outlet for his desires but he had been stupid enough to prefer this cheap slut. Hell, it was over and the damage done, what was the use of grading his infidelity now? He walked out without a backward glance, dismissing Darla as though she'd never existed.

When Ryan left Darla's house for the last time, Cat was already halfway home, pushing the mare to a breakneck speed. When she found herself in front of the familiar mansion and threw herself down from the mare's back, she could barely see the entrance of the house as stinging tears blinded her. Somehow, by pure instinct perhaps, she made her way to her room, throwing the bolt when she was safely inside, locking herself in with the tight ball of misery in her stomach, flinging herself on the bed to weep in humiliation.

On the way home she'd considered different ways to deal with Ryan. She would take a gun to both of them. No, she would kill herself instead. Then she briefly considered a double murder and her own suicide, finally rejecting every thought of retribution. The brazen hussy who had supposedly been her friend had been right. *She'd* driven Ryan straight into the bitch's waiting arms. Even now, they were probably laughing over her indignant, scorned attitude! The thought of continuing to bear his visits to Darla was degrading and she said a quick prayer that God would strike her with a lightning bolt and put her out of her misery! A moment later she arched a brow heavenward, silently canceling the order; and flipped onto her back, changing her mood again as she thought of a way to strike back at Ryan.

Suddenly there was a pounding at the door and Ryan called out to her, ordering her to open it immediately. "Go away! I never want to see you again!" she shouted, glaring up at the velvet canopy above her bed. Silence followed, then a tremendous crash as Ryan threw himself against the door, and it broke. He entered the room, rubbing a bruised shoulder and headed for the bed with a determined gleam in his eyes.

Cat scooted away from the arms that reached for her, but Ryan was quicker and caught her, giving her a shake as she struggled to get away. Finally she faced him with an accusing glare and an attitude of contempt as she waited for him to have his say.

"I'm sorry you had to witness that . . . I never thought you'd find out! It's just as well you did though. We'll have it out now as we should have before." His mouth twitched cynically as he saw the closed, stubborn set of her face. "You made it quite clear what you thought of my attentions. How can you blame me for seeking relief? I admit it would have been more discreet to roam farther from here, but Darla was there and more than willing."

"Blame it all on her—I'm sure you made a heroic stand of resistance before falling on her within thirty seconds!"

Ryan saw it was useless, and cursed. He'd wanted things to change—at least then there would have been some good out of the disgusting situation. He rose and turned to go, telling her he'd have the door repaired in the morning.

"Ryan." He turned with a half-measure of hope. "Don't be surprised if I venture out and strike up an acquaintance of my own. If you can do it, so can I!" It was a childish threat that Cat had no intention of fulfilling, but she wanted to hurt him, to see the hurt on his face.

"Don't ever try it." He wheeled and stalked away without another word. The tone of his voice implied he would kill any man she chose.

That afternoon, no one could have guessed that Cat had spent the morning weeping. She was as fresh and lovely as when she'd left for Darla's house that morning. Ryan was nowhere to be found; and though she asked the servants, not a one knew where the master had gone.

She was in the east drawing room when Avery Simons was announced. As the tall, handsome artist moved across the room to greet her, she dazzled him with a welcoming smile that nearly stopped him in his tracks. There was a difference in the lovely Catherine Nicholls today. For weeks he'd waited for some sign, some indication that she would let him near, and now . . . she seemed to radiate a soft willingness that left him breathless with encouragement. He reached for her hand, drawing it to his lips and pressing an ardent kiss. She seemed to shy. Perhaps she needed to be encouraged herself.

"You're so lovely today. Instead of landscapes, allow me to sketch you in all your loveliness!" Avery considered her the most enchanting of all his students, though he'd never held any hope of luring her away from that dour husband of hers. Now, if he posed her and his hand touched . . . who knew where it might lead?

Cat agreed, curious to test her powers with such an interesting subject. She had no desire to be unfaithful to Ryan. Cat was more curious to see if Avery's kiss would have any effect on her. She let him lead her to the light of the window, watching as he fussed over her position, and his hands became more bold with each passing second. At last he lifted her chin and gazed into her eyes with ardent attention, sliding his fingers to the back of her neck to draw her head forward. He touched her lips with his in an almost brotherly kiss, and Cat felt nothing. Even as he pressed closer and slipped an arm around her waist, she had no reaction.

A sudden roar from across the room separated the two. Ryan plunged across the length of the room like a maddened bull, seizing the scruff of Avery's coat and dragging him away. Cat ran after them, and would have laughed at the sight of the overly amorous artist tumbling down the steps if Ryan hadn't dusted off his hands and turned on her.

Ryan lunged for Cat, missing her agile figure on the first try, lunged again and caught her. He carried her up the stairs, taking them two at a time, entered her room and tossed her down in the middle of the bed.

Cat was a wildcat, spitting, fury, glaring defiance at just another example of Ryan's high-handedness. It was fine for *him* to stray but he judged her in a possessive manner that made her want to scratch the righteous anger from his face. "I hate you," she screamed, rising to a kneeling position, fingers clenched into fists at her side.

Ryan ignored the statement. "Don't ever let me catch you with another man's hands anywhere near you," he threatened solemnly. "I may not have you, but neither will any other man!" Then he turned and walked away, ignoring the shriek of indignation that followed.

In the days that followed, Cat seemed to change. Where she had been withdrawn before, now she was listless, refusing to eat so often that she lost fifteen pounds in the next month. Ryan was seldom home to see the change as she slipped from willowy to slender, from slender to fragile.

Nothing seemed to interest her, nothing seemed to matter as Cat passed day after day wandering aimlessly, sitting for hours in the finished gardens, brooding endlessly.

One day Ryan received an urgent message from Justin de Rysfeld. He would have ignored it but the man who delivered the scrawled note insisted that the contents were true. His master *was* dying and needed to see him. He was a half day's ride south, living at an estate that had belonged to his mother's family.

Ryan didn't bother to make his departure known to Cat, he seldom did anymore. She happened to see him ride off and slipped away into the gardens to cry again. It had gotten to the point where she no longer knew why she wept. Even if Ryan was still seeing Darla, what did it matter to her now? Nothing mattered at all.

Chapter Twenty-two

Will Foster stood in the gardens behind the house, studying Cat's husband as he paced at the cliff's edge. Ryan's back was to Will, his hands clasped tightly behind him. For over an hour now, ever since his return from de Rysfield's deathbed, he had alternately paced and paused, as though he were pondering a weighty problem.

Will shifted impatiently, wondering whether he dared disturb Ryan. He well knew the extent of the man's volatile temper. He'd overheard many, far too many arguments between him and Cat. He rubbed one hand roughly over his bearded face, a face that his mirror's reflection had revealed this morning as worn and tired, with an unruly frame of hair that was beginning to salt with gray. *Cat had to be protected!* He had to see her happily settled at last. Just this morning, while Ryan was absent, he'd happened to catch sight of her seated in the garden. Positive she was unobserved, her shoulders had slumped defeatedly and she had broken into sobs. Shaking his head in worry, he now moved out of the garden and rambled across the wide expanse of well-kept lawn until he stood behind Ryan.

"I was wondering how long it would take you, Foster." Ryan had spoken without turning, startling Will with his knowledge. He turned now, his expression brooding and preoccupied. "Well, spit it out man. What is it you want?"

Will had never felt comfortable in Ryan's presence. The younger man's brooding arrogance always repelled confidences. He seemed to need no one but himself. Yet what Will had to say was important, and he felt strongly enough about the subject to plunge ahead. "I want to know your plans for Cat," he blurted boldly.

Ryan's handsome, angular features, always in control, showed his surprise only by the slight uplift of one black brow. He waited a moment, his gaze sweeping coldly over Will's features before he replied. "I think that is a private matter; something that concerns only my wife and me."

Will's mouth hardened with quick anger. He had his own touch of arrogance and swagger, and no one, including the man Cat had married, could send him packing before he'd had his say! "No, sir, beggin' your pardon, but it's my concern too. Cat's been my responsibility ever since Dev died." He was growing angrier by the minute, for Ryan was regarding him with a cool, almost condescending air. Nothing could stop the flow of anger that now cascaded from him in a roaring, turbulent stream.

"Y'know, I never could figure out what Cat saw in you, but that didn't matter none. It's what makes that girl happy that counts, Nicholls! She wanted *you,* even if she fussed and fumed o'er your high-handed ways." Ryan's face suddenly went pale beneath his dark tan and a stormy glower creased his face. He opened his mouth to speak but Will cut him off.

"Yes, sir, I said high-handed, an' stubborn, too. From the first time I saw you, y'reminded me a Devlan. There was none could tell him anythin' either. I thought you was the one to tame that wild, headstrong little girl."

He paused to take a breath and rumbled on. "I was wrong, Nicholls, dead wrong. You done nothin' but make 'er miserable. Cat's wild an' free, like the sea, an' you didn't tame 'er, you only caged 'er!"

"Are you quite through, Foster?" A muscle ticked in Ryan's face, betraying his anger.

"Yes, I reckon I had my say, much good that it's done." Will refused to back down from the icy glare of Ryan's dark eyes. He had clearly been unable to reach the man but at least he'd tried. He thought a moment, then added his final say. "I lived a lot longer than you, seen more 'a life than you have. There's many a man who'd a died for the love of a woman like Cat. You had her love and trampled all over it." A deep sigh escaped him and he shook his head in disgust. "You sorely disappoint and try my patience, Nicholls!" With this final declaration, he wheeled around and stomped toward the house, completely missing the puzzled look on Ryan's face.

Ryan almost called Will back. The man must be addled! How many times had Cat screamed that she hated him, how many times had she fought him and cursed him for a devil? Did a woman in love act that way? And yet Cat was no ordinary woman, he completely agreed. She was a sensual, passionate beauty. Perhaps she was meant to be tamed by no man who walked God's earth.

Ryan's thoughts turned to the past. Surely he'd given her reason enough to hate him, to distrust him. Hadn't he named her a liar when she'd sworn she had nothing to do with his uncle's murder? And only this morning, Justin had verified her story with his dying confession. When he had arrogantly taken possession of her that day in Tortuga, or later, when he found her again in the Indies, had he ever made an offer of marriage? No, his conscience answered for him, he had merely offered her the ignoble position of mistress. After all that had passed between them, could she have dismissed the resentment and realized she loved him? He glanced up at the house, eyes searching until he found her bedroom window. It was high time they had a talk, an honest open talk that revealed their true feelings. As he hurried toward the house Ryan experienced a suppressed excitement that set his nerves tingling. If he had found a wild, rebellious Cat a fascinating lover, how much more exciting to feel the warm response of her soft and willing body!

Will had sought the solitude of his own room. He lay back on the bed, mulling over the confrontation with Ryan. Next he would have to have a long talk with Cat and find out her plans. Already she looked thin and unhappy. If the poor child stayed here, she'd waste away to nothing.

Suddenly his door slammed against the wall with a loud bang. Ryan appeared in the open doorway, his lean, angular features livid with fury. With more emotion than Will had ever seen him display, he stalked across the room, reaching the bed in two long strides. He stooped, gathering the material of Will's shirt in one hand to jerk him to a sitting position.

"Where is she?"

When Will's face reflected his astonishment, Ryan released him. "I want to know where she's gone, Foster. *Immediately!*" Will had seldom seen such rage on a man's face. He guessed that Cat had finally taken action. Ryan threw a crumpled note on the bed and paced to the window. Will's curiosity was increasing by the second. He picked up the note, smoothing out the wrinkles. The slightest trace of familiar perfume rose from it. He quickly scanned the brief note.

I'm leaving you. We'll both be happier. Don't try to find me.

Will raised his eyes to the man at the window. Ryan's hands were clasped tightly behind his back. Every few seconds, they clenched and opened in impotent fury.

"I found *that* on her pillow," he declared, glaring at Will as though he were at fault. "I must know where she's gone, Will. The servants haven't seen her and none of the horses are missing. She can't have just disappeared!"

A smile flickered across Will's broad, craggy face. It quickly vanished as Ryan stepped forward with a menacing growl. "I knew nothin' about this, but it fits what I told you. You've nothin' to blame but your own stupid pride. As far as love is concerned, you're nothin' but a fumblin' country oaf!"

"I didn't ask your opinion of my character. If anyone knows where she's gone, it'd be you. If it satisfies your meddling mind, old man, I was on my way to talk with Cat, to find out if your addled claims bore any truth!"

Will enjoyed a short laugh at Ryan's expense. "So you've finally decided *you're* in love, eh—and too late!" His expression lost its amusement, turning serious. If she'd disappeared without a trace, he alone knew where to find her. She'd gone to the tunnel of course, as she had once before to escape Ryan. She might still be there. Should he trust Ryan with the knowledge? Cat would never forgive him. He studied Ryan's face, noting the sincere worry there, and made his decision.

"I'll let you know where Cat might be, but you must make me an oath." He knew enough about Ryan's character to be confident he would keep a vow, once given. "Swear you'll leave 'er be if she wants you not!"

Ryan hesitated, torn between a strong desire to force the old fool to tell him what he knew and a desperate fear that this time Cat would disappear from his life forever. "All right, damn it," he cursed impatiently. "I swear. Now, tell me where I can find her."

"I'll have to show you, Nicholls. Have the housekeeper fetch the keys to the wine cellar." Ryan threw him a puzzled glare but quickly moved to obey. Will followed him and ten minutes later they stood in the cellar. He led the way to the brick wall at the rear of the storage area, the only wall clear of stacked bottles of wine. Will pressed one of the bricks, grinning at Ryan's astonishment as an opening appeared, just large enough to permit the passage of a man. As Will held a lantern aloft and lit the way, Ryan followed him through the opening, and found himself in a tiny, windowless room. Three paces ahead, a trapdoor was set into the dirt floor.

"None but Cat an' me know of this," Will explained. "And now you, of course." Catching the iron ring set into the door, he tugged it open, shining the light over the dark hole. "She'll still be down there if she hasn't sailed away," he remarked. "I only hope I don't live to regret this. Just follow the tunnel to the cave." He lit a smaller lantern for himself and after the younger man had climbed down through the opening, handed him the larger. "Remember your vow, Nicholls," Will warned, then the door closed over Ryan's head.

Ryan could hardly believe the existence of the hidden tunnel. He hadn't imagined it could be here and yet, knowing who had built the house, he should have guessed. The air was damp and cool, the walls close to his shoulders as he hurried along, anxious to find Cat. Suddenly the air grew warmer and a pale flicker of light shone ahead. He extinguished the lantern, reluctant to startle her with his sudden appearance. The tunnel widened and he found himself at the entrance to the cave. As he caught sight of her, he retreated, blending into the shadows.

Cat knelt on the floor with her back at a right angle to the tunnel. Ryan could just discern her profile by the light of the lantern she had placed at her side. Dim sunlight filtered into the cave from the cliffside opening. She was dressed in a white silk shirt and men's leather vest and breeches. As Ryan watched, she struggled to raise the heavy ironbound lid of a wooden chest that sat before her. Finally she had it open and began to sort through its contents. She lifted a heavy gold link necklace and held it to the light, smiling as the attached ruby winked a warm crimson red, then placing it in a small leather pouch at her side. Several other equally valuable pieces followed, until she seemed satisfied with her bounty.

Ryan silently pondered how he could approach her without frightening her. As he continued to watch, she turned to the chest again and withdrew a man's coat in a rich shade of midnight blue brocade. Even from his vantage point in the shadows, Ryan could see the excellent tailoring, though the style was somewhat dated. Tenderly the slender hand stroked the material. Suddenly Cat clutched the coat to her breasts, threw her arm across the edge of the chest, and, bowing her head, began to sob. The weeping revealed such pain and suffering that Ryan felt a knife twist of pity within his heart. The Cat he knew had always been so self-possessed, so independent that he was startled to realize that he'd never seen her give way to tears, except in rage. He reproached himself now for the many times he'd deliberately tried to hurt her, to break through her shell of fierce pride.

Ryan couldn't bear to stand by longer, listening to her defeated weeping. Quietly approaching her, he knelt at her side. "Cat . . . darling, don't. . . ." Ryan's soft words of comfort were cut short as Cat's head shot up, and she recoiled, as though he had struck her.

"How did you . . ." Cat clutched the coat more tightly and wiped at her eyes. She felt dazed, dreamy. It couldn't be Ryan! What was more incredible than his appearence in the hidden cave was the glow of tender concern lighting his dark eyes. She had to be dreaming!

Ryan was taken back by her reaction. He'd expected surprise, even fury, but she stared at him as though he were some stranger who had happened to come upon her, or worse yet, an enemy. The lovely violet eyes were glazed and preoccupied with memories of the past. Open resentment battled with hostility, and a mixture of the two, tinged with bitterness, surfaced in her expression.

"I'm sorry," Ryan apologized. "Truly—I didn't mean to startle you. I . . ." For some strange reason he felt like an awkward schoolboy. Perhaps he *was* the country oaf that Will Foster had accused him of being—at least where Cat was concerned. "I found your note and Will told me about the cave. Cat, we must talk—there's been too much bitterness between us for too long. I won't let you go!" He reached out to touch her shoulder, willing her to understand he sought a truce.

"No!" Cat jerked away as if the Devil himself had

reached for her. "Stay away," she pleaded, a note of hysteria creeping into her voice. She inched backward until the wall of the cave was at her back. Everything about her attitude reminded Ryan of a terrified, trapped animal.

Cat's mind ached with strain and confusion. What more did he want from her? Hadn't he caused her enough pain, did he desire to see her suffer longer? The tears began anew and deepened her resentment. Finally he had the satisfaction of seeing her cry!

Ryan was growing impatient and angry. Did she think he had come after her only to beat her? Lord, he thought, had he really treated her so miserably in the past to generate this reaction? Suddenly he reached forward, slamming the chest lid with one hand, grabbing her wrist with the other. She was pulled to her feet with one swift, powerful jerk. Cat clutched the coat closer, as if it were her only protection. Ryan impatiently tore it away and as it pulled free of her tight grip, the sharp sound of the material tearing rent the air.

Cat stared down at the torn coat, lying in the dirt. It had been her father's. Slowly she raised her eyes to her husband's face. Her hand swung back and slammed forward to smash against his cheek in a forceful, satisfying blow. "Bastard, you ruin everthing you touch," she screamed hysterically, and her fists came forward to pummel his chest. She barely realized that tears coursed down her cheeks.

Ryan caught her wrists and shook her, as though she were a rag doll. "Catherine—Cat, stop it, you don't know what you're doing!" He gave her another hard shake but she continued to struggle. Pulling her into his arms, he effectively pinned her arms at her side. "Cat—let go of the past! You've spent a lifetime hating and seeking revenge." His voice softened to a low, husky plea. "Let it be, Cat, it's over now." Though she continued to sob, her struggles ceased. Ryan could feel her trembling against his chest, so close their heartbeats seemed to mingle into one, distinct rhythm.

"Cat, listen to me. As much as you adored your father, he's the root of all your pain." Cat stiffened in his arms and her head rose rebelliously. "No, hear me out," Ryan insisted. He seated her atop the chest, still holding tightly to her wrists. God, he prayed, let me find the right words. She looked so lovely and vulnerable, gazing up at him with wide, liquid eyes. In the struggle, the mass of curls she had pinned so neatly at her crown had come tumbling down and lay in a rich mass of bronze across her shoulders. He suddenly realized how much he would lose if she left him. Dear God, how he loved her—he had to make her understand!

"He had no right exposing you to the life he did. He probably knew that when he left orders with Will to send you to France. He *chose* his life, Cat, but he bequeathed it to you, and he was wrong!" Some of the fierce insistence drained from his manner. "I spent the morning at Justin's bedside. He died while I was there. Cat, he confessed everything, how he blackmailed you, my uncle's part in your father's death—what he did to you!" Ryan's gaze softened with remorse. "I was a fool when I refused to believe you. I know that now. We've both made our share of mistakes, Cat. *I'm admitting mine.*" She seemed calmer now and he released her, holding his breath, waiting for her reaction.

"You've no right to judge my father. *He* loved me, whatever he did!" Her eyes blazed defensively. "And Will had no right to let you come here!" She gazed off into the shadows, sullenly refusing to meet his eyes. "He betrayed me."

Ryan swore an oath, his patience at an end. "Damn it, woman, you're so mired in the past, you can't see straight! Even Will knows your father's gone. He's nothing but dust now! Devlan left you a legacy of hatred and revenge. You give him less credit than he deserves. If he loved you so, he'd not have wanted to see this . . . vendetta continue." He shook his head, frustrated by her stubborn silence.

"You're alive and vibrant, Cat, but no longer the little girl who witnessed her father's death. You're not Cat

Devlan anymore but Catherine Nicholls, *my woman, my wife!* I'll not let you go out of my life again! Damn it all, Cat, do I have to go down on my knees to convince you that I love you?" Her head came up sharply, her eyes fixed on his as she tried to fathom the truth of what he claimed. Ryan's smile was sheepish as he ruefully admitted, "I would, if you insisted!"

Cat drowned within Ryan's black, penetrating gaze. Everything grew dim and hazy and even the low rumble of his voice seemed a great distance away. A small, defiant portion of her mind insisted that he was lying, that it was his demon pride that insisted she stay. Weakness overwhelmed her as a tide of emotion washed over her. She raised a hand to her forehead and spoke, her own voice a thousand miles distant. "Ryan, I—I feel," She never completed the thought as darkness closed about her, shutting out the dim light of the cave and Ryan's startled expression as he caught her limp body.

Slowly the choking gray mists dissolved. As Cat's eyes fluttered open, she found herself lying on the floor of the cave, with Ryan at her side. The deep frown of concern wrinkling his brow eased as she glanced up at him. Her hand moved, touching something smooth and silken. She gazed down to discover that Ryan had taken a length of fine black satin and spread it on the ground for her to lie on. Her eyes sought his again and he smiled apologetically.

"I know it was part of your father's belongings, love, but somehow I don't think he'd have minded." His tone was a tender caress.

Cat felt warm and peaceful at last, sheltered within Ryan's arms. It seemed so natural for him to hold her close. The hatred that had been part of her for so long seemed to have vanished with the mists. "No, Dev wouldn't have minded," she agreed, her own voice sweet and loving. Suddenly she wanted nothing more than to be possessed by Ryan; to feel the safety of his strong arms and the length of his lean, hard body next to hers. Her arms reached up to encircle his neck, her fingers twining in the ebony curls at his nape to urge his lips to hers. Shyly, yet with a growing boldness, her lips pressed his, and she issued a silent prayer that he would not judge her wanton.

A powerful surge of awe and desire pulsed through Ryan. The gorgeous creature in his arms, with her wildly lovely features and flaming fan of copper waves, belonged to him alone. The simple admission that he loved her had wrought this change in her attitude. Her supple arms urged him to hurry, her very posture was a flowering of open desire. Their lips met as his hands tangled in the silken, gold tresses. His need to possess her was overpowering, setting his heart racing madly, his pulse pounding. The light grew dimmer in the cave as the sun lowered in the sky.

Ryan placed tiny kisses at her throat, at the deep vee of her firm breasts. He could delay no longer—his passion was mounting to a fever pitch. He sat up, stripping away his clothing but never taking his eyes from hers. Cat smiled languidly as she slowly, tantalizingly unbuttoned her shirt. The tempting sight of her breasts, set free from the silken bondage of the shirt, aroused his impatience and he eagerly stripped her breeches from her with shaking hands. Her slender body, ivory skin aglow, was vividly sensual against the black satin background. She was a feast set before a starving man, a golden flame burning for him alone. Long, tapering legs, a flat, spare belly, narrow waist, high proud breasts—all of it belonged to him, all of it and that angelic face. His angel now raised her arms to beckon him. He stretched lightly on top of her, careful even in his urgency not to crush her slender form with his weight. Her fingers caressed his back as his arms went around her and his lips nuzzled the warm, velvetskin of her breasts.

Cat moaned as Ryan's tongue teased her nipples until they grew taut with desire, just as his manhood now grew at the junction of her thighs. She felt it pulse there, seeking entry, and she moaned louder, aching to reach down and draw him within her. Her skin tingled with his every touch and the familiar, masculine aroma of his skin inflamed her desire until she reached for him, glorying in the knowledge of what was to come. Never had she felt so strong an urge to be possessed, body and soul; never before had she ached with such a need to feel Ryan's strength within her. Frenzied now, she twisted beneath him in a desperate urge to consummate their love.

Softly, breathlessly, Cat whispered his name over and over, in a litany of mingled endearments. Her heart pounded wildly, her hips moving as a flood of feeling swept her entire body, setting it afire with a building heat.

Suddenly she was on her back. Through langorous, heavy-lidded eyes, she saw Ryan kneel between her outspread thighs. With the glow of the lantern light behind him, he appeared as a magnificent god-animal, his darkly tanned, lithe body poised over her, eager to be sheathed by her warmth. With a love she had never willingly acknowledged before, she surrendered to him.

Waves of intense feeling shook Ryan as he plunged forward to bury himself in Cat's sweet softness. She arched to meet him, absorbing each hard thrust. Their lips met desperately and his tongue invaded her soft, pink mouth. He plunged and her hips met his, again and again until the cave exploded with a blinding, dazzling light and the ground seemed to tremble beneath their coupled bodies. Cat screamed his name as her body seemed to plummet from a steep cliff, spiraling downward to land, not broken and bleeding, but gently as though a bed of rose petals welcomed her.

They lay breathlessly entwined for what felt like an eternity, sweat glistening from every pore, exhausted, sated, awed by the experience. Coupled with the sweetness of fulfillment was the dawning of a shared desire to repeat the performance, over and over again, to taste once more the towering thrill that had transported them beyond earthbound pleasure. Only the knowledge that they had discovered a deep, abiding love, and that tomorrows stretched almost limitlessly before them, allowed relaxation to come.

Cat cuddled close within the strength of Ryan's arms. She had gathered some of his strength to her, enough to bury the past and its memories and look to the future, *their* future. She smiled tenderly at Ryan, reaching up to touch his cheek gently. Perhaps even now, a seed blossomed within her, as it once had, a tiny bit of both of them. His fingers lightly stroked her back and she sighed contentedly, snuggling closer.

"My wildcat's sheathed her claws at last," Ryan noted with a wry smile. "You've turned soft and kittenish, my love. If only I'd discovered the secret of making you purr before now, I'd have saved myself a few scars!" He leaned on one elbow, staring down at her with a mixture of love and cautious reserve. He had insisted *she* bury the memories of the past but found himself remembering her liason with Sean and brooding about the future. She was an alluring flame of womanhood, almost unconsciously drawing men under her spell. Though she had shared the pirate's bed, it had been at a time when she was sure she'd never set eyes on him again. He couldn't blame her for seeking to satisfy the desires he had awakened when he first taught her the pleasures of love.

"I hope we've settled the question of your leaving. You've run from me too many times, Cat . . . you must know now that I would pursue you to the ends of the earth, if need be." He glanced at her discarded disguise and said warningly, "You'll stay here and settle down to a proper life as my wife and the mother of my children. No more running about in men's breeches, no more roving as you please, no more pirating. Is that clearly understood, madame?"

Cat decided to tease him a moment. For some reason, his commands failed to chafe her and she welcomed the feeling of possessive protection he offered. She refused to meet his eyes and her sensuous mouth pouted for the briefest seconds.

"Madame, I'm awaiting your reply. I should hate to restrain your freedom by force."

Cat glanced up, a mysterious smile lighting her face as she stated her terms. "Yes, sir, it's quite understood—but I would strike a bargain with you." Ryan's brows knit as he prepared to negotiate. Cat hurried on, unwilling to distress him further. "I'll not go roving, or command my own ship, or don men's clothing. I promise to stay home and *try* to be demure and modest!" She giggled at the thought, for the two characteristics were foreign to her nature. "In return, you must stay close to home, in case I should feel a sudden, insatiable desire to . . . explore"—her hands moved lightly across his broad, well-muscled shoulders—"or roam, or . . . whatever! Of course," she added, her bright smile turning serious, "you must love me, always love me."

Ryan replied with a delighted grin. His dark eyes crinkled with anticipation as his head lowered over hers. "Oh, I will," he whispered huskily. "I will, indeed!" His lips melted against hers in a deep, sweet moment of contentment as he sealed love's bargain with a tender kiss.

Epilogue

Nine months and twelve days following their tryst in the hidden cave at Canterbury Hill, Catherine Devlan Nicholls proudly produced an heir for Ryan. She was safely delivered of a son they christened Devlan, a strong, healthy child who was to become the scion of a dynasty of strong-willed, staunchly independent men and women who followed. Dev entered the world with a lusty howl that promised he would be as spirited as his beautiful mother and a thatch of ebony curls that matched his father's.

Each succeeding generation prospered and served the bountiful land into which they'd been born. In his middle fifties, Dev served proudly on Washington's staff at Valley Forge. His son, Bryan, was commissioned a captain in the fledgling Continental Navy. Grandson Rian, who left a young wife and two children when he went to serve with General Jackson at New Orleans, helped to repel the British and returned home with only one arm.

Finally, in the fifth generation, there was one male

heir, Devlan Scott Nicholls. His father, having followed General Zachary Taylor to victory at Buena Vista, lost his life on the last day of fighting. His widow remarried when Dev was still a toddling babe and her new husband, Reece Cantrell, adopted the boy and gave him his name. Born at the family estate on the Hudson, Dev Cantrell journeyed west with his parents in the spring of 1857. Reece Cantrell had put Devlan's estate in trust and meant to carve out his own empire in the vast, unsettled northwest. By the time they'd arrived in the southern mountains of Idaho, Carolyn Nicholls Cantrell was pregnant with her second child. Reece had intended to push northwest and settle in Oregon but delayed, for winter was fast approaching, and it was no time to travel with a young boy and pregnant woman.

On a cold, blustery day in February of the following year, the twelve-year old boy returned from an overnight trapping expedition to find the charred remains of the cabin, still smouldering from the flames that had consumed it. His mother lay near the smoking ruins, raped and beaten to death, his adopted father sprawled a few feet away with an axe protruding from his back. Of the baby Jason, born the month before, there was no trace.

The boy would have starved that winter in the wilderness had a band of Blackfoot not come across him and taken him back to their village in the mountains. Dev Cantrell stayed with the tribe, growing into a tall, strong warrior named Senomac. Later, his path was destined to cross that of a young girl named Jennifer Bryant, about whose parents you may have read in *Savage in Silk,* but then *that* is altogether a different tale.